CHEATING DEATH

BOOK FIVE
THE IMMORTAL DESCENDANTS

APRIL WHITE

The Immortal Descendants Series

Marking Time
Tempting Fate
Changing Nature
Waging War
Cheating Death

Cheating Death. Copyright 2017 by April White
All rights reserved. Published by Corazon Entertainment
Palos Verdes Peninsula, CA

Edited by Angela Houle
Cover Design by Penny Reid
Cover images by Shutterstock
Quote in Acknowledgements used by permission of Neil Gaiman

ISBN 978-1-946161-02-4
Library of Congress Control Number: 2016921068

First American edition, January, 2017

"Beware; for I am fearless, and therefore powerful."
-Mary Shelley, *Frankenstein*

Cast of Characters

The Immortal Time – Jera
The Immortal Fate – Aislin
The Immortal Nature – Goran
The Immortal War – Duncan
The Immortal Death – Aeron

Descendants of Time – The Clockers

Saira Elian Devereux – Clocker/Shifter mix. Can Clock to any time and place. Can Shift into a Cougar with the help of the Shifter bone. Native time: Modern.

Claire Elian – Saira's mother, born in 1850. Clocked forward from 1871 to give birth to Saira. Native time: Victorian.

Millicent Elian – Saira's "Grandmonster." Great grand-niece to Claire. Native time: Modern.

Charlotte "Charlie" Kelly – Otherworld Seer, and a Clocker conduit who makes time travel easy for the Clocker she's with. Native time: Victorian.

Valerie Grayson – Took Charlie to 1554 as her ward. Native time: Tudor.

Descendants of Fate – The Seers

Ms. Simpson – Headmistress of St. Brigid's School.

Ava Arman – Twin to Adam and next in line for Seer Head.

Adam Arman – Twin to Ava, boyfriend of Alexandra "Alex" Rowen.

Camille Arman – The twins' mother and current Seer Head.

Tom Landers – Seer/Monger mix, cousin of Ava and Adam.

Archer Devereux – Seer on his mother's side, turned to Vampire by Bishop Wilder in 1888. Native time: Victorian.

Tamerlane "Tam" Roth – Seer/Monger mix. One of the mixed-blood captives rescued from the ghost station.

Descendants of Nature – The Shifters

Will Shaw – Saira's father. Lion.

Mr. Shaw – Medical doctor and science teacher at St. Brigid's, descended from Saira's uncle. Bear.

Connor Edwards – Nephew to Mr. Shaw. Wolf.

Logan Edwards – Connor's younger brother. Able to Shift into any animal.

Liz Edwards – Mr. Shaw's sister and the boys' mother.

Descendants of War – The Mongers

Bishop Wilder – Bishop responsible for infecting Archer with Vampirism and killing Saira's father in 1888. Native time: Edwardian.

Spencer Rothchild – Monger Head in 1871 responsible for the Council massacre that imprisoned Will Shaw and sent Saira's pregnant mother forward in time. Native time: Victorian.

George Walters – Grandfather to Seth Walters. Died in the Underground explosion that split time in 1944. Native time: WWII era.

Seth Walters – Monger enforcer and Saira's nemesis. Currently in possession of the Monger ring with the power to compel.

Tom Landers – Seer/Monger mix. Biological son of Seth Walters.

Raven Rothchild Walters – Seth's niece, Saira's former roommate.

Descendants of Death – The Suckers

Archer Devereux – Seer, turned by Bishop Wilder in 1888. Native time: Victorian.

Tom Landers – Seer/Monger mix, turned by Bishop Wilder in 1428. Native time: Modern.

Sebastien "Bas" Tousi – Shifter Eagle. Moor. Native time: 12th Century.

Bishop Wilder – Monger. Native time: Edwardian.

Mixed-blood Descendants

Saira Elian Devereux – Clocker/Shifter.

Tom Landers – Seer/Monger.

Cole Moore – Raven's boyfriend.

Melanie Moore – Cole's sister.

Tamerlane "Tam" Roth – Seer/Monger, Cole and Melanie's friend, one of the mixed-blood captives.

Other Important People

Ringo – Victorian thief Saira brought forward from 1888.

Bishop Cleary – Bishop at Guy's Chapel, understands the world of the Immortal Descendants.

Rachel – Jewish mechanic who survived the WWII massacre at Oradour-sur-Glane.

Table of Contents

Nightmare

My feet pounded the cobblestones of Covent Garden. Moonlight, and the certainty I would find him this time were my only guides as I ran.

Archer's life depended on my speed and my determination. Panic had replaced the bone-deep sadness that had taken root deep inside me, and I was almost glad for something different to feel.

The London streets were empty and unnaturally silent, and the silver light threw the scene into the high contrast glare of a video game. The shadows were endlessly black and full of menace. I knew I wasn't alone. In fact, everything about this place was a gamer's nightmare. Every wrong move stopped me in my tracks or worse, until I finally learned to navigate each fresh horror and move on to the next.

I kept going though, pushing harder and faster. I knew in my soul that if I could just find Archer this time, I'd beat the game and wake up with him next to me.

I rounded the corner as The Ripper stepped from the shadows. Moonlight glinted on his raised blade. Jack the Ripper, dead by Ringo's knife a lifetime ago, smiled, a horrible grin full of rotten teeth.

"Ah, Pet, ye can't stay away, can ye?" he snarled.

I put on a burst of speed, but he was in front of me again. "Ye'll not escape me this time." He lunged, but I leapt to the side before his knife could slash down and bury itself in my back. No amount of anticipation could erase the fear that coursed through me at the sight of The Ripper. I had died at that corner the first time I saw him there, and woken up with the echo of a searing pain between my shoulder blades.

His snarl lingered behind me as I sprinted down the next street, away from his lethal menace. The pounding of my feet began to match the rhythm of a distant hum. I knew the sound and I hated it, but still I flew toward it like a shard of iron to a magnet.

There, down the next street and tucked into an alcove, was the Seer bodyguard who had murdered young Henry Grayson in medieval France. He had threatened me with rape and death then, and now his knife hung loosely in his hand as if I was no danger to him at all. "Ye came back fer more, did ye, lass?" His voice was oily, and the stench of him hadn't improved in death.

A dozen snarky comebacks flashed through my brain, mostly having to do with the crushed nutsack I'd inflicted on him when he threatened to cut my windpipe. But cleverness was wasted in nightmares, and my fear of him had long-since turned to anger.

So I charged at him.

I ducked down, put my shoulder into it, and rammed him up against the wall. He tried to get the knife up, but like most cowards who attack women, he didn't anticipate that I would be the aggressor. I smacked his knife hand against the bricks and thrust my elbow so hard into his solar plexus that a cloud of hot, stinky air rushed from his lungs. He doubled over with a sucking gasp.

I bolted.

Now the landscape had the eerie quiet of a ghost town, and there was no joy in hurdling broken guardrails or scaling crumbling walls. It was the silence that drove panic into my throat. Silence curled its fist around my heart where memories of Archer lived.

I sensed someone with Monger blood waiting in the wings like a deadly Greek chorus, ready to step out and flay the flesh from my bones. He stayed hidden as long as I continued down the cobblestone road that ended at an alley between a pub and an old theater. I entered the black passageway, and dread wound its way around my lungs.

This was Wilder's place, and no matter which way I ran, I had to enter his rooms at the end of the passage. The door was always open, the table was always set for two, and the sharp scent of my own fear filled my nose as I stepped across the threshold.

"You came," he said in a deep bass voice that still had the power to freeze my blood. He stood and held out the chair for me. My heart slammed in my

chest from the running, and from pure, raw terror. I had tried to escape
Wilder's invitation, but the door had always locked behind me or the windows
wouldn't break, and every object I weaponized against him slipped from my
hands.

So I sat at Wilder's table and he pushed in my chair. He bent his head
and whispered into my ear, inhaling the scent of my skin as he did. "You belong
to me now."

I had tried to break a glass in his face the first time he said that to me.
Now I just waited until he finally stood straight and returned to his seat.

Wilder indicated my plate, which had filled with food. "You will eat."

On the plate was a slab of fresh meat sitting in a pool of congealed blood.
Wilder had the only knife, so even if I'd wanted to eat the barely-cooked flesh,
which I emphatically did not, I'd have had to pick it up in my bare hands to do
so. The metallic smell of blood made my stomach roil in disgust, and when I
began to retch, I pushed back from the table.

I was still gripping the table when Wilder stabbed my hand to it.

Stabbed. A knife. Embedded in the table through the back of my hand.

White-hot, the pain was like the shot of adrenaline I'd been waiting for. I
yanked the knife out of my hand and lunged. The forward momentum carried
me into him and buried the knife in his chest. It also knocked him to the floor
and revealed a trap door under his chair.

Wilder's roar of rage filled the room as he struggled to right himself. I used
my good hand to haul the trap door open, and I dropped down into the
blackness below. The trap slammed shut above me. The bellowing sounds of
rage went instantly, eerily quiet.

The tunnel had a dirt floor, brick walls, and dank air that coated my
skin like wet wool. My left hand burned with pain, but I ignored it and used
my right hand to fumble with the Maglite in my pocket. Even here I knew I
wasn't alone. With just enough light to see the dangers ahead of me, I took off
at a dead sprint.

Rats skittered away from the light, but not before I caught sight of their
eyes glittering at me from the edges of the tunnel. A brick wall sent me down a
branch to the left, and I braced myself.

Slick stepped out of the shadows, hatred naked in his face. The Monger
ring glinted ominously on his finger. I steeled my will against the impulse to
hide.

"The Sucker is already dead. You will fail." The first time I had heard those words, my will had crumbled and I had broken down in tears. Now though, I had finally faced this scene enough times that I could stand my ground against the despair his words induced.

I squared my shoulders. "Out of my way, Slick."

A gun appeared in his hand, and his finger twitched on the trigger. His smile said he looked forward to shooting me. "The power is already mine."

The first few times, it was the gun that held all my attention. Getting shot in a dream felt like getting punched in the chest. All the air whooshed out of me and I woke up gasping. But when I ignored the gun and listened to his voice, the words made me bold. I was determined to prove him wrong — the power wasn't his, and I could change this. But, like any bully, he wasn't alone. Slick's goons had surrounded me — two behind and one more with Slick blocking my way forward.

I lunged at Slick. He shot reflexively, but I anticipated and spun into a tucked roll at the last minute. The shot hit one of the goons behind me, and I heard the wet smack of a bullet entering flesh. Momentum carried me right into Slick's kneecaps. I had rolled so tightly that his body sailed over mine, and he hit the ground knees-first.

I sprang to my feet just beyond Slick and the goons and bolted forward without a backward glance.

I turned right at the next fork in the tunnel, and found an opening in the wall. Holborn Underground station yawned in front of me, and I hurdled the track to sprint down the center line toward the British Museum ghost station where I'd last seen Archer — in 1944, before a bomb exploded and time split.

I was getting close to the end of the game, and adrenaline fueled the burst of power I sent to my legs. The deep, throbbing hum in my ears grew louder the closer I got to Archer. Just around the bend was the spur to the ghost station, and beyond that was a wall of rubble. I'd long since stopped crying at the sight of that wall. Tearing away at it with my bare hands didn't work — I'd tried it and ended up with nothing more than torn nails and bleeding fingers. When Wilder stabbed my hand, moving rocks became impossible.

So I did the only thing I could do — I picked up a piece of chalky rock and began to draw a spiral. It was the source of the humming sound that had pervaded my dream, so I surrendered to it and let my mind choose the way in this time.

Other times I'd tried to imagine the platform where I'd left Archer. I'd pictured it as it had been, and I'd pictured it collapsed and covered in rubble. But the explosion had changed the landscape of the ghost station so drastically that no amount of imagination could open the portal to find him. I had never gone beyond this impenetrable wall of rocks.

This time, I tried something different. I pictured Archer's face. I filled my mind with the planes of his cheekbones, his jaw, the black of his hair, the length of his eyelashes. I had drawn that face on paper so many times, now I drew it in my mind.

And for the first time since the nightmares had begun, I could see him as clearly as if I'd been standing in front of him. The image of Archer, skin as pale and waxy as death, propped brokenly and utterly unmoving against the passage wall filled my brain.

I closed my eyes and drew the final spiral on the tunnel wall. I felt the stretching and falling and humming take me to him, and then I saw Archer's eyes. They weren't closed in pain or healing, his eyelashes didn't flutter against his cheek, and his pulse didn't beat in his throat. His eyes were open and unseeing — as empty as the glass eyes of a porcelain doll.

The eyes of a dead man.

And then I screamed.

# Tom – Present Day

Screaming sirens filled the air and I set my teeth against them as I climbed the stairs out of the Underground. The power was out in the station, so the only lights on the street came from the handheld torches of shocked onlookers.

I was coated in a thick layer of brick dust, but I'd forgotten about the blood until someone shone a torch into my face and screamed, "He's hurt!"

"I'm fine," I croaked through the dust in my voice. Another Good Samaritan joined the first and tried to hand me water. I pushed it away as I became increasingly aware that the lights I saw were coming from mobile phones being used as torches.

Mobile phones.

I was no longer in 1944.

I shoved through the gathering would-be rescuers and bolted for a dark alley. The whole city block had lost its power, and the wailing sirens and flashing lights of rescue vehicles surrounded the blast site. Something had exploded in the Underground.

I'd been down there when it happened, pushed through a spiral in the ghost station under the British Museum – sent by Saira away from the great-grandfather I'd gone to kill.

Once I hit the ground, I had tried to find the spiral I'd Clocked through, tried to go back to 1944 to finish off George Walters before he could spawn the lineage that made me, but I was blind in the tunnel and stumbled down nothing but empty track.

Then the world exploded behind me, and I ran mindlessly up – away from the choking dust that filled the tunnels.

Now, on the surface, I realized I was in London, *my* London, where mobile phones recorded everything and a bloody, dust-covered guy got too much attention on a pre-dawn city street.

I slid around a corner, out of sight of the well-meaning Londoners. What had they seen? I looked down at myself, barely visible in the still-dark sky of early morning. I was filthy and covered in blood, but my 1940s clothes weren't obviously anachronistic in this age. Outwardly, I probably still looked like the eighteen-year-old guy I was, not the ancient, battle-scarred horror I saw in my mind. I felt my chest, my torso, and my face where I'd been slammed against a wall in the blast. I was battered, but I'd heal after a day's sleep.

My body would heal anyway. I doubted the same could be said for the rest of me.

"Tom?"

I stiffened, and my fingers curled reflexively into weapons.

"Tom, it's Ava."

Ava, somewhere in the alley ahead of me. Her voice was a sound from the time before I knew what true pain was, before hope had fled … and that voice was coming closer.

Panic rose up like a vise to squeeze my throat, and I turned to run. And then I remembered who I was and what I'd done. I wasn't her poor little cousin with an emotionally abusive father and a mother who hated the sight of me because I reminded her of *him* and what *he* had done to her. I wasn't anything weak or frail or good or right. There was nothing in me for her to care about and everything for her to fear. In fact, I thought dispassionately, I could kill my cousin now and then disappear as if I'd never been here at all.

She stopped moving. Maybe she heard my thoughts. I took a step forward. "Ava?" My voice was definitely not my own, and I decided to use the croaking to sound helpless. "Is that really you?"

I sensed her hesitation in the dark. I looked for her, but couldn't see her outline – she was still too far away. I took another step forward.

"Adam was in the tunnels when the bomb exploded," she said. "I can't See him." I froze in place. There was a soft desperation in her voice. "I can't See him underground – or Archer, or Tam."

I didn't know what she was talking about. Tam? Archer? Adam, my cousin and best friend, was underground?

I couldn't let Adam see me. He would know in an instant what I'd become, and he would hate me. I knew I should wrap my hands around Ava's throat, squeeze until she broke, and then find a spiral and just … go.

There was a spiral below – the one I'd come through. Maybe it had survived the blast that had sent me scrambling up to the surface, away from the debris.

Had Adam been down there when the tunnel exploded? I scraped together a vestige of my humanity and backed away from Ava. "I'll go down there. I'll go back down to find him." The words came without conscious thought, and I wanted to take them back the moment I'd said them, because her sigh of relief sent a shiver through me. I turned away from her voice, and from the words I knew were coming.

"Thank you," she whispered.

I stepped toward the alley entrance, still wondering why I didn't break Ava's neck and be done with this place.

"I miss you, Tom," she whispered in the darkness.

I closed my eyes against the hope in her voice and then strode back out to the street.

I made my way back to the Holborn station entrance, but the police had blocked it off with caution tape. A large crowd of onlookers were gathered on the street, all milling about, shooting video and photos with their mobile phones. There was a reporter with a microphone talking about "authorities unsure of the source of the explosion," while words like "terrorism" and "another 7/7" were murmured around her. There were enough bystanders that ducking under the tape would draw attention, and with the hushed whispers of terrorism, attention was the last thing I needed. I would have to find another spiral to escape this place before anyone else knew I'd come back.

Rough hands grabbed my shoulders, and the instinct I'd developed to survive a war took over. I turned with a roundhouse kick and my foot connected with a head. The guy went down with a grunt of pain.

"I told you he'd be fast."

I knew that voice. It was the same one that laughed at me inside my head and called me worthless.

"You've become quite extraordinary, haven't you, Tom? Something quite … different than before." Seth Walters spoke with pride. There was no other way to describe the tone in his voice. I had exactly one second to decide what I was going to do with the father's pride I'd never actually experienced before. With one word, I could embrace it and the legacy that was mine by rights: the Mongerness that I had pulled on and worn with a vengeance since I'd discovered who my biological father really was.

"I never suspected just how useful a bastard bloodsucker would be to me." He sounded impressed, and I turned to face the man responsible for my heritage. He wore the expensive Saville Row suit not like he was born to it – which was how my stepfather, Phillip Landers, wore clothes – but as though he had forced its submission and now it served him. Seth Walters did the same to the men who surrounded him – men as ferocious and submissive as beaten dogs. I knew he held their loyalty on a leash, because I'd once been on the end of it.

My father smiled at me.

I went for his throat.

The fragile bones in his neck were my target. They would snap like firewood if I could get my hands on him, and the flash of fear in his eyes made me even more determined. One of his junkyard dogs yelled, and I was dimly aware of a gun, but I paid no attention until one of them shot me. I didn't know who it was, nor did I particularly care, except that the gunshot slowed me down.

Pain jackhammered through my body. Every wound I'd gotten since I drank Bishop Wilder's Vampire blood hit me at once. War wounds, gunshots, stab wounds … I felt blood run in rivulets down my skin, and I rocked backward as I struggled to regain my balance. It was only a second, but it was enough to let dear old Dad slip out of my grasp.

He stared at me, wide-eyed. Maybe because I suddenly looked like the walking dead, or maybe because I was determined to kill him, but he was definitely no longer happy to see me.

His dogs closed ranks around him instantly, and I knew my chance was gone.

The gunshot brought instant attention to our little tableau, and when the screams died down, the crowd began to move in for a better view.

Seth clutched at one of his men – the one who had shot me – which was how I noticed the ruby ring on Seth's finger. He'd never worn a ring before, and this one matched the Monger ring that Saira had described to me as we dug Léon's grave in medieval Paris. Seth wore the ring to compel people with his words, she'd said. Like the Pied Piper with his flute. A wave of fury hit me squarely, and I made an instinctive move toward him as the shooter's finger tightened on the trigger.

"Don't! He's still useful," Seth snarled.

I would never allow myself be useful to him again. I bolted past a startled tourist who had presumably filmed the whole thing on his mobile.

"It's the bomber! Stop him!" Seth yelled with surprising ferocity, and there was a moment of pure silence as his words were processed in so many brains.

And then pandemonium broke out.

With the Monger ring on Seth's finger, people took his words as truth.

Shouting filled the air and frenzied hands grabbed at me. It was suddenly a fair imitation of a gauntlet-run, and I, ironically, felt like the lone human left to face a zombie apocalypse. I might have laughed if my sense of humor hadn't fled long ago. Here I was, a

Vampire, running from zombie Londoners who believed they were stopping a bloody terrorist.

It was utterly surreal.

I ran straight for the Holborn station entrance and got shot twice more for my trouble as I vaulted the police barricade. Again, the gunshots jackhammered me with pain as all the old wounds flared, but worse than that, they slowed me down. It was time I couldn't afford to lose. I swayed on my feet and braced myself against a wall while the wounds closed. The zombies were still coming, and oddly, the person who came to mind was Saira.

The fury returned. Saira had sent me through that spiral – away from the man I was meant to kill. She had betrayed me, but she came to mind for a reason, and I forced myself to imagine what she would do. I pictured her freerunning from zombies, and I realized I could use the bannister-sliding trick she had taught us all so long ago.

I made it to the platform well ahead of the few brainwashed Londoners who had followed me down, and dove off the platform onto the track. My strength was fading, though I wasn't sure if it was from the gunshot wounds or from the coming dawn. I needed a safe place to hide.

I turned down the spur toward the old Aldwych station and hoped that whatever police activity the explosion inspired wouldn't follow me down an unused track. But I couldn't see in the pitch black, and I tripped over cabling on the track. I went down with a muffled curse.

"What the hell?" A voice from a different lifetime hovered somewhere over me, and for the barest moment I wondered if I'd somehow finally died.

"Adam?"

He dropped to his knees next to me and gripped my shirt. "Tom!" he whispered urgently. "What are you doing here?"

"Leaving," I croaked. Blood loss had taken a bigger toll on my strength than I'd realized. Just then, zombie voices echoed down the track behind me, and Adam hauled me to my feet.

"Come on." His voice was authoritative and firm and held a tone I didn't recognize. This wasn't the Adam I'd always known – so easy-going that his size was never a threat to the random drunks that picked fights with the big young guys in pubs.

"Daisy, move the rest of them out to the other track," Adam whispered to someone else as he pulled me into an open doorway. Adam held me up against the wall for a moment, and I let him. It almost felt good to be held in place by someone strong enough to keep me propped up, and when he closed the door behind us, my legs sagged for just a second.

"Are you okay? Are you … hungry?" His whispered voice was still urgent, and as the sounds of shuffling feet died down, I realized that Adam had just protected other people from me. I shouldn't have been surprised that he knew, but it hurt nonetheless.

I shook my head, though he probably couldn't see it in the dark. "You're more in danger from *my* blood than you are from your own."

He let go of me with one hand and a torch flicked on. I flinched away from the sudden light, even though Adam had it pointed toward the ground.

"Ah, bloody hell," he said quietly. I watched Adam's face as he studied me. There was pain, and maybe some sympathy there, but the thing I waited for, the thing I expected didn't come.

"I know I'm disgusting," I managed to croak.

His eyes opened wider and then they narrowed, right before he pulled me into his chest for a hug. Not the pull-in-and-two-slaps-on-the-back guy hug. It was a proper embrace, and I was so surprised I hugged him back.

"You're sodding filthy, covered in blood, and skinny as a rail. You're a mess, Landers, but you're definitely not disgusting," Adam said quietly.

The tears came then, and I pushed him away so he wouldn't see them. I couldn't stand his kindness and I made my voice as hard and cold as I could. "I thought about killing Ava tonight so she couldn't tell you she'd seen me." Adam flinched, and I thought it took some effort for him to shrug casually.

"I think about killing Ava on a semi-regular basis, but in a family of Seers, it's pretty pointless. Our lot knows everything."

A sob caught in my throat. The tears were going to come in earnest now. "Just stop! Nothing will wipe it away. You don't know what I've done." I swiped angrily at my eyes.

Adam stepped back and then squatted on the dirt floor with his back to the wall. He sat the torch in the middle of the passage, light pointed up like a candle, draped his long arms over his bent knees, and looked up at me.

"So tell me." Adam's voice was quiet, and I stared at him.

He was serious.

And he wasn't horrified.

The silence stretched between us. I scrubbed the tears away with the heels of both hands, then finally shook my head and squatted across from him with my back against the opposite wall.

"Evidently you know I drank Wilder's blood." My insides clenched at the memory of having drained his dead body on the false medieval timeline.

Adam nodded. "Saira told us."

Saira. Her name sent another bolt of anger through me and I glared at Adam. "So she also no doubt told you that she would have rescued me from that hell-hole if I hadn't tried to change things."

He tilted his head and regarded me steadily. "She said your friend died and you blamed yourself."

I snorted angrily. "I *blame* myself? Of course I blame myself! The first time I killed him was pure murder. I was hungry and I drained him of every drop of blood."

"The first time?" Adam ground his jaw, which made me perversely glad. He should never be comfortable around me, no one should.

I drove the knife in deeper. "The second time he died was my fault too. I threatened to murder his family unless he put me out of my misery, but he failed and Wilder broke him. I killed him in cold blood, and then I did it again."

"You couldn't help it," Adam finally said. His voice sounded weak to my ears – as weak as the feeble excuse he made for me.

My eyes narrowed. "You forget that half of me is Monger. Maybe I couldn't help the first murder, but the tenth …? And certainly by the twentieth or thirtieth, I should have gained a little impulse control." My tone was laced with irony and bitterness.

Adam watched me for a long moment, then he leaned forward and looked me squarely in the eyes. "You hate yourself enough for both of us, Tom. I can't compete with that, and I have no interest in trying." He stood up and brushed the dirt off his jeans, then held a hand out to help me up. I ignored his hand and stood on my own.

"Who's after you, then?" His casual tone startled me into an answer.

"Zombies."

Adam scoffed. "Because a Vampire in the London Underground isn't bad enough?"

I winced automatically. "Walters is up above. He's wearing that ruby ring and has everyone convinced I'm a terrorist bomber. They follow the ring so mindlessly, they're like zombies."

Adam sobered instantly. "Seth Walters is out of hiding?"

"If he's hiding, he's doing a piss-poor job of it."

Adam muttered a curse under his breath. "I'll be right back." He strode to the far end of the passage and opened the door to speak to someone. Their voices were quiet, but I caught the words "Monger" and "Aldwych station." A few moments later he returned, and the adult confidence was back on him. "That ring's a problem."

"For me, yeah. But why is it a problem for you? Your mother is scary enough to keep Walters leashed, at least around her precious son."

Adam studied me silently, then changed the subject. "Where did you come through? Did Saira bring you with her?"

"I have no clue where Saira is, nor do I care," I growled.

Adam actually looked shocked for the first time since I'd stumbled into his world. "She didn't find you?"

"She found me. Walters wouldn't be a problem now, though, if she hadn't. If Saira had let me kill his grandfather as I'd planned, that ring wouldn't even be an issue."

Whatever Adam was going to say was lost in the commotion of a naked kid running toward us. "Adam! Is Connor with you? Where's Archer?"

I presumed the kid was Connor Edwards' younger brother, and therefore a Shifter, which explained the nudity. "Slow down, Logan," Adam said. "You should be home. Your mum's going to freak out." He sounded worried.

Logan glared at him, then shimmered for half a second and suddenly a huge, maned Lion stood in front of us. It roared so loudly we both literally hit the walls behind us, and for the first time in a very long time I felt actual fear. Half a second later, the naked boy was in front of us again, so mad his fists were balled up at his sides and his eyes brimmed with angry tears.

"Connor and Archer are missing!" he snarled, in a fair boy version of the Lion's roar. "I looked everywhere. If they're not with you, they're under a wall of rubble so solid not even my Stink Bug could get through."

I stared at Logan, and wasn't sure why the words came out. "You have a stink bug?"

I got the full weight of his death-glare. "I *am* a Stink Bug. Who are you?"

Adam ignored our exchange. "You went back to the blast site?"

Logan nodded vigorously. "The whole British Museum station spur is blocked by rubble. I made myself as small as I could and wound my way through the rocks, but all I found was a dead Monger near the entrance. He was crushed in the cave-in."

"How do you know it was a Monger?"

Logan wrinkled his nose. "They stink." He turned back to me. "You stink too, but not as bad as regular Mongers do."

"So I've got that going for me," I muttered under my breath. Logan looked sharply at me.

"Who *are* you?"

"This is my cousin, Tom," Adam said, dismissing the question with a wave of his hand. It may have been unimportant to him, but the easy way he owned our relationship meant everything to me.

Logan's eyebrows furrowed as he studied me, then he shrugged. "Connor told me about you. You're here for the cure?" he asked in a tone that let us know there were far more important things to be discussing.

Adam suddenly studied me with interest. "Are you?"

I scowled. "Am I what?"

"Here for the cure. Saira told you what Shaw's working on, didn't she?" Adam faced me, and it didn't sit well with the Edwards kid, who inserted himself between us and demanded Adam's attention.

"Connor and Archer. How are we going to get to them?" Logan glared at him, but Adam's eyes were still locked on mine.

"If Seth Walters is out in the open and wearing that ring, getting you to Shaw is going to be tough. The Mongers have had eyeballs on Shaw ever since he started working on Archer's blood."

I still had no idea what Adam was talking about, but pieces were starting to fall into place. "Do you mean Shaw's found something that affects Sucker blood?"

Adam nodded, but his expression was strange. "Yeah, that's one of the reasons Saira and Ringo went to find you. They wanted to bring you back here for the cure."

I exhaled sharply. "My God, does it really work?" The idea that something could actually cure the hunger that had driven me to murder Léon was almost too much to imagine.

Logan was exasperated that Adam's attention was still on me. "No one knows. They think it'll either kill you or cure you. It's not like there are gobs of Vampires around to test it on, and if my brother and Archer are buried under all that rubble, you're it." He spun back around and pushed Adam. "Let's go!"

Adam had been watching me for my reaction, but I kept my expression completely neutral. Finally, his eyes found Logan's angry ones. "Take me to the cave-in," Adam said grimly. Logan Shifted instantly from naked boy to enormous Bat, and he shot Adam a look that dared him to keep up.

My feet were still rooted to the floor of the passageway, and Adam stopped when he realized I hadn't followed. He turned back to face me. "You coming?" I shook my head mutely. Adam took a couple of steps back toward me. "Where will you go?" he asked.

"There really is a cure?" I hated how hopeful my voice sounded to my own ears.

Adam nodded. "I can try to get you some eventually, but I have to keep the mixed-bloods we just risked our bums to rescue out of sight of the Mongers. Their safety is my first priority until we can figure out how to get Walters arrested for their kidnappings."

"He'll never be taken in while he has that ring," I said.

Adam sighed. "That bloody ring. Ringo held it in his hand once, but Saira wouldn't let him steal it."

Bitterness edged my words. "Of course she wouldn't, because it's Saira's plan or nothing."

Adam looked sharply at me. "What's your problem, mate?"

I really didn't want to get into it with Adam, since he clearly still had a crush on her. I shook my head. "Nothing. Go, follow the Bat or he'll come swooping back in here like some prehistoric mutant thing."

"I heard that." Logan's once-again human voice came from the far end of the passageway. "And I'm still waiting."

"What are you going to do?" Adam's voice was quietly urgent.

"I want that cure."

Adam made a face. "As I said, I can't help you now. I have to stay low while Walters is anywhere out there with that ring."

"Thanks to the zombie horde up there, so do I."

"Zombies?" Logan's voice piped up from the other end of the passage. The kid must have still been sporting his Bat ears.

Adam ignored him. "The key is the ring. How can we get it away from him?"

I scowled. "Unfortunately, when I went for Walters' throat, I painted a target on my back."

My cousin looked surprised. "You went for his throat?"

"I'd wipe out his whole line if I could. I would have killed his grandfather if Saira hadn't interfered.

I could have gone my whole life without seeing Adam look at me the way he did at that moment. "Tom," he said quietly. "That's your great-grandfather. If you'd killed him then—"

I interrupted sharply. "There'd be one less lethal Vampire in the world to destroy the lives of people he cares about. And," I cut him off before he could protest, "you wouldn't be having the problem with that ring now because he was wearing it then. I could have grabbed it from his corpse, and … problem solved."

The sick-looking horror on Adam's face shifted to surprise, and he stared at me. "Wait - can you go back?"

I shook my head in disgust. "Not on purpose. I have no idea how I get anywhere. When I go through a spiral, I pretty much just Clock where it sends me."

"Saira says it's all about focusing on a specific time or place, and she has to have a picture in her mind of where she's going."

"Well, I don't have any of her blood. I just have her mother's, and Ms. Elian needed the necklace to focus." The conversation was beginning to set my teeth on edge. "And regardless, I apparently can't go where I already was." My voice was bitter. Medieval France seemed so long ago, and yet it was the first place my thoughts went during a conversation about Clocking.

Adam nodded vaguely, but his mind was obviously somewhere else. His eyes finally re-focused on mine. "Saira can take you to the ring, no matter where or when it is."

"Unless I'm missing something big, Saira's not here," I snapped.

"You could leave a message for her somewhere," Adam said. "Or maybe some-*when*." It's worth a shot if it might keep Walters from ever getting that ring."

I was willing to consider anything for the sake of getting the cure, but it sounded ridiculous even to me. "Chances are I'd Clock back like she did before she knew she could direct it. That would put me somewhere around 1889 or 1890. Where could I possibly leave Saira a message that she would find sometime in the future, and where could I also hang out waiting for her to find it and *maybe* come looking for me, *if she feels like it?*"

Logan came into view from down the hall, still naked, and even angrier than before. "Ringo's flat. No one knows about it, and it's totally hidden."

Adam looked sharply at the kid. "How do you know where it is?"

He shrugged. "Ringo told me. It's where I would hide out in London if I had to. Ringo's with her. Seems logical they'd go there."

"It also seems like the mother of all longshots," I grumbled. "But tell me where it is anyway."

Logan had a memory for details that was like being handed a picture, but it was a twenty-first century picture, not the nineteenth century I'd likely end up in, so I wasn't particularly confident in my chances of finding the place.

Once he was sure I'd gotten it all, Logan turned to Adam again with a growl in his voice, and I wondered if there was such a thing as half-Shifted. "Right – if there's any chance at all my brother is still alive, we need to get him out. Now!"

I thought the probability of anyone surviving that blast was pretty much zero, but the kid was actually terrifying in his Lion form. I didn't need to be the one to provoke it again by saying as much.

Adam surprised me by pulling me into another hug. "Come back as soon as you can," he said as he turned to follow Logan down the passage.

"I'll try," I answered quietly.

SAIRA – ALTERNATE PRESENT

Ringo and I had taken to sleeping in the Clocker Tower at St. Brigid's. It was pretty much forbidden on every level, but I thought Ms. Simpson – the one on this timeline – had figured out I didn't really care about the rules, and there was very little she could do about it anyway. Worst case scenario, we'd leave. Best case scenario, we were leaving anyway, just as soon as we could figure out how to get back to the right timeline.

I hadn't slept well since we'd gotten here. Losing Archer had settled over me like a fever that made my skin hurt, and searing agony sometimes lanced the constant, dull, throbbing ache with breathtaking suddenness. It didn't matter that this could be temporary – that on the real time stream the bomb hadn't exploded in 1944 – and Archer was probably still going about the business of trying to find the mixed-blood Descendants Seth Walters had kidnapped. The fact was that he wasn't on this timeline with me, and I didn't quite know how to get back to him.

The nightmare didn't help. It was the same one every time I closed my eyes, playing through my subconscious like a deadly videogame with challenges to overcome and levels to beat. I flexed my hand again before I picked up the pen. The memory of stabbing pain lived in the tissue, even though there'd never been an actual injury, and I was starting to get jumpy when I had to round a corner in dark halls.

"What're ye writin'?" Ringo said quietly. He'd come down the hidden staircase from the tower room where he slept, but I hadn't heard him behind me. His wraith-like powers were getting better, or my own survival skills were slipping. Considering I couldn't beat my nightmare, I was going with survival skills slippage.

"I'm making a list of everything I notice about this time. If we do fix the time stream, I want to record what I can in case …" I faltered, but Ringo finished the sentence for me.

"In case this time gets erased?"

I swallowed and nodded. "Theoretically, that's what happens, right?"

"Right. What do ye 'ave so far?" He flipped a chair around backward and sat across the desk from me. His arms hung over the chair back in the fluid way guys draped themselves across furniture, as if the furniture, not their bones, was the thing keeping them upright.

I worked down the list. "Obviously, the fact that Millicent got married and Elian Manor has been deserted since Millicent's parents died."

"I'm not actually sure ye didn't change that before time split," he said.

"I had a two-minute conversation with Sean Mulroy as I was stepping onto a plane in 1944. No way was that enough to cause something so big. I mean, Millicent is *married*. She has kids and grandkids. That's a huge change from the history we know."

His eyes held mine. "When are ye goin' to see 'er?" He'd asked me that question pretty much every day we'd been here, and I always gave him the same answer.

"I'm not."

"'Er grandkids go to school 'ere."

"Hopefully we'll be gone before term officially begins."

"Students are already startin' to come back. Ye can't stay 'idden from 'em forever."

"Don't push me, Ringo." He watched me silently long enough that I looked back at my list. "Do you want to hear this or not?"

"If she's 'appy, ye're afraid ye won't be able to do what ye need to do." I looked up at him sharply, but my automatic denial died before any sound came out. Ringo nodded. "Yeah, that's it." He thought about it for a moment. "Ye 'ave to think of this time as more of a 'what if' than as somethin' that's actually real."

"These *are* real people, Ringo – people who love and laugh and have lives that matter to them."

"Are ye arguin' to keep this time intact, or are ye planning to fix the breach?"

I ground my teeth. "We're fixing it. Now, do you want to hear this, or not?"

He rubbed the back of his neck and then waved his hand for me to continue.

"No one here knows us. I mean, Ms. Simpson said she'd Seen us, but only in some weird prophecy vision." We had tried to stay away from the adult staff as they were starting to ready their classrooms for students, but I'd run into the cook, Mrs. Taylor, who'd looked through me as if I wasn't actually there, and Ringo's charm had taken days to work on Annie so she'd give him coffee in the mornings.

"Ye're ignorin' the bigger fact that ye don't actually exist on this time stream," Ringo persisted.

"It's implied. I couldn't be here if I did, could I?" I didn't know why I was getting annoyed with him – he hadn't done anything more than state the obvious, but I had an itchy conscience at the idea of messing things up for Millicent.

"And apparently, yer kind isn't quite so endangered 'ere, what with the Mulroys and the MacFarlane Clocker Ms. Simpson said was comin'."

I shook my head at him. "I've never even heard the name MacFarlane among Clockers. How does a Family line just show up like that in the seventy years since the war ended?"

Ringo shrugged. "Maybe the MacFarlane Family was killed by the bomb explodin', or even by the George Walters who lived on the true timeline. Time splits like it did, and anythin' is possible."

"Makes as much sense as any other theory we have about time stream splits." I shook my head to punctuate the irony in my voice. "Maybe, if he's a Clocker, he can go back to the British Museum ghost station and fix the time split for us."

Ringo's expression was suddenly serious. "'Ow are we goin' to change that bomb explodin', Saira? Ye are the only one who could actually Clock into that station, and like ye said, ye can't go where ye already were."

I couldn't meet his eyes so I stared at the list in front of me. "I don't know. I just know we have to figure it out."

Ringo stood and shoved the chair away. "C'mon. Let's go run. Ye can show me yer new moves."

I scowled. "What new moves? We haven't been running since we got here."

"Ye made it further in yer dream last night didn't ye?"

I stared at him. "How did you know?"

He shrugged. "Took ye longer to cry out. Show me what ye did and I'll show ye a new flip I've been workin' on."

It was an offer I couldn't refuse, because stir-craziness made the itchy conscience worse. We'd spent most of the last few days in the libraries of St. Brigid's and Elian Manor, looking for anything that would help us fix the time stream split. Ms. Simpson was busy with start-of-term business, and I didn't really get the sense she was too interested in helping us. I had a place at the school if I wanted it, she had said, but Ringo was not a Descendant, so she couldn't allow him to enroll as a student. Even though we hadn't planned to stick around long enough to attend classes, it chapped both of us that merit wasn't even a consideration in her decision. It was all about blood.

We didn't bother with stairs, and instead, took off across the roof. There was probably about an hour to run before the light faded too much for a rooftop return. We alternated between straight parkour and fancy-trick freerunning. Ringo was definitely better at the freerunning flips and dives, but I had endurance on my side, so if the run was long enough, I could usually pull ahead.

Today's run was farther than we'd ever gone from St. Brigid's, and I recognized the road that led into Brentwood proper.

"Come on," I said when we stopped for a breath, "I'll buy you a coffee." The fading light turned the sky the color of old denim, and it was an odd time of day for most cafés to be open, but we found one near the church and went inside. The place had a cheerful, bohemian vibe, with a big sideboard along one wall full of paperback books, puzzles, and games. There was no one behind the counter, so I grabbed two menus and we sat ourselves in the window.

"I love places like this," I said in a low voice.

Ringo nodded as he scanned the menu. "We should open one. The profit on a cup of coffee is massive."

I smirked. I used to dream of opening a café with big glass cases of homemade desserts, and walls lined with books, until my mom gave me a very eye-opening view of where the money goes. "Well, a cup of coffee here is £1.30, and last time I checked, minimum wage is £5 for anyone under twenty-one, so it takes four cups of coffee times eight hours, thirty-two cups a day, just to pay for the person to make and pour it. Then there's electricity, water, and gas, and a shop like this probably rents for about £1000 a month, so that's probably another eight hundred cups of coffee, divided by twenty-four days a month that they're open, so …" I did quick calculations using math that I swore to my mother I'd never use outside of school. "That's about another thirty-three cups a day. Which means you'd have to see at least sixty coffee-drinkers every day just to break even."

"That's why we have the books," said a voice behind me. I knew that voice. It was usually accompanied by a feeling of nausea, but oddly, there was none this time. Ringo's eyebrows arched up in the only concession to surprise I knew he'd make, and I carefully composed my face when I turned to see Raven Walters, my former roommate and the Monger niece of my nemesis, Seth Walters.

"Because ye sell them?" Ringo said neutrally.

"There's that, but mostly because people come in for a coffee or a cup of tea, get hooked on a book, and then order two more cups, plus a slice of cake before they finally buy the book and go," Raven said in a friendly tone.

Ringo winked at me. "I knew there was a reason I liked readers. They'll be my customers when I open a place like this."

Raven gave him a proper smile and pulled out a little pad to write on. "I'm Raven. What can I get you?"

I was trying to wrap my head around seeing Raven working at all, much less in a bohemian café with a smile on her face. Shock seemed to make my ability to speak run away screaming.

"I'm Ringo," he said with a return smile, after a quick glance at my shocked face. "'Ave I seen ye at the fencin' gym in town?"

My stunned expression turned to him. What game was he playing? Raven shook her head. "I've tried fencing at school, but I'm not good enough at it to justify the gym fees."

"Oh? What school do ye go to?" he asked.

"St. Brigid's." Raven's tone suddenly downshifted into something far less enthusiastic.

"Doesn't your mom teach there?" I said, before I could consider the words that finally decided to make an appearance.

It was Raven's turn to look surprised. "Do you go to St. Brigid's? I've never seen you there."

I couldn't seem to think of an answer that made sense, but Ringo came to the rescue. "Saira has distant cousins there."

Her expression shuttered, and I had the odd sense that she was about to censor herself. "Oh. I don't know too many people at St. Brigid's. It's a big school."

Raven, the Monger mean girl beauty queen, didn't know people? Everything about this conversation was almost too strange to process and my eyes dropped to my menu. "Could I please have a coffee and a slice of apple tart?"

Her voice brightened again, but there was a false edge to her cheeriness. "Sure. The apple tart is excellent. How about you?" she asked Ringo.

"Coffee with lots of cream and sugar, and whatever dessert ye think is best."

Raven opened her mouth to respond to that, but he hadn't sounded flirty, so she closed it and nodded with a smile. "Be right back."

When she was out of earshot I spoke quietly to him. "What are you thinking?"

"'Ow's the Monger-gut?" he countered.

"Non-existent."

"That's what I thought." He leaned a little closer without being too obvious. "I think ye react the way ye do because the Mongers 'ave always been a threat. There's no Monger ring in this time, and the way she's actin', I'd say they might even be a little powerless among Descendants. You saw the way she shut 'er mouth when I said ye 'ad cousins at St. Brigid's. She's afraid, and there's nothin' threatenin' about 'er to ye. So, no Monger-gut."

Raven returned with a tray of our coffees, a big jug of cream for Ringo, and two apple tarts. She smiled at me as she set the tarts in front of us. "You chose wisely," she said.

"Raven, can I ask you something?" Ringo's observations had sent me on a fishing expedition.

"Sure." Her tone was friendly.

"I'm trying to decide whether to go to St. Brigid's, and the only things I've heard about it are from cousins I don't really know. I'd really appreciate a different perspective as I try to make up my mind."

She considered me for a moment. "Do you mind if I ask who your cousins are?"

"They're Mulroys," I said. Whoever the Mulroy kids were, I hoped they weren't jerks.

Raven nodded thoughtfully. "They're young, so I don't really know them. The other Clocker at school is someone I'd stay away from though."

"Why? Who is he?"

She suddenly got busy re-tying her apron. "Like I said, I don't really know too many Clocker kids. I just keep to myself."

I decided to throw caution to the wind and take a potshot at it. "What about the mixed-bloods at school? Are you friends with any of them?"

Raven stared at me like I'd grown a third eye. "Mixed-bloods? There aren't any mixed-bloods. The moratorium makes them illegal."

Damn. I had hoped it was just a Monger thing. "Just because something's illegal doesn't mean it doesn't exist."

She gave me an odd look. "You're not from around here, are you?"

I shook my head. "My mom's English, but I was raised in the States."

"Well, I don't know how they do things in the States, but here Descendant laws don't get broken."

"Why not? Who enforces them?" I asked. Maybe Ringo was wrong about the powerlessness of Mongers. Raven was staring at me in shocked silence, so I prompted her again. "Well, who's the Descendant law enforcer?"

She looked over her shoulder, as if someone else was in the room who could overhear, and her tone was incredulous that I didn't know. "Death, of course."

DEATH, OF COURSE

It was my turn to stare. "Death? Like people get put to death if they break Descendant laws?"

From the look on Raven's face, my third eye had just become a headful of snakes.

"The Immortal Death. You know," her voice dropped to a whisper that was a tad too Voldamorty for my taste, "Aeron."

Right. Death.

"So, say a kid is born to a Clocker and a Shifter, for example. Death just shows up and … what?" I struggled to keep the incredulousness from my tone, but I pretty much failed.

"There would never be such a child."

"Why not?"

"Because a Clocker and a Shifter would never be allowed to be together."

I felt like I was back on my own timeline talking to Adam. "Just hypothetically then. Or say there was a mixed-blood kid no one knew about, how would anyone ever find out?"

"Well, if someone was suspected of being mixed, it would probably be like with any other crime. The person would have to plead their case in front of the Council, and if a decision couldn't be reached, then Death would get the truth."

I wasn't the only one staring at her now. "Bloody 'ell. What does *that* mean?" Ringo's voice was quiet but as intense as I'd ever heard it. Raven's eyebrows furrowed.

"Obviously, he doesn't come 'round much. The Council tries not to call him if they can avoid it. I don't think he's been seen in years."

"But Death himself has actually shown up at a Council meeting? How does someone call Death? What does he look like? Do any of the other Immortals come around?" I knew my eyes were huge in my face, and I was babbling, but seriously, this was massive.

Raven suddenly got all rabbity and scared-looking. "I shouldn't be talking about this." Her voice dropped to a whisper again as she looked around nervously.

I reached out to touch her hand, but she snatched it back like she'd been burned. "I really must get back to work," she said as she hurried away.

Ringo and I stared at each other across the table.

"Death is the enforcer?" he said, shocked.

I stood and fished a twenty-pound note out of my pocket. "I think we need to have another conversation with Ms. Simpson," I said, slapping the note on the table.

"Ye gettin' change for that?" Ringo asked, indicating the money.

I shook my head. "The information alone was worth more than that."

He followed me out of the café, mumbling under his breath. "Books and information. That's 'ow to make it in the café business."

We didn't speak on our run back, and by mutual, silent agreement we made our way directly to Ms. Simpson's private office in the library. She was in and didn't seem surprised to see us when I tapped on the open door.

"It's not a good time, Miss Elian," she said sharply.

"Right now, or in general?" I didn't consider my words before speaking, which was common enough that Ringo didn't even flinch. Ms. Simpson, however, narrowed her eyes as she looked up at me.

"I trust you will be forming your own opinion about that, regardless of what I might say," she said archly.

"Is Death really the Council's enforcer?" I blurted.

Ms. Simpson stood and came toward me. "I believe I told you that it is not a good time. Good evening, Miss Elian." She closed the door firmly, and I heard the lock click. I turned to Ringo, shocked by her abrupt dismissal.

He shrugged. "I guess it's not a good time."

I glared at him and stormed out of the library, suddenly determined to find someone who would answer my questions. Almost without realizing I was doing it, I headed toward Mr. Shaw's office. Ringo kept pace beside me as if he knew exactly where we were going, yet both of us pulled up in surprise to find his door open and the light on in his office.

I knocked tentatively on the doorframe and stepped forward so I could be seen.

The office looked the same as it did on the right time stream, including Mr. Shaw seated behind the big scarred-wood desk. "Yes?" His voice was the same deep growl, but his eyes were wary, and he looked at me without recognition.

"Mr. Shaw?" I said, trying to sound more confident than I felt.

"Are you students?" he asked, beginning to sound impatient. "Because students would know better than to disturb me before the term has officially begun."

This was the blustery bully I'd met when I first came to St. Brigid's School a lifetime ago, but rather than back away in fear as he probably expected me to, I stepped into his office with a smile. "Mr. Shaw, I'm Saira Elian, and this is Ringo."

His eyes narrowed as he studied first me and then Ringo, who had stepped into the office behind me and shut the door. "So?" His tone was dismissive, but there was wary interest in his expression. I took a deep breath and another step closer, but his growl halted me. "I'm busy. What do you need?"

"Information," I said bluntly.

He glared at me. "The library is down the hall."

"Only useful if you know what you're looking for," I retorted.

His glare sharpened at my too-quick comeback. "Saira Elian, you said? Any relation to the Mulroy kids?"

I looked him straight in the eyes, took a deep breath, and dove. "Elian is the Clocker Head Family on the other time stream – the one I come from. There are no Mulroy Clockers in my time."

His eyebrows shot up. "Other …" His voice faded away, but he remained otherwise motionless as he stared at me. He tried to speak, failed, cleared his throat, and finally found his voice again. "Why are you here?"

"Accident."

"And ….?" He was watching me as if I was suddenly going to grow fangs and strike.

My eyes flickered to the shelf where the other Shaw kept vials of various things he was working on, including the salve he had once used on Connor's Werewolf bite, but this shelf was minus the rack of test tubes filled with Archer's blood that I'd become used to seeing.

Right. Without Archer, Shaw had no impetus to work on a cure for Vampirism, and the thought chilled me. My eye was caught by my dad's brass microscope, and my heart was suddenly in my throat in a way nothing else in this time had caused. I took a step toward the shelf and Mr. Shaw stiffened.

"A Ross binocular microscope, circa 1870," I said quietly. He stood then, so fast he knocked his chair over. It landed with a crash, and I turned to face him. "It was my dad's."

His expression shifted so rapidly I could barely register the shock and the horror before he wiped his face blank. "I'd like you to leave my office, Miss Elian." His growling voice was the only thing that betrayed any emotion at all, and I could see I'd pushed him further than he could deal with in that moment.

I nodded. "We'll be out running in the north woods later if you want to find us," I said. I knew he needed time to process our presence before he'd be willing to talk. I only hoped this Mr. Shaw was as curious and fearless as my Mr. Shaw was.

Neither of us turned our back on him until we'd stepped out of the office. When one is faced with a confused and startled Bear, backing away is pretty much the only way to stay intact. Ringo shut the door behind us, and he looked a little worried. It was a rare enough expression that I stopped. "What?" I said, trying not to sound defensive.

"Was that wise?"

I exhaled shakily. "Baiting a Bear? Admitting I'm mixed? Busting ourselves on our visitor status? Probably not."

"And ye just invited 'im to find us in the woods?" Ringo shook his head. "Are ye daft?"

I laughed to cover my nerves. "Apparently so." I took off toward the stairs that led up to the Clocker Tower. "How else are we going to find out what we need to know?"

Ringo kept stride with me, and his voice was tighter than normal. "What is it we need to know, exactly?"

"How to fix the timestream split," I said, exasperated.

"And 'ow is knowin' about this time's politics figurin' that out?"

I threw my hands up. "It's information. That, books, and coffee, and we'd be in business."

A voice I knew like my own called down the hall to us. "Oy! Are you mad standing there?"

I spun to greet it, my relief at the distraction giving me temporary amnesia about the fact that he didn't know me on this time stream. "Adam!"

His answering grin would have made me fling my arms around him for a giant hug if it hadn't been accompanied by an up-and-down leer worthy of the obnoxious player he could be. "Was it as good for me as it obviously was for you?"

I stared at him. "Are you kidding? You actually just said that out loud?"

"Yeah, well, it does me no good to keep it in my pants, now, does it?"

"Ew," I grimaced. "Where's Ava? You clearly can't be let out in polite company."

"Sorry, Adam, who is this?" Another voice I knew piped up from behind him, and I looked past my hulking friend who was currently grossing me out, to find an unfamiliar face.

"Who are *you*?" I blurted, because blurting is what I did.

Adam's leering grin was jovial as he turned to the guy behind him, a slender, elegant, dark-haired, slightly exotic guy who looked like someone I should know, but didn't. "The way she's staring, I think she likes you, Tom."

"Tom?!" I *was* staring. In shock. "You don't look like yourself."

Ringo spoke warningly under his breath. "Saira."

"So the strange girl's name is Saira. Odd, but nice," Adam said.

I dragged my eyes away from Tom and fixed them to Adam. "I need to talk to Ava."

Something in my tone must have finally gotten through Adam's player persona because the look he shot me was coated in slightly less slime. "She's saying goodbye to the fam downstairs. Why?"

Oh boy, I really didn't want to run into Camille Arman, but maybe she didn't hate me yet on this time stream – after all, I hadn't come *here* to steal the Seer cuff from her Family, back when I'd needed to bring it to Elizabeth Tudor. "I have questions, and Ava usually has answers," I said to Adam. My eyes slid past Tom's guarded expression, and I suppressed the shock his face inspired.

Shock, because there wasn't a trace of Seth Walters in Tom's appearance. He was Phillip Landers' biological son, right down to his father's arrogant eyebrow arch. According to Ava, his mother had gypsy blood, which was the source of the exotic coloring on both versions of Tom.

I took off down the hall at a full sprint, away from the narrowed eyes of both guys, and hit the main staircase bannister like a playground slide. Ringo came down the other bannister with even more grace than I'd managed, and the slide felt like a tiny gasp of fresh air in the whole dark tunnel that was this time stream. I turned to find Mr. and Mrs. Arman looking at us with varying degrees of horror, and Ava's face lit up with an ethereal smile.

"Hello, Saira," she said brightly.

Relief poured through me at being recognized, until Ava turned to Ringo. "I'm sorry, I didn't See you. I'm Ava Arman." She held her hand out to shake his, and he took it politely.

"I'm Ringo." Ringo's quick pitying look at my face told me he understood the depths of my disappointment.

Mrs. Arman saw it too and stepped forward to shake my hand. "I'm Camille Arman, but I think perhaps you know that?" She took my hand in hers, and her eyes widened immediately. Mrs. Arman could get instant visions of people through touch – a fact I'd learned the first time I met her. I knew she was a strong Seer, but her daughter was stronger.

"I'm not sure it's a wise idea for you to come to a Council meeting, Saira. Don't you agree, Ava?"

Well, that was interesting.

Ava cocked her head like a bird as she looked at me. Then her head swiveled and she regarded Ringo. "Information and books. Those are the currencies you trade in."

If he was startled, he didn't show it. "That's right."

She turned her gaze back to me. "There's a Council meeting tomorrow at noon. It would be best if you weren't seen, I think."

"Ava—" her mother began, but Ava shook her head.

"No, mother. He has the right idea. They need information." Ava turned back to me. "But what do we get in return?"

"What do you want?" My heart slammed in my chest. Ava didn't know me, but somehow she Saw me – it was enough to feel like this place was real and not just a figment of a very twisted dream.

"There's going to be an attack at the meeting," she said in an eerily calm voice. "You can prevent it."

THE BEAR

Great. Did I have a sign on my forehead that said *disaster magnet*? Ava saw the expressions on my face run the gamut from shock to chagrin, but then cut me off before I could ask any of the questions that raced through my brain.

"I have to run," she said, kissing her mother on the cheek. "Miss Simpson is waiting."

An attack, she'd said. "Wait, Ava—"

She shot me a bright smile. "You are a Clocker. It's the only thing I can See that could possibly change things."

"But I'm not the only one. Why me?"

She shrugged. "You're here and I've Seen you." Then she darted away, her parents said a hasty goodbye to us, and we were left standing in the hall with stunned expressions still painted on both our faces.

Hard to argue with that, but it didn't change the fact that I felt a burning need to run. Ringo seemed to share the desire because he started bouncing up and down on the balls of his feet.

"Food first, then we run," he said.

"Right," I answered. By mutual agreement, we slipped out the front door of the school and around to the kitchen gardens at the back of the massive building. Inside we could see Mrs. Taylor calling swift orders to Annie.

"Think you can get some soup for us?" I asked Ringo.

He shrugged. "I'll see what sort of charm I can lay on."

"Wait … here, take this." I gathered some fresh thyme from a small patch of dirt just outside the walled garden and handed the bunch to him. "See if this helps your case."

He nodded and slipped into the kitchen. I could see him talking to Annie, and she smiled as she accepted the bundle of thyme. That was a good sign. Mrs. Taylor came into view so I stepped back into the shadows, and a moment later Ringo came outside with two bowls of soup with half a loaf of bread laid across the top of them.

"Nicely done," I said.

"We passed a patch of chanterelles on our run earlier. I told 'er I'd bring 'er some tomorrow."

"You're getting better at foraging. You'd make a great Clocker." We entered the garden and sat on a low stone wall. I was hit with a sudden pang of missing Archer – missing all the times we'd found each other in walled gardens. I had to take a couple of deep breaths to open my throat enough so I could eat. I wasn't hungry, and hadn't really been since we'd landed on this wrong time stream, but I ate to keep my strength and because I knew hunger didn't change the ache of missing Archer, it just layered it with a different kind of emptiness.

"What do ye think 'Is Lordship would do if 'e were 'ere?" Ringo asked quietly as we ate.

I thought about that for a long moment. "I think he'd gather information about this timeline – as much as he could."

"To what end?" Ringo didn't sound sarcastic, just curious.

"It's what he does. It's his version of preparing himself for anything, I guess." I wiped up the last of my soup with a piece of bread. "You and I are maybe more practical when it comes to surviving a situation we know nothing about. We look for the basics – food, hiding places, self-defense options – and then figure out how to navigate from there. Archer looks at new situations as if he's playing chess. He studies the board and the players, and then he builds his strategy when he understands the game."

"Maybe we should think like Archer then," Ringo murmured.

I stood abruptly. "Let's go find a Bear in the woods." It was basically the antithesis of what Archer would have done, but thinking about him made it hard to breathe, and I needed air more than just about anything in that moment.

Ringo regarded me for a long moment and finally nodded. "Right."

I let him lead the way so I didn't have to concentrate on anything other than where to put my feet. Running gave me time to think, and thinking was something I'd been struggling with recently. Ringo took us to a section of the woods I hadn't explored before, with big granite boulder outcroppings. We scrambled to the top of the biggest pile and dropped to a seat. The view back toward the school was spectacular, and I watched the distant lights while my heart rate slowed down to something resembling a normal pulse.

"I think we have two problems," I finally said.

I could feel Ringo's raised eyebrow next to me in the dark. "Only two?"

I ignored him and ticked them off my fingers. "The biggest one has to do with reversing the time split. We either have to find someone willing to go to the British Museum station – someone our unwitting selves wouldn't freak out about seeing there – who can change the whole attempted-murder/shooting-the-bomb thing, or we have to stop George Walters from going there in the first place."

"Either of those means a trip back to 1944, and both feel like stumblin' around in a dark room full of wicked blades," said Ringo.

"Right. I know. I'm sick of slamming into things I can't see, so it would be good to have a plan."

Ringo arched a brow. "Listen to yer big talk about havin' a plan. What's our second problem?"

"Ava's vision about the Council meeting tomorrow. If there's going to be an attack, we'd be crazy to go in there completely blind."

"Ye think?" His voice was thick with irony.

I turned to look at Ringo. "I do want to think like Archer would – plan, be strategic, figure out the players and their game. I mean, the political situation here is weird, right? But weird in a way that could be possible in our own time."

"With a massive shift of power, maybe," Ringo said doubtfully.

I shrugged. "Why not? The players are all there, more or less, they're just on different squares playing different roles than we're used to. It's like the rook is suddenly a knight, and the king might actually just be a pawn."

"Mongers are the pawns?" he asked.

I shrugged. "I don't know. My point is that if we learn how this game is being played, it might give us insight into how to fix the problems in our own Council."

"When did ye get so political?" He met my eyes.

I sighed. "I just know we need to go to that Council meeting tomorrow."

"So you've come about MacFarlane then?" A deep voice came from the darkness.

I forced myself to stay still. "Hello, Mr. Shaw. There's room up here if you want to join us."

"Answer the question." He ground out the words gruffly as I turned to look at him. He was wearing clothes, so he hadn't come as a Bear, and the expression on his face was hard.

"Ye're talkin' about the Clocker bloke at St. Brigid's?"

Mr. Shaw snorted. "If he were only a Clocker we wouldn't be having this conversation, would we?"

That statement would probably have sounded really cryptic to someone who wasn't me. "He's mixed?" I asked carefully.

There was a long moment of silence before Shaw spoke again. "When MacFarlane showed up, my class was ABO typing, so I got a look then."

"Blood testing," I murmured to Ringo.

"Yeah. Connor taught me 'ow."

Mr. Shaw hoisted himself up onto the boulder. "Connor who?" he growled at Ringo.

"Connor Edwards."

"You don't know Connor." Shaw said. His wariness was making me tired.

Ringo sighed. "'E's a Shifter Wolf, 'is little brother, Logan, can Shift into any animal 'e chooses, 'is da died before 'e was ten, and 'e's the smartest bloke I know."

Shaw settled back and sounded smug. "You know something about him, apparently, but you certainly don't know him. My nephews are camping with their father this weekend – their very-much-alive father."

My breath hitched in my chest. According to my mom, Connor's dad had died in a car accident with a drunk driver. Was it possible the accident had never happened on this timeline because of something that changed when George Walters was blown up in 1944?

Ringo stared at me. "What did we do?" he whispered.

"I don't know what your game is, but I don't like it," Mr. Shaw snarled.

I tore my eyes away from Ringo's and gave the angry Shifter my full attention – I would deal with the fallout later. I took a deep breath. "Mr. Shaw, you said MacFarlane 'showed up.' What does that mean?"

The subject change seemed to send him off-balance enough that he answered automatically. "Just what I said. We came back from the holiday and there he was – a nineteen-year-old Scottish Clocker, apparently shipped here by his parents to finish his education in England. At first he was quiet, always watching, always paying attention to the least little thing …" His voice trailed off, as though he might have said more, but stopped himself.

"Why did you assume we're here for MacFarlane?"

Mr. Shaw was silent for a long moment and seemed to be searching my face for … something. Finally, he grunted. "His mother's people are Clockers, and I believe he's trying to get back to them."

"Get *back* to them? If he's a Clocker he can place-jump to Scotland any time he wants to."

"The difficulty is, there are no MacFarlanes left in Scotland," he said simply. "I checked."

I replayed his words in my head. "You think he's from a different time?"

Mr. Shaw nodded. "I do."

"Yer blood test showed 'e's mixed. What's 'e mixed with?" asked Ringo quietly.

The Bear didn't look at my friend when he answered. He just spoke the word into the night to be carried away on the breeze. "Monger."

I shook my head. "Who else knows that besides you?"

Mr. Shaw's gaze swung back to me. "No one does."

"We were talking about going to the Council meeting tomorrow, and you asked if we were here for MacFarlane. What does he have to do with the Council if they don't know he's mixed?"

Mr. Shaw seemed to consider his words very carefully before he spoke. "Young Darrell MacFarlane has been accused of a crime, and tomorrow the Council is meeting to decide his fate. This might not be so remarkable if not for the fact that for the first time since World War II, there will be a sitting Councillor for War."

I was stunned. "Mongers haven't sat on the Council in seventy years?"

"There's been no need, as they have no particular skill to speak of beyond making trouble."

I couldn't even wrap my head around the strangeness of this time stream's politics. "So, what happens when there's a Monger Head at the table?"

"Not just a Monger Head, *the* Monger himself is coming to listen to the case against young MacFarlane."

"*Duncan* is coming?" I gasped.

Mr. Shaw nodded solemnly. "And with one Immortal in the room, they may have no choice but to call Death to decide the boy's fate."

My jaw had dropped open, and I didn't even care that I looked like a dimwitted fish. Ringo found his voice before I could remember where I left mine.

"What did MacFarlane do?" he asked.

Shaw surveyed us with a serious gaze. "He stole the Clocker necklace."

INFORMATION

Confusion made my head spin. "He can't have stolen it," I said with a lot more conviction than I felt. "The Clocker necklace isn't on this time stream." And it couldn't be, because my mom had Clocked forward with it from the Council massacre of 1871, so it had skipped over the split and landed with her on the real time stream – the one I came from.

It was Mr. Shaw's turn to look shocked. "Of course it is. All the Family Heads have their artifacts except the Mongers."

"No they don't." His Family didn't either, because I happened to have the Shifter bone tucked down inside my shirt. And since I'd found it in 1889 and basically removed it from circulation, it couldn't have been found by anyone on a time stream that didn't exist until 1944. Ever since we'd landed here I was paranoid about leaving the Shifter bone, or anything else of importance, behind in the Clocker Tower. My daggers were currently strapped to my back under my shirt, and Archer's ring was on my finger. I even had a tin of green medicine next to the Maglite in my back pocket. I was as prepared as I knew how to be, especially since it was the only thing I felt like I had any control over.

"They most certainly do," Mr. Shaw insisted. "The artifacts give the Family Heads their right to sit on the Council. The Mongers lost their right when their artifact was lost in the war."

I shot a quick look at Ringo. He was grimly silent, probably thinking the same thing I was: everyone except maybe the Seers was lying about having their artifact.

"So, Millicent's the Clocker Head?" I asked Mr. Shaw.

"*Lady* Millicent was going to step down in favor of her daughter, but now the change of title is on hold until the necklace is found." Mr. Shaw wore his gruff voice like an accessory. It was especially jarring because I knew what he sounded like without it, and I missed his kindness and humor.

"Mrs. Arman is the Seer Head, right?"

"Only until her daughter turns eighteen next month," Shaw said.

"Really? I've always thought of Camille Arman as more the Queen Elizabeth type – they'll have to pry that crown out of her cold, dead fingers."

Miraculously, Mr. Shaw chuckled. "I would have thought that too. But Ava is clearly the stronger Seer, and a good relationship with her daughter seems to be more important to Camille than power. Of course, thwarting Phillip Landers' ambitions also might have something to do with it."

I'd forgotten that Tom's dad was such a power-hungry jerk. "What about the Shifters? Are the Shaws still banned from leadership?"

Mr. Shaw stood abruptly and leapt to the ground. "As fascinating as this conversation has been, I'll leave you now." He moved away before I could even get to my feet.

"Mr. Shaw! He didn't do it, you know." I called after him.

He paused, the broad outline of him barely visible in the darkness.

"Will Shaw didn't kill the Council in 1871. Rothchild brought in Weres, and they went crazy with bloodlust, killing everyone except my dad, because he had Shifted and could fight them off. He hid the Shifter bone for his brother, Brian, to find. I know where it is, if you want it." My words trailed off because I wasn't quite sure what I was offering. Was I really prepared to give him the Shifter bone from around my neck just so he could finally be the Family Head?

I felt Ringo's tension crackle next to me, and I held my breath. Finally, the sound of footsteps resumed as Mr. Shaw walked away without another word.

"Ye do realize 'e may not want to be Shifter 'Ead?" Ringo said quietly.

"I just told him that the current Head is probably lying about having the Family artifact. I think his honor will kick in and he'll feel duty-bound to expose the fraud." I got up and brushed off my jeans before jumping down to the ground.

"So then, are ye really goin' to leave the Shifter bone on a timeline you mean to destroy?"

"Not holding back even a little bit, are you?" I said grimly.

Ringo landed beside me. "I think ye're right about goin' to that Council meetin' tomorrow, if only to see War and maybe Death in the flesh. But then I think we need to leave this place. Whatever was set in motion with the bomb in 1944 'as left a tangled mess, and I've a feelin' that a storm is comin' to whip that mess into a giant knot. We don't want to get tied up with that, ye know?"

I threw a bunch of drama into my sigh, just to get it out and over with. "I was hoping we could figure out when and where to go before we hurled ourselves into a spiral."

Ringo shrugged. "1944 seems as good as any other time, and better than some."

"Before the bomb? I don't even know if I can get us there."

He shrugged. "Maybe we'll have luck tracing George Walters' movements in the weeks leading up to it. In any case, we'll be closer to the split and much farther away from this political madness."

I sighed again. I was tired of hunting for needles in haystacks. "You're right. It's a place to start, and if we're at your flat, we can stay anonymous."

"That's what I was thinkin' too. Ye all right to run back, or do ye need to do some more dramatic sighin'?"

I threw an elbow into his side and then took off running. Ringo's laughter behind me finally made me smile.

Tom Landers was waiting for us when we got back. He had parked himself outside the Clocker Tower, which was disturbing enough, but when Tom's voice came out of a face I barely recognized, I struggled to keep my expression neutral.

"I need to talk to you," he said to me.

I stopped outside the door because I had a strange desire to keep him out of my space. "What's up?" I tried for casual, but even I could hear the tension in my voice.

"You said I don't look like myself, which implies that you know me, but as someone else. Explain please." He sounded arrogant, just like his dad, with none of the teasing cockiness that Adam did so charmingly well.

I looked him straight in the eye. "No."

Tom took a step backward, as if my refusal had pushed him. "But I've Seen you tell me."

"Then you already know the answers."

His arrogance crumbled at the edges, and a glimpse of the Tom I knew peeked out. "Tell me why you know Adam, then."

I relented. "We're friends."

"Why don't I know you? I've Seen you, so I feel as though I must."

"What have you Seen me do?" I asked. No matter how dumb it was to ask about the future, I could never help myself. I caught Ringo's warning look, but I ignored it.

Tom's expression shifted to something calculating. "An information trade then? I'll tell you what I've Seen, and you'll tell me why I don't look like myself."

That was the piece of the story I really, really didn't want to tell him, and he must have seen the reluctance on my face, because he decided to tempt me. "My vision involved the Council meeting tomorrow."

I exhaled sharply. The Tom I knew hadn't been a particularly distinguished Seer, maybe because he was mixed with Monger, but on this time stream he was a full-blooded Seer – one whose visions I probably shouldn't ignore. "Damn. Okay, you go first."

"Clearly not. I don't know you, and therefore have no reason to trust you," he said.

"What I have to tell you will upset you, and you're going to want to get as far away from me as possible," I said. He looked skeptical. "Okay, fine, I'll give you the first piece, then you tell me what you Saw, and I'll tell you the rest. Does that work?"

He must have practiced Phillip Landers' haughty look in the mirror, because he did it exceptionally well. Finally, he looked around. "Are we really going to have this conversation in the hall?"

I sighed again. Apparently I wasn't done with the drama for the night. "Fine, you can come in." He was a Seer, so he probably already knew where the key was kept, and after tomorrow's Council meeting, we'd be gone anyway.

Tom looked around the inside of my tower in awe. "I didn't know this was here."

I flipped over the paper on which I'd been writing my list of time stream differences and sat on the desk. Ringo draped himself over the back of the chair and left the sofa for Tom. Our seating choices put him at a height disadvantage, which was calculated to take some of the arrogance out of his posture. It worked.

"So, you probably already know I'm a Clocker, right?"

Tom nodded. "Ava told us."

"Well, technically, I don't exist on this time stream." His eyebrows rose, but he stayed silent. "Time split in 1944, and I'm from the other time."

"Time … split." It wasn't a question, but more of a trying-to-wrap-his-brain-around-it statement.

"Yeah."

"Like, it … broke?" The wheels were churning, and I could see him begin to work it out.

"It's more like dropping a boulder into a stream. Water keeps flowing down one side like always, but now there's a new side for it to flow. It's the same river, but with two streams."

Tom looked away for a long moment, and then his eyes snapped back to mine. "And I'm on both timestreams?"

Tom was probably smarter than Adam, a fact I needed to remember. "Yes."

He looked intently at me. "And I look different on the other timestream because my parentage was affected by whatever caused the split?"

Yep, definitely smarter. "Yes, but that's the part that's going to suck, so let's get to your vision. What did you See at tomorrow's Council meeting?"

He sat back and seemed to process my words. Or maybe he was deciding how much to tell me. Finally he looked up and met my eyes. "You have something Death wants. He'll see it, and he'll come after you."

"See what? What do I have?" My heartbeat slammed in my chest, and I took a deep breath to calm the panic that rose with my pulse.

"I don't know; that part was hidden. My visions are more of a *knowing* than something I actually see – they always have been."

Huh, that was an interesting piece of Tom to file away, because it might have come from his mother's gypsy side. I deliberately shifted my brain to practical information-gathering so my heartbeat would quit making my throat jump.

"Should I be worried?" I asked as casually as I could manage.

Tom's eyebrow quirked up. "I've never met Death, but I can't say the idea of him coming after me would be welcome."

Another deep breath. "Right. Well, as interesting as your information is, it doesn't really help me."

Tom glared at me. "So you're not going to tell me the rest?"

I glared right back. "I don't break deals, Tom. I'll tell you the rest. I was just stating a fact. If there's anything else you have that could help me navigate the meeting tomorrow, I'd be grateful for the heads-up."

His defensive posture finally relaxed a little, and then he said, "There's a hiding spot at the bottom of the stairs leading into the Council room."

"I know, I've hidden there before."

"Well, don't this time. Get there early and find a place on the other side of the room."

"You mean trap myself there?" Yeah, no.

Tom met my eyes. "You're never trapped when you have a marker."

My eyes narrowed at him. "You Saw me draw a spiral?"

He shook his head. "It's another *knowing*."

I studied him for a long moment. "Does your dad *know* things like you do?"

His own eyes narrowed. "My mother does. So, my father isn't my father on the other time stream?"

Damn, he was really smart, and I could tell from his expression that I couldn't dodge this one. "Correct."

"Are my parents married to each other?"

"Yes."

"Was it an affair?" His voice was hard.

I held his gaze with mine. "No."

There must have been something in my tone that he understood, because his eyes didn't leave mine until he finally nodded. He got up and paced around the room, studied the curves of everything, and even opened the drapes that covered the painting of the London Bridge. When he turned back to face me, his expression was grim. "What am I mixed with?"

Crap. Really? I had hoped the news of a different father would be enough to forestall this question. Apparently not. I braced myself. "Monger."

The pause was shorter this time before he nodded. "Right. Interesting, but immaterial to me now." Tom strode toward the door, and I jumped off the desk and followed him. He turned to me before he opened the door. "Good luck tomorrow."

"Tom ..." I faltered. I didn't really know what to say, but needed to say something. "I'm sorry," I finally said.

"Don't be. Regardless of the time stream, I'll never know what it's like to have a father who isn't a tosser." He left the room then, and the door clicked loudly as it shut.

My eyes filled with tears for the Tom I had once known, and I couldn't look at Ringo as I reached for the door handle. "I'm going to go wash up for bed. I'll see you in the morning."

"Saira," Ringo said softly.

I shook my head and avoided his eyes. "It's just a little lingering drama. I'll get over it." I took a deep breath and opened the door. I was grateful to find the hall empty, and I closed it behind me so Ringo wouldn't see me cry.

I went to look for Ava in the morning to hear about her vision, but her parents had already come for her. The Council meeting was supposed to start at noon, so at nine o'clock, Ringo and I gathered our few possessions together, strapped our messenger bags across our bodies, and Clocked out of St. Brigid's. I took us directly into the Council room and hoped the early hour would guarantee its emptiness. Fortunately, this Council room was exactly the way I remembered it, and was indeed deserted. I gave Ringo the quick tour of the different Family wall carvings while we searched for someplace to stash ourselves, and I showed him where I'd found the Shifter bone. The problem, however, was that there was no obvious place to hide.

Ringo finally climbed up on top of the huge black marble table and surveyed the room.

"Tom said to hide opposite the door," I said in frustration. We were both very aware of what Tom had said, but hiding in the giant fireplace that was across the room from the entrance seemed a little *too* obvious.

Ringo stared at the fireplace through narrowed eyes. He jumped down off the table and crossed the room to run his hand along the side of the mantel.

"Archer didn't build this one," I said. I had been trying for levity, but the words caught in my throat. No matter how much denial I managed every day, thoughts of him continued to hit me right in the stomach, or heart, or lungs, or wherever my emotions happened to be situated in that moment. I needed to change things so I could get back to him, and that need had become like oxygen to me.

"No, but there might be a common design," he said as he pushed a carved panel and it depressed into the stone around it. I gasped as the back of the massive fireplace clicked, and a small seam appeared in the corner.

I pushed it forward and a dark cavity yawned behind it. I stared at Ringo. "You're a genius. But a common design with what?"

"You told me about the fireplace passage out of the Saint Séverin Abbey. It was meant for Descendants, and I thought ye might 'ave exits from any room ye lot built for yer own use."

I shone my Maglite into the cavity behind the fireplace. I remembered that Old Bailey had been re-built around 1902, and I wondered if the fireplace had been opened since then. It was relatively clean and cobweb-free – which only meant that spiders hadn't discovered it. It was also completely empty.

"No buried treasure," I whispered.

"Too bad," Ringo stepped into the fireplace next to me. It was definitely big enough to stand in with only a little crouching. "Looks big."

"Big enough, anyway." I opened the door wide enough to fit through and looked at Ringo. "Shall we?"

He shrugged. "After ye, milady."

I flinched at the title, technically mine since I was married to the second son of a duke. My fist clenched around my ring, which bore Archer's family crest, and I took a breath to steady my racing heart before I stepped inside the space. I could stand upright as the ceiling stretched up above the top of the mantel, and I realized there were tiny pinpoints of light shining through at eye level. I put my eye to the wall as Ringo carefully pulled the door closed behind us.

"They're spy holes," I said with wonder.

"Makes sense," Ringo said. "So does this interior latch for the door." He demonstrated a simple mechanism that unlocked the catch from the door so it could be closed without trapping us inside. Still, I was nervous when he shut the door and the latch clicked, until he pressed the mechanism and the door popped open again.

I studied the interior walls of the hidden room. The back wall of the fireplace was brick, but the other walls were cement and looked like blank canvases to me. I set my Maglite on the floor pointed up like a candle, and I pulled my fat black marker out of my shoulder bag.

Ringo watched me work. "Escape route?" he finally asked.

I concentrated on blanking my mind of any person, place, or thing as I laid down the five spirals. "Yeah. Somehow I don't think I'd get enough time with the one out there to Clock us out of here if we needed it." I nodded toward the Council room and the big spiral that was carved in the wall.

"What other graffiti should we leave to make our mark on this time?" Ringo asked.

Hmm. That was an interesting thought. Besides spirals and the occasional portrait, I hadn't been doing a lot of art recently. I finished the last touches on the spiral and then handed the marker to Ringo. "You first," I said.

He thought for a long moment, then finally wrote, *Fear not for the future, weep not for the past.* He met my eyes. "They're Percy Bysshe Shelley's words."

"They're appropriate."

He leaned back and handed me the marker. "The Missus 'ad a book of 'is poetry that I read over and over again after ye took yer mother 'ome. 'Is words kept me company the long days I sat next to Archer's bed, and I began to imagine Shelley 'imself was a child of Death."

My eyes opened wide. "You think Percy Shelley was a Vampire? I thought he died really young."

"'E was twenty-nine. They say 'e drowned in a storm. But they also say that when 'e was cremated on the sand 'is 'eart wouldn't burn."

I stared at the words Ringo had written on the wall. They were written for me, I thought, and I wanted to believe both were possible.

I chose a piece of the still-blank cement wall and began to draw while Ringo's quiet voice recited poetry behind me.

"How wonderful is Death,
Death and his brother Sleep!
One pale as yonder wan and horned moon,
With lips of lurid blue,
The other glowing like the vital morn,
When throned on ocean's wave
It breathes over the world:
Yet both so passing strange and wonderful."

He seemed lost in thought for a long moment, then spoke in the same quiet voice. "It was the *lips of lurid blue*. That's what gave me the idea that Shelley was Death's Descendant. Archer's lips were blue for more than a week, and when the color returned, the Missus sent me away."

I knew how much it had hurt Ringo that he hadn't been there when Archer came back to himself after Bishop Wilder had turned him. "He knows what you did. He knows you stayed as long as you could."

"I didn't this time though, did I?" The edge of bitterness in his voice was sudden and violent.

"Don't do that!" I whispered furiously. I wasn't sure why I whispered, except that I might scream if I didn't. "Do NOT blame yourself for anything about that night. We were there to stop Tom from killing his great-grandfather and splitting time."

"Well, we failed," he said brutally.

"Yes, we did. Spectacularly. And we can take responsibility for that. But we weren't the ones shooting. It wasn't our bullets that set off the unexploded bomb. That's on George Walters, and, to be perfectly honest, it's on Tom."

Ringo was silent long enough that I shifted my glare away from him and back to my drawing. "How ridiculous would it be if

Percy Shelley actually *was* a Vampire, since he was married to Mary Shelley, who wrote *Frankenstein?*"

"Ye know 'ow the whole thing came about, don't ye?"

I let out a breath, relieved that he could be distracted. "Yes, this I actually know. Mary, Percy, and Mary's step-sister were staying at a house on Lake Geneva with Lord Byron and some other guy—"

"William Polidori," Ringo supplied.

"Gah! I wanted to know more about this than you." I'd finished the drawing and was moving on to the words. "Anyway, it was a dreary, rainy summer, which was actually a volcanic winter from the eruption of some Italian volcano the year before, and since they couldn't go outside, they started reading German ghost stories, which led to a bet about writing something scary."

"That's good. Ye know details I didn't."

"How about this – did you know the idea for *Frankenstein* came to Mary Shelley in a dream?" I said smugly.

"I did." There was a grin in Ringo's voice. "Did ye know she was eighteen at the time – yer age?"

I liked the game of one-upmanship. "I did. But did you know that Lord Byron's submission was a fragment of a story based on vampire legends he heard when he was traveling in the Balkans?"

"Ha! How do ye know it was based on legends? The first novel that romanticized vampires was written by Polidori after that weekend. How do ye know it wasn't based on the truth about Percy Bysshe Shelley?" Ringo declared triumphantly.

I laughed at his enthusiasm. "I didn't know that Polidori wrote a book about vampires. I bow to your superior education."

"Knowledge. Ye can bow to my knowledge, but yer education's still better." Ringo's smug tone was gone. He had inhaled everything he could get his hands on since Archer and I had taught him to read, but it didn't change his fundamental lack of formal education.

I leaned back from my drawing to take in the whole picture.

Leaving something of yourself for others to experience and remember is sometimes the greatest excuse to live a life that's more than just crossing the distance between birth and death. Ringo read the words I'd written, and there was surprise in his tone. "Archer said that."

I nodded. "To Bas, that night in the farmhouse kitchen."

He looked at the image I'd drawn and said, "That's the Devereux seal, the crowned 'eart on yer ring."

"I've decided it's my new tag. A crown over graffiti means the tagger is going 'all-city.' It came from New York and originally meant all five boroughs. For me I think it means I'm not going to stop until I've done more than just cross the distance between birth and death. I'm going to do something that matters, something Archer would be proud of, and I'm not going to stop searching until I find a way to get back to him."

Ringo studied my tag a while longer, then looked at me with a nod. "It's worthy," he said simply.

I thought so too.

We debated Clocking out to try to find Ava or even Mr. Shaw before the Council meeting started, but I didn't really feel like running around London looking for the Armans, and the idea of returning directly back into the tiny space behind the fireplace without accidentally embedding myself into a wall was a little daunting.

So instead, I drew a chessboard on the cement floor and we killed an hour playing chess with small items from our bags. Lip balm was my queen, and the tin of green medicine was my king, but I kept forgetting if the knight was the new five pence or the old shilling.

I complained often enough that Ringo switched knight pieces with me, so two pound coins became my knights. "Did ye ever see the black knight piece Tom carried with 'im after Léon died?" he asked as he moved his bishop into exactly the place I'd hoped he hadn't seen. My knight would be dead in two moves.

"I have the vague memory of a chess piece that kept moving between his pocket and his hand the night we buried his friend, but I hadn't realized it was a knight." I dangled a pawn in front of him in hopes he'd take the bait and leave my knight alone.

"It was an old piece, 'and-carved in ebony. 'E wasn't conscious of 'oldin' it, but whenever talk turned back to Léon, it came out of 'is pocket again," he said as he ignored the pawn and slaughtered the knight.

I didn't want to talk about Tom, so I changed the subject to the differences between modern coins and the wartime ones that were still in our pockets while I concentrated on the game. The strategic planning that chess required was like a workout for my brain, and when we finally put the pieces away after one win each, I felt a little more prepared to face whatever the Council meeting revealed.

I had just pulled out a handful of almonds and was ready to pop one into my mouth when Ringo shushed me.

"Put it away," he whispered. "Shifters might 'ear ye and smell the food."

I dropped the almonds back into my pocket and joined Ringo at the peep holes. The MacKenzie and both of his sons had arrived, and the room suddenly seemed smaller with all of them in it. His name was his title since he was the MacKenzie clan chief, and it's why he was *the* MacKenzie. He was also the Shifter Head, an actual Highland Bull with the attitude and bluster to match. I'd seen my mother take him down a peg at a Council meeting once, and it was a thing of beauty.

We could hear every word the MacKenzie bellowed, but his sons were a bit less blustery, so their words were sometimes muffled.

"Did ye bring the bone with ye?" MacKenzie asked his older son, a ruddy-skinned brutish-looking guy like his father.

The bone? They didn't have the Shifter bone. So had they brought a fake?

"Course, Da, I'm not as thick as ye like to believe."

"And if they need it tested? What's your plan then?" asked the younger brother. That one was the least bull-like and seemed the most reasonable of the three.

"I'll Shift and none will dare challenge me," bellowed the MacKenzie.

"Challenge you to what, MacKenzie?" A new man entered the chamber. He was about forty years old, tall and well-built, African-looking with very dark skin. He wore a charcoal-colored suit with a topcoat, and had the style and accent of a wealthy Englishman.

My eyes had been so busy taking in the details of the newcomer that I missed the MacKenzie's reaction to him. So I heard the fear and awe before I saw it.

"Sir … forgive me. I didn't hear ye come in," he said deferentially, backing up a step as he spoke.

"I imagine it's rare you hear anything beyond your own bluster," said the man. His eyes flicked toward the fireplace, and I swore he looked into mine. Impossible, of course, but my heart leapt into my throat and I willed myself not to move. Ringo's breath caught next to me, so I wasn't the only one who had imagined the connection.

The man's gaze turned toward the younger MacKenzie men, and it sharpened. "I don't believe I've met your sons." He walked across to the younger and offered his hand. "It's nice to meet you, James. I'm Aeron."

Ringo tensed, and my whole being was suffused with shock. Aeron.

 ## COUNCIL

Death. I even fumbled the word in my brain. If I had been standing in front of him like the MacKenzie, I would have fumbled much more obvious things. Like speech. And maintaining a heartbeat.

Death was in the house.

To his credit, the younger MacKenzie only paled slightly as he shook Aeron's hand, and Death seemed satisfied by something he saw in James' eyes. He didn't even acknowledge the elder brother, who was clearly sweating the introduction but was saved from it by the sweeping entrance of the Armans.

Camille Arman looked like a cross between a runway model and a pixie warrior, which for her, was not as hard to pull off as it sounded. Somehow this fierce Frenchwoman had given birth to my friends Adam and Ava, both blond-haired and beautiful, but without the edge their mother wore like a superhero cloak. Camille went straight up to Aeron and offered him her cheek to kiss as she clasped his hand. "Aeron. You've come."

An interesting choice of words. Not "thank you for coming" or even "why are you here," instead a declaration that required no answer. I could learn from watching the Seer Head.

"Camille, you've aged not a day in the years since I saw you last. I would almost imagine you were one of mine." Aeron's voice was deep and smooth and rolled like liquid off his tongue, and yet the smallest tightening of Camille's smile was the only indication she gave that his words affected her.

Aeron looked at Ava then, and I was proud of her for meeting his eyes straight on. "And this is your lovely daughter," he said to Camille, though he looked at Ava, who smiled graciously as he continued. "It will be a pleasure to work with you when you assume the mantle, Ava." He shook her hand warmly.

I couldn't tell what Ava was thinking from her expression, which was as relaxed and unworried as it always was, but I knew her mother wasn't happy about Death's attention to her daughter.

Adam seemed somewhat … vexed. I had only ever heard English people say it, but vexed was a good description for the slight worry, slight annoyance, slight confusion that warred for dominance in his expression. Aeron turned to Adam and gave him a nod. "Adam," he said quietly.

"Sir," Adam replied. I was impressed at how together he sounded.

Other people had come in, including Ms. Simpson and Millicent. Aeron moved to greet Ms. Simpson warmly with a kiss on both cheeks, and he shook Millicent's hand formally. I couldn't hear specific conversations anymore because the room had gotten too loud, so I watched body language as Aeron made his way around the room.

Aeron.

Death.

I had to mentally shake the shock out of my brain. An actual Immortal was making his way around the Descendants' Council room, greeting people he knew, introducing himself to those he didn't. There was a raging sense of power around him – one that practically pulsed with something not exactly malevolent, but definitely dangerous. It was surreal to watch the people in the room attempt to wear politeness to cover their naked fear. I couldn't look away no matter how painfully people reacted to the idea of Death in their midst.

"It's like watchin' a bloody king, or maybe the king of assassins, make 'is rounds, isn't it?" Ringo whispered.

Across the room, Aeron's mouth quirked up in a smile. I tried to pretend there was no possible way he could have heard Ringo's whisper, but a part of me believed it was entirely likely.

"Shite," Ringo whispered. He believed it too.

There was a commotion coming down the stairs, and a guy I recognized as Raven's older brother came in strong-arming a guy about my age with curly ginger hair. The faint echo of his Mongerness tugged at my stomach.

"The big one is Dodo, the Monger who tried to take me from the Tower," I whispered to Ringo.

"'E's a Rothchild, right?" Ringo's whisper was barely more than a breath of words.

Dodo wore a bulky jumper, and he yanked the ginger to a halt so he could pull it off over his head. Underneath the sweater was a tactical tool belt, its multiple holders bulging with various weapons and hidden devices.

I exhaled sharply. "Raven's older brother. He was a mercenary in Africa." How he managed to get all of that … stuff in a country where guns were illegal was beyond me.

The MacKenzie got in Dodo's face about being armed at a Council meeting, but Raven's brother shoved past him and pushed the ginger into a chair.

"Who's 'e got?" Ringo asked.

The Ginger remained placidly calm despite almost losing his seat from the force of Dodo's push. He had to grab at Dodo's tool belt to keep from going over. Dodo righted the chair, shook himself free, and stepped back to guard the door. I studied the guy. "I'm guessing that's Darrell MacFarlane."

He looked wiry and strong, but with the kind of lean muscle that makes people think they can take him on and regret it when they do. His fingers were tapping out a rhythm on his leg, something that looked vaguely musical, and his eyes were taking everything in.

"'E's a thief," Ringo whispered.

"Why do you say that?"

"'E slipped somethin' from the tool belt when 'e grabbed it. Also, fingers and eyes in constant motion. It's like an itch, thievin' is, and when it's been yer life, ye never stop needin' to scratch it."

I looked at Dodo's tool belt but didn't see anything obviously missing. "You stopped," I breathed to Ringo.

"It wasn't my life, it was my job," he whispered back.

One final person entered the chamber and closed the door behind him. The man was tall like Aeron and looked strikingly familiar. There was enough Michael Fassbender in his features that he owned every pair of eyeballs in the room, and he moved in a powerful, graceful way that reminded me of someone, but I couldn't think who.

The room literally stilled, and in that moment a case of Monger-gut hit me so hard I almost doubled over.

"Duncan." Aeron greeted him neutrally.

Duncan.

War.

I took a deep breath in hopes that oxygen would calm my heartbeat down to something less … loud. This guy's attention was pretty much the last thing I wanted to draw to myself for reasons that weren't coherent so much as they were visceral.

I wasn't the only one, either. The Descendants in the Council room seemed to hold their collective breath, and I could have cut the tension with a knife.

Duncan gave Aeron a charming smile that didn't come anywhere close to his eyes. "Aeron. You've come out of your cave, I see." There was an oily slickness in his voice that Seth Walters had, though I thought Seth could take lessons from this guy. I also noticed an odd resemblance between Seth and Duncan, and I had the fleeting thought that they might be related by more than just their Mongerness. I pushed that unbelievably disconcerting thought as far away as I possibly could. Seth wasn't on this time stream because his grandfather had been blown up in 1944. I didn't need to be seeing ghosts where they didn't exist.

"I believe all the essential players have arrived," said Duncan with the smooth tones I associated with British boarding schools and Parliament. "Ah, Aislin, I didn't see you there, although why you insist on wearing such a dowdy visage, I'll never understand."

My double-take tripled. Duncan was looking directly at Ms. Simpson, and she was positively glaring back at him. "Thank you for that, Duncan. On all counts."

If the quiet gasps and shifting in seats were any indication, War had just outed Fate in front of a whole roomful of people who hadn't known her identity. The looks of surprise on everyone's faces would have been hilarious if the news wasn't so … *shocking*. Ava seemed to be the only one in the room, besides War and Death, who wasn't fazed by Aislin, and I wondered if she'd known.

"There are three Immortals in that room," Ringo exhaled softly. "That's a lot of power concentrated in one place."

I stared at him for a second. "That's like an atomic concentration of power," I whispered. Ava had said there would be an attack that I needed to stop. But they were Immortal, right? Which meant there was no point trying to kill them. Was there?

I looked through the peep hole at the assemblage of Descendant dignitaries, and my think-like-a-terrorist plotting was interrupted by Duncan, who was speaking to the group at large. "As you're aware, my Descendants have been excluded from this Council for over seventy years—"

"Ye've got one of your own with ye here now," the MacKenzie interrupted, "and I can't help but notice how well-armed he is."

Duncan glanced at Dodo in his post by the door. "He's here for the prisoner. If you'd prefer he remove the belt, I won't be responsible for your safety."

The MacKenzie stood to an imposing size. "I would prefer he removes the weapons, and I'll be responsible for my own safety, thank ye very much."

Duncan repressed a smile as he indicated Dodo should bring him the belt. He placed it in the middle of the Council table and met the MacKenzie's eyes. "Does that work better for you?"

Considering the various holsters full of weapons were now well within the Shifter Head's reach, I wasn't surprised that he nodded. The belt was a little lopsided though, and I thought Ringo must've been right about the pickpocket nature of Darrell MacFarlane.

Duncan continued before anyone else could add their objections. "I believe there has been a misunderstanding about our Family artifact—"

"The Monger ring was blown up. That's hardly a misunderstanding," said Millicent archly.

"Be that as it may, excluding my Family is an error that it's long past time to correct."

"*He or she who holds the Family artifact is entrusted with the responsibility to lead that Family in the ways of the Immortal from whence they came,*" quoted Mrs. Arman. At least I assumed it was a quote from some Descendant manual somewhere, since I didn't know anyone who actually used the word 'whence' in regular speech.

Duncan's pleasant, reasonable expression tightened just a little, as though he didn't appreciate Descendant laws being spouted at him. "Of course, I could ask each of the rest of you to produce your Family artifact and prove its provenance, though somehow I doubt that would be fruitful."

"Well, obviously. That's why we're here, isn't it? My Family's necklace has been stolen, and the thief must be brought to justice." Millicent's tone was imperious and commanding, and if I didn't know who she really was under all that arrogance, I'd have been intimidated.

I glanced at Darrell MacFarlane, whose fingers hadn't stopped tapping out their pattern on his leg. He watched Duncan like prey might watch a predator.

I nudged Ringo. "What's Darrell doing?"

"Waitin' for somethin'," Ringo said quietly.

My eyes went to Aeron, who had moved back against a wall. He was watching Darrell intently.

"Of course, the theft of the Clocker necklace," Duncan said to Millicent with galling smoothness. "According to young Darrell's statement, your great-grandchildren brought him to the keep to show him the artifact, and in fact, intended to give him the necklace. However, when they searched the room, they discovered the artifact wasn't in the warded keep – the place you naturally protect all your precious Family heirlooms."

Millicent's mouth tightened into a straight line. "The necklace had been there since my grandmother's time. It's not there now. He stole it." Her glare landed on Darrell, who held her gaze without flinching. That was something.

Duncan smiled. It was a truly disturbing sight. "We shall, of course, need to bring the children in to testify."

Millicent's daughter gasped quietly, and then whispered something in Millicent's ear. The Clocker Head's eyes narrowed as she held Duncan's gaze. "Why are you defending the thief? What is it you want?"

"There is only a thief if an item was stolen. In fact, it seems that your Family's artifact has been missing for some time, yet you have retained your seat on this Council without it. What I want is only what you have already been enjoying – a suspension of the artifact rule, and the reinstatement of Mongers to the Council."

Camille Arman gasped, "No!" It must have been an instinctual response, because it was very unlike her to lose control about anything. Millicent merely glared at Duncan, and the MacKenzie actually nodded his assent. I knew why, of course – his family didn't have their Shifter artifact either – but I doubted any of the other Heads knew that.

Duncan turned toward Camille, and I thought she might have flinched. "Camille, darling, why do you object so strenuously to my Family?"

She took a breath and stood a little straighter. "Because they're bullies and agents of dissent. The day that ring was destroyed was the greatest day in Descendant history."

War's smile broadened and my heart stuttered in fear. "Ah, but you see, our artifact was not destroyed during World War II."

"Of course it was. George Walters was wearing the ring the day he was killed in the British Museum bombing," growled the MacKenzie.

Duncan gestured dismissively. "That ring wasn't ours. We just – how shall I say it – borrowed it from the Pope in 1842 and never returned it."

I stifled my own gasp, but no one else did. Voices rose angrily, and Millicent might have actually fanned herself.

The Monger ring didn't actually belong to the Mongers.

So, what did?

I wasn't the only one who wondered. Camille glared at Duncan, her arms crossed in front of her. "You wonder why I object to Mongers on the Council? You just admitted they stole something you claimed was an artifact, and now you want them reinstated? Does your Family even have an artifact of its own?"

"Of course we do," Duncan said, his tone full of derision.

"What is it?" demanded Camille.

He looked her straight in the eyes and smiled again. "We all have our secrets, don't we, Camille?"

She actually blanched a little at that, and I wondered what sort of secrets Camille Arman had.

"You can't think we would believe your claim that the Monger artifact still exists without proof," said Millicent.

Duncan turned to her. "And yet you expect to retain your seat on the Council despite your claim that the Clocker artifact has been stolen?" She opened her mouth to speak, but nothing came out. Duncan continued. "Our artifact represents our strategic strength. I wouldn't have sired this Family unless I had a strategy to see my aims realized."

Aeron pushed himself off the wall he'd been holding up and stepped forward. His tone was casual as he spoke, yet his gaze on Duncan was laser-sharp. "If I'm to understand you correctly, Duncan, you wish to see the Mongers reinstated as a power on this Council, and you wish to suspend the artifact rule. The first I understand. The second feels too altruistic for you, frankly. Enlighten me."

Duncan's smile tightened, yet remained in place. "Incentive. Time's artifact is missing, and if the rumors are correct, Nature's may very well be, too." The MacKenzie looked like he was about to protest, but his younger son shushed him as Duncan continued. "Our position was denied when it was assumed our artifact was destroyed, and rather than see that happen to those Families, I propose that a missing artifact not be grounds for dismissal."

"I see," Aeron said mildly. "And where is your Family's artifact currently?"

"Where's yours?" Duncan shot back defensively.

Aeron's smile didn't waver. "Ah, but you see, my Family does not have a seat at this table."

Fear seemed to flit across the expressions of several people in the room, and I wondered what else they thought would happen when they asked Aeron to come to this meeting. I saw that coming a mile away.

"I was called here to determine the veracity of this young man's statements of innocence," continued Aeron, the mildness gone from his voice. "I have no interest in the pettiness that seems to have infected this room."

He drew a dagger from under his coat and was by MacFarlane's side in two steps. "Your hand, sir," he snarled at the young man who had jumped out of his seat in terror at Death's approach.

Despite eyes wide with fear, MacFarlane's fingers still moved as if he was tapping a rhythm in the air. Aeron grabbed his hand, and I thought he was going to cut the fingers off.

Ringo started toward the door of our little hideaway but I grabbed his shoulder. "Wait," I hissed. I reached for one of my own daggers with my other hand, as I kept my eyes glued to the peep-holes.

Aeron ran the edge of the blade very lightly down the center of MacFarlane's palm until just the thinnest thread of blood bubbled up. The room was cloudy with tension and fear, and I had an instant flash of a rocky mountain jutting up from a lake, covered in heather. A kilted man thrust a wooden sword at a ginger-haired boy, and the boy parried back with a dagger. He took a knock to the hand from the sword, but didn't cry out, and the man grinned broadly and pulled the boy into a warm hug.

The image was replaced with one of MacFarlane in a rough homespun shirt and the same tartan kilt as the man had worn. His shadow flickered in the light of a candle on a window ledge near him as he stood in a narrow doorway. His fingers tapped their rhythm on a rag-stoppered bottle filled with amber liquid as he watched the street. The door opened, and a white-wigged English gentleman stepped out. MacFarlane drew the rag halfway out, lit the end on the candle, and prepared to throw.

The scene flashed, and suddenly Darrell MacFarlane was in the keep of Elian Manor with two children, a boy and a girl. The children appeared to be directing search efforts, presumably to find the Clocker necklace, and MacFarlane followed their lead.

I shook my head and stared through the peep-holes at the half-Clocker, half-Monger accused thief. Could Ava have somehow sent me visions she'd had of MacFarlane? But she didn't see into the past, and I wasn't touching her. Ringo had gone back to his post at the peep-holes, and I shifted my dagger into the other hand so I could rub my eyes.

Aeron's eyes were locked onto MacFarlane's, and he inhaled, about to speak.

Suddenly, MacFarlane threw something past Aeron, and a huge FLASH filled the room with noise, light, and smoke. The BANG that followed shook the room, and Darrell lunged forward to grab the handle of the dagger from Death. He slashed the blade as he did, and it sliced deeply into Aeron's forearm.

My head instantly flooded full of images that made no sense as panicked screams erupted in the Council room. A smashed cradle held an infant covered in blood, pale as death, while the screams of the mother filled the room. Images of deadly illness, battlefields full of corpses, a drowned child, bloody sheets on a childbirth bed, an old woman keening in misery all swam through my head, and I struggled to focus on the scene in front of me.

Aeron dove forward, but MacFarlane grabbed the tactical belt off the Council table and yanked what looked like a grenade from a holster. He pulled the pin on it, then swung Aeron's dagger in quick, erratic arcs that kept everyone else at bay. He put the table between himself and the enraged Immortal.

"It's a concussion grenade, meant to kill in a six-foot radius four seconds after 'e throws it," Ringo whispered.

I didn't even ask how he knew that.

"We have to get him out of there," I said fiercely.

"'E'll just as likely cut us as them before 'e blows us all up." Ringo's whisper was equally fierce.

I knew that, but as far as I could tell, I seemed to be the only other armed person in the room. I searched for Dodo, but he must have bolted along with several of the onlookers, including Millicent and her daughter. Adam was still there, and the MacKenzies. Ms. Simpson – *Aislin*, I corrected myself – looked worried and was herding the few people left toward the door.

"Take one of my blades," I said as I pulled the other dagger from its sheath. "We'll disarm him if we can, but at this point, I'm pretty sure Death will kill him if we don't get him out." I spoke in my normal voice because the screams in the main room overpowered every other sound.

Ringo was about to unlatch the door when I stopped him with a hand on his arm. "He's definitely not from this time."

The words sank in, and I could see the wheels turn with the impact of them. Finally, Ringo nodded and flipped the latch on the door.

The Council room was in chaos. Aeron and MacFarlane still faced off across the Council table from each other. The younger man's back was to us, but Aeron saw us emerge from the fireplace, and a slight narrowing of his eyes was the only indication that he noticed.

Adam and the younger MacKenzie had moved off to the wall opposite the Family carvings and were making their way toward Darrell, just out of his direct line of sight. MacKenzie had his gaze locked on the explosive device in Darrell's hand and hadn't seen us, but Adam gave me a single nod when my eyes flicked to the fireplace and back.

Two quick hand signals told Ringo everything about my meager plan, and he also gave me a single nod, then slid back to the right of the fireplace to put himself in the way of the only other escape route. I moved along the carved wall until I could step into Darrell's line of sight.

And then I did.

"Darrell MacFarlane!" I called out to him. "I can take you home."

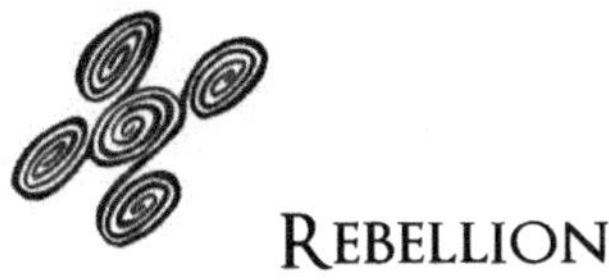

REBELLION

The young, Scottish Clocker/Monger caught me out of the corner of his eye, but remarkably didn't break his concentration on Death, who waited across the table for any chance to take him down. He spoke to me without taking his eyes from Aeron.

"Who are ye, then?" His brogue was thick, and I had to listen hard to understand his words.

"Saira Elian," I said boldly. My eyes flicked to Aeron's face, looking for any sign of recognition or acknowledgement, but his own gaze hadn't left Darrell.

"Ye'll be a Clocker, I take it, from yer name? And ye'll have heard the necklace is missing. So how do ye propose to get me there?"

"I've never been to Scotland, so unless you're a Seer who can send me the image of your home, the best I can do is London. But I can get you to the right year. That's what you wanted the necklace for, isn't it?"

"Why?" he asked.

"Why *can* I do it, or why *will* I?" If I could keep him talking – split his focus between me and Aeron – Ringo and Adam had a chance to move into a position that would effectively trap him between us. I still didn't know what to do about the grenade, but maybe someone else would come up with that plan.

"Why would ye? Ye dinna know me. For that matter, how do I know ye'll take me back, and not straight to prison?"

"Depends what you do with the grenade and the knife," I said sharply. "You can believe me or not, it's up to you, but know this. I'm not from this time either, and I'm leaving now. Come with me, and I'll take you back to whenever you came from, or take your chances with Death."

I felt eyes on me and glanced up to see Duncan shooting me a fierce glare. I scowled as I mentally replayed the events leading up to this moment.

He did this. He wanted it to happen. He somehow knew Darrell's history as a thief, and maybe even that he'd been a rebel. He probably told Rothchild to wear his weapons just so he could make sure they ended up in Darrell's reach.

I spoke out loud to Duncan, barely thinking through what I said. "Too bad Darrell wants to get home more than he wants to do your dirty work, Duncan."

I was baiting War, which was approximately as intelligent as dangling a mouse in front of a cobra with my teeth.

"How dare you address me!" Another wave of Monger-gut hit me, and I was nearly crippled with it.

I looked behind Darrell at Ringo. He had opened the door at the back of the fireplace and then stepped to the side closest to Aeron. Death hadn't seemed to notice Ringo's shift, but he did suddenly notice the dagger that was still in my hand. His gaze burned into mine for half-a-second before returning to Darrell, and I had the very uncomfortable sensation that I'd just put myself in Death's sights.

"So, Duncan," I said, attempting a conversational tone when I really just wanted to run away screaming. "You said your Family artifact is strategic. It seems like you haven't had it since at least 1842, and I'm a Clocker, so maybe I can help you find it?"

I heard Ringo groan behind me, and I ignored him. I stepped forward and Darrell took a step back, which put him directly in line with Adam. I shot Adam a look to see if he was on the same page as me. He nodded. Good.

The only people left in the room now were the Immortals, Adam, James MacKenzie, Ringo, Darrell MacFarlane, and myself.

Everyone else had cleared out, and I heard the far-off sound of sirens coming from somewhere overhead at street level.

Duncan sneered at me. "That you could imagine I would ever need anything from you is the height of arrogance." I didn't disagree, but Duncan wasn't done tearing into me. "You dare to offer your *help*? I would see the end of war before I'd ask you for assistance. You're just a girl."

"Oh, now that pisses me off." I said it before my brain could catch up, but really, I would have said it anyway.

The scorn in his voice matched his face. "Despite your feminine weakness, if you cross me or get in my way, you shall find yourself at the end of a sword."

"A sword has two ends." I hurled my dagger toward Aeron suddenly. "Catch!" I used the momentary distraction to lunge forward and snatch Death's dagger from Darrell's hand just as Adam rushed forward with a full rugby tackle and sent Darrell backward toward the fireplace.

Ringo leapt inside the hidden room and pulled Darrell and me in after him. Adam had stopped just outside the fireplace and looked ready to follow us. "Run!" I shouted at him. My voice snapped him around and he took off toward the door, barely avoiding Duncan's charging rage.

I was already tracing the spiral when the very shocked Scot suddenly hurled the grenade out into the Council room just as Ringo slammed the door shut.

"Oh crap! Grab on!" I had four seconds before the grenade blew. Ringo snatched our bags and pushed Darrell into me as I traced the last spiral. "What year?" I shouted.

Someone hammered on the back of the fireplace, and the Council room was full of shouting.

I was about to yell again when Darrell finally understood. "1765," he called.

"1765," I confirmed to myself as an explosion sent us through the spiral and *between*.

I took us to the Clocker Tower at St. Brigid's. The whole thing had been too fast for me to be more creative than that.

Darrell and Ringo both looked green around the gills, but I was too mad to be sick, so I punched Darrell instead. "What the hell were you thinking? Do you even know what a grenade can do? Don't *ever* pull the pin on a grenade! And then you *threw* it? What if you killed someone in that room? What if you killed Adam?"

Darrell could tell I wanted to hit him again, and he held up his hands in surrender. "The only way I could get out of that Council room alive was on Duncan's coattails," he said.

"Did you have some sort of agreement?" I spat. I was still mad, but reason had begun to return to my brain.

"I worked it out myself," he said quietly.

I looked down at the blade that I'd taken from Darrell. "Taking Death's dagger was a bad idea," I finally said.

"Aye." His tone was actually contrite, and I finally looked at him with something other than rage or fear clouding my vision.

"You still have my other knife?" I asked Ringo. He handed me the dagger by its blade, and I took the silk-wrapped handle in my right hand while Death's dagger remained in my left.

Darrell's gaze was on the daggers in my hands. "They're the same," he said. He was right. Except for the grip, they looked identical. His eyes were wide when he looked into mine. "Why do ye have Death's dagger?"

I shook my head, "I don't." But even as I denied it, I felt the weight and balance of both daggers and realized they felt like a matched pair – like the set I'd had until I threw my own dagger at Aeron to distract him.

Ringo held his hands out for the knives and I gave them to him. The grip of mine was wrapped in silk cord, while the grip of Death's dagger was bare and intricately carved. Other than that, the shape was the same, the size and weight were equal, and the blades were identical.

"Unwrap the 'andle," Ringo said, handing my dagger back to me.

I held it out for him to slit the fabric with the other blade, and then I carefully peeled back the aged silk to reveal the carvings underneath. The two daggers were mirror images of each other.

My eyes drank in the intricate whorls and dips in the handles. They were truly stunning daggers, and I'd never seen even a hint of their beauty until now. I looked up at Ringo. "Archer gave them to me. He said he found them in the room under St. Brigid's after the war."

"After the war. Death could 'ave placed them in the cellar pretty much anytime," Ringo said in wonder, "but since Archer didn't live on this time stream to find them, Aeron could still retrieve them from St. Brigid's. That's why they could be on both timestreams."

"But why would Death ever keep anything at St. Brigid's School?"

"The 'idden cellar room was built for any of Death's Descendants who might become 'Eadmaster of the school, right?" Ringo asked.

I scowled. "Like the Council would let that happen."

We lapsed into silence as we thought through the ramifications. I couldn't wrap my head around any of it, except that Aeron and I had just effectively swapped identical daggers – one from my time for one from his. Maybe that was what Tom had Seen when he said I had something that belonged to Death.

I gave up trying to divine the mysteries of the daggers and returned them to the straps that crossed my back under my shirt. Darrell watched me carefully, and I shot him a glare. "Don't even think about it."

"About what?" His attempted innocence would have worked if his fingers hadn't resumed tapping on his leg.

"You can't have the daggers, and if your fingers so much as twitch in their direction, I'll cut them off."

Darrell flinched back, and even Ringo looked a little surprised at the venom in my tone. "I'm serious. I'm still mad about the danger you put everyone in, and I did you a favor to bring you home. The least you could do is keep your hands to yourself."

He stared at me a long moment, then got up and started poking around the tower room.

"Are you looking for confirmation of the date, or something else to get your hands on, because you're making me nervous," I said finally. I was totally confident I'd brought us to 1765, mostly because I'd never miscalculated a Clock. But the furnishings and hangings would have told me we'd gone back in time even if my Clocking sense was off.

The stone walls were bare except for a tapestry where the London Bridge painting hung in modern times. The desk was the same, heavy carved wood, but the chair had a needlepoint seat and looked like a Chippendale, and the wide-plank wood floor was bare.

Darrell opened a desk drawer and let his fingers run lightly over the quill pens and a small leather-bound book inside. He flipped open the page of what must have been a journal and found the date. "June, 1765," he read. Darrell looked up at me in confusion. "It was September when we left, no?"

I shrugged. "Maybe the Clocker who uses this tower isn't back from summer break."

He closed the journal, and then pushed the drawer shut. He looked out the window at the cloudy sky. "The Clocker who uses this tower is Mr. Grayson. He was my history professor last year."

Ringo and I both stilled. It was one of those say-nothing-and-hope-he-keeps-talking moments.

"My mother sent me to St. Brigid's when I turned eleven, just to get me out of the Highlands, I think. It's where she went to school, and she hoped they could train some of my da's wildness out of me."

"He's a Monger, isn't he?" I said quietly.

Darrell looked startled. "Aye, he is. But my mother said they'd not let me in school if they knew I was of two Families. She also told my brothers and me to choose the Family we want to be associated wi' and stick to it. They've all chosen da's people, so when I leave here, I will too."

"But here, you're a Clocker?"

He nodded. "It's the only way to get the right training. Except the Monger in me affected my skill. My jump back a century and a quarter turned into a jump forward two and a half centuries."

I looked at Ringo. "See, I think that's at the heart of why there's so much prejudice against mixes. The skills are unpredictable and people are afraid of that."

"And then the Mongers got their 'ands on a ring that didn't affect mixed-bloods like it did everyone else, so they fanned the flames of the fear," Ringo said.

"They dinna have it yet, though – this ring. Duncan said they'll steal it from the Pope in 1842," said Darrell.

"What *is* the Monger artifact, do you know?" I asked.

Darrell shook his head. "Da's Family cut us off when he married my mother, but he did tell us Mongers have been searching for it since it was lost in the Crusades."

I snorted. "Figures they'd lose it in a holy war."

"He said the legend was it was worn by a Muslim sultan, then hidden in a Jewish temple and taken to Europe with an ungifted family fleeing the war."

"That's probably why the Mongers sacked the whole Middle East – looking for their Family artifact," I said.

"'Avin' seen War now, I don't doubt ye." Ringo hopped down from the window ledge he'd been seated on. "Darrell MacFarlane, can we leave ye 'ere, or is there another place Saira can take ye?"

Ringo was right, it was time to go. Darrell shook his head. "I can get myself home from here. After all I just saw of politics in the future, I'm not of a mind to announce my return from my ill-fated journey, so I'll be goin' in a back way. As far as they need know 'ere at St. Brigid's, I'll just be one of the many who were lost in time."

I narrowed my eyes at him. "I saw you firebomb the aristocrat, you know. That looked pretty political to me."

Ringo's eyes swiveled to me, and Darrell shook his head. "That wasna politics, it was personal."

I frowned. "Why?"

"The Duke of Cumberland took off my da's hand at Culloden. I was aiming for his leg."

I stared at him. "With a fire bomb?"

Darrell scowled. "If I'd had a grenade instead of a jar of spirits he wouldna have lived."

Ringo spoke quietly. "The Duke 'ad a fit last month. 'E'll die before the year's done."

Darrell turned his surprised gaze to Ringo. "Are ye a Seer then?"

He shook his head. "I'm a student of 'istory, which is a bit of the same thing. We learn it so we don't repeat it. Ye've seen things now that no one would believe, and ye'll 'ave to live with the knowledge. There's good in what ye've learned, but there's danger in it too. It'll be the mark of yer character 'ow ye choose to use what ye know."

Ringo and I left through the spiral that was carved in the wall behind the tapestry. Darrell said he could Clock between places with ease, so he would get himself back to his home in Scotland. I could tell that Ringo's words had made an impact on him, and I guessed Ringo was probably speaking as much to himself as to the young Scot.

I set my mind to the London Bridge in 1944 as I traced the spiral, and it was near sunset as we made our way to Ringo's flat.

We had expected to find Rachel there, but the place was deserted when we arrived. None of Rachel's things remained, and there was no evidence she had even occupied it. I could feel Ringo's disappointment like a heaviness in the air.

"Why do ye think she left?" he finally asked.

Something caught my eye on a roof support post and I pulled out my Maglite to take a look. It was a note, folded over and pinned to the wood with a knife. My name was written on it.

My heart beat faster – in hope, in fear – I wasn't sure exactly which. I had to pull hard to get the pocketknife out of the wood.

I showed the knife to Ringo – the swastika on the grip glinted cruelly in the gleam of my Maglite. "If I had to guess, I'd say this is why."

RACHEL

The note was written with a fountain pen, and the edges of the paper were yellow with age. Ringo held the light so I could read.

"It's dated September 8, 1889." I read, "Saira, I'm here waiting for you. Come find me. Tom."

I stared at Ringo. "This wasn't here when we came before."

He looked grim. "We need to find Rachel."

"You don't think he did anything to her?" I asked. No matter what Tom had become, I refused to believe he would deliberately hurt innocent people.

Ringo contemplated for a long moment before he finally shook his head. "No, but somethin' 'appened, and we need to know what."

I read the note again, then stuffed it into my satchel, and folded up the pocketknife and handed it to Ringo. I didn't want anything to do with a swastika and neither did he because he dropped the knife into a drawer and closed it firmly.

"Let's go up to the British Museum first," he said. Neither of us had even removed our satchels from our shoulders, much less thought of leaving them behind.

"Hang on a second." I pulled one of my daggers out of its sheath and cut a line in the wooden support post where we'd found Tom's note.

"What're ye doin'?

77

"Leaving a mark. We can figure out which timeline we're on based on whether it's here or not."

He watched me carve a crowned heart into the wood. "So, that's it then? That's yer tag?"

I stepped back and looked at the mark, then nodded and sheathed my knife. "I'm a Devereux now."

"'E'd be proud to 'ear ye say it, too," Ringo said quietly.

I shoved back the bloom of pain that threatened to fill my eyes with tears. Grief felt self-indulgent when we still had no answer to the question of fixing time, so I exhaled sharply and looked at Ringo. "Right. Let's go"

It was full dark when we made our way through bomb-damaged neighborhoods up toward Russell Square. The streets were mostly silent, but here and there people still sat on front steps with neighbors, quietly sharing a single glass of beer or wine. An observer would have seen a desolate landscape with small, bright spots of hope dotting it, and to me, that was community.

My community was in a place I couldn't reach, and missing them – my mom, Mr. Shaw, Adam, Ava, Connor, and even Millicent – was like a constant ache in the pit of my stomach. Ringo's presence next to me was maybe the only thing that kept me moving forward when the instinct to hide under the covers consumed every bit of hope I had.

We walked without speaking, and I could only guess at the direction his thoughts took. I wondered how much of his brain was occupied with questions about Rachel. He hadn't talked about her since we left 1944 to go forward, but he hadn't really talked about Charlie after she went with Valerie Grayson either.

I was suddenly intensely curious. "Who would you choose, if they were both standing right in front of you?" I finally blurted out boldly.

He shot me a confused look. "Between 'Itler and Stalin? What are you askin', Saira?"

I sighed dramatically. "You're usually better at reading my mind." Then I scowled at him for making me spell it out. "If

Charlie and Rachel were both standing right here, what would you do?"

He thought about it for exactly one second. "Dance a jig to find them both safe."

I was beginning to regret the question. "But who would you choose?"

He shrugged. "Ye, of course."

I stared at him. "What? Me? What are you talking about?"

Ringo stopped and faced me. "I told ye I 'ad yer back as ye did this thing. Until it's done and time is fixed, I'm with ye."

Oh.

He started walking again, and it took me a second to make my feet work to catch up. "What then?"

"Ye mean after ye and Archer are back together?" He shrugged. "I'll open a bookshop, or a tea shop with books."

"You're serious?"

"I've funds set aside – enough to get set up and see me through the first six months. I'd like to make good on my admittance to the Working Men's College too, though, if they'll still 'ave me."

"You got into the Working Men's College?"

Ringo nodded. "I was on my way 'ome from class when Lizzer 'ad me nabbed, then ye came to get me out of Newgate."

I was so surprised I missed a step off the curb, and his hand darted out to stop my fall. "I took you away from college, and you never said anything?"

He shrugged. "'Elpin' ye seemed more important."

I tried to say something appropriately effusive, but the words got stuck in the sheer enormity of what Ringo had done for us. I lapsed into silence, and then finally took his hand in mine and held it for a long moment.

"Thank you," I whispered.

He squeezed my hand before he let go, and we rounded the corner at High Holborn St.

There, where number 133 had previously stood, was a bomb crater the size of a large house.

I stumbled forward to the edge of the crater. The bigger chunks of broken pavement still hung precariously, though the smaller debris had been cleared already. I couldn't look at Ringo. I couldn't bear for him to see how much I had hoped that there'd been no explosion in the British Museum Station – that somehow we'd found our way back onto the true time stream. I turned away and searched the neighboring buildings for something to rest my eyes on that wasn't damaged or broken.

A lace curtain fluttered in an open window just as a candle blew out deeper in the room. The last verse of *Don't Fear the Reaper* skimmed the surface of my mind, followed by a memory of Aeron's eyes locked on mine. I shivered at the chill that raised goosebumps on my skin.

I stepped back from the crater and finally turned to face Ringo. "Where to?"

His eyes searched mine. He must have sensed my disquiet, but didn't push. "The temple, I think. Then maybe the residence at Guy's Chapel if she's not there."

I nodded. "Good ideas."

We took off running toward the temple. I needed to get out of my head so I didn't spend too long spinning on the image of the giant hole in the ground. Ringo kept his thoughts to himself, but he was unusually serious when we finally arrived at the Bevis Marks Synagogue. There were lights on inside, and Ringo knocked loudly on the heavy wooden door.

After a minute we heard sounds of someone coming, and finally a young man opened the door. I was startled to see him because it seemed like everyone else his age had joined the military.

"Can I help you?" he asked in one of the most beautiful voices I'd ever heard.

I felt like a sailor drawn to a siren song, but Ringo tensed and flinched back. "We're looking for Rachel," he said.

The young man studied us for a long moment, then his eyes widened slightly. "You're her friends from France? Please come in. I'll get her for you."

He stepped back to let us enter, then moved off across the room toward a door at the back. And I realized why he wasn't fighting the war with the rest of the young men. He had cerebral palsy and dragged one leg while the other foot turned in. Ringo and I shared a quick look of surprise, then stepped into the room and closed the door behind us.

"If you'll wait here, I'll find Rachel," he said in that beautiful voice. We stopped at the bench where Archer and I had lain and looked up at the chandelier barely two weeks before, but I didn't sit. It was hard enough to be assaulted with such recent memories of Archer without recreating the view I'd shared with him.

"I think 'e's Other," Ringo whispered when the door had closed behind the young man.

"You mean like Charlie sees?"

Ringo nodded. "She used to point them out to me when she saw them. I started to see signs."

I scowled, oddly bothered by his quick conclusion. "He moves that way because of cerebral palsy, not Otherness."

Ringo looked surprised for a second, then shook his head. "No, it's the voice. Charlie used to say the Fae and bastard angels 'ad voices that made ye weep with the beauty of them."

I swiveled toward the closed door the young man had gone through. A bastard angel? What even was that? The door opened and Rachel stepped into the room. She saw us in one breath and was across the floor in the next. She flung herself into Ringo's arms and then into mine with a great gasp.

"You came back!" Her voice was nearly a sob, and she peeled herself back reluctantly to look at us. The young man had followed her more slowly and stood just off to one side. Rachel turned to him. "Aviv, this is Saira and Ringo – my friends."

The way she spoke to Aviv was equally protective and deferential, and I noticed Ringo tense again. I didn't think Rachel saw it, but Aviv definitely did, and he regarded Ringo with an unblinking gaze as he held out his hand to shake.

"You are welcome, Saira and Ringo. Rachel's friends are friends of the temple," he said warmly. I was truly captivated by that voice, and it made him someone compelling to watch.

"Come, sit. There is still milk for tea, and Aviv made bread today. There is no more butter or jam, of course, but Aviv knows a man with gas rations who will take us to the country next week to hunt the rabbits that run from the harvesters."

She led us down a hall to a kitchenette where a simple table was draped with a clean white tablecloth, and two cups, saucers, and plates were stacked on the sideboard. Rachel bade us to sit while she fussed with the kettle and sliced thick chunks of bread. It was more generous than I thought most people could be with war rations, but she didn't even hesitate.

Rachel chattered on about the work she was doing with children in the temple school. She was teaching French and mathematics, and she had a car to repair with a couple of the older kids. Aviv stood in the doorway of the kitchen while she talked, and Ringo sat so that he could keep an eye on the young man. Rachel invited Aviv to join us, but he declined graciously as she poured the tea. Ringo finally relaxed when Aviv left the room.

"Did you find what you were looking for?" Rachel asked me, as she blew softly across her teacup.

I shook my head while I debated how much to say. "Things were … different," I finally admitted.

Ringo interrupted my halting words, for which I was grateful, even though it surprised me. "What 'appened? Why aren't ye at my flat?" There was an interesting possessiveness to his tone, and my eyes danced between Rachel and Ringo curiously.

She took a deep, shuddery breath. "I did stay – two nights. But then the third day I woke up, and there was … a knife." Fear laced her voice and made her eyes go big.

"The knife was stuck through a piece of paper on a post. I tried to read it, but I couldn't touch the knife. The handle …" Her hand trembled on her teacup, so she pulled it off the table and hid it in her lap. She looked like a child frightened of having done something wrong, and it broke through Ringo's strange reserve. He picked up the hand in her lap and held it between his.

"The man who put it there wasn't in the flat with you."

Oh! I hadn't even thought that she could imagine such a thing. No wonder she was so terrified.

Her eyes shone with unshed tears, and she looked at Ringo with the tiniest hope. "He wasn't?"

He shook his head. "We read the note. It was from 1889. Tom left it for Saira then so she could go back in time to find him."

Her gaze turned to me. "But how …?" She faltered, and I honestly didn't have an answer.

"I don't know. The only thing that makes sense is that when something changes in the past, it instantly affects everything in the present. We had something like that happen with memories of history. After we had changed a thing, all of a sudden the memories of the correct history were in our heads." I was talking about the memories of Joan of Arc.

"But did the old memories get replaced, or were the new ones just added?" Rachel asked. It was an astute question.

"New ones were added, but only for those few of us who were part of the change. As far as we know, everyone else's memories were just replaced."

"It's a big responsibility, no? To be the keeper of the memories?" Rachel asked. I was surprised at how serious the conversation had gotten.

"I hadn't really thought about it before. You're the same though, a keeper of memories." I meant because she was a Jewish survivor of a horrific World War II massacre, but I couldn't say that out loud. She understood, and her voice was solemn.

"I will keep the memories of my village with me until the day I die." She looked at both of us, but her eyes seemed to linger on Ringo's. "I've decided to go to Palestine. I've submitted my immigration paperwork and am just waiting to hear when I can leave."

Nothing obvious changed in Ringo's expression, but the tension rippling under his skin might as well have been a neon sign to me. He exhaled quietly. "'Ow will ye get there?"

"I'm a mechanic. Most others are gone fighting the war. There isn't a lot of money left in the city, but there are still vehicles that need to be fixed, and I can fix them. I have a little money saved from just the short time you've been gone – since Aviv took me in and let me sleep here. He's coming with me." She whispered the last bit, as if she was afraid of Ringo's reaction. But he was finished reacting – I could see it in his eyes – and a moment later the tension left his body.

He squeezed Rachel's hand. "Is there anything ye need? Anything we can help ye with?"

She smiled sadly at him as if she understood what she'd just lost. "I don't suppose you have any influence with the Home Office to help us get our exit papers?"

"Not currently, but we can ask around," Ringo said.

Rachel brought his hand up to her lips and kissed it. "Thank you for understanding. I feel that I'm making the right choice."

Aviv returned to the kitchen with another candle to replace the one that was nearly a stub, and Rachel again invited him to sit. This time he did, and gradually, as we talked, Ringo let go of his wariness.

Aviv told stories of ancient Jerusalem, of the fabled Well of the Souls under the Temple Mount and the Dome of the Rock. He said his grandmother's grandmother passed down legends of the Ark of the Covenant hidden there since the time of the Babylonian destruction of the First Temple in 586 BC, and he described a bit of gold leaf on a sliver of ancient wood his grandmother swore came from the wooden box that held the Ten Commandments.

I settled into the hard kitchen chair and closed my eyes. Aviv's voice felt like rich purple silk velvet that wrapped around my raw nerves, and I thought I'd turn into something vaguely liquid just listening to him read the phone book. Stories about tunnels and treasures under ancient Jerusalem were just a bonus, and if I hadn't already been married, I'd have probably fallen in love with Aviv just for his voice.

When I saw how Rachel looked at Aviv, I knew that she already had.

Ringo and I left the Bevis Marks Synagogue that night with hugs and handshakes, but with no tears. Rachel held me close and whispered, "Take care of him."

"I will," I whispered back.

Aviv kissed my cheeks after he'd shaken Ringo's hand. "A safe journey," he said quietly.

"When we figure out what's next," I answered with a small scoff. His gaze held mine, and when I looked into his eyes I could finally see the Otherness. He knew I saw it, and he smiled.

"Not all those who wander are lost."

I stared at him in shock. "That's not published yet." As far as I knew, J.R.R. Tolkien hadn't even written the "All That is Gold Does Not Glitter" poem yet.

"Perhaps not, but it has been spoken since the time of the angels. Trust the journey itself for the wisdom to make the destination a new beginning," Aviv said in his glorious voice, and I thought I might have just heard an angel speak.

SHINY THINGS

We slept side by side on Ringo's small bed, like siblings or pack-mates. I craved the comfort of a friend, and he let me nestle against his back for warmth. I thought he'd say no when I asked, but there was emptiness in his eyes that felt like a hole in the room, and when he finally nodded and wrapped himself in his own blanket to lie next to me, I figured maybe he needed the comfort too.

The tea was cooling in our mugs the next morning when Ringo finally spoke. "I didn't know I wanted a chance with 'er until it was gone, ye know?"

I met his eyes sadly. "I'm sorry."

His gaze drifted to one of the drawings Charlie had pinned to a wall. "It's probably for the best, all things considered. I wouldn't have made a different choice, so I take the consequences. It was just nice to have that door standin' open for a bit."

I watched him quietly over the rim of my mug. In the year that I'd known Ringo, he'd gone from a thieving street urchin with a smart mouth and a fierce curiosity to this … young man who sat across from me. He wasn't particularly tall, but he was strong and fast and ridiculously capable, and he was possibly the wisest person I knew. He was also my best friend, and it hurt me to see him gathering the pieces of himself and putting them together on his own.

"Should we go get Charlie?" I asked softly.

His mouth quirked in a half-smile. "We'll let 'er bask in luxury for a bit longer."

"Just tell me when, okay?"

Ringo's eyes finally met mine. "I'd like to see 'er when it's all done – when I'm ready to go 'ome."

I nodded and ignored the sharp pain in my heart at the idea that he would ever be ready to leave. It was too selfish to say out loud, but the little voice in my head whimpered, *I don't want you to go*.

"So, should I just draw a spiral here in your flat and Clock us back to 1889 then?" I changed the subject so I wouldn't dwell.

"So ready to see me gone?" Ringo smiled sadly, but I stared at him in shock.

"No! I don't want you to go at all. I meant should we go back to find Tom." I felt sick at the idea that he had misunderstood me.

He met my eyes, and though he still smiled, I could see the seriousness. "I'm glad. I realized I'd never actually asked ye if ye wanted me with ye."

"Right by my side."

His eyes glittered and he scrubbed his fingers through his hair as he leaned back in his chair. Finally, he exhaled loudly and said, "To be honest, I'm not so excited at the idea of a spiral 'ere."

"What, you don't want Doran popping by for tea?" I scoffed. "No worries, the London Bridge is close enough. The question is, do we go see Tom first, or do we dig for answers on George Walters?"

"Either way, I need to find a job for a few days. I figure a couple of days of clearin' rubble, even though money's tight with the war, will feed us better than a month of work with Gosford in 1889."

"Why you? Why not both of us?"

He scowled. "I don't want one of yer lectures about men and women bein' equal. I know 'em all by 'eart, and I believe 'em too. But look at the times, Saira. Women are only just gettin' paid for jobs they've been doin' all along, and the only ones with any real money married it or inherited it."

I set my empty mug down with a thunk and stared at him. "That's it. You're a genius," I said as I got up from the table. Ringo watched me with an amused look.

"'Course I am, but what made ye just now notice?"

I held my left hand out to him, palm down. "Archer's ring. He said it's all I need to access his money. He's not on this timeline, so he'll never need his fortune in this future. I can use it to finance us until we figure out how to fix time, and since that means the bomb won't explode and cause the split, I won't have actually ever spent the money."

Ringo's eyes narrowed as he processed what I'd just said. He watched me for a long moment before he finally spoke. "I don't like usin' yer money when I 'ave two perfectly good 'ands and a strong back."

I exhaled sharply. "I knew you'd say that. So I'll say to you what Archer would – what good is having money if we don't use it when we need to? And frankly, I don't want to scramble for a couple of days of work when the job we have to do is so much bigger than just keeping us fed. So, I'm going to register your protest, and then I'm going to ignore it. Are you cool with that?"

"I'll pay you back," he finally said. It was ridiculous, and we both knew it, but his pride wouldn't let him off the hook.

"Fine. Then I'm paying for your college."

"What? No ye're not."

"Then shut up." I scowled at him for exactly thirty seconds before the grin broke through my self-control, and when his mouth quirked I took his face in my hands and kissed him on the cheek.

"Now we just have to figure out which bank he kept his money in," I said as I gathered my satchel.

"Rothschild's," Ringo said decisively.

I looked up in surprise. "How do you know?"

"He said ye gave 'im the idea the first night ye met. Ye knew Rothschild as a bankin' family, which meant they'd survived to modern times, so 'e took 'is shares of the family 'oldin and moved them into Rothschild's bank."

"When did he tell you all this?"

Ringo shrugged. "Before we went to Bletchley Park. 'E said to make sure ye knew to go there if we needed anythin'."

"Well, now we need something. Do you know where it is?"

He nodded. "It's close. Up on St. Swithin's Lane."

I brushed the dust off my trousers and buttoned my coat up to cover the t-shirt I was wearing while my 1940s blouse dried. Clean clothes were a luxury I indulged in whenever we had plans to stay any place more than a day, and the radiator was currently sporting a colorful display of my underwear. Ringo very pointedly stayed on the other side of the room. "Well, this is as good as it gets. Hopefully my ring will get us in the door, because I don't think my wardrobe is quite up to the standards of a Rothschild client."

Ringo shook his head. "Ye don't know men if ye think they'll even notice what ye're wearin'."

I stuck my tongue out at him as we headed down the ladder and out of the loft flat. It was a business day, but the accountants who currently occupied the main floor of the building were all fighting the war, so the office was shuttered.

There was life on the streets though – older men and young boys working side by side to clear the rubble of a bomb site on one side of the street, while a mother sat on the stoop of her flat, a book in one hand and a sleeping baby on her lap. She caught me smiling at her baby, and gave me a tired wave in return. She didn't look too much older than me, but there were deep circles under her eyes. The baby was probably only about six months old, and I wondered about its father. Was he fighting in Europe somewhere? Was he even still alive? The stories I could make up about her life made 'new mother' just one of many possible reasons for her sleeplessness.

The Rothschild building was an imposing Victorian brick thing that dominated a whole side of St. Swithin's Lane – an ancient, ten-foot-wide alley. We were ushered inside by an expressionless doorman and directed to the front desk.

"May I help you?" The receptionist was probably about fifty, with perfectly coiffed hair as stiff as her sharp upper-crust accent. She noticed my clothes but had the good taste not to cringe.

"My name is Saira Devereux," I began. My hands were sweating, and I stumbled over my last name. "My husband has an account here, and I'd like to access it." I stumbled over 'husband' too, and the first hint of scorn tinged her expressionless face.

"Where is your husband?" she sniffed. The woman was handsome rather than attractive, and with her haughty superiority, she reminded me of old photos of Wallis Simpson, the woman King Edward abdicated his throne to marry. I dubbed her Wally just to take her down a notch in my mind.

"He's not … here," I said lamely. Despite the nickname, Wally intimidated me.

"We do not grant access to our clients' accounts without proper authorization, arranged with the account-holder in person, in advance. It is for the protection of our clients against fraudulent claims from opportunists and thieves, so unless you have the proper paperwork with you, you will need to return with your husband."

Tears sprang to my eyes so suddenly I couldn't clamp down on the pain. If Archer were able to return with me, there would be no need to be here at all. I opened my mouth to respond, but Ringo beat me to it. "Lady Devereux would like to see Mr. Rothschild, please."

Wally started. "Lady—" She clearly hadn't expected the title, and her eyes narrowed. "Do you have proof of your identity, madam?"

Her imperious tone finally startled me out of my meekness and arrogance hit my voice. "Of course I do. And I'll be showing it to Mr. Rothschild, not to his receptionist."

Her gaze was imperious, but I'd surprised her, and I sensed she was weighing her options with me –

back down and take the possible wrath of her boss if I turned out to be false, or stand her ground and guarantee the wrath of Rothschild when I complained about her. She finally lifted the telephone and plugged in a switch.

"A Lady Devereux is here to see Mr. Rothschild," she said into the receiver. Her eyes opened fractionally wider and she looked at me. "Your husband's first name?"

"Archer."

Wally paled and spoke quickly into the phone. "Yes sir. I'll send her right up, sir."

She replaced the phone in its cradle carefully and took a breath. When she finally met my eyes again I almost cringed from the fear in them. "Forgive me, Lady Devereux. I hope I did not offend."

Ringo spoke before I could. "Ye did, but she won't 'old it against ye."

Wally's expression froze. "I do apologize," she said as she stood and directed us to a gilt cage that housed the elevator. "Jones will take you up to Mr. Rothschild's office."

Jones, the elevator operator, smiled brightly as we entered the cage. "Sure thing, Mrs. Blackburn." His smile was infectious and wiped the sourness off my mood. I looked at Wally from behind the cage doors and gave her a nod. It was enough to change the expression on her face from fearful to thankful.

The elevator cracked to a stop on the third floor, and Jones opened the cage door with a cheerful smile at the young woman who waited for us. "There ye go, Aeris. Safe and sound."

Aeris seemed nervous, so I held my hand out to her. "Hi Aeris, I love your name. I'm Saira Devereux, and this is Ringo."

My friendliness seemed to surprise her, but she recovered quickly and shook our hands. "Thank you. This way, please. Mr. Rothschild is waiting for you."

For the first time, I wondered if the bank and wine families of Rothschild were at all related to the Monger Family I knew in my own time. The name was spelled differently, and as far as I knew, none of the Monger Rothchilds were Jewish, so it seemed unlikely. But I braced myself for Monger-gut anyway.

Aeris tapped twice on the closed door at the end of the hallway, then opened it to usher us in. The office had a view down the narrow alley of St. Swithin's Lane, which, from three stories up, looked like a small stream running through London. It was paneled in beautiful, golden wood, and the Persian carpet on the floor was almost as big as the huge room. Mr. Rothschild stood from his chair upon our entrance, and he came around the desk with his hand outstretched and a welcoming smile on his face.

"Lady Devereux?" He lifted my hand to kiss the back of it. Most people would have missed the tiny glance down at my left hand in the elegance of his greeting. I caught it because I was looking for it, and I met Ringo's eyes with a small smile. This guy was good, and had class in spades.

"Mr. Rothschild, it's an honor to meet you, sir," I said with a friendly smile. "This is our family friend, Ringo." Rothschild shook his hand and then directed us to some chairs by the window.

"Please, come and sit. Aeris, if you would bring us some tea, I'd be most grateful." He turned to me. "I consider your husband to be a personal friend. It is an honor to meet you, madam." His smile was genuine, and it gave me confidence I hadn't felt earlier.

The door closed behind Aeris as Ringo and I sat in the big club chairs across from Mr. Rothschild. "Thank you for taking me at my word. When we were married, Archer said his ring would allow me access to his resources. I now find I need those resources to find him and make sure he's safe."

The smile was instantly replaced with concern. "Lady Devereux … it is Saira, is it not?"

That shocked me. "Yes. How did you know?"

"Archer described you to me when I assumed managing control of the bank after my father. He said I should give you anything you ask, and I find I am compelled to offer whatever additional resources the bank has at its disposal if it will help you ensure the safety of your husband."

Tears prickled at my eyes, but a deep breath helped keep them from falling. "Archer is very lucky to have such a generous friend in you, Mr. Rothschild. I hope I have the chance to know you personally as well."

Just then, Aeris returned with a tray full of tea things, which she set down on the table between us. She took an envelope from the tray and handed it to Mr. Rothschild. "As you requested, sir," she said.

"Thank you, Aeris." He turned his gaze back to me as she left the room. "Archer asked me to keep this letter for you. He gave it to me just after the war began and said you may never come to claim it, but if you did, I should deliver it to you immediately."

I took the letter from him with a shaking hand and shot Ringo a worried glance. His answering expression was calm and supportive, and it gave me the strength to open the wax seal that was imprinted with the crowned heart from my ring.

I read silently to myself while Mr. Rothschild chatted politely with Ringo about the state of the London streets since the Blitz. *My Dearest Saira, I find I am overwhelmed with the hope that you will one day read this letter, because that would mean my deepest desire has been realized — to marry you. Thank you for trusting me with your heart, and for believing in me despite the challenges we'll face.*

My heart utterly galloped in my chest with every word he'd written.

Now, to practical matters (I can see your smirk and it makes me smile)—

I did smirk, and my heartbeat slowed to something manageable.

I've converted much of my fortune into gemstones. They'll be easiest to carry and simplest to return to currency wherever you go. Consider finding Ringo to make the deals. I believe he could charm a fortune from the King of England if he set his mind to it.

I inhaled sharply. How did he know? When this letter was written I'd known him only a few weeks in 1888, and yet he had planned for me to come, and he had anticipated what I'd need. Had he made this arrangement with every Rothschild banker since Victorian times?

I blinked away my tears and continued reading. *Take what you need, Saira. Take all of it. Everything I have belongs to you, and the only thing I want in this world is your security, safety, and happiness. You are my reason to smile, and my reason to rise every night and face all the unknowns that an endless future brings. Thank you for finding me, my love, for I am always and will forever be yours. ~Archer*

The men had moved to the window, and Mr. Rothschild was describing the histories of the various buildings to Ringo, but I knew it was really just to give me a minute of privacy.

I needed it.

My chest was like an aching black hole, and my throat burned with the sobs that threatened. I clamped a tight lid on the need to cry, because once I started I didn't think I'd know how to stop. Archer had loved me so much more than I knew, and for so much longer than I realized. He'd told me his feelings, but I hadn't *understood* until now.

Now that he was gone.

I shuddered and took a deep breath to force calm and peacefulness where there was virtually none left. I wanted to run so badly I twitched with the need, and I saw Ringo notice my agitation. He and Mr. Rothschild returned to their seats, and Ringo's gaze held mine as if to make sure I was still able to function. I was, but barely.

"Archer said—" I started, but had to clear my throat. "Archer said there are stones?"

"Yes, Lady Devereux. I can have them brought to you here if you'd like, or I can take you to them." Mr. Rothschild looked concerned, and I didn't blame him. I probably looked like I warranted it.

"Call me Saira, please. And if they could be brought here, that would be great. Thank you."

"Of course. Let me just go to the vaults myself." Mr. Rothschild left us alone in his office, and I held the letter out to Ringo.

He ignored it. "Are ye alright?"

"I need to cry for about three days. Read the letter. You're in it too."

His eyebrows rose at that and he took the paper warily. I practiced breathing while he read. I felt as if I'd forget how to unless I concentrated on each breath.

Ringo exhaled deeply as he handed the letter back to me. "We'll find 'im again, Saira." His voice held so much quiet conviction that I allowed a little hope back into my heart.

I nodded, not trusting myself to speak, and Ringo twined his fingers through mine for a second – just long enough to squeeze the feeling back into them.

"Rothschild is a good man," Ringo said to change the subject.

"He seems like it."

He got up and went to the window, where I joined him. "There's a Christopher Wren church called St. Stephen Wallbrook just over there. It used to be the main focus of St. Swithin's Lane." Ringo pointed to something out of sight. "Rothschild wants to rebuild this place to bring the church and its graveyard back into view. 'E appreciates the beauty of the place."

The office door opened and Mr. Rothschild returned carrying a large, flat black case, about the size of a briefcase, which he held in front of him like a tray. He set the case on his desk and invited me to sit in his chair. Then he opened the case, and it felt like the whole room gasped. Or maybe just my gasp was the loudest thing in my ears.

The case was full of cut and uncut gemstones. Amethysts, tourmalines, garnets, and citrines were the biggest – some were twenty or thirty carats each. Rubies, sapphires, pearls, and the occasional emerald were somewhere in the five to ten carat range, and diamonds bigger than a carat were scattered everywhere among the colored stones. The whole tray glittered with spectacular stones, and when I could finally tear my eyes away from it, I stared at Mr. Rothschild.

"How—?"

Mr. Rothschild said calmly, "Lord Devereux has been investing with us since 1889." He waited a moment for that to sink in, and when none of us reacted to that news with surprise, he gave a tiny nod of his head and continued. "He was a principal investor in the financing of the London Underground and the Rio Tinto copper mines in Spain, among other things. He has been using our Antwerp connections to convert the profits from his various investments into what you see before you. Lord Devereux has an instinct for the technologies that will become the biggest successes, and as you can see, he's done very well."

I touched the tops of the stones lightly with the palm of my hand. "Wow," I whispered. Then I looked at Ringo. "Could you pick out stones you can sell easily? Just enough to see us through …"

Through what, exactly? I looked helplessly at Ringo, but he was picking through the stones on the tray.

He held up a diamond that looked like it was about two carats and asked Mr. Rothschild, "Could this one be sold through yer Antwerp people for sterlin'?"

The banker nodded. "If you like, although Lord Devereux keeps sterling in his account as well. I can withdraw, say, a thousand pounds?"

Ringo shook his head. "One 'undred is more than enough. In smaller bills and coins if possible?"

"Make it two," I said to Rothschild. Then to Ringo, "I'd like to make sure Rachel can get to Palestine."

Mr. Rothschild looked up from his notepad. "A friend of yours?" I nodded. "Was she able to get her immigration paperwork?"

I shook my head. "She and her friend are on the waiting list."

He handed me his business card. "Have them come to me. I'll see what I can do to help."

I took the card and blinked back even more tears. "Thank you, Mr. Rothschild. That means more to me than you can ever know."

He smiled. "It is my pleasure to help. We've done what we can for some of the larger groups helping the émigrés, but it's very difficult to track our successes. Ensuring an individual's immigration sounds quite satisfying, actually."

He plucked two small velvet bags from a pocket in the lid of the gem case and handed one to each of us. "Please help yourselves while I arrange for your cash needs." He stood and left the room, and I turned to Ringo.

"This is ridiculous."

"This is 'is Lordship takin' care of ye." He picked out a couple of small stones and put them in his bag. "I know a dealer we can take these to, but if we go anywhere else than my London, we'll be at the mercy of whatever thievin' gem merchants we can find."

I held up a thumbnail-sized cut emerald. "I've always heard there's no such thing as a flawless emerald." I peered through it closely. "Looks pretty flawless to me."

"The French loved emeralds during the third French empire," said Mr. Rothschild as he returned with a small leather envelope. "The green was considered Napoleon's color."

"When was the third French empire?" I asked.

"From about 1870 until the start of the first world war. But if one were to try to sell an emerald during the period between 1570 and 1800, the market was depressed due to oversaturation from Colombia." Mr. Rothschild's tone was innocent, but he watched me steadily, as if to make sure I understood his meaning.

Clearly the banker knew something of the Descendants, and again I wondered if there was a connection between the Monger Rothchilds and the banking Rothschilds.

"Any other tips for, say, 1889?" I asked carefully.

"Rubies have always done very well in all the markets throughout much of history, the exception being the early part of this century when synthetic rubies were introduced. Anything of a carat or more will equal or surpass the price of a diamond of the same size, especially in 1889," he said.

Ringo gathered three rubies in the one-to-two carat size, and I plucked a stunning three-carat ruby off the tray for my own bag.

"Pearls are good, and easy to sell as well, particularly matched sets." Rothschild said as he picked a pair of creamy white pearls from the tray. He handed them to Ringo for his bag. "But emeralds of that quality," he picked up the one I had set down, "are the most valuable of all. A fine emerald will outsell a diamond or ruby because they're so very rare." Mr. Rothschild placed it in my palm. "Take it. This stone will be worth more if it's sold in the nineteenth century than now."

My hand closed over the emerald and I looked into the banker's eyes. "I think you and Archer became very good friends," I said quietly.

He smiled. "There are times in one's life when a friend is more valuable than all the treasures in the world. When your husband and I first met, I was the same age as he appeared to be. He was that friend for me, and as I grew older, I eventually became that friend to him."

Ringo closed and latched the lid on Archer's case of gemstones, and we both shook Mr. Rothschild's hand. I stepped close to the banker and kissed his cheek lightly. "Thank you for everything, Mr. Rothschild."

"It has been my pleasure, Lady Devereux. Send your friend Rachel to me, and I hope to see you again someday."

We took our leave of the N.M. Rothschild & Sons bank with pockets full of hope. Archer's letter to me was tucked inside my jacket, and when I had secured the bag of gemstones in the holster where my daggers lay against my back, I turned to Ringo.

"We have news and money to deliver, and then I think it's time to go."

Ringo had tucked the cash and gemstones deep into the recesses of his clothes, and his answering nod was instantaneous. "Let's do it."

THE GEM DEALER

Rachel was teaching a class when we stopped by the temple, so we left the envelope and a note with Aviv. He kissed both of us on the cheeks as thanks, and I seriously left there feeling like I'd been kissed by an angel.

It was a weird feeling.

We grabbed some sausage rolls and a wax paper-wrapped cheese from a shop around the corner. I wanted fresh vegetables, but the shopkeeper had sold out. I did buy a lemon for each of us, despite the look of disgust on Ringo's face. It had only been a couple of days since I'd had fresh fruit or vegetables, but I was already imagining scurvy and vitamin deficiency.

Ringo reminded me that he had sometimes gone weeks without something green to eat.

"Which is why you'll never be as tall as me," I said sharply.

"And ye'll never be as fast as me," he snarked as he took off running.

He detoured around a big bomb damage site just south of the synagogue, and it took us into a square I suddenly recognized. "Wait. Stop!" I called to him.

Ringo grinned back at me. "Done already?"

"No, I know this place. What is it?"

He shrugged. "Mitre Square. It's between Bevis Marks and Aldgate."

A flash of a pitch black night and a body on the cobblestones in front of me made my heart skip a beat. "This was where the Ripper killed his fourth victim the night I met Archer," I whispered.

Ringo looked around the square. "I didn't know that," he finally said. "I met ye that night too. I didn't realize the lads and I were so close to 'im then."

And eerie feeling stole over us both, and we practically backed our way out of the square. Only when we'd made it back out to the main street did we start running again, but a little of the abandon had gone out of it for both of us.

We ate in silence in Ringo's flat until the ghosts of the past finally settled back into the shadows of my brain. I cleaned up the little that we had disturbed there, and then slung my satchel across my body. "Are you ready?" I asked.

Ringo nodded. "Ye're thinkin' that if we go back now we'll find 'im sleepin'."

"I'm not sure how much I trust Tom anymore," I said with a sigh. "I wish I did, but he keeps surprising me, and he's too strong to be so unpredictable."

"Daytime is a good time to go searchin' for Vampires, I always say."

"And with a straight face, no less."

We made our way to the London Bridge, and a few minutes later I'd Clocked us to 1889. The day we'd left was sunny and warm, but we arrived in the rain, and despite a sprint, we were soaked through by the time we made it to the alley behind the accountancy offices. We went into stealth mode, as much for the accountants as for the sleeping Vampire upstairs, and made it up into the flat with none the wiser.

It had only been a few months since Ringo and Charlie had left this place, and I thought I could still smell the remnants of the herbal soap Charlie used. Ringo's expression was neutral, but his eyes seemed sad as they scanned the flat.

The drapes were pulled around the twin bed, and I approached it cautiously. A peek inside revealed Tom asleep, and even though my hand shook a bit, I stood quietly and studied him.

Tom's face was gaunt. The angles were too sharp now to have the kind of exotic good looks he'd had when I first met him, and he looked oddly vulnerable, which might be because he had seemed so tortured when he was awake.

Ringo came up beside me and assessed Tom's sleeping form with a glance, then pulled me back from the draped bed.

"We need to go and sell a stone," he whispered.

"I want to be here when he wakes up," I said quietly, but Ringo was already shaking his head.

"I'm not leavin' ye to face a wakin' Vampire alone, no matter who 'e is. If we go now, we can be back before 'e rises."

I glared at Ringo, then yanked the swastika knife out of the post where it pinned the note. I didn't think I was changing anything vital because it had already gotten us here, but despite my momentary bristle at Ringo's bossiness, he wasn't wrong. One less weapon left lying around was one less thing to draw blood.

When we were outside and heading down the alley, I grumbled at him.

"I may not totally trust Tom, but he wanted me to come. He wouldn't go to the trouble of leaving a note if his purpose was nefarious."

Ringo shot me a loaded look. "Really? We stopped 'im from killin' Walters, and then we sent him through a spiral to God knows where, after 'e'd just spent most of a war workin' for the *Nazis*, Saira — ye can't tell me 'e didn't know what side 'e was on. I'd say there's a better than average chance 'is purpose is nefarious."

I didn't say anything, but I didn't really have to. Ringo had made his point, and regardless of what I believed otherwise, I couldn't deny what he'd said. He led us up past St. Paul's Cathedral, and it was a shock to see the neighborhood around it perfectly intact and full of Victorian and Georgian buildings. The last time I'd seen St. Paul's was the night of the bombing in 1944. The neighborhood around the cathedral had been practically obliterated

– barely more than jagged ruins. The memory of it and everything else about that night nauseated me.

The farther north we walked, the better I felt. I'd never explored that part of London, with its crowded streets full of vendors, and seeing its Victorian splendor standing proudly against a backdrop of daily commerce was a unique way to experience the city.

We traveled up Farringdon for a few blocks, but it was a busy avenue, so Ringo took us through smaller neighborhoods. He pointed out Ye Olde Mitre, the second oldest pub in England, and the second time in a day that name had come up. I had a momentary chill at the thought that Jack the Ripper could be around the next corner, much as he'd been in my recurring nightmares. Ringo cut through an alley and finally we arrived at Hatton Gardens.

It was a bustling jewelry district, crowded with small storefronts and tight alleys. We passed a café where two Jewish men haggled over the price of three small stones on the table, and a storefront where an older woman used a tiny chisel to carve a cameo face on a piece of coral.

Ringo stopped so suddenly, I almost ran into his back. We stood at a corner, and he studied the people outside the shops that lined the cross-street in front of us.

"What's wrong?" I whispered at his shoulder.

"Somethin's goin' down," he said quietly.

I tried to see what he'd seen. Older men, mostly Jewish, but some Italian as well, worked behind the counters in the tiny storefronts. A young, dark-haired man leaned against a wall at the corner across from us, two well-dressed men stood outside the window of a shop half-way down the block, and a scruffy blond kid, about ten years old, kicked a can aimlessly toward them down the sidewalk.

"The guy leaning against the wall?" I whispered.

He shook his head. "No, the kid. 'E's too shabby for this neighbor'ood. And the Jewish kids are all workin' in the parents' shops by that age."

The kid had just aimed a kick at the can that would have sent it into the feet of the well-dressed men outside the shop. "Oy!" Ringo called out as he started across the street. The kid looked up, startled, then defiant when he saw Ringo.

"Ye do it and I'll take ye t' Lamb meself." His accent had gotten so strong it was almost unintelligible, but clearly the kid understood Ringo's words.

He glared at Ringo and pulled his leg back again to kick the can. Ringo moved faster than I anticipated and had the kid up against the wall before his foot ever connected with the tin.

"Wot the bleedin' 'ell!" The kid was furious, and the language sounded ridiculous coming from such a young voice. He tried to kick Ringo, who shoved a knee between the kid's legs. The kid howled in rage, and shopkeepers began to emerge from the doorways.

The older of the two men standing by the window turned and spoke to Ringo in a very posh, upper class accent. "Now, see here, young man—" he began, but the kid's howls drowned out the man's voice.

"Ye want another clip in t'stones? Shut it!" Ringo shook the kid, who glared at him.

"Let me go!" the kid said furiously.

The posh gentleman had taken a few steps toward Ringo as if to press his point. I was dressed in my 1940s trouser suit, and I had shoved my hair into one of Ringo's old caps, so I hung back in hopes that no one would pay particular attention to me.

"See here. That child hasn't done anything. You're hurting him." The younger posh man stepped forward to back up the older one, and I thought they might be father and son. I scanned for exits if we had to run.

Ringo spared a quick glance at the two men, then directed his attention back to the kid. "Why don't ye tell 'Is Grace what ye were plannin' for 'im and the marquess."

I wasn't the only one staring at Ringo. His Grace was a duke's title, and the duke looked shocked at having been recognized. "Do

I know you, sir?" he said in a voice so pompous it should have come with its own hot air pump.

"I know yer son," said Ringo as he held the kid with one hand and began emptying the boy's trouser pockets with the other. Out of one came a wire cutter, a bit of broken glass, and a wicked-looking knife. The other pocket held a two-foot-long strand of piano wire, a lock-pick, and a little velvet bag that proved to be full of bits of gravel.

"I'm sure I have no idea who you are," said the marquess with equal pomposity. His voice was drowned out by the boy's protests, but when the knife hit the pavement and the duke's eyes widened even further, the kid wisely shut up.

The duke seemed to have recovered from his surprise at the kid's pocket-contents and directed his attention back to Ringo. "My son has said he doesn't know you," the duke said archly.

Ringo finally let the kid down, but held him tightly by the scruff of the neck. "Lord Devereux the younger has spoken of ye, Your Grace. And in answer to the first question, this one 'ere was about to kick that can between yer feet. Ye'd 'ave either stumbled or reached for the marquess, and the lad would 'ave 'ad the diamonds out of yer waistcoat pocket with none the wiser."

Ringo addressed the next part of his astonishing statement to the kid. "Problem is, 'Atton Gardens is controlled by a fellow called Lamb, and any thief who wants to keep 'is fingers keeps away from Lamb's territory. That makes this one either new or full of 'imself, and both'll get 'is body dumped in the River Fleet within a week."

"Fleet's not a river," the kid grumbled.

Ringo cuffed him on the back of the head. "What do ye think runs under this whole place? Ye stand at any sewer grate in Clerkenwell and ye can 'ear the river flowin' beneath yer feet."

The duke seemed to be stuck on the same part of Ringo's statement as I was. Lord Devereux, the younger son of the duke. This man was my father-in-law.

"Now see here, young man," Devereux began, but Ringo cut him off.

"No, I don't know where 'e is, and it's been a good while since I've seen 'im. But I like and respect 'Is Lordship and would see no wrong done by 'is family.

Devereux didn't know quite what to make of Ringo, and he began to bluster. "But how did you know what I carry in my waistcoat pocket, much less that this young man intended to steal it?"

Ringo ignored the question for a moment as he turned to the kid and shook him. "Listen to me, and listen good. Lamb's territory is all of Clerkenwell, Tok's got the bank district, Riven's workin' 'Olborn, and it's no use tryin' for anything east of Aldgate because Nim's got it sewn up tight. The river's run by Lizzer's gang, and they're meaner than snakes unless ye're river folk. There's a man by the name of Gosford, owns the Sanda. 'E's a good man and a good boss. Tell 'im Ringo sent ye, and then ye work like a dog for 'im. The pay's fair, the toffs leave ye alone, and ye'll learn a skill ye can use in any port city. Best though, Gosford'll give ye a fish for yer dinner when there's ought leftover, and ye'll keep all yer fingers unless ye're lazy with a knife."

Ringo picked the kid's knife up off the ground and flipped it over to the young dark-haired man at the corner. "Yours, I believe?"

The young man caught it and nodded in surprise. "Many thanks," he said with genuine appreciation. The kid scowled, and Ringo turned his attention back to him.

"Or ye can keep at yer thievin' and maybe ye'll see fifteen with all yer fingers intact, or maybe ye'll be dead in one of the rivers that run under us, tunneled over and stinkin' of sewage – unless ye choose a different way. It's not pretty, but there it is – take it or leave it."

The kid's eyes had grown steadily bigger in his head, until at the end of his speech, Ringo had let go of his collar and pushed him away. The kid didn't need to be told twice, and he was gone a moment later. Ringo turned back to Archer's father and brother then, and addressed the duke as if nothing odd had just happened.

"As to yer questions, ye've been pattin' yer waistcoat every two minutes since I saw ye, and the lumps are not bits of sugar for yer 'orse. The kid 'ad a velvet bag full of pebbles to replace the one he planned to nip from ye, and 'e'd 'ave used the knife 'e nicked from the fellow over there if ye'd caught 'im at it."

Devereux's mouth was set firmly, and his eyes narrowed as he looked in the direction the young thief had taken. He held his hand out resolutely to shake Ringo's. "Right, then. I believe I owe you my thanks. Winston Devereux, at your service."

I was actually impressed. My father-in-law had seemed like a pompous old windbag when he first spoke to Ringo, but he had just introduced himself with his first name. Ringo shook his hand.

"Jonathan Starkey, sir, but I'm called Ringo."

I suddenly wanted to meet Winston Devereux, and I stepped forward. Ringo's eyes widened briefly as I held my hand out to Archer's father. "Your Grace, my name is Saira Elian. I am also a friend of your son's, and I've heard quite a lot about you."

Devereux was clearly shocked to be shaking the hand of a woman dressed in men's clothing, but I gave him credit for not faltering. He shook my hand and met my eyes. "A pleasure to meet you, Miss Elian." He held my hand a moment longer than was strictly necessary, and his voice had an edge that hadn't been part of the windbag act. "Is my son well? Is he … happy?"

The word, 'happy' sounded foreign to his tongue, and Devereux dropped my hand as if he couldn't believe he'd just asked such a ridiculous question. I stumbled over the things I wanted to say to Archer's father, so Ringo answered. "'E's in love, and 'is lady loves 'im right back. It's as good a measure of 'appiness as a man can find."

Devereux looked from Ringo to me, and the smallest piece of a smile lifted one corner of his mouth. "Hrmmph," he said finally. "Quite so. If you see him, tell him I've left him the townhouse. If he sells it after I'm gone, he should know I've left something of his mother's …" He shook his head sharply. "The townhouse. That's all he gets. He'll do with it as he sees fit."

He gave a quick bow to me, then shook Ringo's hand again. "A good day to you both."

"It was nice to meet you, Your Grace," I said quietly as he and Archer's older brother walked away. And it was. No matter how Archer had felt about his father, this man had loved him.

Ringo waited until they were out of earshot. "Ye alright?"

I took a deep breath. "Yeah."

"Ye think Archer ever found 'is mother's things in the town'ouse before 'e sold it to the Arman's great-grandmother?"

I shook my head. "No, he would have told me. He thought his father hated him for killing his mother with his birth."

Ringo snorted derisively. "More likely 'e 'ated 'imself."

He led me down a different street, and then turned a corner into a narrow alley. Only half of my attention was on our surroundings – the other half was tied up in knots around our encounter with Archer's father. He had been blustery and pompous, but underneath all the obnoxious trappings of nobility was a man who was actually noble. A man who hadn't known how to deal with the pain of losing his wife, and had failed at showing his youngest son that he loved him.

Ringo stopped at an old wooden door with sturdy new hardware. Ringo knocked twice, then once, then three times, and a moment later, the handle turned and the door was opened by a young girl. She was probably twelve years old and was dressed in trousers. She didn't seem to be masquerading as a boy because her long hair was unbound and cascaded in beautiful dark waves down her back, so maybe her clothing choice was just about comfort or convenience. Something I could relate to.

"'Ello Maeve. Is Yaniv in?" Ringo stood perfectly still while the girl studied his face. I didn't know what she finally saw there that convinced her to let us in, but when she closed the door behind us, she threw the bolt with a solid click. She led us up the stairs to a big open workroom filled with natural light streaming through an entire wall full of windows. A woman who might have been the girl's mother sat by the window cutting a gemstone with a tiny chisel, but it was the older woman, possibly the grandmother, working at the big table in the center of the room who looked up at our arrival.

Ringo caught her attention first, and I was startled to see that her eyes were covered in milky white cataracts. But then she smiled at him and held out her hand in greeting. "Young man, you've grown. You're finally eating, then?" she said in a voice much stronger than she looked. He grinned and took her hand in both of his.

"Ye've not aged a day, Yaniv," he said warmly.

This was Yaniv? The name was masculine, so I had assumed Yaniv was a man. But despite the trousers on every woman in the building, Ringo was the only male I could see.

The old woman laughed in delight. "Found yourself a honey tongue, too. Is she the reason?" Her milky gaze found me and seemed to look beyond my face and into my soul. Her gaze tickled a little, but wasn't unpleasant, and I instinctively stood very still so she could see whatever it was she was looking for.

There was a smile in Ringo's voice as he answered. "She's one of them. Friends'll do that to a bloke."

Yaniv shifted her gaze back to Ringo, and I was left with the sense that I'd just been scanned for the contents of my character. "Are you buying or selling?"

He pulled the small velvet bag from his pocket and emptied it onto the table in front of her. "Selling," he said. Maeve came over to stand behind her grandmother as the woman ran her fingers lightly over the stones from Archer's box. Her eyes remained fixed on Ringo's face, but I had the sense that her focus was all in her fingertips.

She held up a ruby. "Old, this. Roman, I think." She sniffed the stone, then touched her tongue to it. "Sweat and steel. From the hilt of a sword I'll wager."

Yaniv was a Seer, and she seemed to know the minute I'd worked it out, because suddenly I had her attention again. "Surprises you, does it?"

"I've never known a past-Seer," I said simply.

"Surprised my papa too. No one expected a girl, and sure as the sunrise not one with my skill. So, a boy's name, and a man's training for the girl-child of a master stone-cutter. Good thing my papa wasn't so hidebound as others." She said it with a wry smile, and I grinned back.

"Good thing."

She made a lovely hrmphing sound and refocused her fingers on the stones. "It's the history of stones I see," she said. "Useful for weeding out the ones painted in blood."

I thought about the conflict diamonds of the twentieth century, but she wasn't talking about African civil wars. "I don't know what you mean," I said.

She waved me closer and gestured for me to sit across the table from her. "These stones you have here – some are old, some are newer than they should be, but none have the taint of bloodstain around them. This," she lifted the lid from a tray of cut sapphires on her table and plucked one out without hesitation, holding it out for me to see, "was mined by a child who was whipped for hiding it in his shoe. It has the taint of blood and pain, and you'd feel it if you wore it."

She dropped the sapphire back into the box and closed the lid. There were no fumbles in her movements and no pauses in the certainty of her touch. She plucked one of Archer's diamonds off the table and held it to her nose. Then she handed it back to Ringo. "Keep this one, if the lady will let you. Your heart's wrapped in it, and the bride you give it to will know it."

Ringo looked startled and glanced at me reflexively. I grinned and nodded. "Only if you invite me to the wedding."

He looked completely bemused at the two-carat stone in his hand, and he flushed slightly as he shoved it deep into his pocket. "Thank ye," he said quietly.

The old woman had separated out five stones from the small pile and replaced the others in the velvet bag, which she handed back to Ringo. "I'll buy these from you. Standard deal – market price less ten percent."

She nodded at Maeve, who pulled a bag from around her neck and handed it to her grandmother. Yaniv counted out a fistful of gold coins, plus some bronze and copper ones. Ringo produced a small piece of fabric which he handed to the woman, and she wrapped the coins in it tightly. "Smart lad. Keeps them from clinking." I was impressed that he seemed to trust her, and I didn't question her price, or her honesty. It made me pull the small velvet bag out of my own pocket and place it on the table.

"I don't need to sell these yet, I just wondered if you could tell me about them," I said.

The old woman swept Ringo's stones into her own small bag and cleared the work table in front of her, then she nodded and gestured for me to show her.

The big emerald winked at me from the small pile of gemstones I'd collected, and it was the one Yaniv went right for. "How'd you come by this?" Her tone wasn't as sharp as her words were, but the question made me defensive nonetheless.

"I didn't steal it, if that's what you're asking."

The old woman tsk'd. "That wasn't my question. I sold it last month. Young man said it was for the woman he loved."

My heart plummeted to my feet. Archer was here, in this time. How could I not have realized that?

And he'd been right here where I was standing.

I swallowed.

"Does he come here often?" I asked quietly. "The young man you sold this stone to?"

"Are you his love?" she countered.

I nodded, and then finally answered out loud in case she really couldn't see. "Yes."

"He comes every month."

I looked at Ringo, and the expression on his face mirrored the one I thought was on my own – something between shock, hope, and fear. And then he shook his head, and even though I knew he was right, it snuffed the tiny ray of light right out.

If Yaniv knew about the roller-coaster ride my emotions were on, she didn't show it. Instead, she caressed the emerald. "It once belonged to Artemisia Schiattesi. She was an artist in Rome, and some said the emerald was a lover's gift. I prefer to think she earned the emerald on her feet."

I stared at Yaniv. "Earned it on her feet? That's … vivid."

Yaniv shrugged. "Eh, a hard truth is still true no matter how it's dressed."

Maeve snorted behind her grandmother, and I realized again how very remarkable this whole set up really was. Three women, working together in the jewelry trade during a time when men still controlled nearly everything.

Yaniv held the emerald out to me, and I closed my hand around the warm gemstone. "I think I like having a stone that belonged to an artist," I said.

"Your man was pleased by that as well," Yaniv said with a smile.

Her references to Archer were unnerving, and I stood up to go as if he was going to walk in any moment and catch us there. We took our leave from Yaniv's shop with a thank-you and promises to return. I felt Yaniv's milky gaze on my back long after we left the shop, and it wasn't until we were nearly back at Ringo's that I finally spoke.

"We shouldn't see him," I said. He knew I meant Archer because he answered quickly with a shake of his head.

"There's no point. 'E can't help us, and it'll only confuse things later."

That was putting it mildly. Anything I did to change something in history – even something as simple as having an out-of-native-time conversation with Archer – seemed to send a ripple down the time stream and make a new memory that hadn't been there before.

I already felt like we were tap dancing in a minefield every time we Clocked, but part of me didn't care what kind of damage we left in our wake as long as we could fix the time stream split and get back to Archer in the present – the right one, where he was safe and sound and waiting for me.

The days were beginning to shorten, and it was already dusk when we got back to Ringo's loft. The accountants had left for the day, so we debated whether to make a lot of noise or enter the loft silently. In the end, we opted for going in as if we owned the place, which, theoretically, Ringo did. Tom was the interloper in the scenario, and behaving otherwise would put us at a tactical disadvantage.

We had stopped by the Sanda on our way to say hello to Gosford and warn him about the young thief who might come by. Gosford had given us haddock for our dinner and said he'd keep a lookout for the kid. We picked up a couple of eggs, oil, some herbs and day-old bread, and I looked forward to actually cooking a meal.

Tom was sitting at the table staring out the window when we came in. He didn't seem surprised to see us.

"Hello, Tom," I said. I tried to keep the wariness out of my voice, but I obviously failed, because Tom's expression tightened as he turned to face me.

"Thank you for coming." The words seem to strangle in his throat, and my instinct was to growl at him for the cryptic message, so instead I fussed over the food we'd brought.

Ringo nodded at Tom as he bent to light the stove. I found a cast iron pan, poured some oil in, and set it on the heat while I prepped the fish. I avoided Tom's eyes until he finally spoke again in a tone that sounded vaguely normal.

"Can I help?"

I looked up in surprise at his offer. "Sure. Can you make breadcrumbs?"

He nodded and started tearing up the bread. When the fish was deboned and chopped small, I mixed it with the egg and breadcrumbs for fishcakes. Tom didn't speak again until the fishcakes were frying and Ringo had set the table.

"I didn't know you cooked."

I turned the cakes and shrugged. "Survival skills."

"I know about those," he said quietly.

I used cooking as the excuse to avoid Tom's eyes, but when Ringo and I were seated across from each other with food on all three plates, there were no more excuses.

"You know I'm not going to eat. Why did you put food in front of me?" There was an edge to Tom's voice. It was the same edge he'd had when he thanked me for coming.

I looked him straight in the eyes. "It's called being polite, Tom. You don't have to eat it. Archer always offers his to whichever person at the table looks hungriest. You can give it to Ringo or throw it away if you want, I don't care. But it's yours."

Ringo looked back and forth between us. "Ye used to be friends, did ye not? Ye might as well pick the scab off to let the fester out."

"Uh … eating?" I made a face.

Ringo smirked and grabbed the half-eaten fishcake off my plate. "I'll 'elp ye with that, then. Fester gets ye every time, doesn't it?"

Tom pushed his own plate away, then shifted in his seat to face me, arms crossed, wearing an expressionless face. "You go first."

I was tempted to argue that he was the one who called me, but his attitude since we'd walked in had annoyed me, so I inhaled and tried to make my tone as neutral as possible.

"You split time."

THE DEAL

Tom glared at me. "No I didn't. The time stream is just fine."

I scowled. "If you've gone forward, you know it's definitely not fine. The bomb exploded right after you left 1944 and took Archer, George Walters, the Monger ring, and the world as we know it with it."

It was Tom's turn to scowl apparently, and he turned the full force of it on me. "I was just there dodging zombie Londoners because of the Monger ring on Seth Walters' hand."

"No you weren't," I said in a voice full of scorn.

Tom's eyes narrowed. "You Clocked me out of the British Museum station. It was your damn spiral I got shoved into – you should know where you sent me."

Ringo's eyes got big and he stared at me. "Saira, that was before the bomb went off."

The anger drained right out of me. "You went forward? How do you know it was our time?"

Tom's voice was still growly and furious. "Because of the mobile phones. There was an explosion, and everyone had their mobiles out shooting video."

"But how did you *know*?" The edge of desperation in my voice made Tom look at me strangely.

"Ava was there … and Adam. They knew me … knew what I'd become." His tone was still brittle, but some of the anger had gone from it, replaced by sadness or pain. "Adam said there's a cure ..." The strangled sound was back in his voice.

"We looked for you," I said quietly. "It's why we went to Bletchley Park ... to England during the war. We followed you to France so we could bring you back, but then ..." My own voice trailed off and the tightness returned to Tom's face.

"But then you found me and I was the enemy, so you betrayed me instead."

"Oy," Ringo said angrily. "Ye made yer choice, knowin' full well what was right and what was wrong. Don't wipe yer bloodstains on Saira. Ye earned those all on yer own."

I cleared my throat to make my voice stronger. "Yeah, we found you. And you know what, I wasn't wrong when I said killing George Walters would split time, because it did, and now I can't get back home. The spiral sends me to the wrong future."

Tom's glare tried to burn itself into my skin. "Prove it."

"What?" I couldn't believe he just said that.

"Take me to that wrong future. Prove it actually exists, because I don't believe we can change the past enough to split time. We don't have that kind of power." Tom's voice was hard and so bitter.

A million protests went through my head. How could he think that, after everything we'd gone through with Wilder, and after Léon's death? But Ringo beat me to the punch.

"Saira, ye can't take 'im to the wrong future. 'E already exists there." Ringo was angry, and I wanted to scream.

I spun to face Tom. "Do you at least accept that the rules of time travel don't let you be in the same place as you already are?"

He nodded, seemingly reluctant to give me any concession.

"Ringo's right. If I take you with me to the other time stream, we'll either land sometime before your mother gets pregnant with you, or we'll get spit out after you die."

He set his jaw. "I'll take my chances. But take me to school so I can see Mr. Shaw."

I narrowed my eyes at him. "You're looking for the cure. Well, Shaw didn't make one on the wrong time stream, because Archer wasn't there to give him blood."

Tom studied me for a long moment. "Why should I believe you?"

I threw up my hands. "Oh my God! Tom, if you still have any Sight left at all, use it. You don't See things, you *know* things. Look at the future and *know* that I'm telling you the truth."

Tom got very still and quiet. "How do you know that?"

I huffed a sigh. "How do I know what?"

"How my Sight works. How do you know I don't See, I *know?* I've never told anyone that before, not even Adam."

"You told me – on the other time stream." I didn't tell him what I'd had to share to get that information, and I definitely didn't tell him how very different he was then.

Tom sat in silence for a long time. "There's no cure in that future?"

I shook my head. "No Archer, no cure."

"Shaw could have—"

"He didn't."

Tom's gaze finally left mine, and he went very still. "You're sure there's a cure in our time?"

"Yes." I willed him to meet my eyes. "I'm sure there's a serum Shaw hopes is a cure. I'm not sure it works. Mr. Shaw and Connor wanted to test it on Archer, and I don't know if they have yet. I've been gone a long—" my voice broke and I cleared it. "I've been gone a long time. For all I know he could already be cured."

Tom scoffed, and then turned away to walk to the window. He stood there with his forehead against the window frame for long enough that I got up to clear the dishes.

When Tom finally turned around he spoke quietly, and his tone of voice was low and controlled, as if it cost him something to speak. "I need your help."

I searched his face. He met my eyes for a second and then looked away, while barely controlled anger thinned his lips. There were so many things I wanted to know, but I settled for the most pressing question.

"With what?"

He exhaled softly and met my eyes for slightly longer this time before looking away again. "I need to steal the Monger ring."

Had he completely lost his mind? "No."

He glared. "It's your fault they even still have it. You wouldn't let *him* steal it," he tossed his head at Ringo, who was drying his hands, "and now Walters has Adam and a whole bunch of mixed-bloods on the run."

"No," I said again, "you're not laying that on me. And I'm definitely not going to be guilted into helping you get something you could use exactly the way Walters does."

Tom's laugh was an ugly sound. "You think I want it for myself? I don't want anything to do with it, but I'd cut Walters' hand off to get it away from him. Unfortunately, I can't get close enough to him anymore, not after I went for his throat."

My eyes narrowed. "When?"

"When I was just there."

"That was dumb," I said.

Tom glared. "Why?"

"What if you'd turned him instead of killing him? That's all the world needs, another Wilder, only worse."

The jerk actually rolled his eyes at me, as if *I* was the one making *him* tired. "I have to get the ring away from the Mongers so I can get Shaw's cure."

"We've seen the Mongers without their ring," said Ringo, "on the other time stream. Surprisingly, it's not good."

Tom turned on him. "You haven't seen Walters controlling everyday Londoners with that ring. It truly turns them into mindless zombies who do whatever he says." His eyes returned to mine. "He told them I was a terrorist. So long as Walters has the ring, I can't go back there."

"Forward there, not back. And you can't go there now anyway because it's all changed," I said under my breath. I sat back on my heels and considered Tom's words.

Ringo didn't like what he saw in my face, apparently. "Saira," he said in a warning tone.

I ignored him, just for a minute, I told myself. "What do you need my help with?" I asked Tom.

"Clock me somewhere back in time, before any of the Walters ever get their hands on the ring, and I'll steal it."

"And do what with it? You certainly don't get to keep it, and as far as I know, the fires of Mordor already have their ring."

Tom shrugged. "Send it *between*, or give it to the other time stream, I don't care. It just can't be on Seth Walters' hand."

"Saira," Ringo began again, but I cut him off.

"It doesn't belong to them," I said to Ringo.

"But it's not up to ye to take it."

"What do you mean, it doesn't belong to them? Them, who?" Tom cut in.

I stood up and faced him. "On the other time stream, Duncan told the Council that the ring was never the Monger artifact. The Mongers apparently used to have something else – something strategic."

"Duncan?" Tom looked confused.

"War."

He looked appropriately stunned. "You met *War*? What did he say about the ring?"

"Enough to know that the Mongers don't have their artifact on either time stream, and I got the sense it was lost a long time ago."

"How did he look? Was he like a regular guy, or did he have, I don't know, superpowers?" Tom sounded like I'd had a celebrity sighting, and I barely contained an eye-roll.

"His superpower was being a jerk, okay?"

Ringo's quiet words cut in. "Does nobody wonder whose ring it actually is? I mean, if it really does 'ave the power to compel, whose power is it?"

The words sank into the silence of the room, until I finally broke it. "The Immortals know who the ring belongs to. According to Duncan, the Mongers stole it … so maybe we *should* steal it back."

Tom interrupted whatever protest Ringo had been about to make. "You don't even have to be there – just Clock me to a time when I can steal the ring, and leave before I do. That way, if something goes wrong, you'd be able to go back and fix it."

"That's a terrible idea," snarled Ringo.

I looked at Tom, and then at Ringo. "No, it's not. It's actually brilliant." I paced around the room while the wheels spun in my head. I grabbed a climbing rope and monkeyed up it, just to free up the direction my thoughts were taking. I sat on one of the cross beams that held up the roof and let my legs dangle.

"Saira, stay there. I'm comin' up," Ringo commanded from below. I was too busy in my head to do more than nod, and a few moments later he was next to me on the beam. His back was to the upright pillar so he could face me, and the concern on his face dragged me out of my thoughts.

"He's not wrong," I said quietly. It was quite likely Tom could hear us from below, but he had returned to his spot by the window.

"I know what ye're thinkin'," Ringo matched my quiet tone, but his was full of concern. "Ye're thinkin' about 1944." That was exactly what I'd been thinking about, and the fact that he guessed it was a little unnerving. He continued, "There was a gap of about twelve seconds from the time we sent Tom through the spiral until the bomb exploded."

I nodded. "Tom can go back to the moment right after he left. He can stop George Walters from shooting the V-1 and activating it." I was a little breathless at the possibility.

"And 'ow's 'e goin' to do that?" Ringo asked. "George Walters used the distraction of Tom Clocking out as 'is excuse to start shootin'. 'E shot Archer first, then just kept goin'. Maybe the fifth or sixth bullet was the one that hit the bomb, and twelve seconds later, time split."

"It could work," I said stubbornly. "All he has to do is drag Walters and Archer off the platform with us when we go. The bomb could still explode, but if we're all safe, then so is the time stream."

Ringo shook his head. "Ye don't get it, Saira. The only way Tom can change things is if 'e puts 'imself squarely in the way of a 'ailstorm of bullets. 'E wants to live. It's why 'e wants the ring – so 'e can keep Seth Walters from gettin' in the way of 'is cure. 'E's not goin' to risk 'is life for anyone, and definitely not for a Walters."

"I'll make you a deal," Tom called up to us. He didn't even pretend he hadn't been listening. Ringo grit his teeth as his eyes met mine.

I spoke to Ringo. "It's a way to get back to Archer." Ringo held my gaze a moment longer, then sighed, leaned his head back against the post, and shut his eyes. I'd been dismissed.

I stood up on the beam and then jumped to the rope and swung myself down. I landed like my Cat would, with a light, sure foot, then dropped into a chair to face Tom. "It's rude to eavesdrop."

"It's rude to talk about someone behind his back."

"Over his head, actually. What's the deal?"

"You help me steal the ring, and I'll go back for your Sucker."

I studied him in silence, and I felt Ringo tense above us. "Deal or no deal, Saira?" Tom's voice was hard and cold.

"You have to save Archer *and* Walters." I didn't know why Walters was so important, but my instinct screamed that he was.

"No! Walters made his bed. He dies. It's the Sucker alone or no deal." There was barely-contained fury coiled through Tom, and it was about to ignite.

"Then no deal."

Tom's foot lashed out, and he kicked one of the chairs away from the table. It flew across the room, broke against the iron radiator, and knocked the steam valve off. Steam burst into the room with a fierce whistle, and Ringo swung down on the rope like Tarzan. Tom was already crossing the room to the radiator, but Ringo snarled at him, "Get the bloody 'ell out of my 'ouse!"

Tom stepped back, clearly shocked at the rage that contorted Ringo's face. He turned toward me with his mouth open to say something, then shut it slowly and left.

Ringo wrestled with the valve and burned his hands on the blasting steam. I threw him tea towels and then filled a bucket with cold water. A few minutes and several muttered curses later, he had gotten the valve screwed back on and closed. He finally dunked his burned hands into the cold water and sat back, exhausted.

I dropped to my knees beside Ringo on the floor. My throat was closing again with tears, but I made Ringo look at me. "I think it could work. I think he could fix the split."

"Why'd ye say no then?" he asked.

"Because he's only willing to save Archer. I don't know why I'm so sure, but I believe George is the key to the split. And unless Tom is willing to save the man he split time to kill, it's no deal."

THE DEBATE

Ringo dried his hands carefully. "You need green medicine." He nodded, wincing slightly. I got up to retrieve a tin of the salve and Ringo held his hands out for me to apply it. He rarely ever let me take care of him, and I tried to put myself in his place while I did.

"You don't trust Tom," I said.

Ringo's gaze met mine. "'E 'ates ye."

"Hates? That's kind of extreme, don't you think?" I was startled. I knew he was angry as a general state of being, but I hadn't thought it was directed any place specific except maybe at himself.

"'E carries too much pain to bear it alone, and 'e won't let anyone love 'im to share the burden of it. Blamin' ye, that's an easy way to make someone else responsible."

"I think we need him though," I said. "To change things in 1944, we need him."

Ringo flexed his fingers carefully. The skin was red, but didn't look like it would blister too badly. He studied his hands for a moment, then finally nodded and looked at me. "I'll be at yer back."

I hadn't realized it was even a question for Ringo, and it shook me to think he could have chosen otherwise. But we were in his native time, and he could step off my ride whenever he wanted to.

This was Ringo's native time.

I looked at him more closely. "You've aged since we've been here."

He grimaced. "Fightin' with ye will do that to a man."

"No, I mean, you've actually gotten older, all at once. I think you're affected by being outside your native time the same way Clockers are." I studied the beginnings of scruff on his face. Whiskers that I hadn't seen before dotted his jaw, and he was taller than he'd been the last time I noticed his height.

My scrutiny seemed to make him uncomfortable, because he scratched his face and turned a little pink. "What're ye goin' to do about young Tom?"

I grimaced. "Go find him I guess." I looked out the window at the dark night sky. "Will you come with me?"

Ringo rolled his eyes. "As if I'd let ye go out in my town without me."

I kissed Ringo quickly on the cheek. He blushed pink again and I laughed, then made a show of rubbing the kiss off. He batted my hand away and scowled, but I felt lighter with relief that he wasn't still angry. That Ringo had gotten angry at all was remarkable enough, and the fact that his anger had bothered me so much shouldn't have been a surprise. But I was shaken by both, and I realized I wanted to get out of this time. It felt like we were treading water here, and I was ready to jump in the deep end – to do whatever we had to do to get back to Archer.

"Where should we look for him?" I asked as we headed out.

"I doubt we'll need to," said Ringo.

"Huh? Why?"

"Because we are the only plan 'e 'as." We stepped out into the dark alley behind the building and someone moved forward from the shadows. I was startled, but Ringo nodded at him and spoke as though he'd been expecting nothing less. "Tom," he said in careful greeting.

"I apologize for my outburst, and for damaging the radiator. I will replace or repair anything I need to," Tom said.

"It's fixed," Ringo answered. I was impressed that he managed to keep his tone neutral.

"Are you up for a run?" I asked Tom.

"I'm not really a freerunner, Saira," he answered cautiously.

"I know, but you're stronger now, right?"

"Evidently."

I turned to Ringo. "Show us something new."

Ringo thought for a moment, then nodded. "Right. Keep up if ye can. The neighbor'ood's not the best, but it's worth it."

He took off down the alley and turned left, which took us away from the river. Ringo was holding back just enough to make sure Tom stayed with us, but not so much that it was obvious. He kept the showy flips to a minimum too, more like a straight parkour run. Tom's expression was one of grim determination. This wasn't fun for him, but he didn't complain, even as we passed Holborn. We were heading straight back into the jewelry district, except all the shops were closed for business. Ringo finally stopped outside an ornate gothic church, which was only visible from the street when we were standing right in front of it.

He smiled at the confusion on both our faces. "Not goin' to burn up inside, are ye?" he said to Tom. Surprisingly, Tom smirked back.

"Haven't yet."

"There's still time," Ringo answered with enough snark in his tone to get a raised eyebrow from me. The big front door was unlocked, and Ringo slipped inside. I went next, and Tom closed the door quietly behind us.

"What is this place?" I whispered to Ringo.

"St. Etheldreda's Church."

We were in a long hallway that ran the length of the building that seemed fairly small for a church, but had the cold stone smell of someplace very old. A man was speaking in the room next to the hall. We couldn't see him, but his speech was cultured and educated, and his accent was slightly Irish.

"Father Lock'art usually 'as writers or poets readin' their work 'ere until midnight. I've 'eard some very interestin' stories inside these walls, let me tell ye."

I stared at Ringo. "Do you come here often?"

"Well, not anymore, obviously. But yeah, a few times a week. It's a Catholic church, one of the oldest in England, but all kinds 'ave worshipped 'ere." We walked down the long hallway, lit only by a lantern at the far end of the room. Laughter came from the other room, and it sounded like there were maybe twenty people listening to the writer read his work. "And all kinds 'ave read 'ere, too."

We had reached the door to the other room, but I was hesitant to enter. It was lit by several shielded candles, and the light flickered as warmly as the voice that filled the room. I just wanted to linger by the door and listen without a picture of the speaker to influence the way his words landed in my ears. Ringo stepped inside the room and leaned against the back wall. After a moment of hesitation, Tom entered the room too. I had the sense that Ringo's company was preferred over mine.

The speaker's voice was melodic and deep, and I closed my eyes as he began another passage.

"Life is a question of nerves, and fibres, and slowly built-up cells in which thought hides itself and passion has its dreams. You may fancy yourself safe and think yourself strong. But a chance tone of colour in a room or a morning sky, a particular perfume that you had once loved and that brings subtle memories with it, a line from a forgotten poem that you had come across again, a cadence from a piece of music that you had ceased to play … I tell you, that it is on things like these that our lives depend."

I recognized the words. Whoever this author was, I'd read his work, and I stepped into the room next to Ringo and Tom. The assembled group was mostly standing, although there were some people sitting on wooden pews nearest the speaker. He faced the group to the right of the door, so I only caught him in profile, but I could see he was tall and well-dressed, and probably somewhere in his mid-thirties. There was a spectacular stained-glass window behind him, and the candlelight glinting on the colored glass gave the odd impression that the man was standing inside a kaleidoscope.

"Well, my dears, that is all I shall read for tonight. The story isn't finished, though it soon will be, and you'll be able to purchase your own copy to see how it all turns out for poor Dorian. Until then, thank you to Father Lockhart for looking the other way. I hope to prevail upon his good-natured oblivion another time." The audience laughed as the man finished his speech. "I wish you all a good night, and I leave you with the words of my Dorian: The only way to get rid of temptation is to yield to it."

Laughter erupted, and it was lovely to hear Ringo and Tom chuckling next to me. When the speaker finally turned to face our side of the room, I realized why I knew his words. It was Oscar Wilde, younger than most of the images I'd seen of him, but definitely him.

I wanted to meet him. Sometimes I actually loved being a Clocker.

Tom made a move to push off the wall and leave, but I grabbed his arm. "Wait," I said quietly. Tom pulled his arm out of my hand, and I turned in surprise to find him scowling at me. He quickly schooled his expression to something more neutral, but I'd seen that Ringo was absolutely right in his assessment of Tom's feelings. I caught his eye and didn't let go until he looked away, kind of like an alpha would with her pack. And then I smiled, just because I wanted to growl.

"That's Oscar Wilde," I said under my breath.

Tom looked over at the man in surprise. "How do you know?"

"He was reading from *The Picture of Dorian Gray*. I read it my sophomore year."

I moved forward past some of the people who were leaving, and Tom fell into step behind me. I studied Wilde as people shook his hand and said a few words to him. He looked tired and vaguely bored, and I didn't think he was quite famous enough yet to have the disdain that comes with celebrity, which probably just meant he thought most people were idiots. I was beginning to regret my impulse to meet the man.

Interestingly, every person to whom he spoke came away with a happy smile on their face, as if they'd just had their socks charmed off. The last of the people shook Wilde's hand and left, and then a person who must have been Father Lockhart came up, exchanged a few words with him, and began shooing the stragglers toward a door at the back of the room.

Oscar Wilde had gathered his papers from the lectern before he finally noticed us. His eyes landed on me first, maybe because I was tallest, then Tom, then Ringo, who had joined us. And then he smiled.

"Well, aren't you three pretty," he said, his eyes brushing each of us again before landing on Tom.

I stepped forward and held out my hand to shake his. "It's an honor to meet you, Mr. Wilde."

His eyes widened in surprise. He must have thought I was male until he heard my voice. "And quite unexpected to meet you, Miss …"

"Saira. Saira Elian," I said as I shook his hand. He held my hand longer than a standard handshake and studied me.

"*Very* unexpected, Miss Elian. A rare pleasure, I believe, considering your Family's propensity for losing themselves." His eyes were sparkling, and I narrowed my eyes at him teasingly.

"Of course, you can See."

He met my smirk with one of his own. "Only people, my dear. It is perhaps why I am so cynical. Although, according to my father, a cynic is a man who knows the price of everything and the value of nothing, so perhaps the word doesn't apply."

I laughed and shook my head. "You, sir, are trouble."

"Of the most interesting kind." His eyes flicked back to Tom, though he still held my hand. "Introduce me to your friends, my dear. I find I'm suddenly in need of new acquaintances."

For the first time in a long time, I felt like teasing. "I'm not sure that's a good idea, Mr. Wilde—"

"Oh, Oscar, please. Mr. Wilde is my father. And it's an excellent idea."

I bit back the smile. "Your reputation precedes you. You might have to make do with only my acquaintance."

Oscar laughed and lifted the back of my hand to his lips. "My dear, for you I shall endeavor to be on my best behavior so as not to offend any whose constitution isn't on par with your wit."

Ringo's expression was openly intrigued, similar to the look he got when he discovered a new bit of technology. Tom was guardedly fascinated, and some of the hostility had slipped from his face.

"Then I will introduce you. Oscar Wilde, this is Ringo, and this is Tom."

He finally released my hand to shake Ringo's first, which he did with an open smile, and then Tom's, which he held longer than necessary as he studied his face. Tom didn't flinch under the scrutiny, and I was glad to see him study Oscar right back.

The men still hadn't broken eye contact when Oscar finally spoke a little breathlessly, "I do believe I've found my Dorian."

Oscar Wilde

Oscar Wilde finally tore his eyes from Tom and turned to me. "Miss Elian, would you and your friends join me for a drink?"

I looked at Ringo and Tom, neither of whom seemed ready to answer. "None of us really drinks, but I have the feeling a conversation with you would be memorable."

His smile was a sly, creeping thing that began with a shine in his eyes and promised laughter in its wake. "Anything less than memorable is hardly worth our time." Wilde shot Tom another look, then tucked my arm under his solicitously and patted my hand. "Miss Elian, I do believe we should be friends. There is something quite extraordinary about a woman who is quite completely herself. I find that being oneself is an excellent choice, as everyone else is already taken."

He began walking us toward the back of the church, and Ringo and Tom fell into bemused step behind us. Wilde called out in a jovial voice, tinged with the hint of an Irish accent. "Father Lockhart, a favor if you will."

Father Lockhart came to the door with a smile as we approached. "I'll do what I can, Mr. Wilde."

"Would you happen to have a corner with rugs, pillows, a divan, or merely a bench that we could pull up and occupy for the span it takes to tell a story, hear one, shed a tear, and laugh at something ridiculous?"

Father Lockhart looked at the four of us with amusement. "I'll do you one better, Mr. Wilde. You may use the crypt for your stories as long as you ignore the Lockhart-sized fly on the wall and you let me make you lot a cup of tea."

Wilde held out his hand to shake the priest's with a grin. "You have a deal, Father." The priest ushered us downstairs into the gothic-style crypt. It was a beautifully eerie space lit by the lanterns he and Wilde carried, with small stained-glass windows that echoed the spectacular one upstairs. Most of the space was empty except for the pillars that held up the floor above, but there were low divans in one corner, and I had the thought that people might sleep there occasionally. Father Lockhart saw us seated on the divans and bustled off upstairs to put a kettle on to boil.

"How is it that you and a Catholic priest are such good friends?" I asked Wilde. He grinned and stretched his long arms across the back of the cushions.

"The good father and I are in agreement about the aesthetics of this fine church in which we find ourselves. He is responsible for its restoration, you see, and quite possibly for the fact that it remains standing at all."

I looked at Ringo, and he gave me a quick smile. We were like kids who recognized the beginnings of a long-winded tale and had settled in for the inevitable. And, from the way he looked around at us in anticipation, it seemed Oscar Wilde enjoyed having an audience.

"Many a night Father Lockhart and I have sat here, debating the finer points of my Anglican upbringing versus his Catholic conversion, my classical education versus his theological one, my beliefs versus his faith. Indeed, the night I stumbled into this church to debate the merits of organized religion with Bernard, whom Father Lockhart had invited to read from his latest monstrosity, was the night I met a kindred soul. It is a rare and confident man who can appreciate both the wit and the wisdom of one such as myself, who walked in here that night with the firm belief that religion is like a blind man looking in a black room for a black cat that isn't there … and finding it."

Father Lockhart returned with a teapot and a tray of cups. "Ah, but Mr. Wilde, you are neglecting the commonalities in our backgrounds." He met our eyes as I took the teapot from him. "Our Oxford educations could be enough to bind us to each other, but an interest in Catholicism despite an Anglican upbringing virtually guarantees kinship."

I poured the tea into the simple mugs he set out, and his eyes sparkled as he whispered dramatically to me. "Mr. Wilde would like to think he's the most shocking speaker we've ever had at one of our salons, but honestly, Mr. Shaw was far more so."

Wilde scoffed. "You can't compare Bernard's eugenics nonsense to the horror your parishioners experience at my belief that art need not teach, instruct, preach, or for God's sake, moralize."

Father Lockhart smiled fondly at Wilde. "You have complimented my renovation of St. Etheldreda's on more than one occasion. What is art for the sake of sheer beauty more than the staining of glass, or the decorative carving of wood? You are not nearly so shocking as you would like to believe, my friend, though you delight in being the subject of the horrified whispers of bored matrons."

Wilde grumbled good-naturedly, and a phrase came to mind. I spoke without thinking. "The only thing worse than being talked about is not being talked about."

Wilde sharpened his gaze on me. "My dear Clocker, I'll thank you to keep your quotes from my unpublished work to yourself. It might give a man ideas about his future prospects for fame, or at the very least, his notoriety."

I blushed, completely horrified that I'd just quoted from *The Picture of Dorian Gray*, which obviously hadn't been published yet. "Oh! I'm so sorry."

Wilde gave a wry smile. "Although I'll admit to a certain satisfaction that my words have made any sort of lasting impression. In my experience, it becomes rather difficult to live in the moment when one spends too much time anticipating the future."

"Is it not the way of the hedonist to live only for the moment," asked Father Lockhart, "as if the future matters not?"

Wilde laughed, a deep, infectious laugh. "There are those in my Family who believe the future is the only thing that matters. But that's not what I said. To live *in* the moment is vastly different than living *for* it. To be truly present as life unfolds around one is to take fullest advantage of being alive. Take young Dorian here," Wilde indicated Tom, who sat on the floor and was using the divan as a backrest. Tom had been watching the exchange between Wilde and Lockhart through narrowed eyes, and Wilde's sudden attention disconcerted him.

Wilde knew exactly what his effect on Tom was, and seemed to deliberately poke at him. "He has made a bargain with the devil and now squanders the days as too numerous to be worthwhile. One could argue hedonism, and certainly fatalism, but neither would be accurate, would they, Dorian?"

"I'm not Dorian," said Tom through gritted teeth.

"Of course you are." Wilde's jovial good nature was laser-sharp, and Tom was its focus. I held my breath and Ringo tensed beside me. "Except it isn't a portrait that ages with the life you choose to live."

His pause was dramatic, and he waited for someone to ask the question, 'what is?' Tom just glared, and there was no way Ringo or I would step in that pile of poop. Finally, Wilde rolled his eyes and sighed, "Do none of you have a sense for the dramatic moment? Really, what good are you?"

Tom stood up, still glowering. "I'm done here."

Oscar Wilde stood too, and his 6'3" frame towered over Tom. "You'd like to think that, wouldn't you, *Tom*. You'd like to think that the stain on your soul will just spread and spread and spread until finally it consumes you. You believe that only then will you truly be yourself – the man you were born to become. Well, my darling Dorian, I have news for you. It is not your soul that wrinkles like ancient flesh with each act of self-hatred. Your soul is pure light and possibility, and it is the one thing that will resist every act of torture you commit on it."

Tom stood frozen. He faced Wilde with the whole empty crypt at his back, and yet he looked like a cornered, feral thing, ready to flee at the slightest move. "No," Wilde continued softly, as if he could sense the frightened animal lurking beneath Tom's glare. "Your story isn't true just because you keep trying to prove it. It's a story, a made up story; like Dorian exists in my mind, so does your idea of Tom in yours. It is something you told yourself to explain the disgust you feel when you look in the mirror. It is an invention of your imagination, which means no amount of horror will prove it, and the only things you've stained are your hands."

Tom's hands flinched, and I didn't know if it was from the instinct to check them for blood, or a desire to hit Oscar Wilde.

I expected Tom to storm out. I think we all did. But he took a deep breath, squared his shoulders, and nodded his head once as if in acceptance. "You are certainly welcome to your opinion, Mr. Wilde."

We stared in astonishment as Tom returned with dignity to his seat on the floor. And then Wilde burst out laughing and clapped Tom on the shoulder. "I may not agree with you, but I will defend to the death your right to make an ass of yourself, eh, Tom?"

The tension disappeared from the room, though it lingered around Tom's eyes when our gazes met. Father Lockhart got up to make more tea, and Wilde directed our conversations across a vast landscape of topics, from the Roman Catholic Relief Act of 1829, which finally restored most of the civil rights of Catholics in Britain, to the value of an education rich in Greek classical humanistic theory.

Ringo was completely in his element, absorbing information he didn't know, and contributing to the conversation about things on which he had opinions. He had become so much more confident since the days when Archer would regale us with the lessons of his university classes, and neither Wilde nor Father Lockhart spoke to him as anything other than an equal.

Lockhart was passionate about the role of the church in service to the poor, and was very proud of the work St. Etheldreda's parishioners had done in the slums of Holborn.

Wilde's conversations returned again and again to the theme that beauty should be celebrated in art, books, music, and plays for no other reason than its own sake. The way he spoke about books he'd read and things he had studied at Oxford, I had the sense he was two people. His flamboyantly-dressed, sarcastic, and witty public face was the mask, and a quiet, introspective reader with a deep love of learning lived behind it.

Wilde caught me looking at him, and I could see him gearing up to say something clever or cutting, but I spoke first. "Your love of books and learning things reminds me of my husband."

The echo of my words seemed to fill the suddenly silent room. I had spoken without really considering what I said, and I blushed and dropped my eyes so I didn't have to see the questions. Wilde lifted my chin so I'd look at him and said gently, "I should like to know a man with the good sense to choose a woman such as you."

I opened my mouth to ask whether he'd Seen anything about Archer, then closed it again. It didn't matter. Wilde Saw me. He had Seen something in me that showed him loss and pain, and for a couple of hours he had distracted me from it with conversation and laughter.

"Thank you," I said simply. He smiled.

"Now, let me tell you about the time I met the pope."

That shocked me out of my reminiscence. "Which pope?" The wheels began clicking in my head, and I could see Ringo beginning to follow my train of thought.

Wilde looked curious. "Pius IX. Don't tell me you've encountered him on your, shall I say, travels."

"When did he start being pope?" I demanded. It was a clumsy question, but I was digging through my memory banks for every bit of information I had.

"Let's see, I met him when I was twenty, and that was in 1876—" Wilde began, but Father Lockhart interrupted.

"Pius IX was consecrated in 1846," he said quietly.

I turned to Father Lockhart. "Did you know the pope before him, the one from 1842?"

He smiled gently. "I was just twenty-two then, and still an Anglican studying at Oxford. I believe that was Pope Gregory XVI."

"What do you know about him?" I dialed down the demanding tone to something that sounded like reasonable questions, but Wilde was studying me through narrowed eyes.

"Not much, I'm afraid. I understand he was quite conservative and rigid in his views, and spoke out against technological innovations. Gas lighting and railways might increase the power of the bourgeoisie, he said, which could lead them to demand more liberal reforms from the Vatican. He did, however, write a letter condemning the slave trade, so apparently he had his moments."

I could sense Ringo's growing tension, though the others were just intrigued by my sudden curiosity. "Have either of you been to the Vatican? I've always wondered what it's like. Could you describe it?"

Ringo made a noise of protest, but I ignored him. Sadly, both men were shaking their heads. "I met Pius IX when he was on tour, which is quite remarkable really, given that he died two years later," said Wilde.

"Do you have any paintings or drawings of the Vatican I could look at?" I asked Father Lockhart.

"Saira," said Ringo warningly.

"I'm sorry, I have none here," said Lockhart. "I imagine perhaps the Italian or Spanish embassies might have something, but I've never seen their collections."

"We are not running around London looking for paintings of the Vatican," Ringo said with a growl in his voice.

"Why 1842?" asked Tom, finally speaking up.

I met his eyes squarely. "Later," I said. "When there's a deal."

He understood what I meant immediately, and nodded his head. Wilde watched our exchange with a thoughtful expression.

"I have the sense there is a story to be told here, but as it is nearly dawn, perhaps now is not the time?" He eyed Tom meaningfully, and I thought that for all the things Oscar Wilde said, there were a thousand more he didn't. "I should like to hear it one day, if we ever encounter each other again." His eyes traveled around our faces and then returned to Tom.

Wilde stood and offered Tom his hand to help him up. He held it in a handshake and didn't let go as he spoke. "I shall give my Dorian your beauty, but he will not have your soul. It is far too deep a well for him to imagine, much less be privileged to know – a privilege I hope you grant another someday."

Tom's expression remained stoic, but he surprised us all when he clasped Wilde's arm with his other hand in what I supposed was a modern man's version of a Victorian hug.

"I'm very glad to have met you, Mr. Wilde," Tom said.

"I hope we are friends enough for you to call me Oscar."

"Maybe I'll come back and tell you stories someday, Oscar."

Wilde beamed at Tom with a happy grin. "That would be an excellent day, indeed!"

We said our goodbyes to Father Lockhart, and Wilde walked us to the door. I gave him a hug and whispered in his ear. "Take care, Oscar."

He gave me a quick squeeze. "Find beauty in the moments, Miss Elian, because to live is the rarest thing in the world. Most people exist, that is all."

Tom left us on the street corner with the promise that he'd come to Ringo's flat at sunset to discuss our plans and the deal. I asked where he would sleep, but he just shook his head and took off, walking briskly down Holborn. Ringo and I ran silently all the way back down to the river. We arrived just after the sun rose, and I had to drag myself up the ladder to his flat.

Ringo gave me his bed and took the chair with a tired shake of his head at my protests. I didn't close the drapes in case he decided the chair was too uncomfortable, and I watched him settle in and shut his eyes.

"Oscar Wilde went to prison for being gay," I said after a long moment.

Ringo's eyes opened and he regarded me steadily. "People are idiots," he finally said, and closed his eyes again to sleep.

The Plan

Ringo was out when I finally woke up late in the afternoon. I took the rare alone-time to bathe and wash my hair. Basic personal hygiene could always be managed with access to water and a washcloth, but full submergence and soap were a rarity to be taken advantage of.

I debated my wardrobe choices. My satchel had been packed for World War II, and it never occurred to me to pick up any modern clothes during the brief time I was in the wrong future. I had clean underwear and tanks, but the 1940s pencil skirt was way too short to wear in this time. The trousers were great, but desperately in need of a wash and repair. So, I pulled on a pair of leggings I'd packed as a cold weather layer and decided to clean the trousers and stitch up the worst of the damage.

Ringo came back just as I was hanging the trousers to dry. He had two big bags with him and tossed me his satchel when I asked to help.

"There's food in there. Can ye set a table before Tom gets 'ere? It'd be good to actually eat the food instead of arguin' about it, ye know?"

I winced at the memory of the previous night's conflicts and unpacked the meat pies, cheese, and cucumbers. I held up a lemon proudly. "Does this mean you're actually going to have some?"

He cringed. "If ye squeeze it into water, I'll consider it."

"Good man!" I said happily. "I have to keep reminding myself we're not on war rations here, so you can find things like cucumbers and lemons."

"I only got 'em to keep ye from fussin'."

I grinned. "I know. Thank you."

He was unpacking the two big bags and laying things out on the bed. "What'd you get?"

"There's a tailor on Old Burlington St. who works fast and 'ad some outdated clothes 'e could alter to fit us both."

He held up a pair of tan trousers. "These should work for ye, I think." He handed them to me.

"They're so soft," I said. "Leather? Really?"

"Buckskin. The tailor said 'e's never been able to sell these because they were too long and too narrow to fit the men who could afford them."

They were the most gorgeous things I'd ever seen, and I narrowed my eyes at Ringo. "I don't want to know how much they cost, do I?"

He shrugged. "Does it matter? Ye said yerself, if ye fix time, the future the gems came from won't exist anymore. And honestly, the trousers ye've been wearin' are just disgraceful. Those, at least, should do better against yer best efforts to destroy them."

He held up a black pair of trousers and tossed them to me. "And an extra pair in case ye get sick of the buckskin."

I caught the heavy linen trousers and held them up to my waist. They looked like they'd be long enough, and only a little big. "It's nice to have options."

He held up a mid-thigh-length coat, also black, that was narrow at the waist and fuller at the hem. I thought it looked like something Camille Arman would wear with her skinny jeans and red-soled spike heels. "The frock coat should 'ide the way ye fill out the breeks, so if ye don't want too many stares, ye'd best keep it on." He meant my hips, a department in which I was mostly lacking, along with all other feminine curves, sadly. Fortunately for me, the style of these men's clothes was fairly simple to wear and move in and wasn't too far removed from my own twenty-first century style.

He tossed me the coat. "Try it on. 'E can take in the shoulders if 'e needs to, but 'e can't let 'em out."

I had already slipped the soft leather trousers on over my leggings and pulled the frock coat on over my tank. It fit well and still gave me room in the shoulders. The trousers were a perfect fit, and I immediately couldn't wait to wear them for Archer.

The thought hit me like a gut-punch. I looked at Ringo, but he was busy pulling shirts out of the bag, and he tossed me two of them. I caught the fine linen fast enough to hide the tremor in my hand, and was able to still it with a deep breath and move on. The shirts were long enough to sleep in, but the fabric was so thin it wouldn't bunch when it was tucked in.

"These are perfect," I said as I finished dressing. He laid out a couple of kravat-style ties and two hats that looked like the type a gentleman farmer would wear.

"We can get top 'ats if we need them in Italy, but I felt quite the fool tryin' them in the 'abberdashery." Ringo was dressing himself in his own new clothes. I'd seen him in urchin's garb, in medieval French clothes, a wartime suit, and jeans. But I'd never seen his clothes define him as a man before he put on the trousers, waistcoat, and frock coat of the 1840s.

But in spite of all the finery, he still wore the boots he'd gotten in the twenty-first century. He saw me look at his feet, and he grinned. "I can't get better boots than these, so I'll 'ave to contend with being the gent in the odd footwear."

"You look very handsome," I said.

Ringo looked startled. "I didn't mean to."

I laughed, and the pressure around my lungs finally lifted. "Thank you for doing all of this. And especially, thank you for my new buckskin trousers." I kissed his cheek, and when he wiped it away as usual, the rasp of whiskers reminded me he had definitely become his age in this time.

"I didn't even bother goin' to a dressmaker for ye. A man's clothes suit ye, and I figured ye'd fuss about the skirts too much."

"You were right. I *would* fuss. You know how I feel about corsets."

"A particular brand of Victorian torture. Aye, I know," Ringo laughed as we sat down to eat.

"We haven't actually talked about last night, you know," I finally said.

"Ye mean the part about ye decidin' to go to the Vatican to steal the Monger ring in 1842? Ye're right, there was no conversation about it that I remember." Ringo's expression was neutral, but something simmered under the surface.

"We should talk about it."

"What'll ye 'ave me say, Saira?" Ringo's voice was quiet, but low and intense, and his words sounded like they came straight from Archer. "Ye talk about wanting to plan things out, to actually strategize like ye're playin' chess, but I don't see a strategy anywhere in this. Ye don't know what the Vatican looks like in 1842; the only reason ye 'ave a date is because it's when the Monger ring went missin' from there. *And* ye're plannin' to steal it from the pope himself?"

"Only if Tom agrees to go back to 1944 and save both Archer and George Walters from the bomb." Yes, I knew how ridiculous it sounded to be plotting a heist at the Vatican, but Tom might be the only person able to fix the split, and I was fresh out of alternatives.

"I'll do it," said a quiet voice from the top of the stairs. Tom had surprised us both with his silent entrance, and Ringo tensed next to me, his eyes locked on Tom where he stood.

"Come in," I finally said, because neither of the two guys had moved yet. Interestingly, Tom still didn't move until Ringo gave him a curt nod.

I cleared the remains of our meal away, and Tom sat warily between us at the table. He finally met my eyes and exhaled. "If we can manage to steal the ring, I'll do what I can to save both of them."

"Do what ye can?" Ringo shook his head. "Not good enough."

To his credit, Tom's tone didn't harden or get angry when he looked at Ringo. "I'll put every resource at my disposal to the task of ensuring that Archer and Walters survive the bomb."

Ringo studied Tom's face, then he finally nodded. "If Saira's with ye, I'll back ye up too."

Tom's jaw ground as he turned back to me. It clearly chapped him to have the whole deal hinge on my approval. "Saira?"

I studied Tom for a long moment. "I don't really understand why you dislike me so much, and I guess I don't really need to. But if we're going to work together, I need to be able to trust you."

"I won't hurt you, if that's what you mean," Tom said.

"A month ago I wouldn't have even considered that, but yeah, I guess I do need to know I can turn my back to you and not expect a knife in it."

Tom smirked, and somehow the sight of it gave me more comfort than his words would have without it. "You can trust that if I do knife you, it won't be in the back."

Ringo glared, but I laughed. "I think Oscar Wilde was famous for saying something like that."

"It was … interesting to meet him," Tom said quietly, and I sensed that he meant a whole world of things he couldn't, or wouldn't, articulate.

I studied Tom, and he met my eyes. Neither of us flinched, but neither smiled either. Maybe it was crazy to even consider partnering with an ex-Nazi Vampire with a self-destructive bent, but I was feeling nostalgic for a simpler time when he was just Adam's cousin with a fear of heights. Finally, I held out my hand to shake. "Deal?"

Tom took it in his own oddly strong, slender hand and shook. "Deal."

Ringo shoved his chair back from the table and crossed his arms in front of him. "So now that's settled, 'ow the bloody 'ell are we gettin' to the Vatican?"

Ultimately, we settled on the simplest plan of all – public transportation. I knew that the Hôtel de Sens in the Marais district of Paris hadn't changed its façade since the 1400s because I'd looked up a modern picture of it when we got back from our adventures with Joan of Arc. Since France was closer to Italy than England was, it made sense to Clock to Paris in 1842 and then take the train south from there.

Ringo had gotten himself an extra set of clothes which fit Tom, and we had plenty of money and gemstones to sell. It was midnight when we finally decided everything, and given the option of waiting another night and day, we agreed that midnight seemed like a good time to Clock onto a public street in the Marais.

My satchel was packed with all the clean underwear I had, a toothbrush, dental floss, a comb, lip balm, green medicine, a small marker, Sanda's little knife, gemstones, money, a change of clothes, and a copy of Mary Shelley's *Frankenstein* that Ringo had found at a bookseller near the tailor. Apparently, our conversation while hiding at the Council meeting had inspired him.

I was wearing my daggers – I refused to call them Death's daggers because they were *mine* – my new buckskin trousers, and I had my hair tied back in an unfashionable ponytail under the gentleman farmer's hat. The guys both looked like proper English gentlemen, and although the style of men's clothing hadn't changed very much in the past fifty years, they would likely get strange looks on the streets of this late-Victorian London.

We left from the London Bridge, and I found that Clocking with Tom was approximately the same as Clocking with my mom, I guess because he had her blood in him, courtesy of Bishop Wilder. It was slightly easier than on my own, but definitely not as easy as going places with Charlie had been. Her conduit powers were special, and incredibly useful for taking more than one or two other people anywhere.

Thankfully, the square in front of the Hôtel de Sens was deserted when we arrived. The giant old fig tree that had given the street its name was gone, and I had a momentary flash of the battle we fought against the wolves of Paris in that square. I shook my head to clear the image of fighting back-to-back with Archer, wielding short swords while Connor's Wolf battled for dominance over Jehanne's. While I was lost in memories, Ringo was already across the street and scampering up the wall.

"What is he doing?" Tom murmured in my ear.

"Looking to see if anyone's home, I guess."

Considering that Ringo was peering into a window of the giant medieval mansion, it was a fair assumption to make. He jumped down with the grace of a cat and said with a surprised look on his face, "It's full of preserves."

"I'm sorry, what?" Tom said.

Ringo beckoned us to follow him up and over the wall. When we were off the street and in the courtyard out of sight, he said again, "There are big vats and long shelves full of bottles. From what I could see, it's a fruit preserves factory now."

I looked at Tom with an incredulous face, but he wasn't listening, he looked as though he'd been frozen into stone by the sight of Medusa's head. He stared at a fountain set into the wall, and his face had gone utterly bloodless. His breathing was shallow and fast, sweat shone on his upper lip as though he was going to be sick, and I thought that if he had been able to move at all, he would have bolted. And then it struck me where we were.

I had brought Tom back to the scene of his nightmares.

"Come on, let's go figure out where the train station is." I shot Ringo a loaded look, and he grasped my meaning immediately. Tom had been held prisoner by Bishop Wilder here. He'd been tortured, and had infected himself with Wilder's blood so he could survive. He had also watched his friend Léon die here – twice. I couldn't believe I'd even suggested we travel to this place.

Tom moved like an automaton, following us out of the courtyard and down the Rue du Figuier, away from his former prison. His normally near-silent stride was heavy and plodding, and his eyes were a black void.

We walked for several blocks without speaking, and Ringo kept glancing at the sheer blankness of Tom's expression. "Ye alright, mate?" Ringo asked quietly. Tom didn't answer. He didn't even seem to hear Ringo's voice. I touched Tom's arm to get his attention, but he flinched away from me automatically. Finally,

Ringo stopped in the middle of a block of seventeenth-century buildings. We were still in the Marais, but we'd moved out of the realm of the big hôtels particuliers, and the streets had begun to twist and wind around the smaller buildings that had sprung up wherever there was a space to build them.

Ringo sighed. "Get yer daggers out, Saira."

I shook my head. "I'm not drawing blood just to snap him out of his hypnosis."

Ringo was grim-faced. "Not *is* blood." He held my gaze for a beat longer, then deliberately turned into an alley.

Tom ambled after him, probably not even conscious of where he was going. "Crap," I whispered to myself, and I slid my daggers out of their sheaths as I ran to catch up.

I stayed to the darkest parts of the shadows behind Ringo and Tom, and barely two minutes later I felt a presence behind me. I could already see three more people move into place ahead of us, as one young kid who looked to be about Logan Edwards' age stepped into view.

My Monger-gut roiled, the intensity of it taking me completely by surprise. The kid was a Monger, and if my instinct was to be trusted, a dangerous one. He said something menacing in a high, child's voice to Ringo – something in French that I didn't catch – and I dubbed him Chucky, from the horror movie. Tom was the one with language skills here, but his expression was still blank, and as far as I could tell from my vantage point, his eyes hadn't registered Chucky's presence. So it looked like it would just be Ringo and me against Chucky and the five shadows I'd seen. Two of the shadows stepped forward to back the kid up, and when Tom didn't move, I finally had to.

Chucky's eyes flicked to the daggers in my hands when I stepped up behind Ringo. He said something else in French, and there was a leering grin on his face, like he was going to enjoy whatever came next.

"There's two behind us," I murmured to Ringo.

"And one above, in the window. Can ye take 'im out first?"

I glanced up to find the window, spotted my route up to it from door to drainpipe, and nodded.

"Right," Ringo said, "Let's do this."

I bolted for the wall I'd marked for my climb and was on the drainpipe before the three who had shown themselves lunged for Ringo. Chucky had a knife, and the two others with him had heavy sticks. Ringo landed a kick on one of the stick-wielders and disarmed him, and I got up to the window ledge just before the teenaged boy could drop a rock on Ringo's head. I kicked the rock away and slammed the window shut on his fingers. The boy howled in pain, and I dropped back down to help Ringo.

I half expected to see him completely surrounded, but Tom had woken from his stupor and stood back-to-back with him. Each was battling two or three of the thugs, all of whom seemed like older teenagers. I kicked at the back of one's knee and took him down, then had to swipe my dagger at Chucky when he lunged at me.

The dagger sliced across his sleeve and drew blood, and I was instantly assaulted with a sensation of darkness and greed and pain. I shuddered involuntarily and pulled back from Chucky in shock. He lunged at Tom, who smashed out with a fist and caught the kid in the side of the head.

A bigger kid swung his stick and caught Tom in the back with it. Ringo took him out at the knees with his own stick, and Tom kicked him as he went down. He crumpled to a heap next to Chucky.

The two remaining thugs ran away, and suddenly the alley was silent except for our own heavy breathing.

"Merde," Tom whispered into the dark. He looked at Ringo. "What happened?"

"Let's get out of 'ere. I'll tell ye as we walk," said Ringo.

Tom reached for Chucky, but I batted his hand away. "You're bleeding, and that one's bad," I said sharply.

Tom held his hand up and looked at the small cuts on his knuckles. "What's bad?"

"The little Monger kid. Infecting him would be a very dangerous idea."

Tom's eyebrows furrowed as he looked first at the kid, and then at me. Ringo had already started back-tracking out of the alley, and I fell into step behind him. Tom hesitated just a moment, then followed us out.

When we were back on the main boulevard, I fell in step with Ringo. "You took us in there on purpose to find a fight."

Ringo nodded, and I looked at Tom, who had joined us. "Are you back?"

Tom studied us both. "Is that why we were in that alley?" he asked Ringo.

"Sometimes a man just needs to fight," Ringo said as if that were all the explanation that was needed.

Tom nodded thoughtfully. "Yeah."

ARCHER – PRESENT DAY

I fought darkness and pain.

Darkness had been the retreat, but now it was a prison that held the pain close. My groan felt like it came from the earth itself until I realized it *was* the earth that groaned and scraped and moved, even as fire engulfed every nerve ending, every organ, and every inch of skin.

The sound stabbed the darkness and I grabbed onto it, struggling to pull myself up past the pain to the surface of the inky blackness.

"Who's there?" It was my voice that croaked the barely formed words, but I didn't recognize any part of the sound as belonging to me. I only knew it was mine from the rough scrape of it in my throat.

A deep, wrenching sound above, a shower of dirt, and then a shaft of light pierced the dark and seared my eyes. I slammed them shut, but the red glow behind my eyelids held all the promise of a sunrise.

The sun. Sunlight dappled the darkness, and it assured agony.

I could feel the light burn my skin with its brightness, and I flinched away from the pain that was sure to make me scream. But the sounds that filled the cavern were of a machine powering down and then the shouts of men, distant and filled with too much hope.

"We're here!" a voice shouted from the darkness near me. A young man's voice, full of fear and joy and laughter. "Down here!"

The fire I'd expected was still just heat, and I struggled to roll away from the beams of light before they could damage me further. Pain flared with every pull of muscle, and I groaned anew with the effort.

"You're awake," the young man whispered. He had just shouted, and now he whispered as though my consciousness was a secret or a wonder.

"Light," I croaked, again with the voice that wasn't my own.

"They've dug down through the rubble from the blast. We're going to be rescued."

"Burns …" I just managed.

But did it? Did the pain that engulfed me have anything to do with the sun that still shone on my skin?

Cold hands helped push me into the shadows, and I blinked furiously to clear the sun-blindness from my eyes.

Green hair squatted in front of me, and eyes like Ringo's searched my face. Not Ringo. He was with Saira.

Saira.

"My wife …" I croaked.

"Hang on, let me get you water." The green hair moved. No, not green hair. Tam. The mixed-blood friend of Ava's, held captive underground by Seth Walters.

The shouts of men were closer, and the sound of shovels echoed in the small cavern.

"Here," he squatted in front of me again and held a plastic bottle to my mouth.

Cool water touched my lips and I sipped reflexively. "Not too fast," Tam said. "You've only had whatever I could dribble into you for a couple of days."

I looked at him in surprise and nearly spat the water I held in my mouth. Water. I was drinking water. I swallowed, and it went down cool and sweet against my parched throat. I gulped another mouthful, then reached a shaky hand for the bottle. Tam let me have it, and I drank another gulp before I finally pulled it away from my mouth.

"Days?" I asked. My voice began to sound as though it actually belonged to me.

Tam nodded. "Between you and the Wolf, I've become an expert in hydrating the unconscious."

The Wolf. Connor lay curled in a ball of fur against the wall that remained shrouded in darkness. Tam's eyes followed my gaze. "Yeah, he's still out. The bleeding from the gunshot wound stopped though, and his heartbeat's pretty strong."

The shovels above us sent a cascade of dirt raining into the tunnel, and Tam called up. "Hey, watch it!"

"How many of you are down there?" called a man's voice.

"Two. One's hurt. And a w—"

I grabbed Tam's arm and shook my head sharply.

"And a dog."

"All right. Hold tight. Someone's coming down."

Two men, harnessed with ropes, blocked the sunlight as they descended into the tunnel. I whispered quickly to Tam.

"We were exploring the tunnels with our dog when the ceiling caved in."

Tam nodded silently and I held his gaze. "Am I still bleeding?"

He nodded. "You'll need stitches."

I grimaced. "Bob Shaw. St. Brigid's." Exhaustion washed over me.

"I'll do what I can," Tam whispered. The rescuers had reached the tunnel floor and turned on their torches. I was blinded by the light in my eyes, but the voice of the man holding the torch was unmistakable.

"What a lovely surprise to see you, Devereux," Seth Walters said, sounding quite pleased with himself. "You're the injured one, and yet conscious. Isn't that remarkable? Your blood must be very strong."

I still couldn't see anything, and the effort it took to shield my eyes made my arm shake.

"Do it," Walters growled at the other man. Tam stood and turned to face the men, took one step, and crumpled to the ground.

The man behind him held something in his hand, and I struggled to get to my feet.

"This one too."

"Boss ..." he sounded unsure.

"Do it," Walters spat. "I want them both."

I kicked out at the other man has he bent over me, and he grunted in surprise and pain. He lunged, and I felt a needle go into my thigh. My last thought as the blackness around the edges of my vision consumed me was about water.

I drank water.

I was awake in the daylight, and had been touched by the sun.

I was alive.

Saira – The Train, 1842

The first train heading south left before dawn, and a well-spent coin had ensured we got our own private sleeper compartment. Tom climbed straight into his bunk before the train had even departed the station, but Ringo and I were hungry and found the dining car nearly empty except for a woman reading a book by the window. We took a table nearby and ordered bread with butter and cheese and a pot of coffee.

Our voices were quiet, though the clack-clack of the rails would have covered them in any case.

"I shouldn't have taken us to the Hôtel de Sens," I said.

Ringo shrugged his shoulders. "Where else were ye goin' to Clock us? And 'e was fine on the street. It wasn't until I took us into the courtyard that 'is mind left 'im."

I played with the handle on my cup and stared at the steam rising from the liquid. "How many more mistakes am I going to make before I finally screw *everything* up?"

Ringo leaned back and regarded me. "Ye mean split time? Or are ye thinkin' of somethin' bigger?"

I scoffed. "There's something bigger?"

"Well, the time stream split isn't the biggest thing out there to someone like Tom. 'E's got 'is own priority."

"The split affects *all of it* though," I whispered fiercely.

He sipped his coffee and looked around the train carriage. "The physical world was the same in the other future, so it didn't seem like that bomb did more than kill some people."

I stared at him. "*Some* people?"

He met my eyes. "Just a question that ye don't 'ave to answer out loud, but ye may want to know for yerself. If savin' Archer wasn't part of the deal, or if ye couldn't save 'im no matter what, would ye still do what ye're doin'?"

The waiter came to ask if we needed anything else, and I was glad for the interruption. I didn't want to answer Ringo's question – I didn't even want to think about it. Would I care that time had split if I wasn't trying to get back to Archer?

I let my thoughts wander as my gaze drifted out the window to watch the scenery. My mom was on the other time stream, which was a huge downside. But theoretically, I could Clock back to 1870, sometime before she got pregnant with me, and hang out with both my parents – at least for a little while. Right, I scoffed at myself, because that wouldn't cause another split.

I tried a couple of different mental variations on the same theme – trying to find a way to be with the people I loved in some time other than the one I couldn't get back to, but nothing would work for more than a little while.

The direction my thoughts had turned was approximately as comfortable as underwear that didn't fit, and instead of squirming around in them, I reached into my bag for my book.

The waiter moved away to take a bill to the woman sitting near us, and Ringo finished his coffee in silence.

"Did you ever read *Frankenstein*?" I asked him. He had bought me the copy of *Frankenstein; or The Modern Prometheus*, and I'd been waiting for enough uneventful downtime to start it.

"I started it," he said, "but then I got a little busy."

I smiled wryly as I flipped open the cover of the slim hardcover volume and turned the page. Yeah, we'd been busy. There was a signature inside, in delicate, precise handwriting – "To Lord Byron from the Author." I stared at Ringo in shock.

"Where, exactly, did you get this?"

He shrugged. "A bookseller near the tailor. I 'ave the other two volumes with me when you're done with the first. It came in a set."

I showed him the frontispiece of the book. "Did you see this when you bought it?"

Ringo shook his head. "I didn't open it." He studied the inscription. "Odd that she didn't sign 'er name. They were friends, no?"

I touched the signature with reverence, and was startled by a female voice nearby.

"We brought it to Byron in Venice in 1818. I was so proud to inscribe it to him, even if I couldn't put my own name to it," she said in quiet, clipped English. I looked up, startled to find the woman from the nearby table smiling down at us. "The publishers of the first volume suggested that it would hurt sales if it were known to have been written by a woman."

We both gaped at her, completely at a loss for words.

She laughed lightly at our stunned expressions and extended her hand. "Hello. That's my book you have there. I'm Mary Shelley."

"You're … you're … wow," I breathed, finally giving up on finding any word that did justice to what I felt. I'm pretty sure I had the slack-jawed, glassy-eyed stare of a superhero fangirl at a comics convention.

Ringo jumped up immediately and nearly toppled his chair to shake her hand. "Mrs. Shelley," he said with nearly the same look on his face that I wore.

"Your conversation was the most delightful coincidence, as I had hoped to find a way to introduce myself. Please forgive my intrusion, and more importantly, my presumption," she said softly.

"There's nothin' to forgive, Mrs. Shelley. 'Tis an honor to make your acquaintance." Ringo sounded breathless, and Mrs. Shelley seemed amused.

I stood and held out my hand to shake hers. "My name is Saira, and this is my friend Ringo."

She shook my hand solemnly. "I'm Mary. It's a pleasure to meet you."

"Would you …" Ringo hesitated, looking less sure of himself than I'd ever seen him. "Would you care to join us?" He was ratcheting his normal manners up a notch, and it would have made me smile if I wasn't so awestruck.

She smiled. "Would you mind?" Ringo gave her his seat and pulled another from a nearby table, and Mary looked at the book in my hands wistfully. "May I?" she asked.

I handed it to her and she turned the pages carefully, giving me time to find my voice.

"Lord Byron was with you and your husband when you came up with the story of Frankenstein, wasn't he?" I ventured.

"I dreamed it, actually. And yes, we were at Byron's home on Lake Geneva." Mary returned to the signature page of the book and touched the letters of Byron's name lightly. She was a slight woman with a narrow face and big, expressive eyes. Her long hair was thick and dark and pulled back into a low, braided bun. Her traveling dress was simple, but made of beautiful, richly dyed burgundy wool. There was something about her that reminded me of one of Tolkien's elves, only smaller and more approachable. She appeared to be in her mid-thirties, but then I did the math and realized she was forty-two.

"It feels like a lifetime ago," she said softly. She looked up as she closed the book and pushed it back across the table to me. "But I suppose it was. It's been twenty years since Bysshe died, and then Byron followed him two years later." Her laughter was as quiet as her words. "If there is an afterlife for men such as those two, I imagine them sitting by a fire, brandies in hand, debating the finer points of poetry, politics, and the pursuit of happiness. The fire would of course burn to embers as neither of them could be bothered to keep it up, while Polidori scribbled their words furiously in a corner of the room lest they notice him and stop their incessant conversing."

Her eyes seemed to clear from the memory and she gave us an apologetic smile. "I haven't thought about those nights for a long time." She held my gaze for a moment, then glanced at my clothes. "I confess, I've always wondered how it would feel to wear men's clothing but was never brave enough to try. How do you find it?"

"More comfortable than dresses, that's for sure," I answered, relieved that she didn't disapprove.

"I presume most people assume you are male because of your height, though I fail to see how they could maintain that opinion once they really look. I saw you walk in and was struck immediately by your carriage."

"My carriage?" I asked in amazement. I was sitting with Mary Shelley, and she was talking about how I walked?

"The way you hold yourself. You have the confidence of a man and the grace of a woman. It's quite striking, really."

Ringo sighed. "It's a struggle."

This statement seemed to delight Mary, and she turned to Ringo with an amused smile. "I assume you mean it's a struggle to be the companion of someone who risks becoming the target of unwanted attention?"

"On a daily basis," Ringo agreed with a long-suffering tone. I wanted to kick him under the table. This was not what I wanted to be talking about, but she was obviously interested.

"Imagine what it is like when one is a woman," she said simply.

"I do that too, on a daily basis. And sympathy for it is why I 'aven't murdered 'er ten times over for every time she's put 'erself in danger."

"If so, you're a remarkable young man." I wasn't sure Mary believed him, and Ringo's sense of people was finely-tuned enough that he got that.

Ringo shrugged. "Not remarkable. Women are just not somethin' I'm afraid of."

Mary raised an eyebrow in an expression that reminded me forcibly of Archer, and I was hit with a battering ram of missing him. "Please explain," she said.

Ringo settled back in his chair. "I don't know when the fear began, or why, though I imagine it 'ad somethin' to do with childbirth and general competence, but somewhere along the line, men started fearin' women."

I looked for shock on Mary's face, but only found intense interest. Ringo's tone was disarmingly casual, and I loved that he spoke with a shrug, like he was just pointing out the obvious.

"It's the only thing that explains the treatment women get at the 'ands of men, because it just doesn't make sense that 'alf the population of anything is meant to be under the thumb of the other 'alf."

"Half the population of any*thing*?" Mary asked.

"There's no common oppression of females in the animal kingdom," he said.

"Fascinating." Mary said, after a pause to consider.

Ringo shrugged. "It just isn't logical that women are any less 'uman than men, and since I doubt women decided to take away their own rights, it follows that men did it to clap a firm 'and on their own fear."

Mary barely suppressed the grin that threatened, and she turned her gaze to me. "What do you think of your friend's assessments?"

I was thinking it was a very strange and interesting conversation to be having with the writer of *Frankenstein*, but I answered her question. "I was raised to believe I am equal to men and wasn't taught a lot about what women can or cannot do. I pretty much do what I need to do, regardless of whether it's considered 'male' or 'female' behavior."

She regarded me for a long moment. "You speak in an unfamiliar way, but I appreciate what you say." She included Ringo in her gaze. "What you both have said."

Mary stood, and Ringo rushed to pull her chair back. "I find that the rigors of travel have caught up with me, and I believe I shall retire." She held her hand out to shake mine, and then Ringo's. "It was an absolute pleasure to meet you both, and I do hope we'll have a chance to speak further as this journey progresses."

"May I walk you back to your compartment?" Ringo asked gallantly. I stood up too and put her book back into my bag.

"That's very kind of you, but it's an imposition," she said.

"We're leaving anyway, so we'll either follow you out or walk with you," I said.

She smiled. "Then walk with me, and I shall be glad for your company."

Ringo held the door for both of us, and I think he might even have bowed slightly as Mary went through. Mary's private sleeper was actually only two doors away from ours, and as we said goodbye, we agreed to meet again in the dining car later.

There was a tall, fair-skinned man in the shadows at the end of the hall, smoking at the window. The smoke that didn't disperse out the window was sweet, kind of like pipe smoke, or like the clove cigarettes people smoke outside dance clubs at home, and as we got closer, I was struck by a case of Monger-gut.

The man turned away and stepped out of the carriage door before I got a proper look at him, and the Monger-gut faded with his departure. I let out a small sigh of relief as we entered our compartment.

We didn't even try to be quiet in our tiny private room. Tom was out cold, and he had commandeered the bottom bunk, which meant I might have to accidentally step on him as I climbed up to mine, just for being selfish.

I was brushing my teeth at the tiny corner sink when a shadow and the sound of a click, and another wave of Monger-gut, made me look up. Someone had stopped outside our door, but the feeling faded as he moved on. Ringo was already stretched out on the couchette still wearing his clothes, his booted feet crossed at the ankles and his arms draped over his chest.

"Did you hear that?" I whispered.

There was no answer. How was it even possible to fall asleep that fast? It must be a special talent guys have, or at least the ones who hung out with me. I went to the curtained window and peeked out. The hall was empty, and I was too exhausted to worry about imaginary threats, so I unlaced my boots and left them on the floor by Tom's head. I probably needed to check my passive aggression where he was concerned, so as a gesture of goodwill, I didn't try to step on him as I heaved myself up to my bed. The sound of the train clacking on the tracks finally drowned out the thoughts of Archer that spun around my brain every time I closed my eyes, and I was lulled to sleep.

I was violently hurled from my bunk and hit the floor so hard I lost every bit of breath in my body. The sound of metal shredding metal erased any thought of indulging in the pain of the impact, and I struggled to stand.

"Saira! Yer feet!" Ringo yelled at me from somewhere near the couchette.

The bunk wall was at a crazy angle *over my head*, and I was standing on the window in my socks, surrounded by broken glass.

"Don't move! I'll get ye."

I shook my head to clear my vision and orient myself. Night had fallen so the compartment was dark, and the horrific sounds of impact had faded, but they were gradually being replaced by screams of passengers down the hall. Ringo picked his way over twisted metal and grabbed my face in both his hands.

"Are ye all right?" he demanded.

I didn't bother to take stock. I knew my shoulder had taken most of the hit, and I briefly wondered if it might be dislocated, but I nodded anyway. "Fine. Where's Tom?" My voice rasped with an edge of panic I fought to push away.

"Here," Tom said from somewhere over my head. I looked up to find him wedged into his bunk, staring down with wide, frightened eyes.

"You okay?" He nodded, and I hadn't seen him look so much like himself since we buried Léon.

"Climb on my back," Ringo said to me. "I'll get ye out of the glass."

I did what he said, and he piggy-backed me over to his couchette, which was perched at a crazy angle. "Where's yer torch? We need to find yer boots."

My boots, which I'd so vindictively put by the head of Tom's bunk. Right. At least I'd slept in my clothes, so my mini Maglite was still in a pocket sewn into the leg of my trousers. I took it out and shone it around the wrecked compartment. A sigh with a "Bleedin' 'ell," escaped Ringo as we surveyed the damage. We spotted Ringo's satchel first, then my own, then finally my boots, which had been flung across the compartment and were wedged under the window frame where I'd stood.

"What happened?" Tom's voice held the same barely suppressed panic mine had.

"The train derailed and it's on its side," I said. The screams had gotten louder, and a waft of smoke seemed to seep through the cracks in the walls. I stared at Ringo and his wide eyes told me he knew.

"Fire."

The door was still closed, and was at about a seventy-degree angle over our heads. "Tom, can you reach the door from where you are?" I tried not to screech, but panic was edging out whatever calm I had left.

Ringo thrust my boots at me. "Here, put these on. I'll go."

He didn't wait for a response from either Tom or me and paused only to sling his bag over one shoulder before hoisting himself onto the upended couchette to reach the door. It was a sliding door, of the variety that was still used a hundred and fifty years later, and it wouldn't budge.

"It's locked." The first shade of panic crept into Ringo's voice as he yanked harder and harder on the door.

"Break the window!" I said, trying very hard not to completely freak out.

"With what?" Ringo had flipped his grip on the couchette and was trying to kick the window out, but the panes were too small and thick.

Tom had climbed out of his bunk and braced himself against the side of it to kick at the door. It wasn't moving.

I'd gotten my boots on and looked around for something hard we could use. The frame of the window had bent away from the ground it lay on. I wrapped my hand in my sleeve and ripped the metal away from the wall.

The smell of smoke was getting stronger now, and the screams had turned to shrieks that filled the space around us. I handed the metal up to Ringo. "Here, try to pop the lock with this."

The screech of metal scraped my already raw nerves, and then the door slid open.

"Lady and gent, ye need to get yerselves up 'ere and out. The train is most definitely burnin'." An anxious edge was back in Ringo's voice, and I flung the strap of my bag over my shoulder and met Tom's eyes.

"Let's go."

Tom boosted me up to the top of the couchette, and from there I could reach the open door and climb out to the hallway. Ringo was already down the hall at Mary Shelley's door. He had the metal window frame wedged into the seam between the door and its frame, and a moment later he had popped that lock too. He tossed me the metal piece.

"'Ere, go to work on the other doors," he said as he climbed down into Mary's room.

Tom helped me push against the locks, and we'd gotten four other doors open by the time Mary pulled herself out of her compartment with a push from underneath. We had called down to the frightened people inside their rooms and told them to climb out, but only a few seemed to have the presence of mind to climb the couchette like we'd done.

Mary had a small cut on her forehead but seemed otherwise unharmed. Ringo heaved a small valise out of her room before climbing out himself. He grabbed my arm.

"We 'ave to go. The fire's too close."

"Just three more—" I started to say, but Ringo yanked my arm.

"No, Saira – now!" He grabbed the metal piece from my hand and rammed it into the crack in the door at the end of the carriage. He used it to lever the door open, and smoke poured into the hallway. "Let's go!"

I was mad, but it was the kind of mad that comes from being very, very afraid. Ringo was right. The sky outside the train car was glowing bright orange, and a shower of sparks shot into it as I watched.

Ringo and Mary were already through the door, and Tom and I had nearly reached it when I heard the sound of the door at the other end of the carriage being wrenched open. I turned instinctively, and I nearly stopped in my tracks as Death came in.

FLIGHT

Aeron had just entered our carriage. I turned and crawled in blind terror through the door. Tom followed on my heels, and we leapt down beside the overturned train car, then sprinted to the grove of trees where I'd spotted Ringo and Mary.

"Aeron," I blurted to Ringo. "Aeron's here." My heart slammed in my chest, due in larger part to having just seen Death than to my sprint and general state of terror since the crash.

Both Ringo and Mary gasped. Ringo's gasp made sense to me. Mary's did not.

"The man who opened the other door of the carriage? That was Aeron?" Tom said, behind me. I nodded.

Tom blinked. "How do you know Death?"

"Was he tall with dark hair, strong features, the brown skin of a Moor, and the clothing of a gentleman?" asked Mary Shelley quietly.

Prickles raised on the back of my neck as I turned to her with narrowed eyes. "Yes," I hissed. "You saw him?"

She shook her head slowly. "Not tonight."

Awesome. "*When* did you see Death, Mary?"

"The night he came for Bysshe."

The Roadrunner could have dropped an anvil on my head and I wouldn't have been more shocked.

"*Why* did 'e come for 'im?" Ringo asked, even more quietly than she had answered.

Mary's gaze included all three of us. "Because my husband was one of his."

Ringo's eyes flicked to mine in the most subtle *I told you so* in the history of know-it-alls, and maybe because of it I was able to contain the stutter that threatened. Tom couldn't, and Mary's eyes found his.

"I don't know you," she said.

"Mary Shelley, Tom Landers. He's with us," I said curtly. Death was on that train, I reminded myself as I surveyed the overturned cars that were now engulfed with fire. Death was on that train, and Mary Shelley knew him. I was not wild about the coincidence.

Tom's eyes had widened as he registered Mary's identity, but I turned my attention to the wreck. Screams and cries of passengers had quieted in the night air, but it didn't seem as though many people were standing outside the overturned train. And if they weren't outside of it, they were still inside. "What happened," I whispered.

"The doors were locked," answered Ringo. "Who would lock all the doors of a passenger car?"

A memory niggled at the back of my brain. "The man – at the end of the hallway when we got back to our compartment – he was a Monger. I saw his shadow and heard the lock click just before I went to bed." Ringo looked at me for long enough that I got weirdly defensive. "You were already asleep," I said.

He blinked. "It couldn't 'ave been about us. No one knew we were on that train."

"I did," said Mary Shelley.

I turned to face Mary, and the prickles on the back of my neck returned. "Are you a Seer?"

"Distantly." She held my gaze for a long moment, and I waited, knowing there was more. "Aislin sent me."

"Gah!" I yelled in frustration.

"Bloody Immortals," Ringo murmured under his breath.

"What does she want?" I asked Mary. I was near tears, partly from the train crash, and partly from the realization I was in control of exactly nothing.

"I don't know," said Mary, and she had the grace to sound apologetic. "She showed me the image of our meeting in the dining compartment and said I'd be able to help you. She also said you were trying to fulfill the Prophecy of the Child."

There were so many things I wanted to ask, and every question crowded in at once. Ringo didn't seem to have the same issue.

"'Ow'd Aislin come to ye, and why did ye do 'er biddin'?"

Mary nodded. "Both fair questions. Aislin has visited my dreams twice. The first time was just after Bysshe and I were married, the night he was attacked and … turned." She inhaled sharply. "She showed me where to find him and how to care for him as his body changed." Mary's expression looked a little haunted, and whatever anger I'd felt about Aislin's interference melted away. She continued. "The second time was two nights ago, when she showed me our meeting. I don't know how I can help, or why you need it, but I felt I owed her a debt for helping me with Bysshe all those years ago."

"Who turned him?" asked Tom. He had been watching the fire blaze on the train, and flames reflected in his eyes as he asked the question without facing any of us.

"He never knew, and Aislin didn't show me that."

Mary looked pale, and Ringo glared at Tom. "We'll 'ave this discussion later, after we find shelter and transportation. Mrs. Shelley, in spite of Fate's 'and in our meetin', I invite ye to accompany us to Rome."

Mary met our eyes with straight shoulders. "I should be very honored to accompany you. A friend of mine lives outside Rome, and I've sent her a message that I'd like to visit."

Ringo and I looked at each other and silently acknowledged that Aislin was having her way with us, but since we had no better plan, it seemed futile to resist. Ringo nodded at me as if that settled everything, then slung his bag across his shoulder and looked in both directions down the track. "Anyone have an idea where the nearest village is?" he asked.

Mary surveyed the terrain. "I believe south is the appropriate direction." She turned south and began walking toward the tracks. Ringo and I shared exactly one second of a surprised look before we followed her, with Tom at the rear.

Mary approached a man in a uniform with a soot-smeared face who was directing the few injured passengers we'd seen away from the tracks. She asked him something in rapid French, then, when he looked blankly at her, switched to Italian. He answered in a voice that spoke of his sheer exhaustion, and indicated the direction we'd been heading. Mary patted his arm softly in thanks, and I could see how much her gesture meant to him as he swallowed hard. Then he called out to another uniformed man, excused himself, and hurried away.

The air was full of smoke and burning coal, but underneath the acrid smells I caught the sweet scent of clove. I turned toward it sharply and scanned the people along the tracks. There were passengers in formal traveling clothes, some with blood on them, and all looked tired and dirty from the soot. Some people helped the rail workers, while others sat and stared blankly at the flames. One man stood apart from the group and watched silently as he smoked his hand-rolled cigarette. His face was in deep shadows, but the scent of cloves came from him, and I detected a hint of Monger-gut with it.

I touched Ringo's sleeve and tried to be as casual as possible about not looking at the man. "The man with the clove cigarette. That's the Monger," I said under my breath.

The man flicked the still-burning cigarette at a small child who stood nearby wailing pitiably for his mother. The child's cries choked off in surprise as he stared at the man, and before I could move in his direction, the little one took off running. Voices among the people nearby rose in anger, and two men stood up and squared off. The older one of the two threw a punch, and the clove man grinned under his hat.

"Bastard," Ringo said under his breath, and the clove man looked up as if he'd heard Ringo speak. We both recognized him at the same instant.

I froze, and Ringo exhaled sharply. "Duncan," I whispered.

The Immortal War stood about twenty feet down the track from where we were. He wore a light-colored suit and a hat with a brim that hid his face, but somehow his eyes were the most visible part of him. Duncan seemed to watch us for a long moment while the passengers in the nearby group shouted encouragement at the fighters. Monger-gut had stolen all my breath, and I felt utterly sick until finally his gaze slid away from our group. After another moment, he strode off into the trees.

The shouts from the nearby people began to quiet, and the fighters dropped their fists and looked at each other in bewilderment. Mary and Tom had stopped walking to watch us, and when Duncan finally left, we both relaxed visibly. "'E doesn't know us," shuddered Ringo.

"How do you know? I think he locked us in, and I think maybe Aeron was coming to finish us off." I sounded paranoid, even to myself.

"Remember, everyone was locked in," said Ringo. "It wasn't just us."

"Who was that?" asked Mary.

"That was War."

Tom started in surprise, and nearly turned to follow Duncan's path into the woods. I narrowed my eyes at him. "You really want to go after Duncan?"

"No," he said sullenly.

I held his gaze until he looked away uncomfortably. Then I turned back to Ringo and Mary. "We need to get out of here."

They nodded, and Ringo took Mary's valise so she could lift the front of her skirts with both hands and stride swiftly down the tracks, away from the burning train wreck.

We walked for about twenty minutes in silence, until finally the signs of human habitation began to point us in the direction of a village. Mary fell back next to me from her position at the front of the group. "As I said before, the Seer line in my family is several generations removed, and though my mother did tell me of our heritage, she didn't have a tremendous amount of information to share about the other Families. Therefore it is merely my guess that you are a Descendant of Time?"

I nodded vaguely. My brain had been spinning on any possible reason for Death and War to show up at a train wreck in France in 1842, and I'd come up with exactly nothing that made any sense. Were they there because of us? How did they know we'd be there? Had Aislin told them? My thoughts were spinning out of control, and I forced my attention back to Mary. "What gave me away, my clothes?"

"Your ease."

"My ease?" I scoffed. "I feel far from easy right now. In fact I can't remember the last time I felt easy about anything. A lifetime ago, or maybe two."

Mary's expression was wistful. "Ah yes, I understand that feeling. I didn't marry Bysshe until years after I ran away with him. I was sixteen when I left my father's house, and twenty-three when Bysshe died. I lived an entire lifetime during those seven years, and another one since."

My throat suddenly slammed closed, and my heart threw itself against my ribcage. All questions about Death and War fled my brain, and my inability to breathe must have shown on my face because Mary's expression grew concerned. "Are you all right, Saira?"

I nodded silently, and then shook my head when my eyes filled with tears. I wiped them away angrily before they could fall and took a deep shuddering breath to get myself back under control. I felt a sudden kinship with this woman, and the words came almost without thought.

"I met my husband when I was seventeen, and I watched him die the week after we were married. He's not really dead, at least I don't think he is. But I can't get to him …" My voice trailed off uselessly, unable to express any words that mattered.

Mary stopped me and took my hands in hers. "Oh my dear, I'm so sorry!" Her voice was hushed, but the force of her sympathy reminded me so strongly of my mother that I literally burst into tears.

I'd never done that before – burst out crying – around anyone but my mom. It was disconcerting and uncomfortable, and I had absolutely no choice but to give in to it. And then Mary did the one thing I was powerless against while I was in the middle of a snot-fest – she held her arms open.

I hurled myself into them.

I was vaguely aware of Tom and Ringo standing far enough away from us that they wouldn't get hit by flying emotion, but I pretty much lost myself to the feeling, just for a moment, that everything would be all right. Somehow, inside mothering arms there were no problems to deal with, no bad guys to vanquish, no heartbreak to endure. I missed my mom with all the missing I had in me, and I let myself pretend Mary Shelley's arms were hers, that the murmured words of comfort came from her voice, and the fading scent of roses was her perfume.

Gradually, the gush of tears subsided, and I pulled back with a grimace to wipe my face. Mary brushed the hair back from my face and searched my eyes. "The strongest people of my acquaintance are the ones who allow the steam to escape before the pressure builds to explosive levels."

I barked a humorless laugh. "That seemed pretty explosive to me."

She smiled gently. "Merely steam. You'll feel better now."

I returned her smile. "When I can see through my puffy eyes again, maybe. I'm sorry about that."

"My dear, it's what a mother's arms are for."

I straightened my jacket and re-tucked my shirt into the buckskin trousers, which had, miraculously, survived our escape from the train relatively unscathed. "I didn't know you had children," I said to Mary. I realized I knew nothing about Mary Shelley beyond the fact that she'd been married to Percy Bysshe Shelley and had written *Frankenstein*.

"Of my four children, only Percy Florence grew to adulthood," she said. "He's at Cambridge, and is set to inherit his grandfather's baronetcy."

"Three died?" I was struggling with having temporarily misplaced Archer. The idea of losing a child, much less three, was unthinkable.

"Our first daughter came early. I was so young, and she was so small, it was a wonder she even lived two weeks. It was long enough to love her though, and once I'd felt that love, I couldn't imagine a life without it."

Her eyes were clear, but her serene voice caught on the words. She smiled to see the distress in my expression. "William came soon after, and Clara was born a year after that. Little Clara died of dysentery three days after her first birthday. William was two-and-a-half when malaria took him. He and his father are both buried in Rome, which is one of the reasons I chose to heed Aislin's vision. It is long past time for a visit."

"I'm so sorry," I whispered. It was amazing she could still stand after having endured all that tragedy.

She must have known my thoughts, because she looked me right in the eye. "One does what one must to survive. Life is the only possible antidote to death, and living fully is the only way to counter the senselessness of loss."

I was overwhelmed by her words, and I held my hand out to her. She squeezed it in a moment of pure understanding, then she let go and we turned to face the guys.

Ringo was close enough to have overheard our conversation, but Tom had wandered off toward the trees. I caught Ringo's eyes, and he gave me a small, sad smile. I straightened my spine, took a step forward, and then another step. I supposed that's how a person got through the things that stopped them in their tracks. Take the first step, and then the next, and eventually, momentum would pick up where will had left off.

THE KNOWING

We came upon a village not long after that, and after a meal at the local inn with Mary and Ringo, we emerged to find Tom outside the open door of a coach he'd hired. The coachman sat up in front of the rig with a blanket bundled over his lap, a big heavy coat, and a hat pulled down low over his eyes. The two horses were lively and looked strong, and the coach itself looked like it was in pretty good shape.

I raised my eyebrows in a question, and he scowled at me. "I'm not getting back on another train, and I'm sick of walking. I found it – you guys can pay for it."

I nodded. "Thanks, Tom. That was good thinking."

He seemed surprised at my thanks, and his scowl deepened. "The coachman will take us as far as Turin, and we can decide whether we attempt another train from there."

Mary kissed his cheek lightly. "It's perfect," she said. Almost in spite of himself, Tom held his hand out to help her into the carriage. Ringo clapped Tom on the back and then gestured for me to enter the coach, while he walked around it to inspect the wheels and the under-carriage. Mary had taken a seat facing forward and patted the seat next to her.

"The gentlemen won't mind," she said when I hesitated. "It's hard enough to ride in a carriage for a short trip."

Tom climbed in behind me. "I'll spare you both the backward-facing seat." He didn't look at me as he settled across from Mary, but at least he'd lost the perpetual scowl he'd been wearing since we left Paris.

Ringo was still outside speaking in a halting mixture of French, English, and pantomime to the driver, when a little face appeared outside my window.

I shrieked and leapt across the space to the opposite bench, and then I started to laugh. Ringo was at the door a moment later demanding to know what happened.

"An opossum," I managed to say through nearly hysterical giggles, "at the window." As if on cue, a little brown, furry face peeked down from above and looked at us through the carriage window. Its long nose twitched furiously, and black beady eyes looked straight at me as if in accusation for having made such a horrible noise.

Ringo smirked in a way I hadn't seen him do since … well, since before the bomb exploded. "That's Barney. 'E belongs to the coachman's little girl, Amélie." Ringo held his arm out to the little opossum. "Come inside and meet Saira, Barney, and she'll promise not to screech like an owl again."

The little creature put an arm through the window to Ringo's hand, then climbed the rest of the way down and across Ringo's arm to come inside. I held out my hand and grinned in delight as he reached a tentative hand across to me.

"Hello, Barney. I'm very sorry for screaming at you." I peered into his little, beady-eyed face, and his nose twitched as he sniffed my breath. "I'm also sorry I didn't save you any pot pie."

He sat up on Ringo's shoulder and put one of his hands in mine as if I were forgiven. Then the carriage lurched forward, and little Barney scampered back out the window up to the roof of the coach. I sat back in the seat I'd jumped to, next to Tom, and finally felt the tension begin to seep away as I looked at my traveling companions. "The night began with a train crash and a sighting of both War and Death, but it was an opossum that made me scream." There was something cathartic in the laughter that little Barney had inspired, and I thought we had all needed it.

We drove through the night, and just before dawn the coachman stopped to water the horses. Tom came inside the carriage, and with a curt "good night" to all of us, he crawled under the bench beneath me and fell asleep. When we finally stopped at an inn to stretch and eat, I draped a shawl over the seat to protect him from light and casual observation.

I got a good look at Amélie then. She was maybe five years old, and little Barney sat draped across her shoulders, under her hair, hidden from anyone who wasn't specifically looking for him. She was a pretty child, with nearly white-blond hair that she hid under a dirty cap. She wore boys' clothes, and her face was smeared with dirt that looked artfully done, as though she or her father thought the dirt could hide her loveliness. I saw through her disguise in an instant, but it seemed the stablemaster didn't when he took her money and gave her bags of oats for the horses.

I almost strode forward to help her, but Ringo grabbed my arm and held me back. "They'll see yer a woman, and then they'll look at 'er. Right now they only see a dirty child, and it 'asn't occurred to them to wonder about 'er beyond that." I felt a tremor of fear for the little girl whose safety might hinge on how well she could hide in plain sight.

At sunset we stopped for another meal at a tavern outside Lyon, and Tom slipped away in the darkness to find his own sustenance. I'd never questioned it with Archer, and I certainly didn't want to know what Tom ate. This tavern was far less clean and well-maintained than the one we'd eaten in the night before, and the vague uneasiness of Monger proximity hit me when we entered. I made a point of finding a table in the corner where both Ringo and I could sit with our backs to the wall.

We ordered stew from a barmaid missing half her teeth and managed to choke down a couple of spoonfuls before we gave the gelatinous stuff up as a lost cause. Mary's roast wasn't too bad, and the bread was decent, but I resolved to ask Michel about stopping at a farm along our route where I might be able to buy some fresh vegetables and maybe some cheese.

The door was flung open, and a rowdy group of travelers blew in already carrying a jug of whatever they'd been drinking. Mary pulled her shawl more tightly around her, and I saw two older women at other tables get up and quietly slip out the door. The traveling group was made up of five men, all French, and all between about twenty-five and forty years old, if their skin and the state of their teeth were to be trusted. The slight case of Monger-gut I'd been sporting since we walked into the tavern had gotten stronger with their entrance, but so far the loudest thing about them was their laughter. They took a table on the far side of the tavern from us, and a little of the tension left Mary's shoulders.

"During the Bourbon Restoration," she said in a low voice, "the taverns in France were quite dangerous. When Bysshe and I came through France on our way to Byron's house at Lake Geneva, peasants and farmers were starving, and travelers were well-advised to keep one hand on their purse and one on their sword at all times. A tavern like this one could easily become the site of a riot in those days."

"In these days too," Ringo said grimly. Tom had just entered the tavern and wove his way to our table. His gypsy coloring and dark hair didn't mark him as particularly different than anyone else in the room, but his youth and slight build seemed to draw attention from a few of the customers. The Mongerness in him was very faint to my senses these days, but the moment he sat down, I sensed his predatory side pulsing as though I was the one he'd been hunting.

The travelers had noticed Tom, and one of them said something that made the others laugh. I immediately felt like I was in a high school lunch room, and my instinct was to do exactly what I'd always done in school – get up and leave. If I didn't, there was usually a pretty decent chance things would escalate, because I've never been able to back down from bullies, and these guys were shaping up to be classics.

"Watch yer back," murmured Ringo, as Tom took the only seat left at our table – the one next to me. In response, Tom pulled the chair closer to mine and turned it so his back wasn't so completely exposed to the room. There was a spot of blood on his collar, and I wanted to pull his jacket up to hide it, but I didn't think my touch would be welcome.

I leaned forward to speak quietly in his ear. "The group came in already drinking. I think there are at least two Mongers with them."

"I can take care of myself," he growled tensely.

Tom's general state of annoyance at having to be in my presence was back in full force, and it intensified my awareness of his Monger side. I could feel Ringo's attention split between the group of travelers and Tom, and my need to leave the tavern suddenly became overwhelming.

I caught Ringo's eye and stood up to leave just as a man stepped through the door. A man who smelled of cloves and wore a suit of dove gray wool with a silk cravat, and was way too fancy for this dive. He removed his hat and took in the room at a single glance. His Mongerness came at me like a fist, drove the air from my lungs and buckled my knees. Ringo's arm shot out to keep me from falling.

The movement caught Duncan's attention, and a small smile crept across his lips. His gaze flicked from me to Ringo to Tom, and then drifted across the room to the group of travelers.

He went to the bar and ordered an ale, and I caught Mary's eye and jerked my head silently toward the door. She understood and gathered her skirts to rise while Duncan whispered some words to the woman serving drinks. He slipped her a coin and then met my eyes across the room.

Granted, I couldn't take my eyes off him, but the coincidence of his notice was too big. I ducked my head and started for the door. Ringo and Mary were on my heels, and I hoped Tom had gotten the message that it was definitely time to leave.

I reached the door just as the barmaid delivered drinks to the group of travelers. I saw her speak in low tones and then look pointedly at Tom. The energy in the room began to change. Voices got louder, bodies shifted in seats, and the mood was suddenly edgy. It felt as though War's very presence incited anger and violence. One of the men, a big, barrel-chested guy in his mid-thirties, pushed back from the table and called something out to Tom in guttural French.

Tom, in his best imitation of a complete idiot, shot something back at the guy in the same language.

"Oh!" Mary gasped. I spun to find her pale as she stared at the man across the tavern, who was now joined on his feet by two other men in his party.

"What did they say?" I demanded.

"The barmaid told them she's afraid of Tom because there's blood on his shirt."

I scowled. "The barmaid wasn't anywhere near him."

"Doesn't matter," Ringo growled. "Tom just told them to mind their own soddin' business, and that was exactly the wrong thing to say."

And in fact, it was. Barrel-chest had flung a table out of his way and was smashing across the tavern toward Tom, his fellow travelers on his heels. Ringo pushed me out the door, and I grabbed Mary's hand to pull her with me. Ringo dragged Tom out by his coat just as Barrel-chest reached them.

"Michel!" I called to the driver as I ran for the carriage, dragging poor Mary behind me. "Allez!"

Michel took the scene in at a glance and instantly hoisted little Amélie up into her seat before he climbed into his own. I threw open the carriage door and shoved Mary inside before turning to see what was happening behind us.

Men were shouting, and Barrel-chest had a beefy arm wrapped around Tom's neck in a headlock, while the others hurled curses and yelled encouragement. Ringo spun a roundhouse kick to Barrel-chest's head just as Tom slammed his foot into the guy's instep.

He went down with a sharp cry, but two more men, one lithe and mean-looking, the other young and big, lunged forward.

The mean-looking one had a knife, and I could sense the Mongerness of him. "Let's go!" I shouted as I slapped the side of the carriage. Michel understood what I wanted, and he didn't let the horses bolt as he twitched their reins to go.

Ringo pushed Tom forward toward the departing coach, and leveled a kick at the Monger's knife hand before sprinting to follow.

We began to pick up speed, but the guys were still too far behind us. A thrown knife clipped Tom's arm. His face contorted in scary rage and he slowed his run, but Ringo urged him forward. A few of the tavern customers gave chase, but Ringo and Tom were faster, and with the departing coach to motivate them, they got far enough ahead that the men dropped off.

I stood in the open doorway of the coach, and leaned out to call to Michel to slow down, but he was already doing it. Little Amélie faced backward and had apparently already informed her father that the guys needed to catch up. I gave her a quick nod before reaching out to grab Tom's hand and haul him inside. Ringo leapt into the carriage with his usual effortless grace, and the guys fell onto the bench panting.

I glared at Tom furiously. "You're bleeding." I wasn't sure why I was so mad. Seeing Duncan had stolen whatever mental comfort I'd managed to carve out for myself, and somehow, all of it was Tom's fault.

"So?" he shot back.

"So, let me fix it," I snapped.

His glare had daggers attached. "Why do you need to fix everything? Why is it your job? I'm not broken – I'm not even scratched." He yanked off his jacket and tore the buttons off his gashed and bloody shirt to show me his upper arm. The slice from the thrown knife was still there, and I recoiled at all the scars on his chest that had bloomed with blood as the small slice repaired itself.

"Tom!" Horror filled my voice, and behind me Mary cried out.

Tom looked down at his chest and shoulder. The old wounds were disappearing back into the scars they had become, but blood still covered his chest and soaked through his shirt. He made a disgusted sound deep in his throat and yanked the shirt back over his shoulder. It was useless now, torn and stained with his blood, and he hurled it out the window. Suddenly the carriage was filled with his Mongerness.

"You don't get to fix this, Saira." Tom's rage was cold and hard. He ground the words out through clenched teeth, and his face radiated with his anger. "You can't fix me."

Ringo started to say something, but I yelled at him. "Don't!" Then I turned the full force of my glare on Tom. I was sick of his hatred, sick of his anger, and sick of being blamed for everything that had happened. "I don't want to fix you, Tom. I can't fix the anger and the hatred and the self-loathing you wrap around yourself like armor. But the thing I *can* do, the thing no one else in the world can do, is I can take you back to the moment right after you screwed everything up so you can fix it yourself!"

Tom looked like he was about to launch himself at me, and his coiled muscles shook with the effort of controlling his impulse. "I could make you just like me right now."

Ringo moved as if to hold Tom back, but I shouted "No! Let him." I didn't take my eyes off Tom as I answered Ringo's need to *do something*. "Let him turn me, if that's what he needs to do. If that's what it'll take for him to fix the split so we can all get home, that's fine. I can take it."

I finally tore my eyes away from the rage in Tom's face, and when I looked at the anguish in Ringo's, my voice softened and despair choked me. "Archer survived it. I can too. And then maybe if I'm a Vampire I'll be strong enough to stop being afraid of losing him, and Archer and I can go away and spend the rest of time together."

"No, Saira," Ringo whispered.

Tom scoffed, and the sound tore through the carriage. "Archer's dead."

Ringo whipped his head around and glared at Tom. "No thanks to ye!" he spat. "The only 'ope they 'ave of bein' together now is in a future she can't get to unless ye 'ave the stones to fix what ye broke."

"You don't understand," said Tom with eerie calm. "In that future, Archer's dead and buried under tons of rock."

I felt cold prickles of fear begin to creep through my chest. "No he's not," I whispered.

Tom's voice was like ice, and every word had a sharp edge designed to cut. "Remember I told you there was an explosion in the Underground? Adam was down there, and the little Edwards kid – the Shifter – he said he couldn't find his brother or Archer under the rubble. He found a dead Monger, but not them."

My hand balled into a fist, and I cocked my arm back and imagined it smashing into his nose. For the first time in a very long time, I felt my Cat rise up … and I let her.

"Saira?" Ringo warned, as he held my arm back.

Tom smiled, and it was the smile that broke the leash.

My voice was unfamiliar as I met his eyes and answered his hateful words. "You should have kept that to yourself," I said enraged, "because now you're screwed."

I exploded out of my skin and Shifted into the Cougar who lived inside me. She roared, and I heard the horses scream outside the carriage. We lurched to a stop and my Cat threw herself at the door, which burst open and sent me sailing out into the darkness.

"Saira!" Ringo yelled after me, but I ignored him and bounded for the woods.

I could sense him behind me, but I leapt rocks and over tree trunks as though the very act of running could let me escape pain and rage and … emptiness.

It was the yawning emptiness in my heart that stopped me in my tracks.

Do we turn and fight? my Cat asked me in a confused voice in my head. But there was nothing to fight – nothing to vent the rage on, no way to replace the emotional pain with something physical.

My Cat stood in a little clearing in the woods, panting, confused, and drained of the fire that had burned so brightly just moments before. I heard running then, and I sensed Ringo's approach at full speed, heedless of what might be left when he found me.

The rage left me so fast that everything – every ounce of pain and anger and fear that had kept me upright – drained out of me in a rush.

I don't remember Shifting back. I don't remember standing naked in the woods, quivering muscles around my spine unable to keep me upright. Ringo was next to me in a flash, his coat wrapped around me, and his hands supporting me carefully. Standing – even breathing – became impossible.

Ringo lowered me gently to the forest floor. I wrapped my arms around my knees and rocked myself without conscious thought while I stared into the night.

"'E's lying, Saira."

I shuddered. "Is he?"

"Archer's a Vampire. 'E'd survive anythin' to be with ye. And why would 'e even be in the Underground. 'E 'ates it down there."

"Archer, Connor, and Adam were searching for the mixed-bloods." My eyes couldn't focus on the landscape in front of me. Instead I saw the bomb in the ceiling of the British Museum ghost station. "An underground ghost station would have been a perfect place for Walters to hide them." I shuddered, and the motion was entirely involuntary. "If we hadn't changed the past – if that bomb never exploded in 1944, it would still be lodged in the station." My voice was as empty as I felt, and whatever strength I'd used to animate my body was slipping away. I relaxed my arms and loosened the fetal ball I'd curled myself into, letting my head loll on the ground. "I'll take you whenever you want to go, Ringo. Just let me sleep for a minute. I'll be okay."

I didn't even have enough left to say the words – they came out as a strangled whisper. I could feel Ringo's eyes search my face, but I didn't look at him. I closed my eyes and let everything go.

ARCHER – PRESENT DAY

I opened my eyes to blackness. The sheer, impenetrable darkness was the same whether my eyes were open or closed, so I attempted to use my other senses to gather more information.

The air was cold … and damp … and I lay on a stone floor. The smell of something like sewage was faint, but it wasn't exactly that. It was more … animal, and slightly familiar.

I tapped my hand on the stone floor next to me. The echo of the sound told me the space was small, but there was also a vastness to the air. I thought perhaps I was in a cell positioned off a larger cavern. I was certainly underground, but no longer in the London Underground, where the air was dry and smelled of oil and metal.

I also wasn't alone. Someone breathed nearby, and the sound was regular and even. The person was either asleep or had been awake much longer than I and was being careful.

A vision suddenly shattered the darkness in my brain. St. Brigid's School. Claire and Shaw together behind barricaded doors. Camille Arman pacing furiously behind them while a line of armed Mongers stood like watchful sentries outside the gates.

And then it came back to me. An explosion. The sun. And Seth Walters.

"Are you awake?" a young, male voice asked tentatively.

Tam. With green hair. He was a mix himself, with Seer and something else. I listened hard for another breath – a Wolf, or another boy. There was none.

"The Wolf?" I whispered. My voice was completely foreign to my ears, and I tried again. "What happened to the Wolf?"

Seth and his goon had taken us from the collapsed passage. What had they done with Connor's Wolf?

Tam's voice came from about five feet away. "I don't know where he is. Hang on a second and I'll try to let Tink know you're alive."

He was silent, and I ran his words through my brain twice before I realized what he had actually said. "Who is Tink?"

There was fondness in his tone. "A Seer friend of yours. Looks like a little blonde fairy, you know, like Tinkerbell?"

"Ava," I breathed. "Ava Arman. You're her leprechaun."

He snorted. "Because of the hair. I guess that's fair."

I allowed myself a small smile at his tone. "You can talk to Ava?"

"Not with words, only images. She's not answering right now, but when she does, I'll picture you opening your eyes. I already showed her how dark everything is here. Hopefully she'll get it."

"Have you explored this place?" I asked.

"We're in a cell of some kind. The door is heavy wood, and from the feel of it when I kicked, it has a bar across the outside."

"And obviously underground, near enough to the water tables that this place floods occasionally." I said quietly. "Have Walters or any of his men returned?"

"I only woke up ten minutes before you did, and there's been nothing." He was silent another moment, then he moved and his voice came from a few feet higher. "You told me you injected a cure."

The words had no meaning for a moment, and then the memories slithered back. The vial Connor had given me, which I had injected as I lay dying from the accumulation of several lifetimes of injuries. I let my mind wander over my body as I tested for pain. It was there, and I was surprised that I hadn't been consumed by it when I first woke. The fire of gunshot wounds, only partially healed before I injected the cure, the deep, fierce ache of impact injuries, the burning pattern of stabs and cuts seared my torso and back.

I lay there long enough cataloguing my various pains that Tam asked again, "Did it work?"

"I don't know," I murmured, even as I remembered the water and the touch of sunlight. I was afraid to hope.

"You were in pretty bad shape. I did what I could, but that passage didn't have a lot in the way of medical supplies. I was glad to find water at least."

Fear trickled through my veins. "You touched my blood?"

He snorted without mirth. "You were dying. What else was I going to do?"

"You could be infected …" I struggled to sit, and the pain was enough that I nearly didn't.

"It has probably been a couple of days, and I don't claim to be any sort of Sucker expert, but don't you think I'd have started to turn into one by now if I were going to?" The exasperation in his voice gave way to something cheeky. "And if I were a Sucker, I'd need you alive to feed from anyway, so my motives for helping you were completely self-serving."

I began to like this young man. He reminded me, in a way, of Ringo. My mind circled around what he'd said. "Tell me about my wounds. What bled?"

Tam seemed to rearrange himself, and I pictured him sitting back against a wall. "Well, you're a right mess of scars and old wounds, and it looked like you got shot someplace you'd been stabbed before – that was the worst bleeder. Another bullet went through and through, and I can't tell whether the third is still in there or not. For a time right after you injected yourself, you seemed to bleed from all of it – every old scar and wound you had. But I could tell none of those was going to kill you. The dangerous ones are the new ones." A wry smile entered his voice. "I thought Suckers were immortal, but you're pretty much anything but that."

I struggled to pull myself up into a seated position, and every muscle, sinew, and bit of skin hurt doing so.

"Do you need help?" Tam asked.

I did, but I wouldn't admit it. "Tell me what you have learned from Ava."

Tam rustled in a pocket, then groped his way across the floor to me. His hand hit my leg rather than my torso, thankfully. I reached for it, and he helped pull me forward. Then he pushed what felt like a water bottle and a plastic-wrapped bar toward my hand. "Here, I'll tell you while you eat."

My throat closed with some emotion I wasn't prepared to deal with, and then I realized how very parched I was.

I picked up the water bottle and twisted off the cap, then put it to my mouth in an utterly unfamiliar motion. The water hit my lips, so oddly wonderful, and I very nearly gulped it.

"Hey, slow down. You'll make yourself sick," said Tam.

I pulled the bottle away from my mouth, astonished. "It's been more than a century since I could drink water."

He stared at me. "You're joking."

It was the last thing I felt like doing, but I tried to rise to the occasion with irony. "Vampires can only digest the platelets in blood, and we rarely have a sense of humor about it, so no, I'm not joking."

"You're more than a hundred years old?" he asked, incredulous. "You look like you're in your twenties."

I smiled. "I was born when Victoria was queen, and as remarkable as that may be to you, the fact that I've drunk water is far more remarkable to me." I found I was indeed very thirsty, but I took Tam's advice and drank slowly. I didn't think my abdominal wounds would do well with vomiting.

Tam's voice was thoughtful. "Are you hungry?"

I considered his words. Was I hungry? I felt the plastic-wrapped thing he'd pushed at me.

"What is the bar you gave me?"

"Granola. They had packaged snack foods in the passage where we were trapped, so I shoved some in my pockets."

I smiled ruefully. "Is there anything else? I haven't eaten food in more than a century either, and a granola bar wasn't really what I dreamt about as a first meal."

His voice betrayed his wince. "Yeah, that wouldn't be my choice either." He rummaged, then groped for my hand again. "Will almonds do?"

They were in an individual package, but there was at least a handful. "Remarkably well. Thank you."

Despite the fact that the nuts had been preserved in plastic for who knew how long, they were more flavorful than I could have imagined. There were moments that I actually struggled to concentrate on Tam's words because I was so delighted with the sheer overwhelm in my taste buds.

He told me what Ava had shown him before Walters found us, when we were still buried in the Underground. Adam had gotten the mixed-bloods out through the tunnels, but they'd had to spend a full day in a crossover passage before they could travel far enough down the tracks to escape the Mongers who now roamed the streets in packs. Seth Walters had wrested control of London through liberal use of the Monger ring. He now had Scotland Yard reporting to him, and had apparently been seen with select members of Parliament. Much worse, though, were his speeches to the regular citizens on street corners and in city squares, beginning with the night of the bombing. His messages had begun with condemnation of the terrorists who had bombed English soil, and then grew to define who the "terrorists" were.

Ava had shown Tam that anyone with Descendant blood who wasn't a Monger was at risk of being called out as a terrorist. The only reason Bob Shaw and Claire Elian weren't in custody was that they'd barricaded themselves behind new wards Miss Simpson had set around St. Brigid's, along with Adam, the mixed-bloods, and the rest of the Arman family.

So, it had been a vision I'd Seen. Fascinating. My Sight had previously been spotty at best, and those images had been crystal clear.

I interrupted Tam frequently for as much detail as he could remember from the pictures Ava had shown him. The MacKenzie Shifter Head had fled back to Scotland with one son, leaving the other behind somewhere in London. Millicent had also gone to St. Brigid's, and Jeeves had stayed behind at Elian Manor with Liz Edwards. Apparently, Walters wasn't touching Liz because a grieving mother searching for her child in the bomb rubble suited his purposes well.

"You've told Ava that Walters found us, and that Connor's Wolf was with us?" I asked.

"I did – just now when I woke up. She's gone to tell her parents."

Connor's Wolf needed medical attention, but we had no idea if he had managed to escape when Walters took us. He was strong though. He would pull through this. I had no room for any other possibility.

"Did Ava have any news of Saira and Ringo?"

Tam cleared his throat. "Saira's your wife, yeah?"

The new memories of everything that had happened in France, from our walled garden wedding to the confrontation with George Walters and Tom Landers on a ghost station platform, were burned into my brain.

The last time I saw my wife, I had just pushed Ringo into her and sent them both through a spiral. She screamed, and my heart had torn in two. I shoved past the images of fire, blood, and oblivion, and instead, found the picture of Saira's eyes gazing back at me with so much love it drowned out the horror. I absently rubbed the bare spot on my finger where my family's ring had once been and felt an overwhelming sense of peace that it was now on Saira's hand.

"Yes, she is," I said.

"You spoke to her a lot while you were unconscious. A little raving, a little moaning, but always to her."

"That's not surprising," I said. "She's the first person I want to talk to every morning and the last one every night."

Tam was silent for a moment. I heard a drip of water hit the stone floor somewhere in our cell. "That's what love should be I guess." He opened a packet of something plastic and spoke through a mouthful of crisps. "Tink hasn't seen your wife. She did see her cousin though, right after the bomb exploded."

"Tom? Tom was here?" That surprised me, though I wasn't sure why. Saira had sent Tom through the spiral on the ghost station platform right before the shooting began. I'd assumed he'd gone backward in time, but he could have just as easily gone forward.

"He scared Tink. Apparently there was a moment she Saw the violence in him. But when he went in search of her brother in the tunnels, the violence quieted."

"And did he find Adam?" Tom had been Adam's best friend, but the cousins hadn't seen each other since Tom had been turned by Wilder.

"Yes, but Adam won't talk about it. Tom's gone though. He went back to find Saira."

That bit of news was as unsettling as anything else Tam had said. It could be taken many ways, and I realized it wasn't fair to assume Tom meant any harm to Saira, but the last time I'd seen the young Vampire he had been on a most effective self-destructive bender.

Frankly, I didn't trust him.

SAIRA – TRAVELING SOUTH, 1842

Tom had effectively severed the connection between my brain and my spine with his words. I hadn't been able to stay focused, or even conscious, for more than a few minutes at a time since … I didn't really know how long.

Since he'd told me that Archer was dead.

The thought would have been crushing, if there had been any part of me left that felt anything.

No, Tom hadn't *told* me, he'd spat it at me as though I was his worst enemy and the news was his coup de grâce. In a way, I supposed it was.

I didn't exactly lose consciousness when I lay down in those woods somewhere in France. I just lost … will.

I had a vague recollection of Ringo picking me up and carrying me back to the coach. He laid me on the backward-facing bench and then had a heated conversation that I didn't care about hearing while someone – probably Mary – dressed me. My next memory was of waking to the motion of the coach and the concerned face of Mary, who watched me from the opposite bench. Ringo sat next to her, staring out the window at the passing sky, and it seemed to be hard for him to drag his eyes to me. I didn't know where Tom was, and I didn't care.

I didn't care about anything.

I didn't even care that we were still traveling south toward Rome. Mary treated me like a mental patient, which was probably

the only reason I responded to her at all. She fed me and helped me
out of the coach to the privy wherever we stopped. I functioned on
a kind of survivalist autopilot, shivering when I was cold, sweating
when I was hot, but doing nothing about either of them until Mary
noticed and adjusted my clothing accordingly.

Sometimes, to break the deathly silence, Mary told us stories,
but I drifted in and out of consciousness so often I lost the plots.
Later, I saw Amélie sitting solemnly on Mary's lap during the
stories while Barney, the opossum, played with her hair.

Once, Amélie gave Barney a direction in French, and he came
over to my bench and offered me a nut. I couldn't make my arm
move to take it, and Barney chattered at me in frustration. He
finally used one little spidery hand to shove the nut between my
lips. I chewed it a couple of times and swallowed the jagged edges,
and Barney seemed satisfied enough to leave me alone.

Amélie watched me curiously, then tugged on Mary's sleeve
and asked her for another story.

Michel took us all the way to Turin, where he helped Mary
deposit me in a train compartment. I was vaguely unhappy to be
back on a train, but I couldn't muster the energy to protest. In fact,
I didn't think I'd spoken in days. Mary went to buy tickets and left
Ringo to his own devices. I managed to direct my eyes to him, but
he avoided them and sat looking out the window into the night.

Just before the train pulled out of the station, Mary returned
with Tom. He sat in the corner of our compartment, as far away
from me as possible in the small space. I could study him at my
leisure because he steadfastly refused to meet my eyes.

We traveled in silence the whole way to Ancona, alternately
sleeping, staring out windows, or avoiding each other's eyes. I
began to spend more time awake than asleep, and I started noticing
details about my companions.

Mary was very often out of our compartment. She brought me
food and helped me to the privy, but she left the guys alone to fend
for themselves. Ringo was utterly silent, but it wasn't a stealthy
silence – that was too active – it was more the absence of sound

that surrounded him. He wouldn't meet my eyes, and I had the sense that when he did look at me, he didn't register anything he saw. Tom's avoidance of me was much more active, and it seemed tinged with guilt. He avoided my gaze and always sat as far away as it was possible to be. Yet I noticed he didn't leave our compartment very often, and only when Ringo or Mary was there. It was as if he was afraid to leave me alone.

With more detailed observations came more awareness of myself. I began to smell like a long-unwashed body, and my hair, even pulled back into a pony tail, was oily and lank. Mary had been able to get the equivalent of about one meal a day into me, and my normally slim-fitting trousers felt loose and saggy. She had made me use a toothbrush and tooth powder, but I could tell that even forcing that much grooming was wearing thin on her.

Mary was getting sick of us.

"I'm sorry, Mary," I said as she pulled her valise down from the overhead luggage rack at the station in Ancona. My voice cracked and squeaked from disuse, and she started at the sound of it. When she turned toward me I expected to see annoyance and resignation on her face. Instead, she wore the most beautiful smile.

"Hello, lovely. It's nice to see you again."

I must have lost brain cells in the catatonia, because it took a few moments of mulling the sentence over before I understood that she meant *I* hadn't been present.

"Can I help you?" I asked weakly.

Her smile grew even wider. "Yes, you certainly could. If you could walk on your own power to the Rome train, it would help me immeasurably."

I understood enough to nod sheepishly. Obviously I hadn't been carrying my own weight at all, and I was startled to realize I didn't know how long I'd been so helpless.

I stood carefully, and despite the weakness from disuse, my muscles were still toned enough to support me with only minimal swaying. Ringo roused himself from whatever absence he'd been stewing in, grabbed our satchels, and followed us out of the compartment.

"What about Tom?" I asked.

Mary's eyes met mine. "He will meet us tonight at the home of my friend, just outside Rome. He is in a coach, and the driver is under the impression Tom has consumption, so he won't be bothering him until they arrive."

"Oh." The complexity of their arrangement surprised me, and I was momentarily distracted from the effort it took to walk across the platform to the train bound for Rome.

Once Ringo and I were settled in another private compartment, Mary left to deal with our tickets. Ringo had placed himself at the window again, as he'd done since we'd learned about Archer.

Pain seared my chest at the thought of Archer's name, and it surprised me how glad I was to feel it. I hadn't felt … *anything* in days. Even if the feeling hurt worse than any injury I could imagine, it was a feeling. It had substance and depth, and it provoked a physical, mental, and emotional response in me.

I recognized it as part of me, and it made me want to rip more of the bandages off.

"Ringo?"

His head turned toward me slowly, and his eyes were a fraction of a second behind, as if he couldn't bear to let go of the scene outside the window to focus on anything else. When his eyes were finally on mine, I sucked in a breath.

I had never seen emptiness in Ringo's eyes. Not ever. No matter how sad or angry or tired he'd ever been, Ringo's eyes always flashed with life. Ringo did not have dead eyes.

But there was nothing there.

"Ringo?" My voice was suddenly desperate. I needed to see some spark, something that was uniquely Ringo.

He submitted to my searching gaze just long enough to realize I didn't have an actual question, and then his gaze slid away toward the window again. A sob tore from my chest, and I dove across the compartment to sit next to him. I drew his unresisting arm around myself and looked into his face. His eyes were unfocused again as they stared out the window at nothing in particular.

He could have been chiseled from stone for all the animation there was in his face, and I had a sudden urge to slap him, or tickle him, or kiss him – something … anything to get a true reaction.

So I kissed him - on the edge of his jaw, near his ear. I let my mouth linger there and breathed in the scent of his skin. He smelled like home, like family, like laughter and love, and I closed my eyes to remember.

"What are ye doin'?" he ground out through his teeth.

I leaned back so I could see his eyes. They had finally focused on me, and they flashed angrily.

"Waking you up."

"I'm not Sleepin' Beauty," he snarled, "and I don't want to be awake."

I narrowed my eyes at him and pulled his arm away from my shoulders. "Why are we still going to Rome?"

He closed his eyes and sighed. It was the most human and vulnerable sound I'd ever heard him make. "Because I didn't want to be the strong one," he said quietly.

"Oh Ringo."

I put my arms around him and gathered him to my chest like a little boy. He resisted at first, but then his shoulders trembled, and he began to shudder as great, wracking sobs escaped him and bled into the fabric of my shirt.

I held him and we rocked a little in rhythm to the movement of the train, and when he could breathe again without the air catching on a sob, he sat up and screwed the heels of his palms into his eye sockets. He was avoiding my gaze again, so I spun in my seat and laid my head down in his lap facing straight up his nose.

He stared at me. "What the bleedin' 'ell are ye doin'?"

"You're going to need to trim your nose hairs pretty soon."

He glared at me. "And ye need to wash yer 'air. What of it?"

"I missed you," I said. The view up his nose was pretty terrible, and I was going to have to move soon. But not yet. Not while he was still talking to me.

"Ye weren't 'ere to miss anyone."

"I missed me, too."

He swiped at a stray tear and nodded solemnly. "Yeah."

"What are we going to do?"

He started to speak, then shook his head and shrugged his shoulders.

It was an answer I understood.

"Yeah," I whispered.

I watched his eyes, and they watched mine. Ringo had interesting eyes, full of gold flecks and prone to squinting in the sun, or at a fascinating book, or with laughter.

"I liked it when ye kissed me, but then ye smelled me and it got weird," he finally said. The corners of his mouth were tight, like he was trying to hold in a laugh, so I reached up and flicked his nose.

"Jerk," I said as I burst out laughing.

He couldn't keep a straight face, but still tried to hide his laugh behind his hand, so I sat up and tickled him, and he wrapped his arm back around my shoulders to hold my arms to my sides. "Ah, Saira. I love ye too much."

"Too much for what?"

He shrugged and wouldn't say more, no matter how much I threatened him with tickles.

We ended up talking for a long time, mostly about Archer, and some about Mary and Tom. Ringo had told Tom that for whatever wrong he thought I'd done to him, we were now even, because he had hurt me worse than anyone could ever imagine.

At first Tom had stayed away from me, riding up front with Michel and Amélie on the coach. But then, on the train, he had stayed in the compartment with me, maybe afraid of what I'd do if I were ever left alone. Ringo said that before Tom left the train to find a covered coach to travel through daylight, he looked at me with something like compassion.

I almost scoffed at that, but a wave of tiredness hit me and knocked the scorn right out of my voice. "I wish I could make things better for him somehow," I sighed.

Ringo's arm was still around me, and the heat of his body, with the rocking of the train, was like a sedative. I closed my eyes and snuggled in.

"Yeah," he whispered.

MARY'S FRIEND

We arrived in Rome several hours before Tom's coach was due, and Mary had us all taken directly to the estate of her friend, Signora Schiattesi, on the outskirts of the city. I recognized the name, but I wasn't sure from where, and I still felt like I could barely use my brain for more than basic functions.

The instant we entered the walled estate, the noise and crowds of Rome vanished. The house was hidden from the view of the road by massive trees that covered the property in dappled light. A fountain sat in the middle of the drive, and I was seriously tempted to take off my boots and splash my feet in the water.

The villa itself looked like a Moorish palace, rising from the lush garden with towering walls of rich, orange-red stone. Mary explained that the Signora's lover of many years had gifted the villa to her, and although Mary and Percy had stayed there many times, their visits had never overlapped with his.

Mary had sent word ahead about our arrival, so when the coach came to a stop in front of the villa, the doors opened and a woman came out to greet us. She looked to be in her fifties, with long, pure white hair that had been haphazardly tied up with a strip of cloth. Her dress sleeves were covered in red, orange, and brown paint, and two small paintbrushes were stabbed into the bun at the back of her head. Mary bounded out of the carriage like a teenager and flew into the woman's arms, and the woman's remarkably unlined face broke into a delighted grin.

"Oh, Mary! I'm so glad you've come!" she said in Italian-accented English.

"Mia, these are the friends I told you about. Saira Elian and Ringo … I'm sorry, I don't know your family name," Mary said in embarrassment to Ringo.

"It's Devereux," he said quietly. If Mary was surprised, she didn't show it.

"Ringo Devereux, Saira Elian – this is one of my dearest friends in all the world, Artemisia Schiattesi." She smiled proudly and waved her arm with a flourish.

Ringo made the connection just before I did and shot me a quelling look when my hand went automatically to my satchel. He was right, I'd been about to pull Artemisia's emerald out of my gem bag.

"Ye're an artist," he said with wonder and, I thought, admiration.

Her friendly interest shifted into surprised intrigue. "I am. How do you know this?"

He hesitated only a moment before indicating her sleeves. "If the paint on yer sleeves and the brushes in yer hair didn't give it away, yer name would. I saw yer self-portrait in the Royal Collection during a public exhibition for the queen last year." He stumbled very slightly over the last words because last year was probably 1888. Good thing Queen Victoria had such a long reign. He recovered with a genuine smile. "Ye look very much the same, Signora."

She laughed delightedly and shook Ringo's hand. "You are a charming liar, *caro*, but I will accept your compliment with grace and only a little skepticism. I was twenty-three in that portrait your queen collected– I am sixty-three now." She shook my hand with equal grace and a smile that made me feel like I was the only person she saw.

"Miss Elian, I believe I know of your Family. It is very lovely to meet you both." I couldn't tell if she knew my last name as just a name, or as an Immortal Descendant, but based on her association with Mary, I thought anything was possible. Artemisia watched the hired coach drive away with consternation. "But what of your luggage?"

Mary laughed and took her friend's arm in hers. "That is a story best told after baths, with wine. Shall we?" The two women turned and walked into the villa. Ringo and I followed a few feet behind.

"My emerald—" I whispered.

"Shhh, I know," Ringo murmured back.

"Have you really seen one of her paintings?" I watched the women walk ahead of us into the arched entry hall of the villa. Spectacular oil paintings hung on the walls, and I gasped quietly.

"Wow," Ringo whispered in awe.

We stared around us with open mouths and huge eyes, and I felt a tiny piece of the despair that had filled my world with shadows break off and open a window to light. The color and glow emanating from each canvas reminded me very strongly of Caravaggio's work, yet the subjects of the paintings were all women. The men were utterly peripheral to the stories told in the paintings. Artemisia's women seemed strong and capable, like they were the heroines of their own stories rather than men's. It might have been a subtle thing to someone else, but to my eye, it was as obvious as if each painting had been tagged in neon spray paint.

Artemisia sent Mary to her room with a servant and then returned to our sides. "Too much, no?"

"No," Ringo said decisively.

"They're extraordinary," I said at the same time.

"*Grazie.*" She sounded surprised. "It is not often people like them." Her accent was thick and musical, though her English was excellent.

"Who could say a bad word about any of this?" Ringo asked in honest confusion.

"Men, most likely," I responded.

"And some women who do not trust my past," she said.

Ringo studied the paintings for a moment, then finally nodded. "I see it now. Sometimes the weak are threatened by strength."

Artemisia considered him thoughtfully. "Come, after baths, as we wait for your friend, we will discuss women and art, for they are the most wonderful topics in the world."

Ringo shot me a look of "uh oh," and I was surprised to realize I'd smiled. A servant led us to rooms on the second floor of the villa overlooking a glorious interior courtyard with a tiled fountain. My bath was definitely the best thing that had happened to me all week, and afterwards, I dressed in a long, white caftan that the maid had left when she took my clothes away to be cleaned. It had intricate embroidery at the wrists and around the v-neck, and wearing something so pretty felt strange and foreign, as though the insides of me didn't match the outside.

Mary met me in the courtyard wearing a similar gown, and Ringo joined us a few minutes later in a loose white shirt and pajama-like trousers of the same material. Mary explained that Artemisia enjoyed trips to the northern parts of Africa, and whenever she wasn't painting, she preferred the loose robes that Moorish men often wore.

It was full dark by the time we finished a light meal in the courtyard, and it was so nice to be clean and comfortable that I curled into a chaise with a glass of sweet Moroccan mint tea and just listened to Mary and Artemisia talk. They let me bow out of contributing to the conversation until Ringo returned from his walk in the front gardens, but finally, our hostess requested that we all join her in the salon.

The salon faced the gardens and had big windows that looked out on a small, glittering moonlit pond. The room was decorated like something from the Orient Express, with low divans, layers of Turkish rugs, and engraved brass trays on wooden stands to serve as tables. The same servant who had shown us to our rooms – an older Italian woman with an easy smile – brought a tray of glasses with a bottle of Italian wine and then drew back a heavy velvet drape on one wall.

Behind the curtain was a spectacular and horrible painting. A naked, bearded man lay on his back, covered by a red velvet bed coverlet. He pushed against a woman who held him down, while another women grabbed his hair and stabbed a sword through his neck. Blood sprayed from the wound and ran in rivulets down the white sheets of the bed. The violence of the painting was astounding.

Artemisia sipped her wine silently and watched as we took in the scene in front of us. The room was silent for a long moment, and I had the sense that even Mary hadn't seen this particular painting before.

Ringo met Artemisia's sharp gaze. "It's probably a good thing it's not hung in the dinin' room," he said mildly.

She burst out in delighted laughter and waved the servant in who had just appeared in the doorway. A quick exchange in Italian, and then she turned to us. "Your friend has arrived. Shall we see his reaction to Judith before I explain?"

I carefully schooled my expression into something totally neutral and said nothing. Mary stood to greet Tom, and Ringo got to his feet because the ladies did. Tom looked haggard and accepted Mary's surprising hug with reserve. He was tight-lipped but gracious as he met Artemisia, nodded warily at Ringo, and then turned his gaze to me.

"Saira," he spoke formally, "you're looking well."

I studied him in silence for a long moment, then sighed and got up. I took both of his hands in mine and gave him a kiss on the cheek. "Go take a bath. We'll talk in the courtyard when you're done."

He looked stunned but not, I was glad to see, angry. Ringo's eyebrows were up around his hairline, but he said nothing as Tom made his excuses to the ladies and followed the servant out of the salon.

"Quite a tragic young man, is he not?" said Artemisia.

It felt like gossip to talk about Tom with a stranger when he was out of the room, so I ignored the question and looked back at the horrific and beautiful painting. "You were about to tell us a story, I think?" I sipped the light red wine and curled my legs under myself. "When did you paint this?" I studied the people individually, examining fine details so the whole image didn't work on my imagination.

"A few years after I married. My father paid my husband well to accept his *soiled* daughter."

"You're no longer married?" As much as I wanted to ask about her use of the word '*soiled*,' I wasn't walking in that minefield unless she led me there.

"It was useful to cover the birth of my daughter. When she was born, his purpose was finished." Artemisia wore a radiant smile at the mention of her daughter, and it transformed her from a striking woman into a stunning one.

"How is Palmira?" Mary cut in, obviously wanting to skip over the part about Artemisia's daughter's actual parentage.

The gorgeous smile got even brighter as Artemisia waxed poetic about her daughter's marriage and her family in Naples. "Palmira's little son, Doriano, looks just like his grandfather with the same fair hair and the same playful nature, but of course no one would ever imagine their relation."

I was starting to get an itchy feeling at the back of my neck. Artemisia wasn't talking about the husband she'd left after using him to legitimize her daughter's birth. She was describing Palmira's father, a fair-haired playful man his grandson may have been named after? A man no one would think was the boy's grandfather.

I looked at the crease between Ringo's eyebrows and the itch got itchier. His brain was riding the same track mine was, and the train we were about to collide with felt too close.

I suddenly jumped up and smoothed the wrinkles out of my caftan nervously. "I … I need to … I'll be back." I bowed my head slightly to Mary and Artemisia to try to make up for my rudeness and then hurried from the room.

I found myself in the double-story entry hall, staring up at Artemisia's magnificent paintings. I tried not to think, but memories and stories and facts kept intruding on the carefully-wrought blankness of my brain. My hand went to my pocket, where I'd put the emerald Archer had bought for me from the gem dealer who could see the past written on stones.

"Are ye thinkin' about the woman, the art, or 'er lover?" Ringo asked quietly. I'd heard his light footsteps on the stone floor.

"All of them," I said, still looking at the painting. "These two guys, and the one being murdered in the salon, are the only men in her work."

"Do ye find that odd?" Ringo stood next to me and considered the painting in front of us.

"If her lover was the father of her now-married daughter, and she still speaks of him in present tense, where are the paintings of him?" I wanted to know what he looked like. I wanted to know if I was right.

Ringo knew why I'd asked the question, and he considered for a moment. "Where would ye keep a paintin' of Archer?"

I smiled with the sudden wave of memory. "I drew him once, and I stuck the drawing in the mirror of my bedroom."

He spoke carefully. "Maybe we should take ourselves on a tour of the villa."

I met his eyes, hesitated for long enough to look at my good manners and toss them over my shoulder, and nodded. "Yes, let's."

We started upstairs, as the logical place to find the master bedroom, and chose the wing opposite ours. The first two rooms were additional guest rooms, one of which appeared to be occupied by Mary. The third room was at the end of the corridor with a huge bank of windows that faced out toward the eastern garden. It was a huge room, the size of two bedrooms, and Artemisia had set it up as an art studio. Because the floor was wooden, much of it was covered by a large canvas sheet, and cupboards with slots for rolls of canvas dominated one wall. Paintings in various stages of completion were propped against the walls, and two easels stood proudly in the center of the room.

Moonlight made the east end of the room glow and was the only light we used to search the room. The other option was candlelight, which seemed to be a fairly bad idea in an art studio filled with oil paints and turpentine. Ringo strode to the semi-finished canvases, while I poked around in the cupboards first. The smell of the paints was like catnip to me – I inhaled deeply and felt the familiar giddiness that art supplies and small puppies always inspired. I trailed my fingers along the fine sable brushes, the course boar brushes, and a brush I had to smell to guess it was made of squirrel hair. I missed making art. I missed the rattle of the ball at the bottom of a spray paint can. I missed the hiss of the aerosol and the fine cloud of color that misted my clothes on a windy night. I missed the time when discovery was the biggest danger I faced, when gang bangers would give a reluctant nod to a fellow tagger with stealth and skill, and when secret alleys and hidden stairwells were my canvas.

I missed home.

I studied the sketch on the easel closest to the window. The outline was faint, but the image was unmistakably feminine. I smiled at the lush curves of the nude woman who reclined on a bed and looked happily up at a child who might have been Cupid. The painting promised to be beautiful, and I imagined I would see it hanging in a museum someday.

The other easel held a half-complete portrait of a young boy with fair hair and laughing eyes. The boy looked as though he had a secret and was holding back a fit of giggles. The boy had a familiar cast to his face, and I thought I'd seen him somewhere, maybe in the art downstairs?

"Oh … no," I gasped. I hadn't seen this boy in Artemisia's paintings. The few she had depicted were baroque angels with full cheeks and golden curls. This boy – this painting – was done in a post-impressionistic style; the style of artists like Van Gogh and Cezanne *who painted in the late 1880s.*

My suspicion was confirmed.

"I wondered when I'd see you again, Saira." A low, masculine voice came from the doorway, and I forced myself not to jump or turn or move at all.

"Hello, Doran," I said to his painting as Ringo spun to face the man himself.

"Are ye followin' us, then?" said Ringo.

"It would seem, in this instance, that you are following me." Doran's voice was careful and quiet, as though he were measuring his words.

I infused as much casual calm into my body as I could when I turned to face him. Doran looked as he always looked – like the guy who could step off a plane with nothing more than a passport and a credit card in his back pocket and be totally comfortable in any situation.

Doran had always irritated me so much with his enigmatic smile and his dribble of information that I had never really paid more than cursory attention to how attractive he was. The boy in the painting … Doriano – I chuckled – he had the same bright eyes as Doran, the promise of the same broad cheekbones, the same strong jaw.

"Your grandson is beautiful," I said.

I hadn't recognized Doran's expression as wariness until it softened. "He is, isn't he? Palmira was my treasure, but little Dorio – he is a playmate and compatriot and best friend all in one tiny, energetic package."

"Does Artemisia know you're here?"

He nodded, and the softness stayed in his eyes. "Of course. I arrived two days ago and stayed to meet her friend, Mary Shelley, whom I had heard so much about. Imagine my surprise to discover who else had joined us, though I admit, I was less than pleased to see the young Vampire enter the villa."

"Archer's dead," I blurted, and then I realized he meant Tom.

Doran's eyebrows rose. "Is that so? You've managed to Clock back to your own time stream then?"

I just accepted that he knew there'd been a split, despite the fact that we were having this conversation in 1842, before the split had occurred. Nothing about Doran surprised me anymore. I shook my head and Ringo answered for me. "No. Tom did – before the split happened."

"Ah, and you have reason to trust what he says?" Doran took a lantern off a shelf and pulled a Zippo lighter from his pocket to light it. The grinding sound of the striker was so incongruous in this Moorish villa without flushing toilets or running water that I almost laughed.

Warm lamplight bathed the room in the kind of glow Dutch painters loved, and I noticed that Doran actually looked almost relaxed. Almost.

"Lying about it would be pretty counter-productive. He wants to get back to the right time stream so he can try the cure Mr. Shaw's working on. Archer's dea—" I cleared my throat. "If Archer isn't there, it kind of puts a damper on my burning desire to risk myself to fix the split, you know?"

"I see," he said simply.

Doran strode to the window and looked out over the garden. Ringo stepped back, as though he wanted to disappear into the shadows, and I thought it was on purpose. There were a lot of pieces to the puzzle that was Doran, and confronting him never seemed to get me any closer to the answers.

I studied him while his back was to me. He wore a loose white shirt, the kind I'd seen seventeenth-century poets wear in paintings, and his hair was longer than the fashion of the times dictated. There was a spot of blue paint on the elbow of one sleeve, and my gaze returned to the painting of his grandson.

"Do you not age because you're out of your native time, or is there something else going on?" I finally asked.

He exhaled and turned to face me. "Why are you in Rome?"

Not going to answer the question, clearly. "I made a deal with Tom."

This time, only one eyebrow went up, in an expression that reminded me so much of Archer that my heart stuttered.

"Of what nature, may I ask?" He sounded a lot more British when his tone got arch, and I thought about getting annoyed but decided I was too tired.

"You can ask." I paused, and Ringo smirked. I turned back to Doran's painting. I actually loved post-impressionism, and the style was really kind of perfect for a painting of a kid because it often looked like a very talented child had done it. "Do you have a lot of children running around history, or is Artemisia's the only one?"

My question made him angry. I wasn't sure if it was the question itself, or if it was the you-scratch-my-back-and-I'll-scratch-yours nature of the exchange. I probably should have backed off if I really wanted answers, but the apathy I'd felt still lingered, and I really was curious.

Doran must have sensed this, because the squinty-eyed glare I'd gotten had been rubbed away in the kind of tired gesture people usually make when they're too old for this crap.

"Come," he said. "The terrace is a nice place to sit."

Ringo shot me a quick look as we followed Doran out of the studio and through a room that must have been the master bedroom. A big, rumpled four-poster bed dominated one end of the space, and a huge fireplace with low divans in front of it filled the other. I pointed to a gold-framed pencil drawing next to one side of the bed and looked meaningfully at Ringo.

He peered at it in the dim lamplight, then scoffed and shook his head. It was a portrait of Doran, laughing in a way I'd never seen him, happy and in love.

Doran either didn't or pretended not to notice our exchange as he led us through big folding doors to a terrace overlooking the interior courtyard. It was a breathtakingly lovely spot, and I thought that if it were my house I would move my bed out to the terrace to sleep.

We settled into settees so comfortable that I thought it likely they were often slept on. I looked down at the courtyard below. "Were you up here earlier, watching Mary and Artemisia talk?"

He looked down at the places by the fountain where we'd sat and nodded. "I love to watch her laugh. She does it easily with her friends, and there are so few I can allow myself to be seen by."

"You've been coming here a long time," I said simply.

He nodded. "I met Artemisia when she was sixteen. I'd come merely to paint with her father, but I left his studio feeling as though I'd met one of the Muses."

Whether he meant the Greek goddesses of the arts, or his own personal Muse, I couldn't tell, because the reverence in his voice fit both.

"She was nineteen when I returned to discover that two years prior, an art tutor hired by her father had raped her." I sucked in a horrified breath, but Doran continued grimly. "And although she sued him and won, the bastard got away with a slap on the wrist. After that, as one could imagine, Artemisia despised all things male."

Doran studied his hands for a long moment before he looked up at me. "It took two years of trying to make her smile for me to fall irrevocably in love with her."

"Why didn't you marry her?" I asked without thinking.

Pain flashed in his eyes. "I was called away by my father. I was gone for two months and hadn't thought to return the day after I left."

He meant that he Clocked away and should have Clocked back to the next day instead of allowing the two months to pass. I wondered, yet again, what Doran's native time actually was.

"Her father had already paid her dower, and he refused to back out of his agreement with Schiattesi. They were married, and only then did she finally admit that she loved me in return."

"Is Artemisia a Descendant?" I asked him carefully.

"No."

"But she knows about us?"

He gave a slight smile. "It would be rather difficult to explain this otherwise." He indicated himself.

I studied his face for a long moment – longer than I'd ever looked at him before. He looked relaxed here, and a little bit sad. I couldn't imagine what it must be like for him to watch the woman he loved age, although honestly, it probably wasn't any different than a normal human couple who gets old together.

"Tom wants me to help him steal the Monger ring," I finally said.

Doran looked at me in surprise while Ringo sat in the shadows of the terrace wearing his usual inscrutable expression.

"And you're in Rome in this time because the ring is here?"

Ringo leaned forward and spoke quietly. "It went missin' from the Vatican in 1842. The next time the ring showed up in

Descendant records was in 1871 – on Rothchild's 'and – during the Council massacre."

"And you couldn't go there, for obvious reasons," Doran said.

"The only other person we know had it for sure was George Walters in 1944 – he was wearing it when the bomb exploded in the British Museum ghost station."

"The explosion that split time," he said.

"We all spent time in 1944 before the explosion, so going back to find George and the ring before we got there is sort of a needle-in-a-haystack."

Doran shook his head. "Coming to 1842 to find the ring in the Vatican isn't?"

"The pope 'as it," said Ringo in a tight voice. I didn't think he liked agreeing with Doran about anything, and coming here to steal the Monger ring was definitely not his favorite plan.

Doran scoffed. "Which is approximately like saying 'the king has it.' Vatican City has its own army, and despite their ridiculous uniforms, the Swiss Guard are quite deadly."

"Have you ever been inside? Can you Clock us in?" I asked.

"My dear cousin, I cannot help you with this. My involvement in anything you do breaks a great many rules, and puts people I love very dearly in danger." That statement opened a big box of questions, but it was clear Doran's patience had ended. He stood and waited for us to do the same. Considering we were on the balcony of his bedroom, he couldn't exit dramatically without making sure we left too.

Ringo stepped into the bedroom, but I blocked the doorway and turned to face Doran. We were nearly the same height, and there was a familiarity in his face that I found oddly comforting, even though he usually set my teeth on edge. "I'm sorry that we're putting people you love in danger, and I'm really glad to know there are people you love. You've actually been pleasant to talk to here, Doran, unlike every time you've popped by to drop a verbal bomb on me."

He smirked a little, and then seemed to make a conscious effort to smile. It was a nice smile – definitely not something I was used to seeing on Doran's face. "We tend to become slightly more tolerable when there are people who love us."

I smiled in return. "Well, I wouldn't go that far."

He laughed, and the warmth of it was startling. I searched his eyes, which were almost emerald green and strikingly like my own. "I have a feeling that there's a lot more to you than just a Clocker/Shifter mix."

"Everyone has a story, Saira. There's a lot more to you than just a Clocker/Shifter mix as well."

"I have people I love, too - people I may never get to see again if we can't get this ring."

His smile faded. "I can't interfere."

I stepped closer, and I was too close for my own comfort, but I wouldn't break Doran's gaze. I could feel Ringo's eyes burning holes in my back, and I wasn't really sure what I was doing, but I didn't step back.

"Then tell me something true."

"I've never lied to you," he said quietly.

"Tell me something I can use, even if I don't know what it means yet." His resolve was starting to waver. I could see it in his eyes, and I took a half-step closer until our faces almost touched. Tension pulsed from Ringo behind me, but I refused to let go of Doran's eyes. "Tell me about the Monger ring." He flinched almost imperceptibly, but I was too close to miss it. "It doesn't belong to the Mongers, does it?" He flinched again, and my eyes widened. "You knew that?" Doran's eyes had gone slightly flinty, and I suddenly had the sense that the man in front of me knew Duncan – and didn't like him.

My eyes searched his looking for truth. "Whose ring is it? Who is meant to have that power?"

The silence was thick and brittle, and it cracked when he spoke. "Here's something true, Saira. The ring is mine."

A PORTRAIT

It was a verbal atom bomb and he knew it. Whatever open easiness I'd seen in Doran had vanished, as if he hadn't meant to say that out loud. He pushed past me into the bedroom and strode to the door.

"Doran, wait!"

His shoulders tensed and he spun to face me. He was angry – at me? Probably. At himself? Definitely. "I'm leaving now, and I won't be back as long as you remain in this time. You've invaded my sanctuary, Saira – be mindful of that."

His tone was harsh, and he stalked out of the room with aggressive urgency. I turned to Ringo and whispered, "He has a spiral in this house."

Ringo nodded and went after him in the quietest stealth mode he had. My own feet were rooted to the spot as I stared at the open door through which my cousin had just stormed.

He called me his cousin, but was that just an honorific because we were both descended from Jera, the Immortal Time and … Goran, the Immortal Nature? How was it even possible that the Monger ring belonged to Doran? And if it really did belong to him, was he even worse than the Mongers for being the rightful owner of a ring that controlled people's will? The power to compel was a real thing – I'd seen it in action, and its effects were devastating. Who was Doran that he needed such power?

I scanned the room wildly, as if I could find any clue to the mystery of Doran in the place he called his sanctuary. He was right, we had invaded the home he shared with the woman he loved, and part of me wanted to leave right then and there so he could come back. But honestly, Doran had always made me want to throw things, usually at his head, and now more than ever.

My gaze landed on a small painting on the side of the bed I assumed was his. It was of the two of them together, Artemisia and Doran, maybe painted about ten years before, given that her hair was lit with streaks of white, but was still mostly black. It looked like something Maxfield Parrish could have done in the 1920s, in a saturated, neo-classical style that wouldn't be popular for another sixty or seventy years. The most striking thing about the painting, besides the anachronistic style, was the similarity to something else I'd once seen. Artemisia looked straight out of the canvas at me, while Doran gazed at her with utter and complete devotion in his eyes. It was the same way Jera and Goran had looked in the painting of the Immortals at Elian Manor.

It was the way Archer sometimes looked at me when he thought I couldn't see him, and I wished I had a photograph or a painting of us like this. The fact that Doran had painted this of himself and Artemisia made me think I might not necessarily aim for his head when I threw something at him.

I wanted to be alone when I left the bedroom. Or, more precisely, I wanted to be alone with Archer. The sinkhole in my chest felt wide and deep, and I tested its edges carefully. It didn't seem quite so much like the pit of despair and apathy that it had been the past few days, but it still had those freshly-dug sides that could collapse and cause a giant chasm if a wrong step was taken.

The art studio, with all its comforting smells, beckoned to me. I lit a lamp and found a small canvas, and with a charcoal pencil, I began to sketch.

Ringo found me in there about an hour later. He must not have been looking very hard, or he was sick of me and wanted a break from the drama. Probably both. I didn't look up from my drawing when he spoke.

"There is a spiral. It's in the kitchen garden at the back wall."

"Clockers love their gardens," I said, putting a finishing touch on the ring I'd just drawn. It was on my hand as I touched Archer's face. Instead of one person looking out and the other making gooey eyes, we looked at each other. All the longing and missing and love I had in my heart had oozed out onto the canvas and worked its way into the eyes of each figure. I knew Archer's face from memory, but I had stumbled a little on the way his shirt sat against his collarbone, and the way his hair fell at his ear. I had panicked then and had to close my eyes and breathe through the fear of losing any part of my memory of him.

"If I 'ad to guess, I'd say it's practical more than emotional. Ye 'ave less chance of Clockin' into someone when ye come into a garden."

"Why do you think he didn't turn around and go back to Artemisia the day after he left her, once he realized his mistake?" I rubbed some pencil into Archer's shirt to shade it. My mind had been spinning on everything I'd learned from Doran, and this particular train of thought was just the most recent.

Ringo leaned back against a wall and crossed his arms in front of him as he watched me work. "'E said it 'imself. It wasn't until she was married to someone else that she could admit 'er feelin's for 'im."

"So you're saying she had to go through those two months without him, and the whole sham of getting married, just so she could figure out that she really loved Doran?"

Ringo studied me and I met his eyes. "Don't forget what 'e said about 'er bringin' suit against her attacker. Can ye imagine 'ow strong a woman 'ad to be then to do what she did?"

I shook my head and sighed in disgust. "The fact that she could trust another man at all is impressive."

"Exactly. Maybe she needed that time to work through whatever 'eld 'er back from lovin' Doran, so, even though 'e missed out on marryin' 'er, in the end 'e got the prize of 'er 'eart."

I'd gone back to work on my sketch while he talked, and there wasn't really anything else I could do to it except fill it in with color.

I'd been inspired by Artemisia's baroque style, and had worked with the shadows and light on our faces so it looked like we were illuminated only with candles. It was anachronistic in its own right, as the 1800s were considered the era of the romantics, but I liked the effect. We had been in shadows and light our whole relationship, and I wondered, if we'd had more time together, could we ever have found the golden neo-classic light of a Maxfield Parrish painting.

"Archer 'as always looked at ye like that," Ringo said, indicating the drawing.

"I miss him so much." I whispered the words to the canvas, as if he might be able to hear my words through it. I touched the lips on his drawn face lightly, then tucked the drawing into a slot in the wall cabinet. "Maybe I'll get a chance to finish it while we're here," I said as I wiped the charcoal off my hands on a piece of towel.

"Tom's waitin' for us in the courtyard."

I sighed. "I'm kind of done with the drama for the moment, you know?"

"As ye've been known to say, we're steppin' right over that big elephant in the room." Ringo closed the door to the studio behind us as we left.

"The fact that the ring with the power to compel apparently belongs to my mixed-blood cousin?"

We took a different staircase down – one that led directly to the courtyard below. "Makes a person wonder if 'e's one of the good guys, doesn't it?"

The night was still warm, and fragrant from flowers that climbed a wall near the door. I took a deep breath. "Despite … everything, I don't think he's one of the bad guys."

"As much as I 'ate to admit it, I agree with ye."

Tom waited for us at a table near the fountain. The light fall of water was the kind of white noise a person could fall asleep to, and it added to the peacefulness of the space. No wonder Doran called it his sanctuary.

There was wariness in Tom's expression, and I didn't blame him – he probably expected me to go off on him again, now that

I'd climbed most of the way out of my apathy-laced despair. The bath had done him good though, and he must have eaten fairly recently because his resting corpse-face had filled out enough to be considered chiseled rather than emaciated.

Ringo and I sat down at the table. "Have you seen the art here?" I asked him. My question surprised him and I could see the mental switching of gears.

"Not a big fan of men," he said.

I shrugged casually. "We heard a rumor that she got a commission at the Vatican." It's what Yaniv, the gem dealer, had told us about Artemisia when I showed her Archer's emerald. "It may have already happened, or it might still be yet to come, but sometimes these things have a weird way of working out when you need them to."

"You're still going to help me?" Tom asked warily.

Ringo leaned forward. He and I hadn't discussed any of this since we left London. Then again, I hadn't even really thought this all the way through until now.

"On one condition."

"What condition?" Tom's voice was hard and tight.

"I'm giving the ring back to its owner."

Ringo stared at me incredulously. Tom scowled and then looked back and forth between us.

"Wait, I thought you didn't know whose ring it is," he said.

"We do now."

"Saira," Ringo's tone held a warning in it, and my eyes flicked to him quickly before they went to Tom.

"I take the ring to the owner and it'll be out of Monger hands. That's what you want, right?"

"How do you know the owner won't do exactly what the Mongers have been doing with it?"

I shrugged. "I don't. How do I know you won't stab me in the back the next time I turn around? I. Don't. None of us does. But sometimes you just have to trust that you know what's right."

"So you agree that stealing the ring from the Mongers is the right thing?" Tom sat back in his chair and crossed his arms.

"I think fixing the time stream split is the right thing. If stealing the ring is the way to get your help to fix time, then at least giving the ring to its rightful owner takes it off my plate of responsibilities. I don't like the ones I already have; I don't want to add more."

He sounded surly. "I'll think about it."

I laughed completely without mirth. "No, you won't. You'll agree, or I'm leaving tonight. Seriously, Tom, I don't want to be here. So if we can't agree on this, I'm out."

He glared at me and then pushed his chair back from the table. "Fine. When we get our hands on the ring, you can take it to whomever you want, just as long as it isn't either of my fathers or a Monger."

I smiled at that. "Deal. Not your dads or a Monger."

He reluctantly added his own smile, then quickly covered it when Artemisia entered the courtyard. "There you are. Mary has gone to bed and I have no one to talk to." Ringo and Tom rose from their seats at the sound of her voice. I knew Ringo had the habit from having grown up in Victorian England, but Tom's manners were a surprise. She waved them both back down. "Sit, sit. I'll join you."

"Have you ever worked at the Vatican, Artemisia?" Now that I'd actually decided to step in this whole thing with both feet, I was anxious to pull my boots on.

"I have painted there," she said, "for the past ten years."

I shot Ringo a quick, triumphant look, then returned my gaze to our hostess. "I need to get inside the Vatican. Can it be done?"

She sat back in surprise. "Women are not welcome inside the city walls unless they are selling or cleaning something."

"How do you get in?" I asked.

"There's a tunnel entrance that the washerwomen use. A priest leads me through that tunnel to the place I work. I am painting in the Tower of the Winds now."

"Can I go with you? Maybe carry your paints or be your assistant?"

Artemisia studied me for a long moment, and I held my breath. "Doran told me about you. If I take you there, will you leave my house so my heart will return to me?"

I exhaled. "Yes. I just need to see some part of the Vatican's interior, and then the three of us will leave you alone." Artemisia nodded, and I touched her arm. "I am sorry for having caused you both discomfort. We'll be gone tomorrow night if I can see the Tower of the Winds with you during the day."

"Thank you. He is dear to me. I must keep time sacred with him when I can, because it is never enough."

"I understand," I said quietly.

Artemisia and Tom seemed like they were going to be up late, so I said good night and left them to their conversation. I needed sleep if I was going to function the next day, and Ringo followed me to my room. He stood at the window and looked out at the moonlit landscape while I brushed my teeth and washed my face with water from the pitcher on the dressing table.

"Ye're looking for a place to Clock us in?" he asked.

I nodded with a mouth full of cinnamon tooth powder. It was nasty stuff, but it did the job.

I took a sip of water and rinsed. "I'll try to get as much information about the place as I can. I hate going in blind."

He scowled. "Ye and me both." He waited until I'd climbed into bed before he turned around to face me. "Ye're plannin' to give the ring to Doran?"

I nodded. "I don't want it, and I don't want anyone else to have it, so yeah. It makes sense."

"It's a good idea," he said finally.

I hadn't been expecting that. Ringo had taken Archer's job of watching my back so seriously that I sometimes felt like his first answer was always going to be no. "Thanks."

"I'll see what I can find in the way of supplies while ye're with Artemisia. Any requests?"

I smiled. "The Venetians made beautiful glass beads, but they probably don't sell them in Rome."

He shook his head. "Glass beads. Ye manage to surprise me every time I think I have ye figured out."

"Thinking we have anyone figured out is usually our first mistake," I said as I blew out the candle. I was thinking about Doran and the life he'd kept secret.

Ringo closed the door softly behind him when he left, and it was a long time before I could sleep.

Artemisia and I arrived at the entrance to the tunnel at about noon. I was dressed in my own masculine clothes with my hair tied back and a hat to hide my feminine features from a casual glance. I carried Artemisia's box of paints and was introduced to the priest at the gate as her apprentice.

The priest led us through two other checkpoints and by several of the gold-and-crimson-striped Swiss Guard before we were finally handed off to another priest who answered a knock on a very heavy door.

From there we were escorted down a flight of stairs inside the cool, dark interior of a long corridor. The entire place was lined with shelves, and on the shelves were leather-bound bundles of papers. Stacks and stacks of the bundles filled the shelves, and I had a sudden sense of reverence for the place. It felt like a library, but filled with records instead of books. The air wore the heavy scent of old parchment and oiled leather, and the bits of light that drifted down though ceiling grates illuminated the dust in the air like tiny dancing stars.

The priest walked with heavy footsteps, and Artemisia's lighter ones were a sharp staccato above them. I practiced a silent walk, made easier by my rubber-soled boots. The lack of any sound from me seemed to go a long way toward making me invisible to the priest, and I wasn't going to break it with all the questions I wanted to ask. So instead, I studied as much of my surroundings as I could see from our path.

There appeared to be doors set back in the walls of the corridor between a few of the shelving units, but all were closed and likely locked. One of the doors had a noticeably cleaner handle than the others, and I made some assumptions about its frequency of use. That piece of information got filed away, along with the door's location and proximity to the end of the tunnel.

We reached the end of the corridor, and rather than go up the main staircase to what I assumed was the exit, the priest unlocked a door on the right side of the tunnel, then directed us up the winding staircase while he locked the door after himself.

I wasn't a fan of that whole locked door business, especially since the key had been kept not in the lock, but rather on a heavy iron ring attached to the priest's belt.

Artemisia and I made it to the top of the stairs before the priest was halfway up, and I was glad for the distance because I just barely stopped a squeak from becoming a squeal when I saw the room there. It was spectacular and covered in floor-to-ceiling sixteenth-century frescos that spilled color across every surface. The ceiling was about twenty-five feet above my head and painted with glittering stars. Carved into the floor were names of what I recognized as different winds: Tramontana, Scirocco, and Ostro.

"It is the Tower of the Winds," Artemisia said in a hushed voice, "and the most beautiful room in the whole world."

I'd never seen the Amber Room in the Catherine Palace in Tsarskoye Selo, or the Alhambra in Granada, or the Hagia Sophia in Istanbul, but I had seen the Trinity Library in Dublin once on a trip with my mother, and in my opinion, it was what heaven for book lovers looked like. This room, in a tower at the Vatican, made the Trinity Library look like a shoe box.

The priest only stayed long enough to ensure we weren't going to complain to his bosses about him – at least that's what I made up, because the only thing I could understand of his perfunctory conversation with Artemisia was his tone – and then he left us alone in the tower.

Of course I immediately bounded down the staircase to test the door, and yes, he had locked it. I studied the substantial iron lock and thought Ringo could probably pick it if he had the right tools. Then I checked out every nook and cranny of the construction of the staircase and the room until I was satisfied that, with the exception of a window overlooking the roof of the nearby gallery, the Tower of the Winds had only one way in and one way out.

"Do they always lock you in here when you come?" I asked Artemisia as she set up her paint palate.

"Always. They do it not to protect me so much as themselves from me. I am a woman, and so I am dangerous to them."

"They should be so lucky to be corrupted by a woman," I grumbled under my breath.

She smiled. "It is true."

"What was the shelf-lined room we went through to get here?" I asked.

"That is the secret archive."

My interest perked up immediately, as it would with any room that had the word 'secret' in its name. Artemisia laughed at the expression on my face. "It sounds, how do you say … mysterious?" I nodded enthusiastically, and she continued. "The secrets are only those of the popes. It is a library of their letters."

"There could be letters from the English priests who tried to get King Henry VIII's marriage to Catherine of Aragon annulled," I said, not to be dissuaded from the seductive allure of secrets.

"Or perhaps Leo X's excommunication of Martin Luther?" Artemisia supplied. I appreciated that she seemed to share my passion for the controversial stuff in history. She directed my eyes up, about ten feet down from the ceiling. "Do you see that hole there?"

Now that she pointed it out, I couldn't believe I'd missed it when we walked in. It wasn't a large hole in the wall – maybe the size of a silver dollar – but it was definitely a hole through which I could see daylight. "Yeah, what is that?" I asked.

"Every year at noon on March 21st, the sunlight shines through that hole …" she traced an invisible line with her finger "… down to the center of the floor. It is the spring equinox."

"This was built as an observatory?" I asked in awe.

She seemed surprised I knew such a thing, and she nodded. "*Osservatorio*, yes, and there was a time Queen Christina of Sweden stayed here when she first came to Rome."

I helped Artemisia spread a canvas sheet on the floor under the section of wall she was currently restoring. "I don't know anything about Queen Christina of Sweden."

Artemisia sat cross-legged on the floor and began to touch up the ship in a scene that looked vaguely biblical. I sat next to her, and she handed me a brush from the bun at the back of her head.

"Take this. You can restore the frame."

My heart stuttered and I didn't trust myself to speak. I could actually help restore a painting in this magnificent room? The idea that my work could contribute in any small way to the grandeur that was the Vatican was incredibly humbling, and I set myself to the task of repainting the chipped details of the frame around the fresco she was working on.

As she launched into her story, Artemisia seemed unaware of the huge honor she'd just given me. "Queen Christina was the daughter of the Swedish king – I do not remember his name, but he ruled in the early 1600s. She was adored by her father, who instructed that she be educated as a prince would be."

"Same thing happened to Elizabeth Tudor," I said unthinkingly.

Artemisia seemed a little startled at the familiarity in my tone. "Perhaps not so odd a coincidence as some might think. They were both quite accomplished women."

"I'm guessing your father only saw your talent, not your gender, when it came to training you as an artist. I went to school in a place where men and women are educated equally," I said, weighing my words carefully.

Artemisia looked thoughtful for a long moment. "To go to school would be a remarkable thing. Doran has taught me much about history, but there are things I don't know to ask." She studied the detail of the work I was doing on the frame, then looked at me in some surprise.

I smiled as I concentrated on the shading so the swirls of paint looked like they'd been carved from wood. "I've had some training, yes. My mother is a painter."

Artemisia seemed delighted by this information. "Please repair any part of the fresco that attracts you. I do this part so I can sit and talk with you while I work, but you may paint any part of the walls that you wish."

I grinned and continued my work on the frame while I asked, "Would you tell me more about Queen Christina?"

Artemisia laughed and proceeded to tell me historical anecdotes about the seventeenth-century Queen who had been crowned as a king, declared her intention never to marry, and then abdicated her crown after ten years to convert to Catholicism. "Christina liked that Catholics valued virginity as Lutherans did not," Artemisia said.

I couldn't help the bark of laughter that escaped. "The value of virginity? That's almost as bad as the concept of a dowry. It's like 'here, let me pay you to take my daughter off my hands so I don't have to feed and clothe her anymore.'" Too late I remembered what Doran had said about Artemisia's father paying a higher dowry to get her husband to take her, and I cringed. "I'm sorry, that was callous of me to say."

Artemisia shook her head. "No, you are correct. The only dowry I would allow Palmira was a chest of china and linens. I wanted a love-match for my daughter, and happily, she found one." She contemplated the fresco in front of her, and then looked at me. "My church cares for the poorest and weakest of humanity, yet I, too, find the value placed on virginity to be oppressive, as it has been the means to control women."

Our conversations turned to art – to the baroque style she favored, which was one likely reason she was the artist chosen to restore the Tower of the Winds, and to the various styles with which Doran consistently surprised her. She always demanded an education in whatever style he used, and was under strict instructions to keep her knowledge to herself.

I asked Artemisia whether she had ever had a problem with the fact that Doran wasn't aging. She shrugged, "And what would be the purpose of that? My time with him is limited to the span of my life. I will not waste a moment of it considering something as fleeting as my own beauty."

I liked Artemisia. She was an interesting companion, and working alongside her was as inspiring as it was challenging. We worked side-by-side for about five hours, only taking a short break for some bread and cheese.

I did go check the door at the bottom of the stairs again, and then I borrowed some white paint and used my fine brush to paint a nearly invisible spiral onto the wall right behind that downstairs door. The stairwell wasn't lit properly, and when the door was open, the spiral would be hidden behind it. I'd gotten good enough at disassociating myself from Clocking when I didn't want to that I didn't even feel the familiar hum in my bones as I completed the design. I studied the stairwell and then pictured it with my eyes closed just to make sure I could Clock us back here tonight.

When a priest finally came to escort us out, Artemisia and I had finished the restoration of two whole panels of the painted wainscoting. On our way back through the archives, I tried to find any more doors that looked as utilized as the one with the shiny door handle, but as far as I could tell, that was the only one. The corridor was utterly silent, but the priest hurried us through it like his pants were on fire and the bucket of water was outside.

I was surprised to find that there was still daylight, because it had been so dark and gloomy in the archives. When we emerged at the other end of the tunnel, Artemisia's coach waited for us. Once we were inside with the door shut, she sat back and breathed a sigh of relief.

I narrowed my eyes. "You were nervous about having me with you."

"There is a bishop close to the pope whose sole responsibility is the 'reformation' of the fallen, the lost, the heretic, and the infidel. He knows I am a *fallen* woman, and I have felt his gaze on me as I've gone to and from the tower to work. I felt it again today." She held my gaze. "I love that tower, Saira. If there is God anywhere on Earth, His spirit infuses that room with all the color and light and beauty of His being. That room is *my* church, and to be denied it would be like blinding me."

I stared at her in shock. "And you risked that for me? I'm so sorry. I would never have asked for your help if I'd known what you stood to lose if you were caught."

She reached over and touched my hand gently. "*Cara mia,* Doran has told me enough that I would help you where he cannot. I've done what I can now. The rest is up to you."

I took her hand and squeezed it. "Thank you," I whispered fervently. I looked out the window at the city as we passed it by, and I wondered how I could possibly repay all the people who had helped us.

"You must succeed," Artemisia said quietly, as if she'd read my mind.

She was right.

Vatican Night

Ringo, Tom, and I left for the Vatican at midnight. Artemisia gave us permission to come back to her villa to sleep safely if we needed to, but it was understood by all of us that she would prefer we didn't. I had gone to Mary Shelley before dinner to explain our plans and to thank her for having cared for me – for all of us – when I couldn't.

"My dear, there is a time in everyone's life when they lose someone they hold very dear, and nothing is so painful to the human mind as great and sudden change. Just as the most useful help one can give a new mother is to cook and clean and manage her other tasks so she can care for her babe herself, it is also the most useful help one can give the newly bereaved. You needed to find your own way through the labyrinth of pain, but at least I could keep you safe while you did so."

I had hugged her for a long time. "Thank you, Mary. I felt mothered by you, and it was the nicest feeling I've had in a long time."

Her eyes were shiny when she kissed me on both cheeks. "I am glad Aislin's vision sent me to find you. Live now, and be happy, and make others so."

We Clocked through the spiral Doran had carved for his personal use inside the walled garden, and it was an easy transition to the bottom of the stairwell in the Tower of the Winds. Ringo wanted to work on the lock immediately, but I made Ringo and

Tom climb the stairs to see the spectacular room at the top of
them.

The effect of the frescos was very different at night by the
light of the small flashlights we carried, but the gasps of
appreciation from the guys were the same as mine had been. I
showed them the work Artemisia and I had done that day, and then
pointed out the small hole high up in the wall, perfectly positioned
for the equinox sun. I had described everything I'd seen in the
secret archives earlier, and we all agreed that the well-used door was
a good place to start our search for the ring, since it seemed to be a
place to store things valuable to the popes. Ringo went back down
the stairs to work on the lock while Tom lingered in the tower
room and stared up at the walls.

"Artemisia calls it her church," I said quietly.

"If this were a church, I might actually believe in God again."
Tom turned away and left the room without a backward glance.

It only took Ringo about five minutes to pick the lock on the
door, and moments later we were inside the secret archives of the
Vatican. The grates in the ceiling provided the only light, and
whatever moonlight there was outside gave the space a dim glow.
The grates also meant we couldn't use our flashlights, because
artificial light might be visible to someone outside. My Shifter sight
came in very handy at night. As long as there was a little light, my
Cat could adjust my eyesight to see in the dark. Tom had enhanced
eyesight as a side effect of the Vampirism, and Ringo was a former
thief, so none of us were blind.

I reached out as far as I could with my Cat's senses, and I felt
the stillness of the room in every corner and around every
bookcase. We barely breathed as each of us used whatever skills
we'd developed to determine the obstacles we faced.

When Ringo finally exhaled, I knew he felt the emptiness of
the room too, and I stepped out into the main corridor. The guys
filed in behind me, and we clung to the bookcases, away from the
barely visible bands of light that shone down through the ceiling
grates. Ringo tried the handle on every door we passed, and every
one of them was locked.

The well-used door was also locked, and there was no key above the door lintel. The priests at the Vatican didn't have the lazy or over-confident habit of leaving the key close by, so Ringo went to work very quietly with his lock picks.

I used the time to poke around the bundled letters in the stacks. There was an embossed letter "G" on the spine of one stack, and I unwrapped the leather and then bent over the letters so I could shield my flashlight with both my palm and my body.

I couldn't read Latin, but I thought I recognized the name *Galileo* written on the page. The handwriting was beautiful – tight and elegant – and I wished I could trace the letters to learn the style. It was with reluctance that I finally re-tied the leather around the bundle and replaced it on the shelf.

I heard a barely audible click, and then the door opened. I didn't say "you're a genius" out loud, but my slight squeeze on Ringo's shoulder told him anyway. I was about to step through the open doorway first, as had become my habit, but Tom stepped in front of me and shot me a look that dared me to challenge him. I almost did on principle, but then waved my hand in the universal 'you first' gesture. I was tired of battling him.

I was tired of being at war.

Ringo caught my eye as he paused to close the door behind us. He was tired too, and I was forcibly reminded that he was only there because he felt compelled to watch my back. He had no other horse in this race, and I thought the strain of *not* saying what he really thought was wearing on him.

I waited for him, and he stopped beside me. I leaned in so I could breathe the words instead of whisper them. "What's wrong?"

He shook his head, then flicked his gaze down the corridor. This passageway was lined with closed cabinets, and the available light was much dimmer than in the main archive. Tom was about ten feet ahead of us.

"Reach out with yer senses," Ringo breathed in my ear. "Somethin's not right."

I was startled by his certainty, and I let my Cat come to the surface again. My gaze down the corridor sharpened, and I could sense something just outside her range. Something … no, whatever it was, it had gone.

I had tensed, so Ringo knew he was right.

Tom was too far ahead for us to verbally warn him, so we ran silently to catch up. I slipped in front of Tom to block his way, but Ringo tapped him on the shoulder and then instantly ducked when Tom spun around fist-first.

He was about to say something, but Ringo's face silenced him. I tried to hear past the pounding of my own heart, but there was too much motion left in the air around us. It took a few seconds for everything to still again.

It was there again – the something I'd almost felt before. It was closer now and … there it was.

"Monger," I breathed silently.

They both heard me though, and so did my Cat. She came up even closer to the surface of my awareness and used her senses to feed me information. "In the next room," I mouthed as I gestured toward the door at the other end of the passage.

Tom crept forward and leaned his ear to the door. If it was possible to be even more silent than before, we were, and the air barely even moved around us. A distant-sounding clearing of a throat made the hair on my arms stand straight up, and all of us visibly tensed. Then the sound of slippers scuffed the floor on the other side of the door, and I held my breath. Finally, they moved away, growing fainter until eventually a door opened. When it closed again and there was silence, I remembered to exhale.

Tom held a finger up to forestall any whispers while he tried the doorknob carefully. It was locked, of course, and I almost laughed out loud at myself for imagining it could be anything else. When the silence in the other room continued, Ringo knelt down in front of the door, and with the precision of a surgeon, picked the lock and opened it – even faster this time than the last.

No one moved, and Tom's tension had leaked into the air around him until I could feel it crackling like static electricity. Ringo finally took a tentative step forward, and then another, and this time I was right behind him. Tom fell into step with us as he shut the door silently behind him.

A single lantern had been left burning on the desk, and I looked back with a moment of panic to find the door we'd come through had disappeared. But it was just hidden in the paneling of the wall, and Ringo had already found the catch to release it.

When he was satisfied that he could open it again, he gave me a quick thumbs-up and we ventured farther into the room. The fact that the lamp had been left lit made me nervous, so I looked around for places to hide. There was a long settee with a high back against a far wall that might offer a short-term solution if someone came in unexpectedly. There was also a large cabinet across from it that looked like it could hold one or maybe two of us in a pinch.

Tom went to the desk and rifled through it quietly.

"What are you looking for?" I whispered.

"You felt a Monger, right? Well, every Monger in this place is a potential ring-bearer. I just want to know whose office this is." He was growly, even at no volume, and I looked sharply at him.

"What's wrong?" I peered at him in the dim light of the lantern. Stress was visible in his face, and every muscle in his body seemed tightly coiled and ready to spring. My own expression filled with concern. "Seriously, what's going on?" I whispered.

Tom fingered a sharp, dagger-shaped letter opener on the desk. The biting words he had been about to fling drained away, and he sagged very slightly. "I don't know. I can't get enough air …" His whisper faded as he shifted his eyes away. He wouldn't meet my gaze and I shot Ringo a worried glance.

Ringo held up a hand for attention, and then we all heard it – the return of shuffling footsteps.

Ringo dove behind the settee while Tom and I leapt for the cabinet. We pulled the cabinet closed just as the office door opened.

I was smashed against the back wall of the cabinet with Tom's back pressed against my front. I could feel the pounding of his heart in my own chest, and a wave of Monger sickness washed over me. I stifled a gasp against his back and clutched at him to keep my knees from buckling. Tom had never affected me so strongly before, and my Cat practically screamed her danger warnings in my head.

I struggled to control my instinct to fling open the door and bolt, and forced myself to concentrate on slow, rhythmic breaths. Finally, my heart rate dropped enough that I could think logically.

Tom's Monger half had usually only caused a vague sickness in me, except during the war when he was a direct danger to us. Maybe he still hated me, which was entirely possible, but I had never been this sick around him before, even at his most dangerous.

So maybe it wasn't Tom who was making me ill.

I made my fingers relax their grip on Tom's coat, and he exhaled softly. My tension had affected him too, or maybe it wasn't just because of me – maybe the person who had just entered the office was the source of distress for both of us.

I had reacted so strongly that I hadn't been able to hear movements around the office. When I focused my attention back to the person in the room, I heard what sounded like the shuffling of papers on the desk. I forced my Cat's natural flight instinct down and got my panic responses under control.

The paper shuffling stopped, and the chair scraped back from the desk. I held my breath. Tom's heart hammered into my chest through his back, his shoulder blade dug into my chest, and he practically quivered with strung-out tension. I had the random thought that he would not be my first choice of someone to spoon with on a cold night.

The shuffling footsteps resumed, and I sincerely hoped the person was headed back out the door. The Monger sickness was still in full force, but I had managed to rein it in to the point that I was functional, and my hearing was super-tuned to the motions of the person in the office. So when the shuffling footsteps halted suddenly, my stomach lurched.

There was a pause, and then, "You there!"

The voice was male and English, but more than that I didn't have time to register because Tom threw open the door and lunged out of the closet.

I stumbled into the room and then stared in utter horror as Tom hurled himself at Bishop Wilder.

228

THE BISHOP

"Noooooo!" I screamed. My Cat surged to the surface wanting to break free, and I struggled to hold her back.

Ringo threw himself at Tom, but Tom had locked onto Wilder with the iron grip of every corded muscle in his body.

"*Aiuto!*" the bishop bellowed as Tom plowed him into the desk. Ringo tried to grab Tom's arms to pull him off Wilder, but Tom didn't even seem to notice. He was completely focused on killing the man who had tortured him.

Tom got one arm around Wilder's throat in a headlock and pulled back with all his strength. The man's windpipe was being crushed, and he was turning red under Tom's grip. Wilder flailed wildly, knocking papers off the desk as he grabbed for something to break the hold that was strangling him.

I wrestled for my own control, forcing my muscles to lock so I couldn't Shift. The sound of pounding feet in the hallway outside the office caused a fresh surge of fear to fuel my Cat's grab for power. I couldn't tear my eyes from Tom and Bishop Wilder, but I couldn't move to help Tom without losing my grip on my human form.

"Watch it, Tom!" yelled Ringo as Wilder grabbed the letter opener and plunged it into Tom's hand where it gripped the desk.

My nightmare had come true.

Tom roared and scrambled for the knife. Wilder spun out of his grip as Tom yanked out the knife and freed his hand. Blood spurted from the stab wound and then blossomed from multiple old wounds in his torso, but before Wilder could dance out of the way, Tom lunged forward with the knife.

"No!" I screamed.

The office door slammed open and knocked Wilder out of the way just as Ringo grabbed Tom's elbows to hold him back. Tom yanked himself free, but the four Swiss Guard who charged into the room stood between Tom and Wilder with deadly halberds crossed.

Tom could have easily wrenched his arms from Ringo's grip, but with two quick moves the guards would have taken his head off with their halberds. I took a step forward and stumbled.

"Tom!" I cried out in anguish. "You're bleeding."

He blinked as though he only just became aware of his surroundings, and looked down at his hand, still clenched in a bloody fist. A wet stain of blood had spread across the back of it where the letter opener had gone in, and his palm was smeared with it.

Wilder snarled something in Italian to the Swiss Guard who tried to help him up, and he shook off the help. Wilder turned his eyes to Tom in a hateful glare.

"You will pay for this!" he growled in English. Then he gestured toward us and gave a command in Italian that sounded like "take them away."

The three of us were unceremoniously marched out of Wilder's office by Swiss Guard who neither knew nor cared who we were or what we had to say. But honestly, there wasn't anything *to* say. We had been caught inside the Vatican after hours, in a private office, and one of us had attacked a bishop. It didn't get much more red-handed than that. The guards were so well-armed they didn't even bother to search us for weapons. We had left our bags at Artemisia's villa, and the only things I carried on me were my daggers, a small tin of green medicine, and my mini Maglite.

I studied the guards that surrounded us. They moved with calm efficiency and utter certainty of their deadliness should we make a wrong move. Despite their ridiculous crimson-and-gold-striped clothing, they moved with the coiled confidence of a special forces unit, and I knew it would be very bad for my health to resist whatever they planned for us.

We descended to a level deeper than the one on which the secret archives had been housed, and it suddenly hit me that we were going to the dungeons. I had never heard anything about dungeons in the Vatican, but of course it had them. To punish heretics, the Catholics had invented some of the cruelest tortures in history, and a city ruled by the pope would be the headquarters for that kind of nastiness.

So, we had that to look forward to.

The walls around us were made of stone blocks, and the air was cold and smelled fetid, like damp gym socks that had been dipped in blood before being tossed in the corner to mold. I stumbled on a step and Ringo's hands flashed out to steady me, even as the guard closest to me shoved me backward.

"Thank you," I said under my breath to Ringo. He was glaring at the guard and didn't hear me. I looked closely at him and realized he was just barely keeping it together. I glanced at Tom and found him also wound tighter than a spinning top. I, on the other hand, was completely and possibly disturbingly calm about the whole thing.

The lowest level opened into a decent-sized room. One of the guards who had lit our way with a lantern went in first. Rats skittered away into the darkest corners to escape the light, and I watched in idle fascination as one rat ran across the floor in such a panic that he fell through a metal grate. There was a scuffling movement below, a terrified squeal, and then silence.

Something was down there.

Hopefully we weren't about to join it.

When the guard with the lantern had decided there were no unexpected boogymen in the corners, he said something to his fellow guardsmen and all four of them filed out of the room without a backward glance at us. The heavy wooden door slammed shut, and the crossbar thunked into place on the outside.

We were left in complete darkness.

My Maglite was out of my pocket and on first, though Ringo was right behind me in the illumination department. He went straight to the door to check how locked in we actually were, and I turned to Tom to see how the stab wound in his hand had healed. Before I could speak, Tom seemed to just crumple in place, sinking into a heap on the dirt floor.

"Tom!" I rushed to him, and Ringo warned me with a sharp tone.

"Watch 'is blood, Saira!"

I ignored Ringo, sank down to my knees in front of Tom, and reached for his face. I cradled it in one hand while I shone the flashlight at it with the other. Tom stared at nothing and didn't even blink in the light.

"Hey," I said softly. Somehow the different tone of voice drew his eyes to mine. He stared at me in silence for a long moment, and then his eyes began to fill with tears.

"He's here," Tom whispered.

I pulled him to my chest and held him close. He didn't make a sound or touch me in return. The shivering began then, and I clutched him to me and tried to quell his tremors while I gently rocked him.

"Shhh," I murmured. "You're safe, Tom." It maybe wasn't the best thing to say to someone in a dungeon, but at that moment it wasn't a lie.

Gradually the shaking subsided, and Tom pulled back from my embrace. He scrubbed at his face and left a smear of pink behind on a cheek from the blood on his hand.

"Are you still bleeding?"

He cleared his throat and shook his head. "It closed up when they were bringing us down here."

"That took too long though." I looked at the hand that had been stabbed. His coat and shirt sleeve were stained dark red. "You lost a lot of blood."

He barked a bitter laugh. "I don't miss it."

"If ye don't mind me askin'," growled Ringo, "what the bloody 'ell is Bishop Wilder doin' 'ere at the Vatican?" His street accent had been diminishing bit by bit since I knew him, but he reverted back to it with gusto when he was angry.

"How did he know I was here?" There was genuine anguish in Tom's voice, and Ringo snarled, clearly impatient with Tom's self-pity.

"'E didn't know ye. 'E didn't know any of us. 'E's dead. We killed 'im in 1429 after Orléans, and we burned 'is body. That's not the man who tortured ye, Tom. That's the man who will." Ringo's tone was harsh, and his words felt like a slap.

"I'm sure you mean to be helpful, Ringo, but seriously?" I said.

Tom looked like a cornered animal again, and I reached out to him. "Hey, it's going to be okay. We're going to get out of here, okay?"

A rustling sound came from beneath the grate in the floor and we all froze. Whatever was down there sounded bigger than a rat. Much bigger.

I looked up at Ringo with a question in my eyes, and then an ancient-sounding voice cracked. "Saira? Is it really Saira Elian?"

My eyes widened in shock, and Ringo strode to the grate and stood over it. He shone the light down into it and then inhaled sharply. "Jesus, Mary, and Joseph," he said in a stunned voice.

"They had little to do with it," said the voice again from beneath the grate. There was the tiniest hint of humor in it, and suddenly I recognized the speaker.

I got up from the floor so suddenly I almost fell. "Bas?" I cried out, half-panicked, and totally horrified. I stared down through the grate and swayed against Ringo at the sight of our friend, for it really was our friend Bas, the eleventh-century Moorish Vampire we'd spent time with in France – first in 1429, and then again in 1944. "Oh God! What are you doing here?"

"Despite pretensions to the contrary, I'd say God is scarce in this place at the moment," he said, squinting up at me. Ringo shifted the beam of light away from his face, but not before I registered the extent of the horror that the beautiful man had become.

He was emaciated, and his normally warm-toned brown skin
was ashen and gray. His cheekbones and jaw, formerly strong and
chiseled, were sharpened bone under taut bearded skin, and the
bones that circled his neck looked like a metal collar. Old scars
covered his bare torso, and his only clothing was a pair of tattered
cotton trousers stained dark with dried blood.

The hole he stood in was a stone-lined pit, just deep enough
that he couldn't reach the grate over his head, and just wide enough
that he could sit but not stretch his legs or arms out to rest. Ringo
had already bent to grip the heavy metal grate.

"Saira, 'elp me so it doesn't fall on 'im."

I quickly threaded my fingers through the holes in the grate
and lifted. It was heavier than I expected, and even with two of us,
it was hard work to pull the metal high enough to clear the stones it
was seated in. When we finally hauled it to one side, Ringo laid flat
on the ground and hung his torso into the hole, reaching his arms
down to Bas.

"'Ere, take my 'ands," Ringo said.

Bas shook his head. "No. It's been too long since I've eaten.
I'm dangerous to you."

I huffed and leaned back over the hole to see him. "You look
approximately strong enough to catch a turtle, and I'll slice a vein if
I have to so you can have my blood."

Ringo spoke in a grim tone. "Between the two of us and our
knives, ye can eat if ye don't get greedy. But ye'll 'ave to lick the
blood when it runs down our skin, because we can't afford yer
infection."

Tom came to stand by the edge of the hole. He looked down
at Bas, and his tone had an accusatory edge. "I know you."

Bas peered up at him, squinting through the indirect flashlight
beams. He regarded Tom for a moment. "I don't know you."

Tom shook his head. "Yeah, during the war. You were in the
church that burned."

Bas' eyes shifted to mine. "I have a feeling that is an
interesting story."

I looked pointedly at Tom. "It hasn't happened yet."

Tom looked startled for a moment, then he turned his accusing look to me. "How do you know a prisoner in the Vatican dungeons?"

I nodded. "Bas helped us get to Orléans." The part I didn't say was *so we could fix a time stream split and get back to kill Wilder and find you*, since I was pretty sure that was what fueled Tom's hatred of me.

Tom regarded Bas for a long moment, and I had the sense I was watching a dominance battle in the wild. Maybe it was a Vampire thing, or maybe it was a man thing – whatever it was, the whole thing was done wordlessly, with the eyes. Bas never broke eye contact with Tom, which was very interesting given his pitiable condition. And despite how young he was, Tom didn't look away.

"What happened to you?" Tom finally asked.

"Let's get him out of there before we start grilling him, okay?" I was impatient to do something to help him so I could Clock us all out of there.

"We still haven't addressed the fact that I'm exceptionally dangerous to you all right now," Bas' tone was mild, but I sensed tension and maybe urgency underneath his words.

"Not to me, you aren't," Tom said.

I made a sound of frustration, but Bas tilted his head a little as he regarded Tom. I was reminded that Bas had been a Shifter Eagle before he'd been turned, and he hadn't lost the gestures of a bird of prey.

"I was drained of my blood and apparently expected to die in this pit. I was unconscious when they threw me in here, so I'm not entirely sure of his motives." Bas relayed the information as if he were listing ingredients to a recipe, with no emotion whatsoever, but I gasped out loud anyway.

"Whose motives?" Tom asked carefully.

Bas waved weakly in a dismissive gesture. "The bishop who deals with all the heretics, one of which I've been assured repeatedly I am. An older, distinguished English fellow of Duncan's Family."

"Wilder." Tom said in a flat tone.

Bas looked mildly surprised. "Yes, that's the name. Wilder. You know him?"

Tom scowled, and I struggled to contain the scream of frustration and horror that had been building since we encountered Wilder in this time.

There was an echo of sound somewhere above us – the clang of something metal – and I jumped.

"Saira, get started on a spiral," Tom ordered. I almost resisted, but he had already turned to Ringo. "Help me lift him out, but I'll do the pulling." Tom gazed grimly at Bas. "You can drink from me until you're strong enough not to need them, but know that I will kill you if you try to take more than I'm willing to give."

There was another clang above us, but closer. It sounded like doors slamming shut. "Do it, Saira!" Tom's tone didn't allow for argument, and I was a little surprised I didn't push back automatically. Instead, I grabbed one of my daggers out of its sheath, knelt down to the hard-packed dirt floor on the opposite side of the pit from the door, and started to carve spirals into the dirt.

Tom switched places with Ringo to reach down into the hole to grab Bas' outstretched hands, while Ringo held Tom's legs. Between the two of them they yanked the other Vampire up fairly easily, and they were all at my side as I finished the fourth spiral.

"Hang on to me," I said as I concentrated on the image in my mind. "I'm taking us back to the Tower of the Winds." I was dimly aware of hands at my waist and Tom's voice speaking to Bas.

"You don't touch her. Here … take my arm."

And then we were Clocking, and there were more people with me, so it was harder and it hurt more. The tile floor of the stairwell leading up to the Tower of the Winds was cool under my hands, and I pressed my cheek to it to steady myself while the dizziness passed. When I could sit up again, I found I could see by the flashlight still clutched in Ringo's hand. Tom and Bas were apart from us by a foot or two, and when I saw them, I recoiled with a start.

Bas held Tom's arm to his mouth, and he was sucking greedily at a vein. "Stop!" I cried out reflexively, but Tom's grim face turned to mine.

"I've got this, Saira."

He had this. I shifted my startled gaze away from Tom and Bas and busied myself crawling up the stairs to the painted room. I crossed to the window shutters and cracked one open to look out at the night sky.

Tom brought Bas up the stairs, then murmured something under his breath to him. A few minutes later, Tom came to stand beside me at the window. The view from the Tower of the Winds looked out on a long, straight tiled roof that connected to another complex of buildings at the upper end of the rectangular gardens.

I turned to study his face as he looked out the window. "Are you okay?" I asked quietly.

"No, but blood-loss isn't my issue," he answered.

I looked behind me. Bas sat on the floor near the door, his head in his hands and his back heaving with each breath. He was so painfully thin, but his skin was less ash-colored, and his cheeks had a slight flush to them.

I returned my gaze to the view outside and asked Tom, "So, what next?"

"I kill Wilder," he said simply.

"Again?" My voice was tired. I was tired.

Ringo stepped up behind us, and I knew he'd been listening. "Ye'll just splinter time again if ye do," he said.

Tom closed his eyes and took a shaky breath. "Why is he even here?"

"That's a good question. Why would an English bishop of the Anglican Church who has a reputation for being the man who punishes the 'eretics be 'ere at the Vatican?"

"He's a trusted advisor to the pope, and he's a Catholic bishop, not Anglican." Bas' voice was stronger than it had been in the dungeon, and he certainly had no problem with his hearing.

Ringo met my eyes and then strode over to Bas. He sat across from him, just out of arm's reach, but at his level. "What do ye know of 'im?"

Bas' gaze sharpened on Ringo. "What, specifically, do you want to know?"

"We're 'ere to find a ring. Blood-red stone set in gold – belonged to the popes until it disappeared in 1842."

"I've seen the ring."

Tom swiveled around and glared. "Where?"

"Encased in stone," said Bas.

Bas struggled to stand, and Ringo reached out to steady him. I caught my breath, but there was no aggressiveness in Bas at all. Tom's blood must have satisfied enough of his hunger that he could control himself.

He shuffled to join us at the window, and Tom made room for him to fit in next to me. I snaked my arm around Bas impulsively and gave him a quick squeeze. "I'm so sorry for what you've been through," I said.

He held himself stiffly for a brief moment, then exhaled, and squeezed back. "It wasn't the worst thing I've survived." He disentangled himself from my arm, and I realized he'd hesitated so he could test his reaction to me. Apparently his control was still a little shaky.

Bas held onto the window frame and looked out at the view. He closed his eyes and took a deep, satisfied breath. "Thank you," he said to no one in particular. "I've missed this."

"How long were you down there?" I asked.

Bas opened his eyes to meet mine. "I came here to argue for the rights of the Jews in the ghetto of Rome. They live behind walls, can't own property, die of disease and starvation from flooding, and have been treated as less than human by the Vatican for hundreds of years. My mistake was attempting to use a theological argument. The pope isn't overly fond of being enlightened on his ignorance of biblical canon. That was six months ago."

I stared at him in horror. "Six months?"

He smiled. "It was much worse to be a Moor in Lisbon during the Crusades, believe me."

"Tell us about the ring," said Tom quietly.

Bas nodded and pointed out the window to the right side of the big building at the end of the complex. "That is the Cortile del Belvedere. Gregory XVI often conducts business there because the Bramante Staircase allows him to take a carriage all the way up to his offices – he has become lazy in his power. When I challenged Gregory on his understanding of canon, he went to a stone sarcophagus set back near the wall and gestured for guards to remove the heavy lid. Then he reached into it and removed the red-stoned ring, which he slipped onto his finger. He then proceeded to tell me all the ways I was going to humiliate myself in front of his cardinals and bishops, with orders for self-mutilation, self-condemnation, and sheer self-effacing nonsense. When I calmly told him I would do none of those things, he called me a heretic and had me removed to the dungeons immediately. It was there that your Bishop Wilder followed me and had me subdued by several of his guards armed with halberds. Crossed at one's throat, halberds can be remarkable deterrents to sudden movement. It was thus that I found myself bound in chains, drained of my blood, and unceremoniously left to die in the pit in which you found me."

Tom's breath came a little faster as he looked at me. "That's definitely the Monger ring."

I included Ringo and Bas in my gaze. "When Wilder saw that the ring didn't work on Bas, he must have wanted his blood."

"But why? Clearly you know a great deal about this bishop," Bas said.

Tom spoke grimly. "The Bishop Wilder we knew from 1888 had a penchant for genetic testing …" He must have seen confusion on Bas' face because he sighed and tried to explain so a man of learning in the 1840s could understand. "Testing the components in blood to figure out bloodlines – particularly Descendant bloodlines. He collected samples from all the Families, especially those with remarkable skills."

I answered Bas' next question before he could ask it. "We think he figured out that Vampires assimilate some of the gifts of the Descendants from whom they drink. At least that's how he became able to Clock through time – he kidnapped and drained my mother in 1888, nearly killing her in the process."

"It sounds like ye both assume 'e's already a Vampire." Ringo said, his gaze shifting between me and Tom.

Bas answered before either of us could. "He's not."

"What?" Tom shouted as I squeaked. "He's not? How do you know?"

"He was too careful with me. He wore leather gloves at all times and would never touch me with his bare skin. Instead of leeches or cutting a vein, he used goose quills sharpened to a fine point to draw the blood away cleanly."

Tom had paled. "He did the same to me, so he could keep me alive without infecting me."

Bas looked sharply at Tom. "This bishop is the one who turned you?"

Tom looked away, and then finally nodded.

"When?"

Tom finally met his eyes again. "A long time ago to you. A lifetime to me."

Bas turned to me. "This is because of the skills of your Family?"

"Yes, but he should be dead. We killed Bishop Wilder in 1429. Not drained and thrown in a pit to regenerate – killed with decapitation and fire." I shuddered at the memory. "He had Clocked there from 1554. And he had Clocked *there* from 1888, which was when we first met him. He was the man responsible for turning Archer." My voice faded out at Archer's name. Bas would want to know about Archer, but I didn't want to talk about him yet.

"Do you believe 1888 is within Bishop Wilder's natural lifetime?" Bas asked.

It was a very good question, and clearly Ringo thought so too. "'E only got Clocker skills after 'e bled Saira's mother in 1888. 'E was already a Vampire by then, and there were records for 'is education at Oxford in the 1840s."

"Records can be falsified. I've been doing it for centuries. This is the 1840s, and he's clearly not a student at Oxford now, is he?"

No, he clearly was not.

"Does he look the same now as he did when you first knew him?" Bas asked

"Yes, he does. So, he must already be a Vampire," I said.

"Or he's been alive for fifty or so years and will be infected soon enough that he retains the same appearance. He will then falsify his records later to accommodate his agelessness."

Bas sighed. "There is something else, something far less tangible, which is why I hesitate to even raise it." He leaned back against the window shutter and crossed his arms over his desperately bony chest. He was still shirtless, and the sight of him was uncomfortably close to pictures I'd seen of war refugees.

He spoke to Tom. "I was a Shifter before I was attacked, and though I can no longer assume my Eagle form, I still have his senses. I knew my Vampire attacker was a predator before I ever stepped into that alley, because my Eagle sensed him."

Bas continued. "When the Bishop followed me to the dungeons, I got no sense of predator from him. I sensed the Monger in him, but more as a wish for dominance rather than a predatory nature. That is the true reason I don't believe he is a Vampire."

We were silent for a moment, digesting the information. Tom looked out the window. "Six months ago he may not have been, but he has handled your blood since then, and it's possible that things have changed."

"Ye attackin' 'im with blood on yer 'and could do it too," murmured Ringo.

Tom clenched his jaw tightly, and I knew he'd heard him. That kind of thinking could cause an existential crisis of epic proportions, and now was not the time.

"Guys? Focus. Bas knows where the ring is kept. I say we go get it and then get the hell out of here. Worrying about Wilder and whether or not he's already infected is not our problem. In real time, he's dead. We just have to keep reminding ourselves of that, got it?"

"'E may be dead, but 'e can still kill us in this time," grumbled Ringo.

"That's not helpful, and you can just take your pessimistic self away from here if that's all you've got." My hands went to my hips, and I glared for all I was worth.

Apparently I was funny, because Ringo and Tom looked at each other, Ringo cocked an eyebrow, and they both did a very poor job of hiding their smirks. So I ignored them and focused on Bas.

"How do we get there from here – the place where the ring is kept?"

"The way is full of Swiss Guard and locked doors. If you were a cat, you'd cross the rooftops …" That was all he needed to say. I was out of the window and crouched on the ledge before anyone but Ringo realized what happened. Ringo knew because he was right on my heels.

"What are you doing?" Bas looked horrified.

I grinned back at him. "Wouldn't you know, I *am* a Cat." And then I dropped out of sight.

Archer – Present Day

He came to gloat.

Seth Walters and his men remained outside our cell when they opened the door, guns drawn and aimed into the darkness. The light from the main cavern behind them was dim enough that they couldn't immediately see into the corners where Tam and I had arranged ourselves, and I was able to catch a glimpse of ceiling support columns and brick arches.

Finally, after some fumbling by one of the men, they shone a torch at us, which effectively burned our vision into uselessness.

"I suppose the question one should ask is how much longer do I need to keep your food alive before you indulge, Devereux?" Walters sneered as he shone the light on Tam.

"That was a rhetorical question, I suppose." I was very glad that Tam and I had spent our waking moments in conversation so my voice was steady and strong.

"Oh no, not at all." Walters said. "I had hoped my son would come to me willingly, but he made a tactical error, and now I'm afraid I'll need to motivate him into compliance."

"I fail to see my place in your plans, Walters, just as I fail to recognize your right to include me in them," I said, marshalling as much arrogance as I could into my voice. The memory of the way my father had spoken to underlings occasionally came in handy.

My superior attitude had done what I'd hoped – it had made him angry. Angry people made mistakes, in my experience, and given my current physical condition, I was going to need him to make several.

"Oh, I have the right, Devereux. The ring gives me the right. You could try every bit of your aristocratic charm on the men with me, but they'll never go against my orders. Not them, and not the thirty-one thousand London constables I control. This city needs some cleaning up, and I'm the man who will see it done properly. So, yes, I definitely have plans."

It took a herculean effort on my part to say nothing. I'd gotten a piece of the information I needed, but not nearly all of it, and I hoped that my silence might goad him into speaking further. I still couldn't see, and I was tired of having the torch light shone in my eyes. Regardless of how I felt, Walters knew nothing of the cure, and therefore couldn't help but believe I was a Vampire, and I saw no point in disabusing him of that notion. I gathered every ounce of my will and forced myself to stand. My motion was slow, but it was controlled and smooth, and I heard Tam inhale quietly.

One of the torch-holding men took a step back, and I blinked to clear the blinding glare from my eyes. "The power to compel is not the same thing as leadership, and one does not inspire the other. You are not a leader, Walters, you are a bully and a coward of the worst kind. The fear you believe you inspire is merely the fear in which you constantly live, and it undermines the very leadership you profess to have. Strip a bully of his pulpit and he becomes a cowering, quivering thing. Strip you of your ring, and you, too, will cower. You will never lose the fear because it defines you, and the very things you seek to annihilate will be those which ultimately destroy you."

I held myself up by sheer willpower, and I fully expected to be smashed in the face with the butt of a gun. I felt Tam tense beside me. I didn't know if his instinct would be to jump in to help me or jump to the side to avoid the blows that were surely coming. I didn't want him in the line of fire, so I took a step forward. The torch-holder stepped back even farther, and finally, Walters spoke.

"You have no idea who you're talking to. Your arrogance has just signed a Wolf's death warrant. I had toyed with the idea of dangling its life in front of you as inducement for good behavior, but I think now I'll just kill it to make the point that you are not in control here. I am."

Walters stepped backward and slammed the door shut. The darkness was absolute, and my legs gave way as I crumpled to the floor.

"Look, Connor's a Wolf. He has better survival instincts than all of us put together," Tam said as he moved to help me sit upright against the wall.

"I really hope you're right. You and he are part of a select group – people I consider my friends – and I'm very afraid that group is becoming ever more limited as time goes on."

"You're bleeding again," he said quietly. I could see nothing, so I assumed blood had seeped through my shirt again under his hands. This constant state of pain in which I was living had become quite boring and I said as much to the young man who had kept me alive in the days after the tunnel collapse.

He laughed at the idea that anyone could find pain boring. "You're kind of a badass, you know?"

"No, that's my wife. She's definitely the badass of the family." The thought stoked a different kind of pain.

"Have you had any more of those weird, implanted memories of her from after 1944?" he asked.

I swallowed with difficulty. "I haven't, and Ava hasn't heard from her either, I take it?"

"Not since the last time you asked, which was what – an hour ago?"

A sort of dread had begun to take up residency in my abdomen, and another leaf of it unfurled. "I'm very afraid that something significant happened when I pushed them through the portal."

"You don't remember anything else from that moment? Just a flash, and that's it?" Tam settled back against his own wall. They were positions to which we'd become accustomed through long conversations while we'd been prisoners together. Among other topics of discussion, I had given Tam a thorough recounting of the various adventures that had brought me to the Underground to search for him and the rest of the mixed-blood captives, including the new memories of the time I had spent with Saira in 1944.

"That is indeed it," I answered. "And then my memories revert back to the ones I've always had, but in an odd way – as though Saira had never been there at all."

Tam was silent a moment. "What do you think it means?"

I exhaled, and hated to put words to the private fear I'd harbored like a suppurating wound. "That time has split yet again."

"But Tink's cousin came back … I mean forward from then."

"He was sent through the portal several seconds *before* the bomb exploded."

Tam was silent as he worked it out in his head. "But you were there for the explosion, and yet you're here now. So, could that mean there's a time stream on which you're dead?"

I couldn't imagine having left Saira alone on any time stream, nor would I ever allow myself to think of her as injured or dead, so I reverted to humor to cover that which didn't bear consideration. "Until just recently, I was considered a walking corpse on this one too."

Tam huffed something that wasn't laughter, but could have been close. "You joke about being a Sucker, but from what you describe, you weren't dead so much as … suspended."

"That is my understanding of the rudimentary medical explanation for my condition, yes."

"And the cure you injected …?" he left the question dangling.

"Re-started the process of cell-death in my body. In a sense, I suppose, I needed to begin to die in order to properly live."

The silence stretched out for a long while until my green-haired Seer-mix friend spoke again. "When you think it through, it's what we're all doing – dying a little bit more each day as we wander through life. It kind of makes you want to look around and notice all the little things along the way."

In that remarkably clear way young people sometimes have of viewing the world, he was absolutely right, and I'd had a very long life in which to discover the truth of his words. "It is amazing how complete a life can feel when it is full of the little things," I said quietly. My mind had filled the darkness with memories of Saira that scrolled past my vision as though I'd captured each frame of them on film.

Tam interrupted my thoughts, and his question became one of the small things that life had taught me to catalogue as meaningful. "What does Tink's voice sound like?"

I smiled, although he couldn't see it. "Ava speaks softly, and yet every word sounds as though it is shot through with light. Her laughter is where you hear it best – like crystal prisms that dance with sunbeams when they clink together in the breeze. You'll hear it yourself soon enough, and it'll become one of the little things you store away to remember."

He settled back into silence, maybe imagining laughter he hoped to hear, as I heard Saira's rich, throaty voice echo her words of love in my mind.

"Or perhaps, it's the biggest thing of all."

SARCOPHAGUS

I stifled an involuntary laugh as I ran across the rooftops of the Vatican. It had been fun, at least for Ringo and me. Tom had to be convinced not to look down, and Bas needed a bit of extra time to make his way out of the window, but all of us did it without incident. Bas seemed to be getting stronger as his body assimilated the blood Tom had given him, and his face was regaining some of its former beauty. He definitely still moved like an athlete, though more long distance runner than power lifter, and he took the lead to guide us across the tops of buildings in which priests slept and guards stood watch.

The ground beneath us was sloped, but the height of the buildings compensated for the elevation change so that by the time we reached the Cortile del Belvedere, we were just two stories above the earth. The only reason Tom made it at all was that it was nighttime, so he didn't have to know how very high up we had been.

One tower on the far right side of the main complex was higher than the rest of the roofline, and I could see windows at the top. Bas led us to it, but the windows didn't open, so we had to risk breaking a pane. Tom wrapped his arm in his coat and punched the top of the window. The broken bits fell inside onto a tile floor with a smash and we held our breath. We heard no shouts of alarm though, and after a long few minutes, he pulled the rest of the broken glass out of the frame and set the pieces down carefully on the roof tiles.

Ringo dropped down first, and when he had done it safely, the rest of us followed in his footsteps. I shielded my Maglite with my hand so I could see where we were, and when I did, I almost yelped in astonishment.

The tower held the most amazing circular staircase – well, less a staircase and more like a ramp. There were steps, but they were far enough apart that a pack animal could climb them. The staircase had an up ramp and a down ramp, which gave it a sort of double helix look. The view past the columns and down over the railing went all the way to the floor two stories below. It was like looking into the heart of a seashell.

"Wow," I whispered in awe.

"Bramante designed it in the 1500s so the pope could ride a mule or a carriage all the way to his apartments. Those vestments can get heavy after a long day," Bas whispered back wryly.

We followed the twisting path down a level to the entrance to the second floor, and Bas took the lead again. There were enough windows that the rooms glowed dimly in the moonlight, making flashlights unnecessary, though I had to fight the instinct to switch mine on just to see the ceiling decoration. The halls were large and filled with statues of horses. It reminded me a bit of walking past the Elgin Marbles that had been stored in the London Underground during the Blitz – sort of eerie, like silent sentinels watched every move we made.

The biggest hall had the feeling of a formal audience room, and Bas led us past Etruscan horse statues to a large stone sarcophagus at the back of it. Bas and I took one side, and Ringo and Tom the other, but even with the strength of two Vampires helping, that stone lid was almost impossible to move, much less move silently. My wrists had cramped with the strain by the time we finally moved it enough to allow my Maglite in, which I promptly dropped to stifle a scream.

"What the bloody 'ell is that?" Ringo gasped. The light had fallen into the sarcophagus, which apparently was not just for show.

It shone through the eye sockets of a skeleton that was dressed in full regal vestments and covered in glittering jewels.

"It is a Catacomb Saint. I did not realize the Vatican had kept any of them," said Bas quietly. "A cache of remains was found under Rome in the sixteenth century. The skeletons were sent out as martyrs to the Catholic churches in countries such as Germany and Poland. They had been having trouble maintaining a Catholic presence, and the martyrs were meant to impress."

Tom reached down to pluck a ruby and gold ring off the finger of the skeleton. "And look what we have here." He held it up to show me. "Is this the Monger ring?"

I peered closely at the blood-red stone set into a heavy gold band, and I looked at Ringo for confirmation. He stared at the ring as though it had teeth, and then nodded. "Yeah, that's it," Ringo said.

"It is the same ring the pope wore when he condemned me for heresy," Bas agreed.

"We should go," I said with a degree of urgency that seemed to come out of nowhere. I was suddenly very antsy; anxiety crept up my spine as though the skeleton was shaking its bony finger at us and saying we were fools to think we'd get away with this.

The feeling was strong enough that I didn't wait for agreement. I scanned the room for something to leave a spiral on, and found a wooden cabinet that looked like prime real estate. I quickly removed a marker from my pocket and started tagging the side panel of the cabinet.

A wave of Monger sickness suddenly punched me in the stomach so hard I almost vomited, and I staggered backwards from the impact.

"Give me the ring." A voice that pierced my soul with a shiver of fear echoed in the cavernous room. I looked up to see Duncan, the Immortal War, glaring at us from across the great hall.

I swallowed a terrified shriek and hurried back to work on the spiral. My hand shook, and I missed one of my lines. I shut my eyes and concentrated on calming the trembling that had taken hold of my courage so I could finish drawing the spiral.

"Sod off," said Tom, and I looked up in shock. Ringo and Bas looked equally surprised that Tom had just pulled an inordinate amount of either courage or stupidity out of his pocket like a red flag, which he now waved in front of a bull.

"What did you say to me, boy?" Duncan boomed.

"I'm not your boy," Tom spat. Ringo and Bas were edging back toward me.

"Don't, Tom," I hissed.

"You should listen to her. I wouldn't, but you should." Duncan's tone was derisive, and I couldn't tell if he knew who I was and his insult was personal, or if he was just generally being a pig.

He strode into the hall with the swagger of a warrior, as the fear churning in my guts threatened to consume every ounce of self-control I had left. "Give me my ring," he said menacingly.

I was nearly done with the third spiral, but my hand shook so hard I had to switch the marker to my left hand so I could shake out the right.

I looked up to see Tom defy Duncan. "No," he said clearly.

Duncan hadn't broken his stride, and Ringo's voice was urgent in my ear. "Finish it!" he hissed. Tom didn't have a weapon that I could see, but I couldn't imagine Duncan had any less than ten on him.

He was War, after all.

Ringo raised his voice. "Tom," he called in a low voice, "back away."

Duncan stalked forward. His glare burned holes in Tom as though his eyes were laser beams.

"Last chance, *boy*," Duncan's sneer was palpable, and I unconsciously stood and pulled one of my daggers out of its sheath.

Tom took a halting step backwards as he finally seemed to understand the trouble he was in. I saw Bas edge toward a display of halberds crossed on the wall to our right, and I knew he and Ringo had already had a whole silent conversation between them.

Then Duncan lunged, and everything slowed down.

His sword came out of a scabbard on his back.

Bas flung himself at the halberds and wrenched two off the wall.

Tom stumbled backwards.

Duncan's sword swung down in an arc.

I threw my dagger.

Ringo hurled himself at Tom to knock him out of the way.

The ring clattered to the floor.

Tom bellowed in pain.

My dagger sank into Duncan's chest.

It seemed to barely affect him, except that his eyes went wide, and pure, unadulterated hatred filled me with rage.

It wasn't my rage I felt though. I suddenly understood, with utter clarity, that it was Duncan's hatred that coursed through me. The purest anger and deepest desire to kill rolled off him and wrapped icy talons around me until the moment he grabbed the hilt of my dagger and ripped it from his chest.

My other dagger was out and in my hand when Duncan flung the first one at Tom, but Ringo had changed Tom's trajectory and the dagger merely nicked his arm.

Another flash of rage surged through me, but this one was red hot – so very different than the pure, cold hatred that was Duncan's. Threaded through that burning rage was a ribbon of bright light, and an instant later, the feeling was gone.

Two things happened simultaneously then – Bas swung a halberd at Duncan, and Bishop Wilder charged into the hall like a madman. "I'll kill you for what you've done to me!" Wilder shouted at Tom. He waved a sword with sweaty, wild menace, and rushed forward like a crazed man with nothing to lose.

The scene took on the surreality of a nightmare as the metal of deadly weapons clashed on one side of me, and Ringo and Tom scrambled for weapons on the other.

Wilder was older, but he had stayed fit and strong, and the way he held the sword as he raced toward Tom was like a Norse berserker. Tom lunged forward toward the sarcophagus. He plunged his hand inside and withdrew a glittering, ceremonial sword.

He sprang forward to meet Wilder's charge, but Wilder was already swinging. His sword bit into Tom's thigh, neatly slicing into the muscle and effectively hobbling him. Old wounds bloomed all over Tom's body, and the most recent slice in his hand pumped fresh blood. He had to dodge away quickly to avoid a killing blow while his body attempted to heal itself.

Ringo tossed me my fallen dagger and grabbed a short sword from the sarcophagus for himself. We each held woefully undersized weapons as we backed closer together and prepared to fight.

The halberd was not the most effective weapon against a sword, but Bas had gotten a few good swings in against Duncan. War was clearly the better fighter, and he was aiming for decapitation, which was the only effective way to end a Vampire in battle.

Bas saw this as obviously as I did, so he switched tactics, surprising us all. Bas flung the halberd at Duncan, then used the instant distraction to dive for the Monger ring, which still lay on the floor. He tucked and rolled in an impressive feat of athletics, then emerged in the clear and sprinted for the far door. Duncan hadn't anticipated this, and I could see momentary indecision on his face as he debated killing us or chasing the ring.

The ring won, which had clearly been Bas' objective, and the odds of survival suddenly shifted slightly in our favor. Duncan roared in rage as he gave up the fight and sprinted toward the door after Bas.

The clash of metal dragged my attention back to Tom and Wilder. They were on the other side of the sarcophagus from Ringo and me. Wilder was attacking Tom with a ferocity I'd only seen once – right before Archer had killed him in France. Tom fought back hard, but he didn't have Wilder's obvious sword skills, and the stab wound that had re-opened in Tom's hand was bleeding freely over the hilt of the sword, making it slippery and hard to hold.

Wilder growled at Tom under his breath, lunged again, and stuck Tom's shoulder. Tom nearly fell, but at the last moment twisted his body so he was under Wilder. He drove his sword upward, so it pierced Wilder's torso up to the bloody hilt. Wilder lurched backward in shock, and Tom flinched away, suddenly horrified.

I used the distraction to jump onto the sarcophagus and fly off it with my best martial arts kick aimed at Wilder's head. My foot connected and Wilder fell backward. The sound of his skull impacting the tile floor was sickening. Tom staggered to his feet and stood over Wilder. He kicked Wilder's sword away, then reached down and pulled the ceremonial sword out of the bishop's stomach. Wilder's blood on the blade seemed to mix with Tom's from the hilt, and I knew that if Wilder didn't die from his wound, he'd be turned.

My eyes connected with Tom's as the time-bending, mind-blowing irony of what had just happened to Bishop Wilder smacked us both in the face. "I'm going after the ring," I said breathlessly.

Tom looked down at Wilder, then back up at me and Ringo. "Let's go." He picked up the ceremonial sword with his uninjured hand, and we raced from the hall.

Battle Fatigue

The clash of metal on metal rang out in the stair tower, but when we got there, the only evidence of the battle that I could actually see in the dark was the stain of bloody handprints on three of the columns.

Then another clash, and I realized they came from two rungs of the stairs below us. Tom raced down the spiral, but Ringo and I had the same thought. I shoved my daggers back into their sheaths, and Ringo stuck the sword in the back of his belt. I aimed my Maglite at the columns one level down, and then we both climbed onto the railing and jumped across the center to the level below us.

It wasn't a difficult jump, but if we missed, we'd be dead. There were about a million ways we could die on this night, so one more or less didn't really seem like a big deal. Tom was just rounding the corner when we leapt down to the next level, where the clang of metal on metal was loudest.

Ringo threw me a hand sign and we split up – he went left, I went right, withdrawing my daggers as I went. I had to put away the Maglite to hold my daggers, and it took a second for my eyes to adjust to the near dark, and when they finally did, I wished they hadn't.

Bas lay on the herringbone-patterned tile, bleeding from stab wounds all over his body. Duncan stood over him as if debating whether or not to cut his head off, but instead, he reached down and plucked the Monger ring from Bas' unresisting fingers.

"Noooo!" I screamed, as I flung both of my daggers at Duncan. They both stuck in his flesh – one in his torso and one in a shoulder, and I was assaulted again by the purest rage imaginable. The intensity of it combined with concentrated Monger-gut rocked me back on my heels and drove the breath from my lungs. He gripped both daggers, ripped them out of his body, and flung them away to clatter somewhere in the darkness.

I tripped over Bas' sword, which had fallen to the tile before he did, and I lunged for it blindly as Duncan laughed.

"A girl with a sword. How … amusing," he sneered.

His fist flashed like lightening, smashed into the side of my face, and knocked me backward as if he held a hammer. I slumped to the ground and pain slammed through my head and body. I expected the sharp side of his sword to drop on my neck at the next moment.

"'Ow's this for amusin'," growled Ringo, as his sword clashed with Duncan's, and he parried the lightning blows Duncan rained on him.

Ringo drew Duncan away from me, and I crawled over to where Bas lay in a growing pool of blood. He looked up at me. "Don't touch me dear girl. Your Archer wouldn't care for me to infect you with my immortality."

I gasped a shocked laugh through the stars in my vision. "I have to get you out of here."

I'd lost my marker, and searched around me in the dark for something to draw with, conscious of the clanging weapons behind me, but not daring to look up. I heard Tom yell something about having my daggers as he joined the battle, and I barely kept the sobs from choking my throat and blinding me with tears. I finally pulled my Maglite out of my pocket and dipped the end in Bas' blood that had pooled under his shoulder.

He coughed wetly, and I knew his body wasn't healing fast enough to cope with the blood that filled his lungs. I swallowed a sob and drew faster.

The hum of the spiral had started, and I didn't have the concentration to shut it down. I called out through the sobs. "Ringo! Tom! Come!"

"Hold on to me, Bas," I said through tears as I dipped my torch into his blood and began the fifth spiral.

There were more clangs of swords, and then finally Duncan's angry voice. "Enough!" Then the wet sound of a sword running through flesh, and a gasp that sent a chill to my bones.

I sobbed hard as the hum of the spiral filled me. "Please …!" I felt one hand grab my coat, and then another hand clap on weakly as the spiral drew us into it. I barely had enough focus to see a walled garden in my mind before my vision blurred and everything went black.

I grabbed onto the echo of my own name to drag myself to the surface of consciousness. I was on a settee in a large room I didn't recognize. Mary Shelley bent over me pressing a cool wet towel to my head. It felt so good to be touched by gentle hands, and I wanted to close my eyes to revel in the sensation for a moment. Her voice urged me to look at her, so I finally did as she asked.

"Saira, my dear. Can you see clearly? Are you alright?" Mary's voice sounded mild, but there was an undertone of frantic to it that told me I'd been unconscious for more than a couple of minutes.

Then everything came rushing back to me, and I tried to sit up.

"Where are they?" I tried to struggle against her hands, but I had no strength, and my vision swam with the motion.

She gently pushed me back and smoothed the hair from my face as she spoke in a soft voice. "Your friends are alive, and they seem to be healing. Tom …" Her voice caught, and I realized she had come to care for Tom during our journey south. She cleared her throat. "Tom was hurt quite badly, but he has taken some blood and he's finally stable. Your new friend, Bas, is it? He, too, was injured severely, but he seems older, more resilient somehow." She said the last words with a faraway expression, as if she was talking to herself. When she snapped back, her eyes found mine. "You and Ringo managed to avoid the worst of things. Perhaps you're just faster than they are?" She smiled. Her attempts to make me feel better were generous, even though they were misguided.

"I want to see them." My voice sounded weak to my own ears, and I tried again. "Please, can I see my friends?" That one came out how I meant it – with conviction. They were my friends – all of them – friends and brothers.

"I'm 'ere, Saira," Ringo said softly from somewhere behind Mary. She stood up and gave him her seat on the edge of the sofa next to me, and I reached out for his hand.

"Will ye live?" he asked. The very slight twinkle in his eyes told me he was okay, despite the fierce bruises on his face and a bandaged hand.

"Nope. Not going to survive this life. How about you?"

He chuckled. "Keep me out of my own time and I'll live forever. Or at least until some Immortal War god or rabid Vampire decides to take their piece of me."

"They didn't get one, did they?" I asked, suddenly not joking at all.

He held up his bandaged hand. "'Tis nothin' but a scratch. That bloody bastard can fight though. 'Alf the time I thought 'e was toyin' with us, at least until 'e got bored and decided to run Tom through."

I gasped and sat up, managing it with only a little dog-paddling in my head rather than the full swim. "Is he okay? Mary said he's stable."

"'E is now. It was a trick gettin' the bleedin' to stop when we couldn't touch 'is blood. Doran finally came to 'elp us, and once we 'ad pressure on the wound, it started knittin' together."

Ringo looked at me with a deadly serious expression. "Tom's been 'urt bad in 'is short life – worse than Archer ever was. 'E's not 'ealin' fast like 'e should, and I'm not sure 'e could come back from another one like 'e just got."

The sheer magnitude of accumulated injuries that Archer had sustained was the reason Mr. Shaw and Connor had been able to develop the cure for Vampirism. The problem was, the Vampire had to be in an extreme state of weakness for the cure to have a chance of working, and no one knew if he'd survive that part of it, much less the cure itself.

I exhaled sharply, then sank back into the cushion of the sofa while I watched Ringo's eyes search mine. He knew what I was going to say before I said it, and I could tell he agreed with me. "Then Tom can't go back to that ghost station to fix the time stream split. The chances of him getting shot by George Walters are too high."

Ringo was quiet for a long time, and finally he nodded at my prone position. "Sit up and give a man some room, would ye?"

I smiled and pulled my legs up under me so he could sit next to me. He leaned back against the cushions and closed his eyes as he spoke. "So, will ye come back to 1889 with me and find 'im there?"

The words felt like molten lead poured into me – too heavy and toxic to answer without thinking the whole thing through, and my head hurt too much to concentrate. I leaned back next to him, reached out for his hand to hold, and closed my own eyes.

"When I keep in mind the fact that we all die in the end anyway, the choices don't suck as much," I said. Exhaustion wove its way through my voice.

Ringo barked a short, mirthless laugh. "So at least ye've got that goin' for ye."

I turned my head to face him, and his eyes opened to look at me. Our heads rested against the backrest of the settee about six inches apart. "Why do I have to choose what to do next?"

"Because ye choose yer life or ye become a victim of it. That's 'ow it works."

"It's too much responsibility." I knew I was whining, but Ringo was probably the one person in the world I could whine to.

He rolled his eyes. "Bein' responsible for yerself? That's called bein' an adult. Bein' responsible for other people? That's a parent, and ye're not one of those yet, so ye don't get to make choices for anyone else."

"But Tom—" I started to protest, but Ringo cut me off.

"No. Ye choose yer life, and I'll choose mine. Because I like ye, I might take yer choices into consideration, and if I were married to ye, I might base my choices on yers, but they'd still be mine to make. It's why ye don't get to choose whether or not Tom goes back to fix the split. Ye can choose not to take 'im there – that's yer choice. And ye can choose to release 'im from the piss-poor deal ye both made, that's yer other choice. But ye don't get to tell 'im 'e can't do it, just like it was wrong of ye to say to Archer 'e couldn't take the cure because ye were afraid to lose 'im. Ye choose yer life, and let others choose theirs."

I was quiet a long time before I finally nodded. "They're sleeping?"

"Bas and Tom? Yeah. Tom brought back yer daggers by the way. They're in yer bag."

I nodded my thanks. "Is Doran still here?"

"'E's up in the studio, paintin' I think."

"Will you help me get up there? You know, catch me if I swoon, or whatever it is that happens when you get conked on the head by War."

His eyes looked worried as he searched my face. "Ye're alright then?"

I nodded. "You?"

He nodded.

I held his gaze for a bit. "Tom was the one who infected Wilder."

"Seems likely."

I closed my eyes with a defeated sigh. "This Clocking thing needs to be left to the grown-ups. I keep messing things up."

"Ye're 'uman, Saira. We make mistakes, and then we fix 'em. That's what we do. The grown-ups in my book are the ones who don't turn their backs on the fixin'."

He stood and held out his hand to help me up. "C'mon, I'll escort ye upstairs, just to make sure ye don't *swoon* and knock yerself out."

The villa seemed very quiet, and Ringo told me that Artemisia had gone to visit her daughter in Naples. Mary had planned to leave too, but then we arrived, so she stayed to care for us, and Doran had come soon after we did.

I was mostly just achy, and my head hurt where Duncan's fist had smacked me, but unconsciousness seemed to have been the rest I needed, because I felt remarkably decent.

Late afternoon sunlight shone through the big window in the studio, and Doran sat with his back to the door working on a large canvas. He didn't turn when we came in.

"It seems that War is not your biggest fan," he said dryly.

I scoffed. "The feeling's mutual."

Doran was putting detail into the view out of a large window in the background of his painting. It was another Renaissance style formal portrait, remarkably similar to his painting of the Immortals that hung in the Elian Manor keep. Now that I'd seen three of them in person, I could recognize them easily.

They were arrayed on thrones in a room that reminded me of drawings I'd seen of the Greek gods on Olympus, except the view out the window was of islands set into a deep blue-green sea. In this painting, Aislin faced forward, and her young, beautiful face reminded me a lot of Ava's, except with a sharp, focused look in her eyes rather than the dreamy one Ava usually wore. Duncan was still actor-handsome, but because I'd seen the deeper ugliness in person, that was the only thing I noticed about him in the painting. Jera looked down at her empty hands, and something about her pose made me unbearably sad for her. Goran looked angry, but his eyes weren't focused on anything in particular, and that made him seem sort of helpless. It was unsettling that such a powerful man looked so lost. The space between Goran and Aeron was there in this painting too, and I almost imagined I could see an empty throne. I blinked and the space was bare again, but something gnawed at the edges of my brain – something to do with that space.

Interestingly, Aeron's expression was still forbidding, but in a way that no longer inspired fear in me. It was a different reaction than I'd had when I saw him on the train, and I wondered if my encounters with War had shown me what a proper bad guy actually looks like.

"Are these their natural faces?" I asked Doran as I came up to stand next to him.

"You suppose I know their natural appearance?"

I turned to watch his face. "You do though. That's where your chair should go, isn't it?" I pointed at the empty place between Nature and Death, and his reaction was exactly what I'd expected – absolutely nothing. Not a twitch, not a flinch, no scoff or surprise. Nothing. I took his utter lack of reaction as confirmation. "What are you the Immortal of? The big five are already accounted for, so what's left?"

With supreme control, Doran returned his attention to painting the whitecaps on the ocean outside the window. "Where will you go when you leave here?" he finally asked.

I shrugged. "It depends."

"On?"

"On what Tom and Bas want to do."

He let that hang there for a long moment. "What do you want to do?"

I decided to stop messing with him. I pulled a stool over and sat so I could study his painting. He was very good – one of the best artists I'd ever seen – and it was pretty intriguing to watch him work.

"I honestly don't know. I still want to fix the time stream split, but asking Tom to help me isn't really an option anymore."

Doran's eyebrow raised, but he said nothing.

"We almost got your ring back, by the way. Unfortunately, Duncan kicked our collective booties and then walked off with it."

"Ah, so that's how it went missing in your history books," Doran said quietly.

"What would you do with it if you got it back?" I was getting used to this whole not-answering-the-question way of communicating with Doran, or maybe it just annoyed me less now.

Doran shrugged. "It's a nice ring, but I'm not really big on jewelry. I might only bring it out for special occasions."

"Occasions … like what?" Maybe he wasn't answering because I wasn't asking the right questions.

"Oh, you know, times when people needed guidance to follow their path, or when the right words could make the secret dreams of the heart grow into something real and true."

Sentimentality from Doran? Be still my heart.

I willed him to look at me, but he wouldn't meet my eyes so I forged ahead. "If you were wearing your ring right now, what would you say to me?"

He leaned forward to dab a little gold into the whitecap, but not before I caught the barest hint of a smile. Again, he shrugged. "I might tell you that your original plan was a good one, and 1944 would be an interesting place to revisit."

I met Ringo's eyes over Doran's head. "Huh." I said in my best non-committal voice. "Maybe someday I can find that ring for you."

"Maybe someday you can. I've heard you know a good thief." Doran leaned back and regarded the painting for a moment, then dropped his brush into a jar of mineral spirits and stood up. He leaned over and kissed me on both cheeks. "Goodbye, cousin. I'll leave you to the careful ministrations of the remarkable Mrs. Shelley."

I reached into my pocket for the big emerald I'd dug out of my satchel. "Hey Doran?" He raised an eyebrow and I put the gem in his hand. "This would look really good on Artemisia, don't you think?"

He stared at the spectacular stone, and something soft and wistful came into his expression. If I hadn't known better, I might even have thought he got a little misty-eyed. He looked me in the eyes. "Thank you, Saira. I think you have excellent judgment."

He turned to shake Ringo's hand. "Keep each other safe, will you? There are people who would miss you." He included me in his backward glance as he left the room.

A Choice

I sat outside with Mary as we sipped Moroccan tea and watched the sun set.

"Why did you write *Frankenstein*?" I asked her.

"Because I was afraid to," she answered immediately, "and I knew if I didn't do the thing I feared, the fear of it would eventually control me."

"Beware, for I am fearless and therefore powerful," I quoted. It was the line from her book that had stuck with me.

She laughed. "I am not fearless, Saira. I never have been. I am, however, not afraid to face my fears, to look them in the eye, perhaps shake their hands, and then ask them to move out of my way. Sometimes they follow me, and sometimes they're so shocked when I confront them that they just melt into the background. But I do not allow them to stop me anymore, and because I am no longer afraid, my fears have no power to dictate my actions, or, for that matter, exert control over my dreams."

"What do you dream of, Mary? Your husband is dead, your son is grown – what is the carrot dangled in front of you that makes you wake up each day?"

She smiled at me in a way that said she knew why I was asking. "Bysshe's dreams were so grand, so full of individualistic philosophy that I believe his own renown would have fulfilled them. My mother's dreams were easily defined by a woman's place in relation to a man. Education was the foundation of her dreams –

an equal education for men and women to give them equal standing in society." She took a sip of her tea and looked up to see Tom standing in the doorway. She smiled and gestured to him to join us.

When Tom had seated himself, Mary continued, and I let my eyes wander over Tom's wounds. "My dreams," she said, "have always been much quieter than my husband's or my mother's. My dream is to have mattered to the people I love; I would like my world to be a little richer because I am in it. And perhaps, if my words can find their way into someone's heart, to give truth to an idea, or voice to a question, that is reason enough to rise and face each day."

Something in my heart shifted profoundly in that moment, and I felt a weight move to one side where it felt easier to carry. Mary turned her attention to Tom and held out both hands for him to take.

"My dear, how do you feel?" she asked him with genuine warmth in her voice.

He had gotten outside on his own, and he didn't appear to have been moving especially slowly. I didn't miss the wince when he sat down though, and he had the drawn, pale look of bone-deep exhaustion. His hand had a thin bandage around it, which surprised me. The wound should have healed by now. "Like a sushi chef just sharpened his knives on me," Tom said dryly.

I laughed and was surprised at how long it had been since anything Tom said or did was meant to be funny. His own expression was startled, as though he hadn't expected my response, and then he gave me a very small, very tentative smile.

"This is taking a bit," he held up his bandaged hand, "but I think everything else is closing up fairly well. I might need to go out and hunt tonight though. I'll see if Bas is up for a run in the forests later."

I put my hand out and touched his arm. I expected him to pull it away, but despite a little flinch, he left it in place on the table. "I'm not going to hold you to our deal," I said.

Then he did pull his arm away, and the warmth left his eyes. "You don't trust me to do the thing without screwing it up like I did this time." There was no question in his voice. Nothing but flat anger.

I was so tired of fighting him – it's all we had done since I found him in France. That little bit of a smile had meant so much more to me than I realized – I couldn't find any anger of my own to match his. I just sighed and sat back.

"You didn't screw anything up. We're all just trying to do the best that we can and get through this thing despite some pretty horrific odds. We wouldn't have Bas if you hadn't been with us, and Tom, *you fought War* and survived." I rubbed my head; it was starting to ache again and I wanted to lie down. "We didn't get the ring. That's reason number one to not hold you to the deal. I didn't keep my end of the bargain." He was about to protest, but I cut him off. "And two, I don't want you to get hurt again. I don't know how you're up and moving around right now, but your injuries have accumulated to the point that I don't know if you could come back from a gunshot wound anymore."

He was still glaring at me, but whatever he'd been about to say had died on his lips. I pushed back from the table, and weirdly, he got up as a show of manners. The kindness of it made my eyes prickle with tears.

"My head hurts again. I'm going to go lie down for a bit." I reached out to touch his arm, and this time he didn't flinch away. "I care what happens to you, Tom. You matter to me."

Mary looked worried, and I shot her a grateful smile. "Good night, Mary. Thank you for taking care of us all … again."

The interior of the villa was cool and dim, with just a few lanterns lit in various rooms. I didn't want to brave the stairs again, so I curled up on the same settee I'd woken on and drifted off to sleep. My dreams were full of fragments. Images and snatches of conversation were scattered through a landscape of restlessness. Archer was there, and Ringo, and even Tom and Doran, but none of their faces gave me the answers to whatever unsettled me.

Whispered voices finally dragged me up to consciousness, and I opened my eyes with something like relief to be free of the restless dreams. Ringo sat on the floor with his back to the settee where I slept, and Tom perched on the other settee. Bas sat on the floor opposite me with his back against an ottoman. He was the first to notice I was awake, and he smiled so warmly at me that the restless edge of my dreams calmed.

"Hello, Saira," he said in his beautiful, deep voice. The desperately chiseled bones in his face had softened, and his striking looks were back. He was still thin, but he seemed strong and well-fed.

"You're back," I said softly, and he laughed.

"Yes, I am much recovered thanks to you and your friends."

"I'm glad." I smiled happily. With Bas in it, the world was a better place.

"We've been talkin'," said Ringo. I sat up, gratified to find that despite not sleeping well, my head was no longer pounding. Our satchels were next to him on the floor, and I looked over at Tom. The small leather field bag he usually carried was on his lap.

"Are we going somewhere?" I included them both in my question.

Tom very deliberately reached into his bag and removed something, which he then placed on the low, round brass table between us. I recognized the object as if it was from a dream, or maybe a different lifetime – it was the black knight chess piece he'd been carrying in medieval France when we finally found him.

"This belonged to Léon. I took it from his body after I accidentally killed him." There were tears very near the surface of his voice, and I suddenly got how hard it had been for him to say *accidentally*. "It had been his father's, and grandfather's before him, and was the only piece left from a set that had been in their family for generations."

He looked down at his hands. "I ended that family when I took Léon's life. I took this piece that night, and every time I look at it I think I have to do better than I've done. I have to *be* better than my family and my blood."

Tom inhaled deeply, as though trying to find courage, and then he met my eyes. "I stopped carrying it on me for a while. I deliberately turned my back on anything that reminded me there

was something worth striving for. Without that knight in my
pocket, I lost whatever good I'd had left in me."

I protested, "It's still there, Tom. I saw it." He shook his head
and looked ready to contradict me, but I wouldn't let him. "No
really, I did. My daggers – these …" I pulled one from my bag and
laid it on the table next to the black knight. "They belong to
Death." At his look of astonishment, I held up my hand. "It's a
long story, but trust me, it's true. When anyone's blood touches the
blade of one I've thrown or used, I get an instant impression of …
their soul, I guess. It's like seeing who they are at their deepest
level, but through a feeling and sometimes color. At first I thought
it was just adrenaline from fighting or something, but last night I
realized I'd actually been seeing the truth of people in their blood."

I turned to Ringo. "That's why Death blooded MacFarlane at
the Council meeting on the other time stream – I must have seen
what he saw because I was holding its twin." I stared at the others,
wide-eyed. "Death is the judge because with these—" I picked up
the dagger with a degree of awe, "—he can know what's in a
person's soul."

I replaced the dagger in its sheath at my back while I spoke.
"My daggers hit Duncan last night, and the pure evil in him almost
took me out at the knees. But then he threw one at you, Tom, and
it nicked your arm, remember?"

Tom looked at me like I was barely keeping it together, but he
nodded. "Well, I saw what was in your soul then, and there was a
band of bright light in the middle of it. You are a good guy, Tom.
In your deepest, truest heart, you are good."

The shock on Tom's face was palpable, and then tears filled
his eyes and he wiped them away before they could fall. He picked
up the black knight from the table and cradled it in his hands,
looking down so he didn't have to see anyone's sympathy.

"It's time to take it out of my bag and carry this in my pocket
again. I've had enough hate for a lifetime, and none of it has made
me feel better about what I've done." He tucked the black knight
into the pocket of his trousers, gave his face one last wipe, and then

met my gaze. "I want to go back to 1944 with you. If there's any chance we can fix the split and go home, I want to be part of it."

"You wouldn't be part of it, Tom, you'd be all of it. I can only get you there, to the moment just after you left the platform. The rest is all you," I said softly.

He sputtered a laugh. "I'm not really well-known for my good choices under pressure."

"Just as long as you don't make stupid ones that get you shot," I said severely.

Tom scoffed and leaned back on the settee. He might have said something else, but Bas interrupted. He was staring at the now empty table, and seemed to be deep in thought.

"I once knew a man who carried a black knight in his pocket when he went into battle," he said quietly. He seemed very far away as he spoke. "It was during the Crusades. I'd been conscripted into the English King's forces and sent to Jerusalem to aid Richard's effort to take the Holy Land back from Saladin." Bas seemed to focus on us again, as though he were telling the story rather than just recounting the memory.

"After the battle of Arsuf, Saladin and his small force retreated to Ascalon, where Richard the Lionheart was certain he could win. But when we arrived at Ascalon, we found the city deserted and the towers destroyed. In dire need of resupply, we were easily bested in battle and never even saw the Holy City itself before we were beaten back."

Bas met our eyes as if to underscore the importance of his words. "The opposing leader, Saladin, was an expert tactician who spent most of his life in a fierce fight against the Crusaders. He was a warrior, and the most noble war commander I'd ever witnessed. When he took Jerusalem from the Crusaders, he freed slaves and allowed those who could not afford to pay his ransoms to leave the city unmolested. Despite his Kurdish heritage and Muslim faith, Saladin summoned the Jews to return to the city and permitted Christian pilgrims to visit. He sent two horses to King Richard to replace one that had fallen at Arsuf, and at the time of his death, not long after the treaties were signed, he had but one piece of gold and forty pieces of silver. He had given the rest of his treasure to the poor and did not even leave enough to pay for his burial. Saladin was known in Europe as a most chivalrous knight for his generosity and fairness, even in battle, and in the Muslim world, he was regarded as a leader of great heroism."

Bas looked directly at Tom. "Saladin was also a Monger, and it was in *his* pocket the game piece could always be found."

Ringo and I glanced at each other with a 'Whoa. Didn't see that coming' look, while Tom gazed down at the black knight that he flipped over and over between his fingers.

He finally looked up and met Bas' eyes. "Even though War himself is a proper wanker, you're saying it's still possible for his Descendants – notably Saladin, and possibly even me – to be decent human beings?"

Bas smiled warmly. "Yes. I have seen it with my own eyes, and it is not so rare as you may think."

Tom smiled a little at that, and it was good to see the smile could come back. "What are you going to do now, Bas?"

Bas leaned back with both arms behind his head and appeared to contemplate the ceiling. "Well, I suppose I should probably make myself scarce from Rome for a few years – at least until I've outlived this pope. It's a shame, really, because there is much work to be done here."

"It's pretty hard to do God's work from the bottom of a pit, though," I said.

He laughed. "That is true. The conversations are interesting though."

"Between you and God?" my voice squeaked.

"I certainly hope so. The number of things He knows about me would be rather awkward otherwise." Bas grinned.

"Remember what we told you about European Jews in the 20th Century," I said. Obviously, he had paid a little attention to my warnings when I'd first met him, because when we saw him in 1944, he was a Catholic priest helping to hide Jewish children. None of us had mentioned that meeting to him this time though. That was still a hundred years in his future.

"I remember. Your Archer was also quite adamant I avoid England during my Protestant days, at least until Her Majesty, Elizabeth Tudor, was firmly on the throne. That was excellent advice, and I quite enjoyed my time in London in the latter part of her reign. I became rather fond of going to the theater then. The Globe was a particular favorite of mine."

That got Ringo's attention. "Ye mean where Shakespeare put on 'is plays?"

Bas didn't bother to suppress his grin. "He was a fascinating man to ply with drinks in the tavern after an opening night. Perhaps one day you can convince Saira to take you to a show. The opening night of King Lear was quite spectacular."

Ringo's mouth fell open, and he turned to me, but I interrupted before he could speak. "Not a good idea." I said sharply.

"But—"

"Not. A good. Idea." I used my best mom tone and he scowled, so I arched an eyebrow at Bas. "Really?"

He grinned, obviously enjoying himself. "My experience of time will only ever be linear. I've lived far too long to ever skip my lifetime the way you young people can. But, just as you can warn me to avoid certain future events, I can also make suggestions for those in the past that you may want to attend. It is fair play, is it not?"

He got up off the floor and dusted his clothes. "Well, my dear friends, I thank you from the bottom of my heart for rescuing me from the Vatican dungeons. Beautiful Saira," he took my hand and kissed the back of it, "I feel we shall meet again, and I look forward to circumstances that might allow for leisurely conversations about life and love and God and history."

I gave him a big hug that seemed to startle him, but then again, he had only known me for a brief time in medieval France, so he had yet to experience our conversations around the kitchen table in Oradour-sur-Glane. "Where will you go?" I asked him.

He shook Ringo's hand as he answered. "I had thought to travel to China. There are Muslim persecutions there that I could be of use in quelling, and I've heard tell of Shaolin monks whose temple to Buddha is also a school. I think I should like to spend a decade or two in study."

He clapped Tom on the back as he shook his hand, and the comradery between them seemed genuine. "Your path has opened before you, young friend. I wish you wisdom and faith on your journey forward."

Bas strode from the room, and turned only long enough to make a gesture I associate with 'thank you.' I looked at Tom in surprise.

"Was that just sign language? As in ASL?"

"I think so," he said, with as much confusion. "Hey, Saira?" he asked.

"Yeah?"

He made the same 'thank you' gesture, and then he smiled.

SAIRA – 1889

Ringo got older the minute we landed at the London Bridge.

We had arrived the hour before dawn and ran to Ringo's flat just to test out our injuries. We had decided to give Tom one more day of healing before we Clocked directly into the British Museum station, and he didn't care where he slept. We'd made a promise to leave Artemisia's villa, and there was a war on in 1944. In 1889, Ringo could reset to his natural age, and we could stay one more day in a familiar place before we stepped into so much danger and uncertainty.

Ringo and I sat at his table nursing cups of tea. Mary had sent us with enough food to feed five people, so we didn't need to leave the flat if we didn't want to, but neither of us really had an appetite. Tom had made a bed for himself on the floor away from the windows, and I watched him idly for a moment while my tea cooled.

"He's aged too, even though he should look the same as he did before." I'd been studying the lines in the corners of his eyes. When his eyes were closed, I barely saw the difference, but when they were open, I could see the telltale shadows of too much experience in them.

I shifted my eyes to Ringo's face. We hadn't been away a long time, but when the change is sudden, it's noticeable. More whiskers glinted in the light, his jaw and cheekbones stretched the skin taut, and his hands and forearms looked corded with lean muscle.

"Ye've changed," Ringo said to me. I started at his words, not aware that he'd been studying me too. "Ye're eyes 'ave seen more, so they dance less when ye're restin'. And when ye smile now, it's deeper, maybe even truer, but it's not so often, and I miss the ready laughter." His look was appraising over the rim of his mug. "Ye can run longer now than I've ever seen ye go, but ye're not as reckless with yerself. Ye've felt what it is to be 'urt and it makes ye careful."

Ringo had never owned a mirror, but he'd found a piece of one when Charlie had lived here with him, and he got up to find it. It had been a long time since I'd studied myself in any mirror – a long time since I'd cared what I looked like beyond my ability to blend into whatever year I found myself.

I studied my face in the shard of mirror. Up close my eyes held less laughter, and my mouth was completely neutral when I wasn't smiling. My eyebrows were nice though, and I liked my cheekbones – they made interesting hollows and planes in my face. They were balanced by a jaw that let me get away with dressing like a man if a person didn't notice the long eyelashes. I'd gotten stronger, and lean muscle had settled in, and I knew I would rarely ever fit the world's idea of feminine beauty. But I could be graceful when I wanted to be, mostly when I was running, and my body was strong enough to do what I asked of it most times.

"Ye're beautiful," he said quietly, and I shook my head.

"There's nothing conventional about my looks."

Ringo shrugged, "Conventions are more of a guideline than a rule."

I burst out laughing. "You watched *Pirates of the Caribbean*?"

He tried, unsuccessfully, to hide a smile. "Connor and I were tryin' to decide which characters we were more like."

I laughed. "So, who's Jack Sparrow?"

He snorted. "Neither of us. We're both Will Turners, though I wouldn't mind bein' a bit more Elizabeth Swann."

My eyebrows furrowed. "Why?"

"Well, Will is fairly obvious for us – 'e's loyal, and brave, and will fight to the death for people 'e loves. But Elizabeth is a natural leader, and she's a great battle strategist. She also says exactly what she means, even if it offends someone more powerful. Mostly, though, she inspires people to follow 'er, like she did all the pirate kings. Connor and I both agree ye're the most like Elizabeth of all of us, and we're glad to be yer Wills."

I shook my head at him but couldn't hold back the smile. "That might be the nicest compliment you've ever given me."

"Nah, when I said ye could run for longer than ye used to, that was nicer."

He pulled a small silk bag from his pocket and slid it across the table to me. "'Ere. I found this for ye in Rome."

I'd forgotten that Ringo had gone shopping in the city when Artemisia and I were in the Tower of the Winds. I untied the little bag, and a bead strung on a piece of leather fell into my hand. It was Venetian glass of a beautiful amber color swirled through with gold, vaguely eye-shaped, and utterly breathtaking. I looked up at him in wonder. "It's so beautiful."

He wouldn't meet my eyes, but got up to tie the leather around my neck. "It reminded me of yer Cat's eyes," he said quietly. The bead nestled in the hollow below my throat, and I touched it reverently.

"Thank you, Ringo." I turned to hug him, but he dodged my embrace. He went over to the post where I'd carved the crowned heart, touched it lightly, then hauled himself up the climbing rope that dangled from the ceiling. He sat on the cross beam and leaned against the support, didn't invite me up, and didn't meet my eyes. I left him to the only solitude a person could get in a single room loft.

I rinsed the mugs and dried them, then re-checked my bag to make sure I had everything I wanted to Clock with. Ringo still hadn't come down from his perch after I'd done whatever washing I could manage with the limited facilities, so finally I called up.

"I'm going to nap for a while. Shove me over if you want to sleep too."

"I won't be doin' that," he called down quietly.

"Why not? The bed's big enough," I said as I lay down on it. I wasn't sure what the night in the tunnels would bring, and I felt like rest and food were the only ways I could prepare myself.

He mumbled something that I couldn't have heard right, because it sounded like he said "no bed's big enough." I turned down the noise in my brain so I didn't wonder about it too long, and I finally drifted to sleep, my hand on the cat's-eye bead at my throat.

Ringo still wasn't wild about the idea of a spiral in his flat, so the three of us made our way back down to the London Bridge after dark. I wasn't concerned about getting the exact day and minute right on this Clock, because it was the actions on the platform I needed to hold in my brain.

Tom, Ringo, and I had hashed out the incidents of that night in as much detail as each of us could remember. It was pretty fascinating to dissect the whole thing as if it was a scene in a movie we'd all watched but had interpreted slightly differently.

Tom's recall of the night had been quite different at first, colored as it was by his anger and the hatred he felt for the whole Walters family. The memories that Ringo and I had were more similar, but there were still differences in what our brains put emphasis on. The thing that was clearest in my mind was landing in the bishop's attic and realizing that Archer wasn't behind us. The thing Ringo remembered best was the moment he shoved Tom through the spiral. The thing neither of us could completely recreate was what happened right after that. Both of us had been focused on Tom, so we hadn't seen how George Walters got the gun from Archer, or how Archer moved right before Walters shot him.

We also had no idea how this was going to work. Based on both Tom's and my experiences trying to Clock to a place we already were, the theory was that if I directed us to the moment Ringo had tackled Tom and sent him through the spiral, and Tom held that same moment in his mind, he would be spit out, for lack of a more technical term, at the moment he disappeared. The part none of us could guess at was what would happen to me and Ringo.

As I saw it, there were a couple of possibilities. One was that we would hit the platform the moment after we left it. That would be fine if Tom managed to disarm George before he shot the V-1 rocket and armed it to explode. If the bomb went off again just like it had the first time, we'd Clock into an explosion. Which would suck.

Another possibility was that we'd get shot out on the wrong time stream after we left 1944 to go forward. And the third possibility, always a favorite, was that we'd just get lost *between* times, never to emerge again.

What we mostly realized as we talked through all the possible scenarios was that this job was dangerous for all of us, and in the absence of hazard pay, or fame and fortune and everything that goes with it, we'd have to acknowledge to each other that this sucked, but no matter what happened, *we* would know what being heroic felt like.

I had already traced three of the five spirals on the bridge support, and both guys had a hand gripped on my belt – one on either side – when I turned quickly and kissed each one on the cheek. "Love you guys." I really meant it. Even for Tom.

Ringo recovered first. "We'll get through this," he said with determination.

"Thank you," Tom finally said, quietly.

And then we Clocked.

ARCHER – PRESENT DAY

Tam and I had been surviving on the one meal a day they left for him. The Mongers still thought I was a Vampire and seemed to hope that I would start feasting on my cell mate when I got hungry enough. The truth was that the idea of ever tasting blood again was enough to make me a vegetarian.

But we were weak. The lack of food was a big part of it, but I was also still healing from a gunshot wound that fortunately didn't seem to have festered, and neither of us had moved more than our twenty by twenty cell would allow. At least our captors understood that a dehydrated human would make a poor source of blood for a Vampire and had regularly refilled a bucket with water in one corner. There was a drain in the opposite corner, and we had figured out the cell must have housed animals at one time. That explained the vague smells that still lingered in the air, and the clump of moldy straw we'd found. The drain was useful for our waste, though it did little to cover the rank odor that we lived in.

We had lost all sense of day or night, and Tam had taken to checking the time and date whenever he connected with Ava. She kept a calendar on her phone and would show him that, as well as whatever notes she had taken about things that were happening. For people who communicated only via images, it was surprisingly effective.

That was how I knew it was a Tuesday morning the next time they opened the cell. Tam and I had discussed all the various options for getting out, from surprising our captors with an attack, to playing daytime-dead. Ultimately, because I was still fairly weak, I thought a variation on the second option might yield the most interesting information. Walters' presumption that I was still a Vampire was the key to such a feeble plan, and I sincerely hoped that his arrogance made him as resistant to new thought as I needed him to be.

Three Monger bodyguards entered the cell with guns and torches drawn. I immediately played dead, and Tam knew not to resist them in any way.

"What are you doing?" Tam asked. I could hear the fear in his voice wasn't entirely feigned.

"Taking the Sucker for a little stroll. What do you care?" one of the Mongers said.

"Good. Keep him, why don't you? He gives me the creeps." I was proud of Tam for that.

A comically evil chuckle from a gruff-voiced Monger, "What? You don't fancy being the main course? Yeah, we'll see what we can do about that."

Two of the men grabbed my arms, while the third one presumably kept his gun trained on Tam. It was amazingly difficult to make my body go completely limp when I would have cheerfully fought with and beaten the men holding me if I had still had my Vampire health. They half-carried, half-dragged me from the cell as though I were a drunk they'd found passed out in the street. There was a feeling of powerlessness in my mortality that I hadn't expected, and I wondered if all men felt this or if I was particularly susceptible due to my change in status. It bore consideration at a time when I wasn't being unceremoniously bumped and jostled to an unknown destination.

"They really do go out cold, don't they?" This Monger sounded younger than the others. He gripped me under my right shoulder, and it was just tentative enough that I sensed his fear of me.

The Monger at my left shoulder was the gruff one who had threatened Tam. His grip was much harder than it needed to be, and he suddenly pinched the tender skin under my bicep. It was everything I could do not to hurl a punch.

"You could probably cut his throat and he wouldn't react," the gruff one said. I could hear the cruelty in his tone, and I thought the younger one could too, because he shivered.

"You wouldn't want to get his blood on you though. That's what the boss said. If there was blood we had to stay away because it's so contagious."

"You ever think about why the boss is keeping him?" the gruff one asked.

"We're not paid to think," the one who wasn't part of the carry team said. He was behind the other two, which meant he could see my face, though the beam of his torch wasn't trained on me.

"Seriously, though. Why keep a highly contagious Sucker unless you want his blood for something?" The gruff one was spinning conspiracy theories, but it was something I'd considered as well.

"You think he wants to weaponize it?" the young one asked.

"No. That would be stupid. Why turn people into something you can't kill? Nah, I think it might be the opposite – make an army of soldiers who can't die." For all his nastiness, the gruff one wasn't a complete idiot.

"Shut up, both of you," said the one at the rear.

"But what if the soldiers didn't want to be Suckers? Or what if they turned on him after they were infected? No one can control Vamps – they're too strong." The young one's fear made him tremble.

"Or what if …" the gruff one spoke in low tones meant only for the young one, "he wants the blood so *he* can be immortal. I was there when that kid jumped him after the bombing down at Holborn. I heard what he said to him right before. He said he never expected a bastard bloodsucker to become so useful to him. 'Course after that he told us to shoot the kid, because he was a terrorist after all …" The gruff voice faded, as if he wasn't quite sure about the terrorist part of his own statement.

My mind raced furiously. Walters had said Tom was part of his plan, but he was now keeping me on ice, so to speak, in an underground cell. *Could* he be planning to infect himself? That seemed ridiculous considering the limitations of daylight and sustenance a Vampire necessarily had, but until I understood Walters' plan, I had to consider even the most ludicrous options.

We turned a corner and a door slammed open. "What the hell?" Seth Walters' voice sent a surge of anger through me, and I had to force every muscle in my body to remain utterly limp.

"Sorry, sir. You said to bring him right away."

His sigh of frustration made me absurdly happy. "Fine. Put it on the table and strap it down."

It? Charming.

"Who is that?" a feminine voice asked. I'd heard the voice before.

The men heaved me onto a metal table. I did *not* want to be strapped down, but in my current physical condition, I doubted I could prevail against three armed Mongers. The powerless feeling was magnified as the men strapped both wrists and ankles with zip ties.

"Nothing that concerns you, niece."

Walters' niece, Raven. I could sense her eyes on me, and her hesitation. She couldn't know who I was, as she'd never seen me in person, but perhaps she'd heard of me.

The gruff Monger finished with the last zip tie and then flicked my nose like a schoolyard bully as he walked away. Raven gasped, and that surprised me more than the flick did. Sympathy from a Monger? That was new.

The door closed, but the silence remained. Walters finally broke it with impatience. "Finish what you wanted to say. He can't hear you."

She hesitated a moment longer, then finally took a breath. "I'm not going back to that school."

"It wasn't a request, Raven." Walters sounded angry. There was a knock at the door, and his voice was aggressive and frustrated. "Come!"

The door opened, and Walters' tone became businesslike. "You brought everything you need?"

"Yes, sir," a man's voice said.

"Good. I need two liters. See that you don't contaminate it."

"Sir, one unit – half a liter – is the usual donation. He probably only has five or six liters in him."

"I said two liters." Walters didn't wait for confirmation. "Jaeger, stay in here with the doctor. I'm going to walk my niece out."

I heard Jaeger enter, but Raven wasn't finished. "You can't make me go back, Seth."

"Can't I?" he sneered. "I know about your mongrel boyfriend. I could have taken him twice, but I was hoping you'd come to your senses before I had to." He paused to let that sink in, and I thought I heard a tiny intake of breath from Raven. He continued with even more menace. "If you go back there with him, they'll let you in to save his life. And be very clear, Raven. If you get into that school and do exactly as I tell you, you *will* be saving his life."

He must have taken her arm, because they moved toward the door. She was so angry her voice choked back tears. "Mother won't let you do this!" she snarled at him.

Walters' voice was saccharine. "My sister-in-law brought this on herself when she left St. Brigid's, and in fact, she'll do exactly as I say. You all will." His voice cut off when he kicked the door shut behind him, but not before I heard him mutter, "One way or another."

A band tightened around my upper arm, and I felt the doctor tap inside my elbow. "Two pints is too much," the doctor said to Jaeger.

"Do what the boss said," he answered in a bored voice.

The needle went in, and I wondered idly if Walters would actually test my blood before he used it.

SAIRA – GHOST STATION, 1944

I knew the moment Tom left my side. I couldn't feel it, because *between* robbed me of all physical sensation beyond cold, but there was a moment when he was just *gone*.

And then we landed.

Underground, on the platform, with the smell of metal and dust and blood filling the air.

I was on my knees, and I was afraid to open my eyes. And then opening them was worse than anything I could have imagined.

Tom lay on his back in front of me. His eyes were so very afraid as he stared up at the ceiling.

"Tom!" I cried out. His chest was covered in blood. There was so much of it that I couldn't tell where he'd been shot. A bloody bubble burst at his lips as his eyes found mine and he tried to speak.

"Oh God, Tom," I sobbed. I tried to gather him to myself, but Ringo knelt down next to me and shouted my name.

"Saira!" I guessed he'd been doing that a couple of times already, because his tone was frantic. I looked up into his face and focused on his eyes.

"Take him to Shaw!"

Mr. Shaw. Mr. Shaw was a doctor and he could do something. I reached back for the wall and blindly traced the spiral we'd come through, while the other hand clutched Tom's arm through the bloody remains of his shirt. As the spiral pulled me through it, I looked up.

Archer was on the platform. He knelt on George Walters' chest while Ringo stood over them with a gun trained at Walters' head. His eyes found mine.

"I'll come back," I whispered, or maybe screamed, before everything was gone.

Saira – Present Day

Mr. Shaw. Go to Mr. Shaw. I didn't have a location in my head when I Clocked with Tom, I had a man. And when I landed in a room with no portal, that man stood at a microscope in front of me.

"Mr. Shaw." I didn't know if it was my words or my sudden appearance that made him jump, but he was beside us in an instant.

"Good God! Is that Tom?"

"He's been shot." My voice was strangled through sobs and gasps. Tom was unresponsive, and Mr. Shaw had to peel my grip off him.

I suddenly saw in my mind exactly how it had happened. The memory of Tom throwing himself in front of the hailstorm of bullets from George Walters' gun flooded my brain.

"I can see that," Shaw growled. "He's still infected?"

"Yes, but he wants the cure." I tried to lift Tom up onto the table, but couldn't do it by myself. Shaw was putting on latex gloves, and I registered that I'd brought Tom to Mr. Shaw's laboratory at school.

"Wash your hands, Saira," he said sharply to me, pointing to the sink in the corner. His tone of voice broke through my single-minded focus on Tom, and I obeyed. By the time my hands were clean, Mr. Shaw had lifted Tom up to his work table and torn through Tom's shirt. Tom's chest was a ruin of stab and gunshot wounds, and everything seemed to bleed at once.

I swallowed a sob and looked at Mr. Shaw. "What can I do?"

"Up on the high shelf there are vials. Blue plungers on the syringes. Bring me one." He was all business until he roared, "CONNOR!"

I jumped at the fierce command in his voice and found the vials he meant. I pulled one out of the rack and brought it to Shaw.

"Glove up, buttercup. You're not immune." His voice made him sound half-Bear, and I reacted instantly to his direction.

Connor came racing into the room, out of breath and concerned. His eyes went wide at the sight of me. "Saira?" There was so much wonder, awe, and concern wrapped up in his voice that I would have hugged him if I wasn't so afraid for Tom. Then Connor saw him on the table and practically pushed me out of the way in his hurry to get gloves on. "He's still infected?" Connor asked me, breathless.

"Yes, he's still infected!" Mr. Shaw roared. "Bring that vial here and do it!"

Connor plucked the vial out of my hands and took it to Tom. Mr. Shaw had a pair of bullet forceps in hand and was digging into one of the holes in Tom's chest. I knew they were bullet forceps because he yelled at Connor to get the other pair from his kit.

Connor called to me, too intent on injecting the contents of the vial into Tom's arm. "Saira, the kit is in the cabinet. It's like a tool box, only cleaner."

He finished plunging the substance into Tom's vein and then dropped the used needle into a biohazard bin. Suddenly, Tom began to convulse on the table.

"Damn it! Connor, get over here and hold him down!" Shaw growled.

"He's bleeding out. It's too much," said Connor.

"It's the damn cure. I don't know how Devereux survived it, injured as he was."

Wait, what?

"Archer? Archer's here???" I screeched.

"No, he's not here. Damn it, Connor, hold him!" Shaw pulled a mangled bit of lead from the hole in Tom's chest and dropped it into a metal tin. The plunking noise was somehow louder than anything else in the room.

"Where is he?" I was close to panic, and whatever hold I had left on sanity or control felt wafer-thin. The tremors in my body felt like a greyhound dog waiting for the gate to lift so it could run. I needed to run – *to Archer* – more than I'd ever needed anything in my life.

"Walters has him. Get my suture kit! There, in the box." Shaw was focused on the freely bleeding wound in Tom's chest, and he was all business, with no room for anything but saving Tom's life. The convulsions were slowing down, but the blood seemed to be pouring from Tom's body.

Seth Walters had my husband. My hands fisted and I took a breath to fight down the Cat who wanted to claw her way out of my skin.

"He's going to die from blood loss if we don't get him some now!" Shaw snarled.

"Take mine," I said, ripping off my jacket. It was something to distract me from every instinct I had to race out of there. I needed to think, and to have a better plan than just the blind need to *find him*.

"You'll kill Tom. No Descendant can survive blood from another Family," Shaw said as he swabbed the hole with gauze.

"We don't have any ungifteds here at school. Would a pure Seer work? Maybe Adam? They're related," Connor said. He was putting pressure on some of the other bleeds while Shaw took the suture kit from my hands and threaded the needle.

"We just don't know what mixed-bloods can handle," Shaw said. Then he blinked and looked up, as if suddenly aware of something. "Ringo. Get him! He's a universal donor."

Connor looked at me with some mix of fear and expectation on his face. I shot Tom one last quick glance, then nodded. This was something I could do. "I need to draw a spiral here."

Shaw growled at me. "Classroom next door. Go!"

I raced out of the laboratory and into the empty science classroom next door. I went straight to the chalkboard and drew the fastest spiral of my life. Three words pounded in my brain like a heartbeat. *Archer is alive. Archer is alive.* I focused my brain on the scene I'd just left behind on the ghost station platform. Archer had subdued George Walters while Ringo covered him with a gun.

I must have arrived moments after I left, because Archer was still looking at me. The scene was still the same, except Tom was on Mr. Shaw's table in the present.

Had it been the right present? Yes! Mr. Shaw had asked if Tom was *still* infected.

I looked up. The metallic skin of an unexploded bomb gleamed above me. Archer was alive. George Walters was alive.

Tom had repaired time!

Ringo took a step toward me, and Archer stood up. George Walters scrambled backwards, suddenly free of the weight on his chest. I could see the instant debate in his eyes – go for the gun or run away and live to fight another day. He flung himself off the platform, and Archer lunged after him.

"Let him go!" I yelled.

"'E 'as the ring, Saira," Ringo said.

I winced. Now was not the time. "Let him go."

George Walters disappeared down the track, and I ran to Archer and threw myself at him. He caught me in his arms and I crushed my mouth to his. It wasn't a kiss so much as it was me tasting his life and his breath and the beat of his heart. I held his face in my hands and gripped his eyes with mine. "I love you," I said. "And I'm going back to you." Every ounce of pain and fear and hope and truth was poured into those words, and then I did the hardest thing I'd ever done.

I let him go, grabbed Ringo, and ran to the spiral.

When Ringo's blood flowed directly into Tom through what Mr. Shaw called a 'battlefield transfusion,' and all Tom's wounds had been stitched closed, we finally heard the events of the past several weeks. Mr. Shaw wouldn't let anyone else come into the makeshift operating room, but he sent word to my mom and Adam that we were here.

Connor told us that Adam had gotten all the mixed-blood captives out, and though it took a couple of days for them to make their way to St. Brigid's, they had been able to sneak past the few Mongers that Walters had originally set to surround the school. Since then, there had been many more guards added and several attempts made to get in – none of them successful yet because of Miss Simpson's wards.

Connor had woken up under a blanket in the bombed-out passage of the ghost station, mostly healed from his wounds because of the time he'd spent as a Wolf. He'd been able to sneak past the rescue workers and make his way back to school in his Wolf form, and then discovered that his mom's search for him had been broadcast around the city. From Ava's green-haired leprechaun, Tam, they learned that Walters claimed to be holding Connor, so when Connor showed up, they'd been relieved to find that had been Walters' pathetic attempt to control Archer.

Tam was also responsible for all the information they had on Archer after the explosion, and through his Sight-sendings to Ava, they knew Archer was alive and recovering from his wounds. The two of them were being held by Seth Walters and his armed Mongers someplace underground in a cell that smelled like animals.

Ringo's eyebrows furrowed. "An underground stable? I know of only one, under Camden Town. In my time, they kept the pit ponies that worked on the railways there."

"I need to talk to Ava," I said.

"Not in here," growled Mr. Shaw. His gaze had been locked on Tom since he had removed the IV from Ringo, and he didn't seem willing to leave.

I paused at Tom's head and brushed the hair back from his closed eyes. Mr. Shaw seemed about to stop me from touching him with my now un-gloved hands, but I ignored him and leaned down to whisper in Tom's ear. "You need to live."

Then I followed Connor out of the laboratory and we stepped into the classroom next door.

My mom practically leapt across the room at me, and I was caught in her arms before I could even say her name. She was crying, and it made me cry, which frustrated me because I didn't have time for tears. "Mom, I need to talk to Ava," I said in her ear.

She nodded and stepped back. "I know, honey. I wanted to go to Archer, but I can't do what you do." That surprised me, and I gave her another quick hug and turned to Ava.

Ava reached out and touched my hands with both of hers. "Here. Here's what I know." I loved that about her. She knew, without me telling her, exactly what I needed.

Blackness, and then a door opened, and behind some Mongers were columns and some arches made of brick.

She let go of my hands and then gave me a hug. "I'm scared for him, Saira. I'm scared for them both," Ava whispered in my ear. She hadn't been sleeping much, and her eyes looked a little haunted. "Tam is worried. They took Archer away hours ago, and he hasn't seen him since."

I closed my eyes and inhaled sharply. *No – nothing could happen to Archer now that I'd found my way back to him.*

Strong arms encircled me from behind, and Adam's voice spoke in my ear. "You brought him back."

I turned and flung my arms around my friend. The tears I'd put on hold in my mom's arms came gushing out in Adam's. "You got them out," I said, half-laughing, and half-sobbing. I kissed his cheek and he wiped my tears off with a smile.

"I have to go," I said to him. "I have to get Archer and Tam."

"Take me with ye," said Ringo, but I shook my head.

"I need to bring them both back. I'm too slow with four."

"I'll go with you." My mom looked fierce and strong and very, very determined. There was a look in her eyes that I knew I'd inherited, so I didn't bother to argue. Apparently Ringo knew that look too, because he pressed something into her hand.

"Take this. It's loaded," he said quietly.

I stared at the gun Ringo had just given my mother. It was the gun he had picked up off the platform in 1944. I hadn't known he'd carried it forward.

My mom pocketed it carefully, then held my hand as I began to trace the chalkboard spiral I'd drawn earlier. "Do you know where we're going?" she whispered to me.

"No. I just know I'm going to him."

She searched my eyes, then finally nodded and took a deep breath. "I've missed you," she said quietly.

"Me too, Mom."

The nothingness of *between* seemed colder and darker than before, and it took every ounce of my concentration to focus on Archer. I forced my mind away from the memory of his embrace on the ghost station platform. I did not want to go back to 1944 – I needed to find my Archer *now*. So instead, I put everything I had into wanting to hold the *human* man. I imagined a man who could walk in the sun, who recovered from wounds one day at a time, who could watch a sunrise with me from a roof.

I imagined a man I could grow old with.

The landing was tough - my knees hit the brick floor hard enough to hurt, and my mother's gasp told me we'd been *between* for a long time. Illuminated by an overhead work light, the room we were in was empty except for a table in the middle.

A table on which Archer lay.

My mom's intake of air became a sob, and she rushed forward. I hushed her unthinkingly while I drew my knife from its sheath. The door to the room slammed open and a Monger rushed in, gun in hand. I pulled my arm back to hurl the knife in it, but before I could let go, my mom smashed the gun Ringo had given her down on the Monger's temple and he crumpled to the floor.

I stared at her in shock. "You just pistol-whipped an armed man."

She looked shaky and a little stunned at her own actions.

"You're pretty badass, Mom," I whispered as I slit through the zip ties at Archer's ankles and wrists. "Archer!" I leaned close to his ear and whispered loudly as I shook his shoulders. He didn't seem to have fresh injuries, although there was a cotton ball taped to the inside of his elbow. They'd taken blood.

He started to come around, though his eyes had trouble focusing for a few seconds. "Saira?" he whispered. It sounded like he didn't believe what he was seeing, so I pulled his hand up to touch my face.

"It's me," I said. "We have to get the leprechaun and go."

He tried to smile, but it came out lopsided. "Help me up," he said. His voice sounded crackly, like he was dehydrated, and I wondered exactly how much blood they'd taken from him.

My mom got on the other side of him, and between the two of us, we got Archer to his feet. "Hi Claire," he said quietly, and she kissed his cheek, which made him smile.

"Which way to your cell?" I asked quietly as we maneuvered around the Monger my mom had knocked out. When I put my hand to Archer's chest his heart was pounding, and his breath came too fast like he couldn't get enough air.

"This way." Archer directed us down a long open center hall full of support columns.

"Ringo said this place is under Camden," I whispered as we walked. Archer seemed to be counting his steps, and his eyes were closed.

"The stables for the railway horses. I should have remembered," he said. He sounded far away, and my mom looked over at me with the same worry I felt. The place felt strangely empty, and I didn't like that there had only been one guard. When Archer finally stopped and whispered, "Here," my radar for danger was pinging like crazy.

My mom reached for the door handle, but I stopped her. "Wait," I whispered. I sent my Cat's senses out to see what sort of predators might be lurking in the shadows, and I found what I'd feared.

"There are Mongers in there," I breathed. I almost cried, because I felt at that moment like I was the strongest person among us – and that wasn't an encouraging thought.

We backed away from the door and tucked around a corner from the cell where at least three Mongers waited with Tam. I had no idea if Tam was even still alive, and I wished with all my heart that Ava was there with us.

"Archer, can you reach out to Tam?"

He shook his head. "I haven't tried. Ava's the one he communicates with."

"But your Seeing skills should be better now that you're fully human, right?"

He barked a quiet laugh. "I'm not entirely sure how human I am – they've taken a lot of blood from me, and I'm not strong – but I'll try. If I can, what should I tell him?"

The problem was, I didn't know. My mom whispered urgently. "How many Mongers are in with him, Saira?"

"I think three. I've been running down our assets in my head, and they're not good. One gun, two daggers, two Clockers, and a Seer."

I looked over at Archer – my husband. He was so pale, and weaker and thinner than I'd ever seen him. The scruff of a beard grew on his face, and it shocked me. I'd never seen hair on his face before, and it made him somehow more vulnerable and stronger-looking at the same time.

My mom broke my silent contemplation. "And a Shifter, don't forget that."

My eyes widened, and I grabbed at the Shifter bone I still wore under my shirt.

"I've got him. He's scared, but he's alive," Archer said.

The bare bones of a really bad plan were beginning to form in my mind. "If he can get close to the door, I'm going to come through as a Cougar. As soon as they stop shooting at the door, he should dive through it."

Archer looked at me like I was insane.

"It's a crap plan, but it's all I've got. My Cat is low enough to the ground that they'll probably miss. If Mom shoots into the room at around chest height, and Tam and I stay low, then you can kick the door closed as soon as we're back through it."

He held my gaze for a beat longer, then narrowed his eyes. "It's a spectacularly crap plan … but I have nothing better. The downside to taking the cure."

"Yeah, we're going to be talking about that."

He reached for my hand and whispered, "I can't wait." There wasn't a sarcastic-sounding tone to it, and I smiled. Archer closed his eyes, and I knew he was relaying my instructions to Tam.

"Mom, if I have to draw a spiral, it'll take too long. Do you think if I start it, you could, I don't know, hold it open for us?"

"Is such a thing possible?" she asked with awe in her voice.

"I think so. I drew one in 1944 with no specific Clocking location in mind, and somehow I held it open long enough for us to be pushed into it. Then, once I was in it, I focused on where to go."

She looked skeptical, but then nodded. "I'll do what I can, but you'll have to draw it."

I pulled out the piece of chalk I'd pocketed from the science classroom and drew on the brick just around the corner from the entrance to the room. It was out of the line of fire, but close enough to reach if either of us got injured, and at this point, I was feeling *very* vulnerable.

I carefully cleared my mind of any destination as I drew, and my mom watched me closely. When I'd finished the last spiral, I handed the chalk to her. "Can you feel it in your mind?" I asked.

She wore a startled expression. "Yes, I believe I actually can. It's as though there's a great, yawning hole in the wall behind that spiral. But everything in it is the blackest of blackness."

"Yes, that's it," I said as I began stripping out of my clothes and handing them to my mom. I paused for the briefest moment. "Archer," I whispered to him.

He opened his eyes and found me.

"Like my trousers?" Impossibly, the buckskin trousers Ringo bought me had survived, and I flashed him a quick turn in them, wearing just the trousers and a camisole.

Archer smiled a tired yet appreciative smile. "Very much."

I leaned over him and gave him a quick kiss. "I look forward to you showing me how much," I whispered. His eyes flashed with interest, and I hoped I had inspired him enough to stay conscious until I could get him to Mr. Shaw.

I finished stripping, then whispered to them, "Love you both," before I Shifted.

Archer moved into position right outside the door, and he propped himself against the wall to stay upright. His hand stroked my fur as he whispered into my Cat's ear. "One, two, three."

He pulled the door open, and I streaked inside the nearly pitch black cell as gunshots blasted into the empty doorway. My Cat's vision was perfect, and I spotted Ava's leprechaun just inside the door as I barreled into the legs of the first Monger. He went down with a yell and crashed into the second guy. The third stopped shooting so he could see what was happening, and Tam lurched out of the cell and into the dim light of the main cavern. More shots were fired – a couple of them even came from outside the cell. My mom had reached her arm around the door frame and was shooting wildly into the room to cause confusion.

I hurled myself through the doorway before the Mongers could regroup to go after Tam. The door slammed shut, and Archer dropped the wooden slat across the front of it. Then he collapsed onto the floor at my feet. My mom yelled, "Tam! Get him!"

Feet were pounding on stairs, and I knew we had just seconds left. I moved behind Tam as he heaved Archer's arm up over his shoulder and half-carried, half-dragged him to my mom.

A Monger rounded the corner just as Tam and Archer got to the spiral. I spun and roared my biggest, scariest roar at him. He pulled up short and stared at me just as Archer reached out and grabbed the ruff of my neck.

And then we Clocked.

I forced the image of the science classroom into my angry Cat's brain, praying that an animal's vision would be enough to Clock us to the right place. We landed after just the right amount of time *between*, and I was gratified to see it was the place I meant to go. Tam was quietly sick in the corner, Archer was unconscious, and my mom called for help with him. Ringo and Adam were on either side of him in an instant.

They laid him down on the floor while Connor ran to get Mr. Shaw. My mom motioned me out into the hall, and I followed her into another classroom. She dropped my clothes and shut the door.

"Shift and get dressed."

I mentally thanked my Cat for her help, then did as my mom said. When I was pulling on my boots she dropped down in front of me to capture my gaze.

"We're in trouble, Saira." I really looked at my mom for the first time in weeks, or in my case, a span that felt like several lifetimes. She looked worried and tired, but she looked more beautiful than I'd maybe ever seen her. Being in love with Mr. Shaw suited her.

"Seth Walters is controlling people with the ring. Yeah, I heard."

"He blames you for the fact that there is any resistance at all. None of us are safe, but if he catches you, I'm afraid of what he'll do. What we just did to get Archer was necessary, but it can't happen again, honey. You can't put yourself in his way like that."

My mom was terrified. I'd never seen her so afraid, and I felt like I needed to comfort her. "Mom," I started, but she interrupted me.

"You're stronger and braver and smarter than anyone I know, but I want you to seriously consider something, Saira. Consider taking Ringo home, and then you and Archer go away somewhere, to some place or time where none of this can touch you. Just live out your life with him safe from the hatred and the danger. We'll survive here, but I wouldn't if something happened to you."

I finished pulling my boots on and then pulled her to her feet. I hugged her with everything I had, and I said into her hair, "I love you, Mom, and believe me, I get your fear."

She stepped back and searched my face. "Something happened," she said, and I nodded.

"Yeah, something happened. Archer died, and I was alone …"
My eyes filled with tears, but I put a firm clamp on the waterworks
– I did not have time for this. Not yet. I took a deep breath to push
the sobs back down.

My mom pulled me back into her arms. "Oh, Saira! I hoped
you would never have to know that pain, even for a minute."

"But I do, Mom – we both do. We all get our share, so no, I'm
not going to let you or anyone else take it on just because you can
bear it. I can bear it too, and if we all stand together, maybe we can
stop just *bearing it* and instead, *do something*."

She stepped back and wiped the tears off her face with a laugh.
"You top me by five inches, so I've looked up at you for some
time. Now I find that I look up *to* you as well. It makes me very
proud that despite my best efforts to give you no upbringing at all,
you've become a remarkable woman."

I held her hand as we left the room. Even if nothing else on
this time stream was right, my mom was here, and she was worth
all of it.

THE SITUATION

Mr. Shaw and Connor had taken Archer into the laboratory where another table was cleared for him. He was hooked up to an IV of fluids, but he was still unconscious and horribly pale.

"He needs blood," said Mr. Shaw when I entered.

"But the infection is cured, right?" I asked.

Connor was looking into a microscope and nodding. "Yeah, no active infection. He's just an AB-positive Seer." He stepped back to let Mr. Shaw confirm.

"Whoever took blood from him took too much. An infusion is the fastest way, but I have no idea how the mutation has changed his body," said Mr. Shaw after he had looked into the microscope.

My eyes traveled over Archer's pale-as-death face, then to Tom, who was breathing on his own, but still unconscious. "It all comes down to blood, doesn't it?" I wasn't really speaking to anyone but myself, and I turned on my heels and left the room.

Adam was still pacing the science classroom. "Ava's gone off to find Ringo and the leprechaun showers and fresh clothes."

"Would you give blood to Archer?"

Adam registered my words for exactly one second before he stepped forward and began rolling up his sleeve. "Let's go."

Twenty minutes later, Archer was still out cold but looked much better with a bag of Adam's blood draining into him. Adam sat in a chair sipping orange juice and met my eyes after studying the two unconscious guys on the tables. "I guess blood type compatibility is really the only difference between us anyone should ever have to worry about, you know?"

He said what I'd been thinking, and Connor spoke from across the room. "It's bad enough for regular people to figure out who can get whose blood. Add in our Family types and it just gets stupid."

"What about me? Who can I give blood to?" Suddenly that mattered, because the last two hours had been all about blood.

Connor came and sat next to me, and I barely resisted hugging him. Despite the fact that he had just helped to save the lives of two people, he still had teenaged-boy sensibilities. So, I bumped his shoulder with mine, and he bumped mine back. It was boy for everything from 'hi' to 'thank you for being awesome.'

"I started testing the mixed-bloods Adam brought in, and I'd like to start mixing for compatibility with each Family. You're right that it really only comes down to who's blood can save whom, and given the mixed-blood immunity to the Monger ring's power, I'd say they have some extra benefits."

Adam scoffed. "Kind of shoots down that whole 'mixed is bad' b.s., doesn't it?" He was looking at his cousin when he said it.

"Tom and I went through a pretty rough patch for a while, but I'm a huge fan," I said. "He was stupidly brave and totally self-sacrificing, and he did it all to get back here to you. The biggest part of getting cured was your acceptance."

Adam's eyes filled, and he wiped them angrily. "That's such complete bollocks. He's always had my acceptance. Tom has been my best friend since we were kids, and for him to think I could ever believe otherwise …" His tone was harsh and he turned away.

I gave harsh right back to him. "He heard how you spoke about Archer. He heard what you said about Mongers when Seth split you and Alex up. And then to find out he is one and became the other? Of course he thought you would hate him."

I knew he'd get it, and he did. He turned back and looked stricken. "I didn't know. I only knew what everyone said."

"Right. That's what happens." I softened my tone. "We parrot the prejudices of our parents, and they continue until nobody even remembers why we hated those people in the first place. According to Descendant laws, I was supposed to have been killed when I was born," I nodded at Tom, "and him too. How much would that suck?"

Adam took a deep breath. "So what do we do? How do we change things?"

I shrugged. "I just know that I can't let the prejudices slide. No one gets a pass on hate or intolerance around me. From now on I say something, and I don't care who I'm talking to."

Connor chuckled. "I'd love to see you take on Mrs. Arman."

Adam scoffed. "You won't have to, because I will."

I included them both in my smile. "You guys, I love you, but I stink and I need a bath." I hopped off the table and Connor wrinkled his nose.

"I wasn't going to say anything, but—"

For that he got a poke in the ribs before I headed to the door. "If either of them wakes up, will you kiss them for me and tell them I'll be right back?"

They both wrinkled their noses at that, and I left the laboratory with the first lightness I'd felt in a long time.

After a shower and a hurried meal, I got waylaid by my mom and the Arman adults. They wanted all the details of everything that had happened while we were gone, but much to Mrs. Arman's chagrin, I said no. I told them to call a general meeting of everyone currently at the school, and we would tell everyone at the same time. I was definitely done with the control of information that had been practiced by the Families for far too long.

When I finally made my way back to the laboratory, I found it empty, but tracked Mr. Shaw down in his office, where he was taking Archer's blood pressure. Archer's hair was wet, and he wore his own clothes, but not the ones he'd had on before. I was surprised at that, but was too busy grinning to follow up yet.

"Hi, handsome," I said as I slipped into the room. "How can you possibly have been up?"

His answering smile made my heart do giant happy dances in my chest. "Hello, beautiful," he said, then tossed his head at Mr. Shaw. "Ask him."

Mr. Shaw ripped the Velcro open and wrapped up the BP cuff as he peered into Archer's face. "You're a hundred and fifty-odd years old, but all your readings are of a very fit, ridiculously healthy man in his early twenties. Notwithstanding the various stab and gunshot wounds, you barely look worn in."

"But the infection is completely gone?" Archer asked as he unrolled his sleeve.

"There seems to be an odd genetic residue which puts you a little closer to the mixed-bloods than to the pure Seers, and I found the same component in Tom's blood, despite his mix. The infections in your bodies had done most of the work on the gunshot wounds before the cures were injected, and based on your condition, I'd say you both still have much better than average healing times. Perhaps it's something to do with telomere programming …" he mused, and then shook himself back to the conversation. "I suppose you both need time to make your own blood before I start drawing it though." Mr. Shaw smirked at himself as he stood and looked at me.

"No running for a bit. It'll take a few days of good food and rest before he's re-made the blood he lost. The green-haired boy did a good job with both you and Connor."

Archer added for my benefit, "Tam took care of our wounds when we were trapped in the tunnel." Then he turned to Mr. Shaw. "Are you finished with me?"

"For now," Shaw grumbled. There was a hint of a smile at the corner of his mouth, and impulsively, I went over and kissed his cheek.

"Thank you, Mr. Shaw. You're pretty good at this whole life-saving business, you know?"

He narrowed his eyes. "Yeah, well, I'm not too happy about how often I have to do it around you, young lady."

All traces of humor fled as I answered. "Neither am I."

He cleared his throat and then ducked his head to put away his medical kit. "All the wings of the school are full. We had to give away your room, Saira, but no one else knows where yours is." He looked at Archer, who nodded.

"Thank you."

"We're married," I blurted for no apparent reason except that I didn't want Mr. Shaw to think … actually, it didn't matter what he thought. I threaded my fingers through Archer's, and he turned my hand over to trace his signet ring on it.

Whatever Mr. Shaw might have said in that moment was lost. All I could see or hear was the smile on Archer's lips when he said, "I know."

He didn't let go of my hand as we left the office and headed toward the main hall. "Where are we going?" I asked.

"I've never shown you the interior staircase to the cellars, have I?" he said with a smile.

I was intrigued. "No, you haven't."

We turned down a small hallway which must have been used by servants when the school was first built. "No one remembers it. Even Ringo was surprised when I told him how to get me some clean clothes."

"Where is Ringo?" I asked suspiciously.

"After he ran a couple of errands for me, he said he was going to find Connor to go running through the school. He had some anxiety to burn off after the past several weeks."

I scoffed. "My version of anxiety-relief looks like curling up with you and sleeping for about three days."

He squeezed my hand with a quick grin, then led me through a well-concealed doorway under the back staircase and down to the cellar below. The hidden catch slid the shelving unit on the false wall to one side, and we found Archer's hideaway set up for a picnic dinner.

"Ah, Ringo outdid himself," said Archer happily.

The small table had a cloth on it, and there were plates, cups, and silverware for two. Archer lit candles around the room while I unpacked a basket that had been left beside the table.

There was fresh, crusty French bread, still warm from the oven and wrapped in a clean cloth. Fresh, salty butter and hard cheese were in a chilled container, and sliced roasted chicken and the last of the garden tomatoes rounded out the sandwich options. For dessert there were grapes and tiny chocolates wrapped in paper, and bottles of water and wine completed the feasting options.

"Wow, Mrs. Taylor is amazing," I marveled.

"She is, but actually, I think Ringo charmed Annie into helping him put the basket together." Archer smiled. "I told him the only things I'd eaten in a hundred years were a handful of nuts and some granola bars."

I looked at him, aghast, and his expression shifted to concern. "What's wrong?" he asked as he came to me.

I took his face in both of my hands and I kissed him. "You're here and you're alive. If I live a thousand years I will never take either of those things for granted."

He kissed me back. "Good. Don't." He took my hands from his face and kissed the backs of each of them. "Mrs. Devereux, would you join me for my first proper meal in more than a century?"

I smiled, happier than I could remember being in a long time. "Mr. Devereux, it would be my pleasure."

We sat, and ate, and talked, and laughed, and cried for what felt like hours, always touching, always holding hands. He told me that the memory of our wedding in the church garden was the one he had kept returning to every time the pain set in, and it was the thing that had allowed him to endure the endless darkness of the cell where Walters had kept them. I thanked him for the gems he had collected, and I recounted the true history of Artemisia's emerald.

The time I'd spent with Mary Shelley fascinated Archer, and the events of the other time stream intrigued him. War was a bastard, he said, but my encounters with Death made him thoughtful. The fact that we'd run into both Bishop Wilder and Bas sent him pacing around the room with questions about every detail of their words and their actions, and the revelations about Doran dropped him back in his seat in astonishment.

His own revelations about Walters' plans for Raven and the things he'd guessed about Walters' desire for Archer's blood were especially concerning, and we agreed that getting the ring away from Seth Walters was the highest priority. The rest of the political nightmare that the Immortal Descendants faced could be dealt with after the power to compel was out of the equation.

We had long since moved to Archer's bed and lay curled up together on top of the blankets. The cocoon he made for me with his body wrapped around mine felt like the warmest, safest place in the world. He played with the ring on my finger as we talked, and I made him take his shirt off so I could first examine and then trace every scar, every wound, every bruise and scratch on his torso. And when I'd kissed them all, we made love.

The hours we spent together felt more intimate than any we'd spent besides our wedding night. We exposed our most hidden fears and revealed our secret hopes to each other, and I'd never felt so peaceful as I did then.

We slept for a while, then talked some more.

"I hope you'll move in here with me, at least while we're at St. Brigid's." Archer's voice was more tentative than I liked, so I teased him in return, telling him I would move in with him, but only if he hung a disco ball from the ceiling for impromptu dance parties.

"Done," he said, and at the look in his eyes I thought I might regret that particular tease.

I knew I'd put off the inevitable facing of the music that waited for us upstairs, and after kissing a couple of dozen times, we packed up the food dishes and took them back to the kitchen. We used the inside steps again to avoid Monger eyes, because despite the walled garden, we weren't invulnerable from above if someone were high enough in the trees.

Mrs. Taylor and Annie fussed over me in the kitchen, and Archer and I fussed over the delicious food they'd packed, and after a giant fuss-fest, we finally made our way to the library to find Miss Simpson.

It was full dark outside, but Miss Simpson's office light was on when I knocked on the door.

"Come in, Saira," she said from behind her closed door.

I opened it slowly and we entered the small office. Miss Simpson looked exactly the same as she had always looked, but I couldn't see her without seeing the glorious Renaissance version of Aislin that Doran had painted.

"Hello, Aislin," I said quietly. I dipped my head slightly as a gesture of courtesy. It was one I'd learned in Elizabeth's court, and it seemed to soften the hard edges around her mouth.

She studied both of us for a long moment, then finally sighed and gestured to chairs for us to sit. "Can I get you tea?" she asked.

I smiled. She didn't really want to be having this conversation, and yet her English politeness had been worn so long it was like a second skin. "No, thank you. We won't take up a lot of your time."

She answered with her own smile. "Time is something of which I've perhaps had far too much."

She broke the ice, so I dove right in. "Do you remember the other time stream?"

Aislin sighed again. "As a distant memory, as though it happened long ago to someone else, as though I heard it in a story once."

I sat forward. "On that time stream there were some good things, but there were some things that didn't work, too. I'd like to have learned my lesson about those without having to actually try them out."

Aislin gave me the first non-wary smile since we walked in. "A very wise perspective from one who is not of my direct Family."

"I'm not going to ask you what you See about what's coming up, because you won't tell me anyway and I don't love rejection," I said, only half-joking.

Aislin's eyes sparkled, and I caught a glimpse of a striking, ethereal, young blonde woman – her natural form.

I forged ahead. "I know the ring Seth Walters is wearing to compel the masses doesn't actually belong to the Monger Family." That got an eyebrow raise, which made me oddly proud. It was no mean feat to surprise Fate. "But I've seen what happens when there's a power vacuum for Mongers, and that's not great either."

Archer watched me with as much interest as Aislin did – I hadn't really thought this part through and was making it up as I went. "So, we need to get the ring out of Monger possession, but we can't just leave them without their artifact. They are like troublemaker kids when they're bored and have nothing to play with – they stir stuff up just to see it explode."

Aislin's mouth twitched, but she managed to keep a straight face, so I continued shooting rapid-fire questions at her in hopes she might actually answer one or two. "Duncan said their artifact went missing, and I was wondering if you had any information about it that you'd be willing to share – like what, exactly, is it? What can it do? When and where did it go missing? Where it might be now? Anything you know could be helpful in getting the right artifact back to the right Descendant Family."

"Why is this your task, Saira?" Aislin finally asked.

"Why isn't it?"

I surprised her again. I might actually have to start keeping score. She opened her mouth, then closed it, then finally opened it again. "But you're just a girl," she said.

She should have kept it closed. Nothing, not one thing in the world actually pissed me off more than those three words – *just a girl.* Ringo knew this for sure, and yet not even he ever baited me with them – not ever. I could sense Archer's gaze sharpening, and I knew he got it too.

I smiled at her. She should have been afraid of that smile, but she didn't know me well enough. "You know, Duncan once said something similar to me, and I figured his words came straight from his sexist little heart. But now you too? I actually expected more from you, Aislin, because that word 'just,' when used as an adverb, means 'only' and 'no more than.' By using 'just' that way, you're saying there's something greater than being female, and you've implied that being female isn't enough."

Aislin's eyes narrowed at me, but I would win the eye-narrowing stare-off because I was mad, and I was right, and she knew it. So I raised an eyebrow in an imitation of my favorite of Archer's expressions. I'd been practicing it in a mirror, and I knew it made me look disdainful. "And because there's nothing greater than female – male is equal to but not greater than – and being female is clearly quite *enough*, I figure you must have used 'just' as a synonym for 'exactly, precisely, absolutely, perfectly,' – as in 'just what we need.' In which case, I have no argument with you." I leveled her with the nicest, most polite smile I had in my repertoire. "Do I?"

Archer chuckled under his breath, and I loved him for it. His amusement was worth at least two points, since I was keeping score.

And then she surprised me. She gave me the same eyebrow, but with less disdain and more appraisal. "Perhaps you might be up to the task after all."

It took a lot not to splutter. "Because everything that's happened this year wasn't enough?"

"Most of your behavior has been in reaction to something. Admittedly, you react decisively and often very well, but they are reactions nonetheless. You have good instincts for the workable choices, but with a few exceptions, you haven't sought preemptive change."

I opened my mouth to protest with examples, but then shut it again. For whatever it was worth, she was right. My mom disappeared; I went to find her. Time split; we fixed it. The Monger ring became a problem; we tried to steal it. I hadn't actually gone out and tried to make the world a better place.

"So only seeking preemptive change can make me worthy?"

She smiled. "No, but the strength of your conviction gives you a greater than average chance of succeeding."

"Aislin, we can dance around my worthiness all day. I don't actually care if you think I'm up to the task, unless that's a reason to hold back information, in which case, yes, I'm up to it." I sighed. "Our immediate problem is all about getting the power to compel out of Monger hands. This thing I'm talking about is what comes next. What fills the vacuum when the ring leaves Monger hands?"

She studied me for a long moment before she finally spoke again. "We have an edict against interference. It is actually written into our laws to prevent the sort of puppet-mastering that Duncan is so very fond of."

"Neither of you are big rule-followers, then. He had a hand in the theft of the ring from the Vatican in 1842, you sent Mary Shelley to meet us on the train, and he was responsible for locking us into our compartments when it crashed outside Paris."

Aislin scowled. "I sent Mary precisely because I Saw his interference, and you needed a fighting chance."

"You couldn't have come yourself?" I asked.

The light in her eyes had dimmed. "As I said, there is an edict against direct interference, and I would lose my right to speak at our Council and my ability to sanction the others if I indulged in the practice myself."

I had a sudden inspiration, based on my interactions with Doran. "Maybe I'm not asking the right questions then. Let's see …" I tried to think of something she could answer without volunteering anything.

Archer got there first. "Have there been any prophecies about the Monger artifact?"

Aislin smiled. She understood our game. "There was one made by one of my family in Jerusalem long ago." Her eyes went slightly unfocused as she recited the rhyme.

> *"When man of War*
> *And Sight portends,*
> *What great one lost,*
> *And young one sends,*
> *The first one seeks,*
> *The hurt one mends,*
> *What War begins,*
> *The dark night ends."*

I sighed. "I kind of love the poetry even though your Family frustrates the heck out of me." I scribbled down the words and shoved them in my back pocket.

"Any other prophecies we should be watching out for?"

She grinned. "Just your favorite."

I smirked, and recited.

"Fated for one, born to another
The child must seek to claim the Mother
The stream will split and branches will fight
Death will divide, and lovers unite
The child of opposites will be the one
To heal the Dream that War's undone."

I rolled my eyes. "Every time I hear that thing I think of more people it could fit. I might just be the one who tripped over it once and fell down with a thump right on top of it."

"Perhaps. But perhaps it was there to trip over because you were meant to fall on it."

I stood up to go and couldn't hold back the laugh. "Arguing with Fate is considerably less painful than sparring with War, but it doesn't mean I'm ever likely to win."

"Oh, I don't know … your words can be quite provocative, especially when you wield them with careful logic and clear purpose. You might be surprised at the battles that can be won with those weapons."

We left her office and I whispered to Archer, "Why do I feel like that was something I should pay attention to?"

"I have the feeling that anything Aislin says is something to which we should all pay attention." Archer's tone had a smile in it, and I took his hand in mine.

"You're pretty hot when you're grammatically correct."

He laughed. "You're not so bad yourself with all that talk about adverbs."

Archer kissed me just as Ringo came loping around the corner. "Hey!" I said happily. "Where have you been?"

He rolled his eyes in a perfect imitation of Connor. "I'm not the one who took a five-hour lunch," but then he grinned, and I was so glad to see the easiness back in his manner.

Archer let go of my hand and gripped Ringo on both shoulders with a serious face. "Thank you. That was, in truth, the most exquisite meal I've ever eaten, and whatever favors you called upon to make it happen will be repaid a thousand-fold at your bidding."

Ringo stared at him in surprise, then looked at me. "Did he revert back to a Victorian when he lost the Vampire bit?"

I smirked teasingly. "Not necessarily." I held his gaze long enough that Ringo caught my meaning and blushed. That made me laugh, and I looped my arm through his to continue walking down the hall.

"I was sent to get ye. The solarium's full of people waiting to talk to ye," Ringo told us.

I took a deep breath. "Right. Well …" I turned to look at both of them. "This should be interesting."

A Mixed Gathering

Every seat in the solarium was taken, and I realized this was what the school would look like if it was at maximum capacity. Ava gave me a big hug when I walked in, and then she made a formal introduction to Tam, who had only ever seen me in my Cat form. I went straight in for the hug, which surprised him, but he gamely hugged me back.

"Thank you for taking care of Archer for me."

"You're welcome," he said simply, and the twinkle in his eye reminded me a lot of Ringo, just like Archer had said it did.

There were a lot of people in the room I didn't know, although the way Adam was greeting them as he worked his way across the room toward me indicated they were most likely the mixed-blood captives he had rescued. I'd been horrified when Archer described the conditions in which they'd been kept, especially when I saw an older woman seated off to one side. Adam made a point of going over to greet her, and I appreciated his kindness.

I made a beeline for my mom and Mr. Shaw who sat with Millicent on one side of the room. Millicent stood up when she saw me coming, and she shocked me with a giant hug.

"You've returned safely," she said with a relieved smile.

I tried to shove the guilt away when I hugged her back, but my embrace was extra hard, and she sensed it. "I need to talk to you," I said quietly. "Later, okay?"

She looked concerned. "Of course, darling. I believe I am the one who has put you out of your old bedroom." She laughed at my startled expression. "It's the same one I had when I was a girl at St. Brigid's," she said in a whisper.

I kissed her cheek. "You're awesome," I whispered back.

I said hello to a couple of other people, then spotted Tom sitting in a chair in the shadows by the door. I caught his eye, and he smiled grimly at me. Archer detached himself from my side and strode across the room to him. They spoke for a few moments, and then Archer shook his hand and came back to my side. "We're meeting Adam, Ava, and Tom later in the library," he said quietly.

Mr. and Mrs. Arman stood on the opposite side of the room from my mom and Mr. Shaw, and I hoped that was just an accident of the crowd, rather than by design. When Ringo went over to greet them and Mrs. Arman gave him a hug, I felt better.

Adam stepped to the front of the room and got everyone's attention. He had a leader's natural presence, and he actually seemed comfortable in the role.

"As you all know, some things in our world have become pretty dire, and since the explosion at Holborn, Descendant politics have spilled over into the rest of the city. We're all here because it's a safe zone from anyone who intends harm – Miss Simpson's wards around the school have held, so the guys who intend harm aren't able to get inside the gates or over the walls."

He looked around the room and grinned affably. "But as much as I like you all, I'm not so keen to stay here with you forever." There was a general murmur of laughter, and I was surprised to see Adam's girlfriend, Alex, slip in to stand next to Ava. I hadn't known she was back from France, and as much as it sucked for her to be trapped here, I was glad to see her.

"So, here's the deal. Everyone out there is under Monger control; everyone in here is not. That means we—" he gestured around the room, "are the only ones who can change things."

There were more murmurings, this time without laughter.

"Some of you already know Saira Elian, but most of you haven't met her yet. She's a Clocker, obviously, but she's also mixed, and she's been spending a lot of time bouncing around the past trying to figure out what the Mongers are up to. She wanted everyone to be together so she could tell you all what she's learned."

Adam held his hand out to me, and I stepped forward to join him at the front of the room. It was kind of surreal for me to be the one in focus, since I'd spent most of my life doing everything I could to blend into the background.

"Hey, you guys?" I said to the mixed-blood Descendants around the room. "Good job surviving."

That statement was just odd enough that it made a couple of people smile, and then, when they processed it, a couple more did too. I looked around the room, trying to memorize faces. These were the people who could stand up against the ring's power, but a lifetime of living in fear of discovery might be hard to override.

I laid out the two biggest facts I had. "There was a time stream split in 1944, and I Clocked to a different future. It was a future where the Mongers had no ring—" there were gasps and murmurs, "and there I learned that the ring doesn't actually belong to the Mongers." The gasps and murmurs grew louder, and phrases like "take the ring" started to ripple through.

"So yeah, they can't have the ring; they actually have no right to it. And because we can't be compelled by it, we need to come up with a plan to somehow get it off Seth Walters' hand and out of Monger control."

There was general agreement around the room, but I wasn't done. "But before we start figuring out how to do that, I need to be really straight with all of you." I looked people in the eyes, and I made sure to include my mom, Mr. Shaw, and the Armans. "If we manage to get that ring, we can't keep it."

I saw a couple of expressions harden at that, so I directed my words to the narrowed eyes in the group, including Mrs. Arman, and surprisingly, Adam. "It goes back to the Family it belongs to, and not only that, we need to do whatever we can to find the Mongers' actual artifact and make sure they get it."

There were some actual cries of outrage at that, and a couple mutterings of "who does she think she is." Even Mr. Shaw looked unhappy at my words, and the grumbling in the room was getting louder. I caught Ringo's eye and he nodded, then stuck two fingers in his mouth for a piercing whistle. I always wanted to be able to whistle like that – it shut everyone up instantly.

"You don't have to listen to me, and you certainly don't have to do what I say. But here's the deal; things need to change. The prejudice against mixed-bloods has to end. In fact, mixed-bloods *and* Death's Descendants should have a seat at the Council." There was more muttering and outright grumbling, and I glared around the room. "Are you kidding? There are what, about forty mixed-bloods in this room? You people have been hiding, sometimes even from your own families, because someone, somewhere, decided they didn't want to share their power. We're going to have to share every single one of our assets to defeat Seth Walters at his messed up power-play. If we manage to pull this off – and that's a huge if – we *cannot* go back to business as usual."

The grumbling quieted a little, and I still had their attention. "I can't force you to make changes, but I can put a spotlight on things that I think need to change. You could look at me and say, 'she's eighteen, what could she possibly know about Descendant politics?' or you could ask me what the other time stream was like when the Mongers had no teeth and grew fangs to compensate, and you could wonder why the mixed-blood moratorium was put in place, when clearly, we all exist. And you could take the lessons of the past – and I have a lot of them to share, believe me – and pick them apart for the truths that we should apply now."

I looked around the room, and then took a deep breath. "We have members of every Family here right now, plus two Council Heads and a whole bunch of very smart people. I'll tell you my stories, but I want yours too, and when we all know each other a little better, we'll have an idea of all the skills we bring to the table. Then we can make a plan to go after the ring."

Archer's smile was like a thumbs-up, and I saw similar looks on my friends' faces around the room. Adam piped up from across the room. "Hi, my name is Adam Arman, and I'm a Seer. My skills include reaching things in high places, running off at the mouth, puking through spirals, leading people through the London Underground, and generally knowing everything except … you know … the things I don't." People laughed, and then Tam piped up.

"My name's Tam Roth, and I'm a mix of Seer and Monger." That statement got a couple of raised eyebrows, my own included. "I can communicate with other Seers using pictures in my head, and I don't know what the Monger side does except make me want to break the rules I think are stupid. And the rules against Suckers are some of the dumbest rules we have. I just spent more than a week with a Sucker, and he is a fairly excellent human being."

I would have hugged Tam again if I'd been close enough, but then Archer spoke. "I'm the Sucker, or at least I used to be. My name is Archer Devereux, and I'm a Seer. I was infected with the mutation that caused my cells to stop dying in 1888." There were outright gasps at that, but Archer met the eyes of the people around him. "Thanks to a cure that Bob Shaw has developed, my cells are happily dying away, which means I can walk in the sunlight and eat proper food. My skills are much diminished now that I'm no longer a Vampire, but among them I count friendship, love, and a long life spent honing a not-inconsiderable set of survival skills."

"You're more than a hundred years old?" a woman near Archer asked in awe.

He nodded. "I am."

Her stare turned to a huge smile. "Wow," she said, and the tightness in my chest let go.

There were others that surprised us, some that drew gasps, and a couple of people made my eyes tear. Dorothy Charles, a lovely grandmother of three, was a distant mix of Clocker and Seer. She had no particular skill, she said, beyond an extraordinary memory. She remembered two young people sliding down the hand rails at Aldwych Station during an air raid in 1944, and though she was a child in her mother's arms at the time, she distinctly remembered watching Archer and me on the platform that night. Twin girls about Logan's age named Beck and Bauer were with their Shifter/Seer mix mom. They proudly declared their ability to Shift into any bird, which, of course, Logan had to answer with his own all-creature Shifting skills. I predicted an exotic bird and animal Shift-off in their future.

When Tom finally spoke, he sounded as though he'd been drawing strength from the acceptance in the room. "My name is Tom Landers. I'm a Seer and a Monger, and I've been a Sucker too. For a long time I thought my only skill was hurting people, but I'm pretty tired of that, so I'm ready to try something new." Adam moved next to him and clapped a hand on Tom's shoulder in support. "I'm also Seth Walters' biological kid, so I've got that going for me," Tom said wryly. Adam barked a laugh, and that seemed to give other people permission to chuckle. A woman near him reached out to grab Tom's hand for a quick squeeze, and the sympathy startled him. Then someone else began their own story, and he exhaled in relief. Adam leaned over and whispered something in his ear, both of them snickered, and I could tell Tom was going to be okay.

A couple of hours later, everyone in the room had introduced themselves, and we hashed out some ideas to deal with the Mongers that surrounded the school. It was actually pretty awesome to watch Alexandra Rowen sit down with Colin Zhang, a Shifter Owl whose mix with Seer made him an especially effective hunter, to plan the traps they would set in the woods. And Mr. Shaw's discussion with Michael Baretsky, a chemist with a mix of Shifter Badger and Monger, about the compounds he had used to create the cure was deeply technical and highly engaging for both of them. My favorite plotters to eavesdrop on were Ringo, Connor, Logan, and Tom. Ringo and Connor would come up with the most outrageous uses for Logan's various animal forms, Logan would Shift into that animal, and then Tom would spin his little chess piece in his hands and pull their plans apart. As I listened to Tom's explanations about why a leopard or a snake wouldn't work in the scenario they had proposed, I realized he had a really tactical brain and should definitely be in on the planning side of things.

Archer caught my eye and tossed his head very slightly toward the door. I nodded, excused myself from my mom and Mrs. Arman, and followed him out of the solarium. When we were out of sight, he swung me around to kiss him, then rested his forehead against mine. "You were magnificent."

I smiled and kissed him again. "It was good, wasn't it? I feel like it's a start."

"I didn't know how you would do it, but I was totally confident that you *would*. Come, Ringo will send the others to the library, and I'm taking advantage of the few moments we still have alone to do this." He kissed me again, but then just wrapped his arms around me and held me close. "Do you remember that kiss you gave me on the platform in 1944, just before you Clocked away with Ringo?" he asked.

I hadn't been expecting that change in topics. "Of course I do. The last time I'd seen you a bomb exploded, and then I thought you were dead."

"I didn't know that at the time."

I stared at him, and then horror began to dawn. "The only thing you knew was that Tom, who had been a massive jerk all through France, suddenly reappears and steps in front of the bullets he basically instigated in his zeal to kill George Walters." What had I done? "And then your wife freaks out and barely says a word to you before Clocking away with him as he's dying. Then, when I come back, I spared just enough time to kiss you, and then I drag Ringo away without another word. Oh my God, Archer! I'm so sorry!"

Archer laughed at the horrified expression on my face. "After you Clocked out with Tom, Ringo told me about the time stream split. He also told me that he was so glad I was alive because he'd been about to fall for you."

I narrowed my eyes. "What do you mean?"

He smiled. We'd begun walking toward the library, and he took my hand in his. He ignored my question and continued. "He had decided he would have to ask you to take him home and then send you away, because he didn't want to be in love with you."

I huffed. "Obviously I'm not in love with Ringo, but would it really have sucked so much that he would send me away?"

"It would have for him. He'd seen how you looked at me the night we married, and he felt you'd never have the same love in your eyes for anyone else. He wasn't jealous per se, but he'd seen it, so he knew love like ours existed, and he wanted the same thing for himself."

Archer must have seen the ten thousand things I thought about crossing my face, because he touched the cat's-eye bead around my neck and smiled. "Ringo would have been crushed to lose your friendship, but he was convinced it was the only option for him if I was truly gone. I'll admit, I was a bit jealous when he told me, especially when I realized everything you had gone through together."

"There was *nothing* to be jealous of. I love Ringo so much I want to squeeze him – sometimes in my arms, sometimes around the neck," I teased, and Archer laughed. And then I got serious again. "But you … you are my heart."

He took my face in both of his hands and he kissed me softly. "Thank you. And the kiss you gave me on that platform before you took him away with you, it told me exactly that."

I searched his eyes. "I'm sorry I didn't come back to say goodbye properly."

He smirked, "Who's to say you won't still? I mean, what if we argue and you want to run away to your first husband?"

I delivered myself into his arms and kissed him soundly. "What an interesting idea …"

MONGERS

We turned to head into the library and stopped dead at the sight of Raven and her boyfriend, Cole, standing just inside the front doors. For her part, Raven was just as surprised to see us, and her eyes locked onto Archer's with the look a deer gets in oncoming traffic.

I recovered first. "Hello, Raven." My voice was calmer than the pounding of my heart suggested, mostly because my Monger-gut was more muted than usual around my former roommate.

Her eyes flicked between Archer and me, and she finally cleared her throat. "I'm here to see Miss Simpson."

"Have you decided to spy for your uncle, or are you here to resist him?" Archer asked in a pleasant tone. Raven's eyes widened in horror, and Cole took a step forward.

"Here, I don't know who you are, but you don't speak to her that way," Cole said. Raven clutched his arm to pull him back next to her, and she swallowed convulsively.

"Seth threatened Cole," she said quietly. Cole looked at her sharply, obviously surprised by the news.

"You didn't need to bring me here to protect me," he said to her. There was an edge to his voice, but I couldn't exactly tell what it was. Not anger, and not 'I'm too manly to need protection,' – it was more like 'thanks for caring so much.'

"I didn't want him to use you against me. If Seth ever got you, I'd do anything he wanted." Raven's voice was pitched low for his ears, but she was too emphatic to be quiet.

"So I repeat my original question, Miss Walters. Are you here as a Monger mole, or are you willing to betray your uncle?" Trust Archer to cut right to the point.

Raven met Archer's eyes with a proud look. "My priority is keeping us alive and safe."

"Where's your sister, Cole?" I asked.

He didn't like the question, but he answered it anyway. "Melanie's safe and none of your business." Then he stepped forward. "Do you have a plan to go up against Walters and the armed Mongers out there?"

Archer seemed to size him up, and for his part, Cole wasn't backing down. Cole was probably a couple of inches taller than Archer, but Archer had lived a very long time, and nothing intimidated him. It took about thirty seconds before Cole looked away.

"Yes, we do have a plan," Archer said simply, having established his dominance.

"I need to talk to Miss Simpson," Raven repeated. She wouldn't meet Archer's eyes.

"I believe she's in her office," he said calmly.

Raven nodded once before they turned into the library and closed the door behind them.

"We can't meet in there until she's gone," I whispered to Archer.

"I think that even if she agrees to work with us, we can't tell her more than her own small part in anything we do. She is susceptible to the ring's power, and despite her motivation to keep her young man safe, her uncle holds too much sway over her life."

Ringo came running down the hall with Connor, and I could hear several others behind them, including Adam's girlfriend, Alex, and her cousin Daisy, who had helped Adam lead the mixed-bloods out of the Underground. "Meetin' in the library, no?" he said, seeming surprised to find us still in the entry hall.

"Raven's in there with her boyfriend." I tossed my head toward the library doors, and Ringo's eyebrows arched up in surprise.

"The big bloke from the fencin' gym?"

"He's a mixed-blood. She says she's here because her uncle threatened him," I answered.

"Who?" asked Adam. He was pushing a wheelchair with Tom in it, while Ava and Tam trailed behind with Alex and Daisy.

"Raven Walters. She's here with her boyfriend, Cole, and they're meeting with A—Miss Simpson now."

Tam looked stunned. "Cole? Cole Moore is here?" I'd forgotten they were friends. Cole and his sister, Melanie, had been with Tam when he was kidnapped.

I nodded, and Tam looked so happy, it made me disposed to like Cole a little better.

"So, where can we hang out to talk?" Connor asked.

"Our tower's out. It's where Miss Simpson put the parentals," said Adam.

"Mine's out too," I said. My mom had been using it as her office since she started teaching at St. Brigid's, and I was pretty sure she and Mr. Shaw used it as their private getaway space.

"There are people in the Shifter Tower too," said Connor. He looked at Adam. "You ever get into the Monger Tower?"

Adam shared a look with Tom, and there was something mischievous in it. "Once."

"Would anyone be in it?"

Adam and Tom suppressed grins. "Not unless they broke the lock."

I arched an eyebrow at the two young men who looked like guilty toddlers. "Because you hid the key?"

"Maybe?" Adam said, and Tom burst out laughing.

"Yer goin' to 'ave to take us there now, ye realize?" said Ringo in a tone that suggested a dare.

Adam met Tom's eyes with an impish wink. Tom looked away and said, "You guys go on."

"Not a chance," said Adam as he crouched down in front of Tom's wheelchair, his back to Tom. "Hop on, Home Slice."

Tom barked a laugh. "Home Slice? No way am I getting on your back. You'd drop me."

Ringo looked at me and patted his shoulder meaningfully. I hopped onto his back, piggyback style, and he didn't even waver. I challenged Tom. "We'll race you."

Adam growled playfully at Tom. "Get on, Cuz. I'm twice his size – we've got this in the bag."

Tom had no choice, so he scowled, but he also seemed to be having fun with it. The moment he climbed onto his cousin's back, they took off like a shot. Archer and Daisy laughed and raced after us, and I heard Ava say something about catching up in a minute.

Ringo carried me a lot more easily than I could have carried him, and he let Adam lead the way right up until we reached the top of the stairs at the last hallway. I had never explored the entire school, but evidently Ringo had, because he put on a burst of speed and slammed a palm on the door at the end before Adam could reach us.

"Done!" he said, winded, but not doubled over like I would have been. I slid off his back and shot Adam a snarky smirk.

"Got it in the bag, huh?"

"You weigh less than my beefy cousin," he said, panting. Tom hopped down off Adam's back and only winced a little as he hit the ground. I looked him over carefully.

"You okay?"

"I'm fine," he said with another scowl. But then he seemed to force himself to soften his tone. "I got used to the insta-healing powers of being a Sucker," he said, just as Archer, Alex, and Daisy arrived. Archer nodded sympathetically, breathing hard from his run.

"Me too," he agreed.

I tried to be subtle, but I couldn't help giving them a quick once-over to make sure none of their recent injuries had re-opened.

"So, where'd ye 'ide the key, Arman?" Ringo had swept the top of the door lintel like I did every time I came to a locked door.

This one was heavy wood with a big iron lock, which meant the key would be big too. He came away with a handful of dust, but no key.

Adam just smirked and looked at me. "You think I'm lazy. Where'd we stash it?"

I stepped back from the door and examined our surroundings. We were at the end of the hallway, and there was a window on the outside wall. I tried the lintel of the next door down, and Adam scoffed.

"Boring," he said.

There was a pillar with a statue on it set into a niche on the opposite wall. I examined the statue – it was a man done in a classical Greek style, dressed and kitted out like Ares, God of War. I smirked and ran my hand along the back side of it.

I found the key just where I thought I might, taped onto the booty of the statue. I held it up with an arched eyebrow. "Really?"

Adam laughed in delight. "Figures you'd go for the arse."

"Figures *you* would," I retorted.

I handed Adam the key. "Here, you go first in case it's booby-trapped."

Adam handed it to Tom. "You do it."

Tom scoffed. "Coward."

He fitted the key into the old-fashioned lock and turned it with a clear grinding noise. "How long has it been since anyone used this tower?" Alex asked Adam.

He shrugged, his hand on her back in an easy gesture of affection. "No idea. Do you know?" He looked at Archer.

"Not since I began keeping a room here after the war. I didn't go to St. Brigid's as a young man. My father wasn't aware of my mother's Sight," he said.

The inside of the tower was dark, and all the furniture was draped with heavy canvas sheeting. The room didn't have the chill of the wards that the Seer Tower had, and none of the Monger-gut feeling I'd had downstairs with Raven was present at all.

I turned to Tom and whispered, "I just realized I don't get Monger-gut from you anymore."

"You think it's because of the cure?" he asked in a low voice.

I shook my head. "No, I think it's because we're friends." I spoke louder, to the whole group. "When Ringo and I were on the other time stream, we ran into Raven working in a café."

"Bookstore," murmured Ringo under his breath, and I smiled.

"A tea and coffee and cake bookstore," I corrected.

"Wait, Raven was working?" Adam asked in obvious disbelief.

I nodded. "Yeah. And she was actually pretty humble and nice." Skeptical eyebrows rose all around the room. "The strange thing was, I didn't get the Monger-gut thing I usually have around them."

Tam and Ava had just entered the tower room. "What's Monger-gut?" Tam asked. He looked around the tower with something close to awe, and I realized he hadn't gone to school here either.

"I think it's the Shifter part of me, probably modified by my mix, that recognizes Mongers as dangerous predators," I said.

"Do you get it from Suckers?" he asked as he peeked under a drape on the wall and then pulled the cover off a gold-leaf and oil painting. "Whoa, who's the warrior?" A cloud of dust rained down when the cover came off, and it took a second for the dancing dust motes to settle.

The painting was done in a distinctly Middle Eastern style and showed a long-bearded warrior wearing a helmet draped with chain mail. Archer pulled open a window drape to put light in the room, and then stood in front of the painting.

"Salah al-Din Yusuf ibn Ayyub," he said reverently.

I caught Ringo's and Tom's eyes, and all of us wore the same surprised look. "Saladin?" I said.

Archer nodded. "One of the greatest warriors in history, and certainly among the most noble."

"Why is he hanging here?" asked Adam.

"Saladin was a Monger," I said, the light dawning. I turned to Archer. "This is who Bas saw in battle just before the Third Crusade."

"You guys know some cool people," said Tam in awe, stepping forward to examine the painting more closely.

"Saladin's sword was apparently made in a process that is now lost to technology. Crafted in Damascus from wootz steel, which originally came from India, Saladin's sword was very high-carbon steel, which made it extremely strong and light and able to hold the finest edge. Legend says Saladin's sword could clean-cut fallen silk or slice a pillow in half." Archer explained.

"Do you think his sword could have been the Monger artifact?" I asked.

"Bas said the last 'e 'eard of the Monger artifact was in Jerusalem durin' the Crusades," said Ringo.

"I suppose it's possible …" Archer didn't sound convinced.

"Seems weird that it would be another weapon though, since Death has his daggers." I hadn't put my daggers back on since we returned, and I felt a little naked without them.

"Hang on – Death has daggers?" Adam said.

So I told them about having basically traded identical daggers with Death.

"What can they do?" Ava asked.

"I'm not really sure, but I think the blade sort of reads a person's character through their blood." I waited a beat to drop the other shoe. "I saw Duncan's soul when I threw my dagger at him."

There were gasps from my friends, and Archer gripped my hand tightly. "What did it look like?" he asked.

"Take a dose of rage and magnify it to the intensity of a black hole. Then add a streak of pure malevolence, and there you have Duncan."

"Nice to know I'm descended from such a prince," grimaced Tam.

"Leprechaun, you and my cousin are a couple of the princeliest guys I know. Saladin was one of you too, and he was a proper hero," said Adam.

The staircase to the upper tower room was hidden in a way that was similar to the Clocker Tower, and Adam delighted in showing everyone the secret catch at the back of the wardrobe. He and Tom hadn't climbed up there before because he hadn't known how to access the stairs until he met me, so it was a surprise to all of us to find a single round table in the middle of the room.

Ringo and Ava flung open the drapes, and the light shone like an arrow on the tabletop. Tom was the last one up the steps, and he saw my face before he saw anything else.

"What's wrong?" he asked.

I dragged my gaze away from the table and up to his. "I think I know what the Monger artifact is."

THE KNIGHT

The entire surface of the table was painted like a chessboard, with the pieces set up, ready for battle. All the pieces were beautifully carved from a heavy wood and they looked worn from handling. The dark pieces weren't actually stained – they had been carved from ebony, and the shapes were distinctively elegant. Every piece on the board was accounted for except for one black knight.

"Show me Léon's piece," I whispered to Tom.

His eyes were riveted to the board, as he drew the chess piece he had been carrying around with him since Léon died in 1428 out of his pocket. With a shaking hand, he placed it on the empty square.

It was a perfect match, and the table seemed to hum with energy.

"Pick it up," I whispered urgently.

Tom retrieved the piece and held it tightly in his fist. His eyes met mine, and the shock in them was palpable.

"How could Léon have had a piece from this set?" he asked. "He wasn't a Descendant at all."

"Léon was Jewish, and you said the piece had been in his family a long time," said Archer. "Maybe it came from Jerusalem."

"Bas told us about Saladin carrying a black knight piece in his pocket. What if this is that piece? Saladin was there, in Jerusalem. It could have been lost after he won the city." I knew I was grasping

at straws, and then I pulled the scrap of paper out of my back
pocket and read the prophecy Aislin had given me.

"When man of War
And Sight portends,
What great one lost,
And young one sends,
The first one seeks,
The hurt one mends,
What War begins,
The dark night ends."

The silence was almost louder than my voice until someone
said, "Whoa."

Ava's eyes gleamed with understanding. "It's not *night*, the
opposite of day – it's *knight*, the black knight of chess."

"But why a chess piece for the Monger artifact, and what can it
do?" asked Adam.

Archer seemed lost in thought as he moved a white pawn
forward two spaces. "Chess is an ancient game of strategy." He
moved a black pawn forward one. "Each piece is granted its own
very specific move." The white bishop slid all the way out to the
edge of the board. "Offenses are plotted several turns ahead." He
slid a black pawn forward to block the white bishop's attack on the
queen. "And the weakest defenses …" The white bishop took the
black pawn, "become the strongest attacks …" He moved the black
knight out from behind its pawn to take the white bishop, "when
the knights are in play."

Tom had followed the chess moves with a kind of mesmerized
fascination, and at the end, he looked into my eyes with an
expression of complete astonishment and said, "I think I know
how to steal the ring."

It was agreed that only a very few people would know the
entire plan, and everyone else would be fed just their piece of the
puzzle. This was not only to protect the game, but also the players,
since no one could tell someone else what they didn't know.

It was after midnight when we finally left the chess room in the Monger Tower, and we all understood now why the Monger artifact was a chess piece. Every facet of the plan could be acted out on the board, and every possible attack and defense could be anticipated.

Tom was utterly brilliant at it. When he physically held the black knight in his hand, he could spot every flaw and weakness of every part of the plans we discussed. He tried it with different pieces, and he tried it with the knight in his pocket. None of those options worked – only when the black knight was in his hand did his strategic brain turn on and practically light up. The rest of us tried it too, but only the leprechaun, with his part-Monger blood, could feel a difference in his tactical thinking, and it was agreed by all that Tom's strategies were by far the best.

When each of us understood our own jobs, and plans had been laid for the next day, we finally said good night and went our own ways. I grabbed Ringo's hand before he turned toward Connor's room. He was taking Logan's bed, and Logan would sleep in the shape of a Kitten curled up at the foot of his brother's mattress.

"Do you want to come with me to get Charlie tomorrow?"

He nodded, and I didn't like that I couldn't see his expression in the dim light. "Yeah, I'm comin'."

"You don't sound happy about it."

"I know 'ow I feel, I just don't know 'ow she does."

He turned and disappeared into the shadows of the bedroom and closed the door softly behind him.

GRAYSON MANOR – 1554

I left a note on the whiteboard just outside Mr. Shaw's office that Archer, Ringo, and I had gone to 1554 to bring Charlie back with us. I didn't add the words 'if we can,' despite the fact that none of us was at all certain she'd want to come.

But we needed her. Charlie's conduit abilities would make a huge difference to phase one of our plans – no one else I'd ever Clocked with had made transporting a lot of people so easy, and our plans depended on being able to take a lot of trap-builders into the woods past the Monger perimeter patrol.

Ringo brought us fresh scones and coffee that he'd scored from Annie, and Archer, with new appreciation for all things food-related, proclaimed him the very best man he'd ever known. It was early – only a few people were moving around the school – and we'd decided to leave from Archer's cellar room.

I knew how to get us into the same cellar in 1554. It's how we'd gotten back to Tudor England before, and it made sense to cut down on the number of variables I had to face Clocking us there. I was dressed in my clean buckskin trousers and boots for a slightly modified version of a sixteenth-century man. The capes we all wore were our concession to the times, and I was hoping we could avoid being seen by anyone but Charlie.

The trip backward was long and cold. The time we spent *between* seemed longer during the big backward leaps, and I spent the first few moments after we landed trying to keep my scone down.

"Everyone okay?" I whispered to Archer and Ringo. Archer reached out for my hand and I marveled again, as I'd done ever since we were reunited, at how warm his skin was. Ringo just nodded and got up to make sure we were alone in the cellar.

"He's struggling with this," Archer murmured as his eyes tracked Ringo in the dim light.

My heart hurt for Ringo. I had spent nearly every waking moment for the last several weeks with him, and I had learned to read his silences. This one was cloaked in self-protection, and it was the kind that could turn into a hard shell if he remained wrapped in it for too long.

He pronounced us alone in the cellar, so we could use our normal voices.

"If Henry was still here, this would be so much easier," I said sadly.

"If 'Enry 'ad lived, Lady Grayson wouldn't 'ave brought Charlie 'ome with 'er. She would 'ave her own son." There was an edge to Ringo's voice that I hoped wasn't bitterness.

"Valerie planned to leave court soon after she returned from France, correct?" Archer asked.

"That's what she said. And since we don't know what Grayson Manor looks like or where it is, we can either go upstairs and find someone to tell us, or I can try Clocking us directly to Charlie."

Neither Ringo nor Archer looked too happy about that option. I had explained that it was how I'd found Archer twice – the first time on the platform in 1944, and the second time in the Camden Catacombs.

"My greatest concern is that you don't know Charlie as well as you know me, and that might get in the way of being able to Clock directly to her."

"I know what she looks like – that's what I have to visualize," I protested.

"Ye know what she used to look like. Who knows what changes good food and fortune 'ave made to 'er." It wasn't bitterness in Ringo's voice. It was ... regret?

"Well," I sighed, "you know her best, but you're not a Seer, so I can't See her through your memories of her. You're going to have to paint a picture of her with your words."

He looked startled. "'Ow do I do that?"

"Tell me about the time you spent together in your flat. What were her habits? What did she like to do?"

Ringo looked thoughtful and settled himself back against a pillar. "Well, since she'd spent most of 'er life dressed as a lad just to survive, she preferred skirts when we were 'ome. She asked me if I'd sell some of 'er drawin's to buy 'er a lady's clothes. I took the ones with children in them down to the bookseller and sold them as illustrations for books. 'E said 'e knew a publisher who would want more of them, so what ye saw in our flat was just a part of what she'd drawn."

Charlie's drawings of the Otherworlders she saw among regular people were magical and totally perfect for children's books. The ones that had decorated their flat were the kind of illustrations that inspired storytellers to write.

"I was able to buy a skirt and two blouses at the same shop where I found yer trousers, and when she put them on the first time, she cried." Ringo's voice got a little gravelly with emotion. "She cried that someone 'ad thought 'er drawin's were worth money. She cried that she could earn money on 'er feet, and she cried that I'd gone out and bought 'er somethin' that wasn't necessary. It wasn't food, and she already 'ad a lad's clothes – it was just somethin' nice that she'd wanted for 'erself."

Ringo looked away from us and took a deep breath. "So many things 'ad caused 'er pain in 'er life, she didn't know 'ow to be 'appy. Those clothes made 'er 'appy in a way I'd never seen from anyone, and I resolved to do everythin' I could to see that smile again, even if it came with tears."

He looked down at his hands. "I used to steal to survive. It's the most selfish thing a person can do – take from another to feed 'imself. Charlie began sellin' 'er drawin's to the bookseller to buy food for us, so I started usin' the money I earned from Gosford to buy 'er paper, pens, books, and cloth. We were takin' care of each other with what we'd earned from our own labor, and for the first time in my life, carin' for someone else was more important than feedin' myself."

I reached out and took hold of one of his hands, and Archer took the other. It was an unconscious show of solidarity, but the connection between them gave me a sudden flash of Charlie. "Archer, give me your hand," I said with urgency. Ringo tried to let go, but I gripped his hand hard. "No, don't." Archer took my hand, and through his Sight, an image of Charlie came into focus. It was hesitant at first, but then the image got stronger as I felt Ringo relax. His eyes closed as he remembered Charlie, and his face suffused with love. In that moment I knew I could find her.

"Okay. Got her," I said quietly.

I let go of their hands and went to the spiral wall. "You can stay here, and I'll pick you up on my way back if you like."

I laughed at how fast both of them made it to my side. I took a breath, fixed Charlie in my mind, and began to trace.

The room we landed in was dark except for a seam of sunlight shining under the heavy velvet drapes. The time *between* had been brief, and I was able to stand up without dizziness immediately.

"Who's there?" someone whispered.

I debated my options for how to answer as my eyes adjusted to the darkness. We'd Clocked into a bedroom, dominated by a massive four-poster bed draped with swathes of fabric, and the person who had whispered sat up suddenly with a gasp.

"Ringo?" It was Charlie's voice, but not her accent – this one was soft and clipped with posh precision, and her tone held so much hope that my heart squeezed in my chest.

"It's me," he said, as he got to his feet and strode to the bed.

Charlie scrambled out from under the covers and hurled herself at him. "It's you," she breathed.

He caught her in his arms, and she held him for all she was worth. I couldn't see much of her face, buried as it was in his shoulder, but then she started giggling and I knew it was happiness that drove her.

There was surprise in Ringo's voice when he finally pulled back. "Are ye well?"

I opened the drapes just enough to put a beam of light into the room, and Charlie caught my eye. "Thank you for bringing him," she said a little shyly. She ducked her head, then met his eyes and smiled. "You're here."

"I am." His voice was full of emotion and he cleared his throat. "Char?" He sat on the edge of her bed, and she sat next to him. Shyness had dampened some of her enthusiastic greeting, but her fingers reached for his, and she seemed relieved when he held her hand. "I 'ave two questions for ye."

She looked into his eyes with some mix of hope and trepidation. "Yes?"

I held my breath, wondering what he would ask.

Ringo exhaled. "The first question will 'ave to wait, but I promise ye I'll get to askin' it."

"Very well," she said softly. He touched her face to bring her gaze back up to his.

"The second question is a 'ard one, and I'm sorry to 'ave to ask it of ye."

She took a deep breath and tried not to look nervous.

"Would ye come with us now? We need yer 'elp – somethin' only ye can do or I'd never put ye in danger – and we can bring ye straight back after if ye like." He sounded so nervous, and the expression in her eyes went from hope to fear to anger. The anger surprised me until I heard the words that were attached to it.

"Of course I'll come with you – whatever you need. If it's something dangerous, you'll want me at your back. I've learned archery now, so I don't need a frying pan anymore, but you will not bring me straight back until you've asked the second question."

Ringo stared at her, and I had to admit, her confidence startled me too. And then he smiled, and her fierce expression softened into a huge grin. She stood up and made a shooing motion. "Go over there while I change into my clothes. Saira," she looked at me with shining eyes, "perhaps you'll help me?"

She ducked her head in a quick curtsy to Archer, then smiled and held her hands out to me. I gave her a hug. "It's so good to see you, Charlie."

She drew me around behind a screen into her dressing room. There were several elaborate gowns draped over a rack, and several more in simpler fabrics for day wear. The whole room had been full of beautiful furniture, with museum-quality rugs and artwork that made it clear she'd been living in luxury.

"I assume trousers will be the best choice?" she asked, as she took in my own wardrobe.

I nodded with a grimace. I knew how much she liked dresses. "Just at first. Then you can have full run of the attics at St. Brigid's."

She smiled and dug into a trunk. She pulled out a pair of dark trousers that were similar to tights, but thicker. "I had these made for riding. Long skirts are quite hard to move in, aren't they?"

I laughed. "They're the worst."

She quickly pulled off the linen nightgown, and I noticed that her tiny frame had gotten stronger. She saw my surprise and smiled shyly. "Lady Grayson understands why I've taken up riding, climbing, and archery, though no one else on the estate can fathom it. If I hear 'just a girl' one more time from someone hired to teach me, I might have to resort to the frying pan again."

I laughed out loud and marveled at this young woman who now had natural confidence threaded into her bearing and her voice. She'd lost the accent of the street, and the unconscious fear that had hovered around her since we'd first met was gone.

She was dressed in a tunic and the leggings, and was pulling on her boots when Ringo knocked on the screen. "Do ye need to see Lady Grayson before we go?" he asked.

She looked at me. "I'd like to speak to her properly, but I don't yet know about what."

I nodded. She needed to know if she was going for good or just for a short trip. "I can bring you back here to the moment just after we leave – does that work?"

A relieved smile crossed her face. "That would be perfect." She stood and pushed aside the screen. Ringo's gaze lingered on her face, and then he stepped back to let us go first.

"After you, miladies."

RAVEN

We clocked straight back to Archer's cellar, and the difference was astounding. With Charlie along, I barely felt the effects, and both Ringo and Archer seemed immediately fine. This was what we needed to take the trap-builders into the woods.

In terms of real time, we'd been gone less than an hour, and I bounded upstairs to let Mr. Shaw and my mom know we were back. I ran into them in the hall, just having come from a meeting with Alex Rowan and the others who were planning the traps.

Mr. Shaw grinned. "You're back!" he said happily, and my mom looked behind me hopefully.

"Did you bring Charlie home?" she asked. She might have missed Charlie almost as much as Ringo had.

"She's with Ringo in the kitchen. We took her from bed without any breakfast."

My mom kissed my cheek. "I'll just go and see what she needs," she said as she hurried away.

"Your mum has missed having someone to take care of," Mr. Shaw said fondly as he watched her go.

I reached up and kissed his cheek. "Maybe you and I should stop being so tough and self-sufficient all the time. We could probably allow for a little care-taking every once in a while, right?"

He chuckled. "I will if you do."

"You're on."

I walked with him to his office, and he filled me in on the various kinds of traps that had been planned for the woods that surrounded St. Brigid's. We discussed some of the finer points, including the use of the Shifter animals to lure the Mongers away from the school. As far as we could tell, there were about thirty or so men surrounding the school, armed with guns that were illegal to carry in England. Because they had tried and failed to get in past the wards, they seemed to be engaged in a modern day siege – blocking anyone from getting in with food and supplies, and hoping to starve us out. Clearly they had never been in the cellars, or they would have realized how long Mrs. Taylor and Annie could feed us all on the supplies they had in stock.

When the Mongers first came to St. Brigid's after Seth Walters took over, they only guarded the front gates. But when Adam had led forty mixed-bloods into the school through all the various entrances he'd discovered around the property, Walters had apparently pitched a raging fit and placed guards all around the walls of the school grounds.

"By the way, Miss Simpson allowed Raven Walters and her mixed-blood boyfriend to stay here last night. There are those among us who aren't happy having a full-blooded Monger in the school, but the headmistress was adamant that she be allowed to remain."

"Hmm. Maybe she Saw something that includes Raven." I shrugged, and Mr. Shaw looked hard at me under furrowed eyebrows.

"I was under the impression that you and Miss Walters were not the best of friends," he said suspiciously.

"We're not."

His eyes narrowed. "So why aren't you afraid she'll act as a spy for her uncle?"

I looked Mr. Shaw straight in the eyes and said with complete seriousness. "I want her to."

He regarded me for a long moment, and then grunted in a distinctly Bear-like way. "Right."

"Any chance you and Mr. Baretsky can whip us up some incendiary devices?" I asked in my most innocent voice.

Laughter exploded from him. "I'm sure we'd be delighted to."

I grinned and waved goodbye, then took the rest of the hall and a flight of stairs at a run. I ended up outside a familiar door with my heart pounding much harder than it should have with such little exertion. I knocked, and a familiar voice called, "Yeah?"

I opened the door carefully and stepped into the room I had once shared with Raven. The look of shock on her face was similar to the way I felt.

"Can I come in?" I said.

"What do you want?" Raven's voice was snarky and defensive.

"To talk … without teeth and claws if we can."

She snorted derisively, but waved her hand toward my old bed. I sat on the edge, and she pushed herself backward on her own bed against the headboard, with her arms wrapped protectively around her knees.

"So, your uncle wants you here to spy for him."

She paled. "I didn't know who the man on the table was," she whispered.

"Who do you think he is?" I asked. I wondered whether Seth had told her Archer was a Sucker, and if so, I didn't necessarily want to disabuse her of that notion.

"He's with you, right? I mean when I saw you guys together it made sense that Seth would hold someone that was important to you." She shook her head. "I have never understood why you matter so much." She sounded annoyed.

"It's because I'm mixed." I shrugged. "And mixed-bloods are immune to the powers of his ring."

Her eyes widened at that information. Interesting. She hadn't known. "How do you know you're immune because you're a mixed-blood?"

I scoffed. "Why do you think he wanted all the mixed-bloods out of the way? They're the only people who can't be compelled."

"Why didn't he take Cole then?"

I shrugged. "Maybe Cole is your uncle's leverage against you."

She opened her mouth to answer that, but shut it again. The defensive glare in her eyes faded, and she rubbed her arms as if she was cold.

"I'm tired of all the games, Saira. If you have something to say to me, just say it."

I studied her across the room. She looked worn out, and it made her look young and vulnerable. "I'm sorry you got caught up in all of your uncle's politics." I didn't know why I suddenly felt sorry for her, because she had certainly never been nice to me. But if things had been different – if her Family hadn't played power games and stuck her in the middle – she might have been more like the café waitress Ringo and I met on the other time stream.

I'd surprised her. "Thanks," she said uncertainly. "I am too."

"We need to take him down, you know?" I said.

She nodded, and clutched her arms tighter without looking at me. "I know."

"I saw a time stream where the Mongers had no power. It wasn't good."

She met my eyes and narrowed her own. "Why tell me that?"

I shrugged. "I met you on it. You worked in a café that had books, and you were nice."

She scowled. "So I'm nice when my Family has nothing. Good to know." I chuckled. She was silent for a long time before she finally said, "The café in town?"

"Yeah. They have good tarts."

"Apple's the best." She looked at me. "Weird conversation to be having."

"Yeah." I stood up. "I guess I just wanted to say that if we can actually pull this off, the leadership of the Council is probably going to change, along with the rules that discriminate against mixed-bloods, and probably Suckers too. But I made them promise not to take away the Mongers' power."

"You think they'll listen? You're just a—"

"—if you say 'just a girl' I might start throwing things."

She grinned, and something dangerous glinted in her eyes. "I was going to say just a student. I once threw my brother's phone out the window when he told me I couldn't fence because I was *just a girl.*"

I scowled. "Your brother's a jerk. And you're a way better fencer than he is."

She scowled back to cover the grin. "Yeah. Probably because I fence *like a girl.*"

I found Ava and Tam sitting in the dining hall with Cole. Tam's green hair was the brightest thing in the room, and it provoked smiles from everyone who caught sight of it. I grabbed a cup of coffee and sat down next to Ava. Cole scowled, but I was beginning to think it was his resting face, so I didn't take it personally.

"Morning, Saira. Did you just get up?" Tam asked with a cheeky grin.

I shrugged and said casually. "Just got back from 1554. You?"

Tam gaped, and Ava laughed at his reaction. "Do you just flit around in time?"

"Not usually. Most of the past is pretty stinky, and the meat's too salted. No, I needed to collect a friend."

Ava turned to me with her ethereal smile. "Will Charlie stay?"

"I don't know. She's waiting for Ringo to ask her, I think."

"To ask her what?" asked Tam.

Ava gave him a sweet smile. "You'll know the answer to that question when you're ready to ask it."

Tam rolled his eyes with an easy grin, and said to Cole, "You'd think you'd get all the answers when you hang out with Seers. Instead, you just get more questions."

"Does your name mean anything specific, Tam?" I asked, after Cole had grunted an indeterminate word.

"Short for Tamerlane, from the poem."

"I don't know the poem. Wasn't there a conqueror, kind of like Genghis Khan, named Tamerlane?"

Tam nodded. "The poem's sort of based on him, but it's about a guy who chooses his job over the girl he loves, named Ada – after Ada Lovelace, Lord Byron's daughter. Huh - kind of like Ava."

Tam seemed startled by the similarity. "Anyway, on his deathbed, Tamerlane is full of regret because he made the wrong choice."

"So, are you named after the conqueror, or the poem?" I asked.

He quirked an eyebrow at me. "Good question. My mum always felt like Ada with my da, and I guess she named me so I'd think through the regret factors before making choices."

"Consequently, you're a troublemaker who doesn't let people slide on crap behavior," murmured Cole. There was affection under his hard tone, and I sensed a deep friendship between the two guys.

"I just came from talking to Raven," I said to Ava, and Cole's attention swung to me.

Ava smiled serenely. "She wants different things now."

I shot a glance at Cole, who was scowling again. "Yeah, I believe she does. I just don't know if she'll actually help us," I said.

"Sometimes the question just needs to be asked," said Ava. She had a completely peaceful expression on her face, and Tam barked a laugh at something she must have shown him mentally.

I rolled my eyes and stood up. "I can already tell that you guys are going to be intolerable to be around. I thought the twin-speak was bad …"

Cole pushed back from the table. "You're like the blasted Borg together."

My mouth quirked up in a smile as he fell into step with me. "A Next Generation reference? That's awfully geeky of you."

He shrugged with his perpetual scowl. "Resistance is futile." I was surprised that Cole walked out with me, and even more surprised when he spoke again. "I knew Walters was coming for you."

I stopped walking, then slipped into a classroom. He followed me in, and during the few moments of stalling, I'd managed to get my initial rush of anger under control. "What did he have on you?"

"Walters knew about me and Raven. He said he'd leave Melanie alone if I just let him know when I saw you. I knew he'd come after us eventually, and I hadn't been able to follow when they grabbed Tam, so I figured I'd set you up, then get you sprung, just so I'd know where to find him."

I nodded slowly. "Makes sense." And it did. He hadn't known me and certainly had no allegiance to me. "Would you do the same thing again – now?"

Cole studied me for a long moment, and I saw him work through all the ramifications of my question. His eyes narrowed, and he finally answered. "If you needed me to."

So, he'd figured some things out. Whether he was with us or just smart, I didn't know, but I was hoping that what Seth Walters represented was a big enough deterrent to choose us.

"Would Seth buy your complicity?"

A slow nod. "He knows I'm helping Raven do what he ordered. He doesn't know she's told me everything."

I met his eyes. "It would suck to be betrayed."

He shrugged. "You don't have my loyalty – that belongs to Raven."

I nodded. "So maybe your self-interest is enough."

THE PIECES

Cole and I went our separate ways, and I was startled to run into Olivia at the top of the stairs. "Aunt Sanda sent me to make sure Lady Millicent was taken care of," she said. "Sanda and Jeeves won't leave the manor house to the Mongers, and Mrs. Edwards won't leave Jeeves. So between them and the gardeners, there are enough people there to be a deterrent."

I was glad Liz and Jeeves were with Sanda at Elian Manor. Of course if he really wanted to, Seth Walters could compel them to leave, but Olivia was right. Enough gardeners with shotguns would deter the easy land-grab attempts.

"Are you heading up to see Millicent now?" I asked.

"Just for a minute. Then I wanted to go up to the attics with Charlie. The girl needs clothes."

I laughed. "And you're the perfect person to go vintage clothes shopping with her."

She sparkled as brightly as her eyes. "Yes, I am."

I tagged along. I'd been putting off the conversation with Millicent, and it was time to rip off the bandage.

Olivia tapped on the door to my former bedroom, and Millicent's imperious voice called to come in. I opened the door to a veritable palace inside the relatively small room.

The rug Archer had brought me was the only thing of mine that still remained in the space. There was a now a double four-poster bed draped in gorgeous green fabric, an exquisite silk tapestry hanging on the opposite wall, and a credenza beneath it that looked like it had belonged to nobility. Millicent sat in a chair by the window reading on an iPad, which might have been the most startling part of the picture.

She looked up to see us, and a smile lit her face. "Saira, it's so lovely to see you."

I crossed the room to her and kissed her cheek in greeting. "I like what you've done with the place," I grinned.

"It's completely excessive and utterly outrageous. But it fulfills a fantasy I had as a young girl at this school, and that has made it totally worth the effort."

She saw Olivia behind me and beamed at her. "My dear, it is so good of you to come. Sanda worries that I don't know how to fetch my own tea, which is ridiculous of course. But I do find I'm in need of a procurer of things, and I'm told you know the attics of this school perhaps better than anyone else?"

Olivia beamed. "They're not as well-stocked as the Elian attics, but none can beat them for variety."

"Ah, brilliant. Well then, when I graduated from St. Brigid's I was in such a hurry to begin my life that I accidentally left behind a small valise that my mother had insisted I bring in case of an emergency. I always assumed it was a medical kit or some such thing, but when my mother died, she asked me where that valise had gone. I honestly could not remember where I'd left it until now. Returning to stay at this school has brought back so many delicious memories of my youth, I find I very nearly want to skip down the stairs as I used to do when I was young." Millicent's smile gave her the look of a much younger woman. Her Clocker blood made her age much more slowly than normal people, and even though she appeared to be in her sixties, her actual age was closer to ninety.

She held Olivia's rapt gaze. "So, if you would be so kind as to search the attics for a brown, crocodile-skin valise, about the size of a medical bag, I would consider your time here well spent."

Olivia grinned and did a little curtsy. "It would be my pleasure, ma'am." Then she shot me a quick grin and ran from the room.

"You know her people are native to this island?" Millicent said.

I nodded. "She said she was related to the Pictish people of Wales."

"Her blood is bluer than yours or mine," she confided proudly, as if Olivia's heritage was her own doing.

"It is? Why is Sanda a servant then?"

"That's just what she does," Millicent dismissed the idea with a wave of her hand. "Who she is, is a descendant of the first nobles of Britain."

I looked sideways at her. "So, what's your feeling about mixed-bloods?"

Millicent looked confused. "Why do you ask?"

Something was strange about her. Millicent and I had made our peace a while ago, but she had been so bitter about my parents' marriage when we first met. "I ask because you're currently surrounded by us, and you've been living under a political moratorium against mixed-bloods for centuries. I just wonder where your personal feelings lie on the matter of mixed-bloods' rights."

She gave me an odd look. "But Saira, my husband was mixed."

Her husb—? Even my brain stuttered on the word. My mouth fell open, and Millicent gave me a disapproving look. "My dear, you look like a fish. Please close your mouth."

Well, at least she was still Millicent.

"I didn't know you were married." She'd said he *was* mixed. I didn't think I committed any major faux pas by speaking in past tense.

Nonetheless, she gave me a sharp look. "Don't be ridiculous, of course you did."

And all of a sudden, I did know. It was as though a door opened and the information poured into a formerly empty chamber in my memory. It was a stunning feeling, and my words came without conscious thought. "When I left a few weeks ago, you had never married." I inhaled sharply. "Your husband was Sean Mulroy?"

"There, you see? You knew."

I shook my head. "Not until just now. You told me a story about Sean – that he was the one that got away – before I went back to 1944. I met a pilot named Sean Mulroy when I was there – I mean then – and I mentioned that if he ever met you, he shouldn't be scared off so easily."

My heart was pounding at the thought that I could have changed something so big. Millicent looked out the window thoughtfully. "He was always so pushy when he thought I was being too proper." Her voice trailed away softly.

"Did you have any children?" I asked the question even though I thought I already knew the answer from the implanted memory.

Millicent seemed to shake herself and come back to the conversation. "No, we never did. Sean was able to hide his Descendancy from the Council, and we spent most of our married years in Ireland. We were afraid that if we had children, their mixed heritage would be revealed. So, you asked about my feelings toward the mixed-blood moratorium?" Her eyes glared fiercely. "I hated it and everything it meant for my family."

For the first time, I noticed that Millicent wore a thin gold wedding band on her left hand. I took her hand in mine and held it. "He's gone now?" I asked softly.

Her fierceness dissolved into a tender, faraway look, as though she were turning the pages of a treasured photo album, and she nodded. "We had twenty very happy years together after the war. My father eventually learned to love Sean as I did, but we spent most of our time together at our cottage in Galway." She smiled. "He was my best friend and the love of my life. He teased me when I got too serious, cherished me when I got too strong, and reminded me that no matter who I was to the rest of the world, to him I was his treasure."

She sighed. "My mother outlived Sean, so he never had to see me become the Family Head." She looked down at our entwined hands, and her fingers brushed the gold of my wedding ring. She looked up at me in surprise. "What is this? Are *you* married?"

I nodded, still speechless at the story of her time with Sean. Tears prickled my eyes – happy that she had found love, but so sad for her loss.

She clapped my hand in both of hers. "Oh Saira! Tell me everything!" There was so much excitement and joy on her face. This Millicent was a different person, with so many different life experiences than the lonely woman I'd left behind.

So I did tell her, and I made us tea, and I had a totally enthusiastic audience for my stories of our time in France. She was especially interested in Stella O'Brian, and she clutched her hands to her chest at the romance of our wedding in the church garden.

Telling Millicent the story of the wedding allowed me to relive all the joy and love and excitement of marrying Archer, and I sensed that she got to relive some of her own joy in marriage too. When the tea was gone and her energy began to flag, I kissed her cheek and thanked her for such a wonderful conversation.

She walked me to the door and took my hands in hers before I left. "I'd like to give you a wedding present if I may," she said softly.

I started to protest. "Oh Millicent, you don't—"

"—Don't you tell me what I can and can't do, young lady," she said sharply, and then smiled. "I'd like to give you my cottage in Galway. It overlooks the Cliffs of Moher and the Aran Islands, and there's a beautiful walled garden at the back of it."

I couldn't find my voice, but my face must have said the words because Millicent's smile grew wider and she kissed my hands. "You're welcome, my dear. It makes me so happy to think that the house where Sean and I lived so happily will again be filled with love."

I went up to the attics to see how Olivia and Charlie were doing and found them in the middle of a vintage shopping spree. Charlie said the guys were out on the roofs, so I slipped out of an open dormer window and climbed up to join them.

Archer and Ringo sat on the warm tile enjoying a rare sunny day. Archer had his eyes closed, his face tilted toward the sun, and a happy smile on his face when I joined them. "Hello, beautiful," he said, in complete contentment.

"Hi." I couldn't get enough of the look of his skin in the sunlight. He was still very pale, but the beginnings of a tan made his face glow. Ringo smirked at the look of wonder I wore.

"I give 'im twenty more minutes and 'e'll be burnt to a crisp," he said with amusement.

"Shhh, I'm in heaven right now." Archer rumbled. "I have the most extraordinary wife in the world, the sun is shining, and I'm warm. And if my best friend would shut his trap, I could properly wallow in all my good fortune."

I settled back between them and turned my face to the sun. "Millicent was married," I said finally. I peeked an eye open to see Ringo staring at me in shock, and Archer still smiling serenely.

"Yes, I know," said Archer.

Ringo shot me an accusatory look. "It's what ye said to that pilot, isn't it? That Mulroy chap? Ye said somethin' about Millicent and it changed things."

Archer frowned slightly. "I remember that conversation." He was silent a bit longer, then he opened his eyes and looked at me. "She hadn't been married when you left?"

I shook my head. "No." I looked at Ringo. "They were married for twenty years and had no children." I could see him process that information the same way I had. No children meant minimal impact on the time stream, so not a big chance that I'd caused a split. "And she was happy," I whispered to him.

He seemed to come to a conclusion and nodded once. "Good. I'm glad she 'ad love."

Archer watched our exchange with concern. "I don't like that I remember something differently than you do," he said.

"I didn't remember it until she and I talked," I mused, and then I gave myself a mental shake to change the subject. "She gave us their house in Galway as a wedding present." Archer's eyes widened in surprise, and I added, "It's on the Cliffs of Moher, overlooking the Aran Islands."

"That is spectacular country."

I linked our fingers together. "Want to go when this is all over?"

His smile lit me up all the way to my toes. "There's nothing I'd love more," he said.

I took a deep breath of joy, and then turned my brain back to the business we had to finish first. "So, have you guys spotted all the Mongers out there?"

Ringo pointed out the fifteen guys they'd spotted and places where others might be hiding. They had set up a perimeter just outside the school walls, with some of the men using the closer trees as high perches to be able to see into the grounds. "Since we've been here," Ringo said, "they've done one full shift change."

I looked at where the sun sat in the sky. "It's afternoon, so they're doing a standard three-shift day?"

Archer nodded. "Seven to three, three to eleven, and eleven to seven. It means our best chance is at midnight – an hour after the shift change."

"So that puts my trip outside the walls at about one a.m.?"

"Our trip. There's no way Walters would believe I'd let you go anywhere without me, not even Elian Manor, and especially not at night."

As twingy as that made me, I shoved the fear down and kept my expression as neutral as I knew how to. "Right, sorry."

"Well then," Ringo said, as he stood up and brushed slate dust off. "I think it's time to properly admire some ladies' dresses, and then get to work."

He had a grin on his face as he left us, and I thought it might be in anticipation of seeing Charlie's fashion show. Archer touched my arm as I moved to stand.

"Wait," he said quietly. I sat down again and turned to face him as he continued. "I do realize it's hard to know what you can expect or rely on with me now – now that my body is mortal again."

My heart beat a little faster. He'd seen my hesitation and he knew why. The thought that he could wonder about my trust in his abilities made me feel sick. I opened my mouth to speak, but he raised his hand. "I know you love me, and I know you trust me, but what you don't know is what to expect from me at your side in a battle."

"Your sword skills—" I began, but he interrupted.

"—are excellent, as are my knife skills, my aim, and my reflexes in hand-to-hand combat. I wasn't kidding when I said I had exceptional survival skills. I've spent more than a century and a quarter honing them, and I promise you, though I can't heal like I once could, and I may be slower, I am no less capable of avoiding injury now than I have ever been."

I took a deep breath, and this time he let me speak. "I know that, Archer. I'm just scared. I lost you, and I survived – so I know I can do it. But I don't want to do it. For the first time in my life I'm actually wondering what it would be like to grow old, because for the first time since I've known you, I can hope that we'll grow old together."

"Which is why we go together," Archer said softly. "I'll always be afraid to lose you, my love, but I've learned to trust that you won't be reckless with your life, as I hope you trust me. When I gave you this ring," he said, fingering the flaming heart, "I gave you the promise of my future. I have earned many, many years of sunshine with you, and I intend to collect."

He kissed me softly as the sun dipped down below the tree line, and the warmth seeped in and wrapped itself around my heart.

Raven found us after dinner in the library. She and Cole had been looking for us for a while, and she seemed exasperated when she sat down.

Tom got up and gave her his seat, while Archer, Ringo, and Adam scooted around the table to make room for two more chairs. When everyone was settled, Raven turned to me. "I need to tell Seth something." Tom tensed, and Raven noticed. "You know I have to," she said to him. "He sent me here to spy, and if I go silent, he'll hurt Melanie."

I stared at Cole. "You said your sister was safe. Does he have her?"

He scowled. "I didn't have a place to move her. I even tried her friend Olivia, but could never reach anyone."

I rubbed my temples. "Because Olivia's here. Why didn't you bring Melanie?"

"Because then he'd know we were running. This way there's still a chance we have people to go home to."

"Do you even like your people?" Adam asked Raven. "I mean, your brother's a prat, your mother's the Rothbitch, and your uncle's Seth bloody Walters."

Her glare was hard, but her voice was quiet. "They're all I have."

"No they're not." Tom's hands were fisted on the library table. "They're not all you have. I'm here, aren't I?" She stared at him, and he didn't look away. "I mean, your uncle generously donated to my creation, so we're first cousins." The scorn in his voice was directed at his father, but Raven flinched.

She continued to stare at Tom, and he held her gaze until she finally looked away. Her expression was angry, but her voice held frustration. "What can I say to Seth?"

"Tell him the truth. We're meeting about something, but you don't know what. You think we don't trust you, but Tam and Cole are friends and they spend a lot of time together, so maybe you'll have more to report tomorrow," Tom said, and she scowled. He had unclenched his fists and was spinning his chess piece on the table in front of him.

"It's not enough. He'll want to know who's here and what they're doing."

He shrugged. "Tell him."

She glared at him. "You're pretty confident he's not going to start going after families."

"He probably doesn't have confirmation that I'm here, but that's fine – he can know. And there are forty people here because he brought them all together. If he wanted to go after their families he could do that any time. Anything he wants to know about the people who are here – tell him. You get brownie points for observation, and then he maybe forgives whatever you're not telling him until next time." Tom spoke confidently, though the edge in his voice grated my nerves. Raven finally nodded.

"Do you want him to know you're here, or you just don't care?" she finally asked.

He stopped spinning the chess piece and put it away in his pocket. His jaw clenched, and he forced his eyes to meet hers. "I tried to kill Seth Walters last time I saw him. I even went back in time and tried to kill his grandfather so he could never be born." Raven blanched at that. There was Walters blood in her veins too. "His brand of evil doesn't scare me – I've seen and lived through much, much worse. If it helps you to tell him I'm here, do it. I. Don't. Care." Tom took a deep breath and softened his tone. "I'm not going to lie to you, cousin. I may not volunteer the information, but I won't lie."

Raven looked down at her hands and then used them to push back from the table. She met our eyes. "Miss Simpson let me keep my phone – I'll use it to text him. If anyone wants to see my text history, you can."

"Thanks, Raven." I said quietly. We watched her leave with Cole, and then I turned to Tom. "That was a nice thing you did – to claim her as family."

He barked a mirthless laugh. "She might not think so. I'm not exactly a poster boy for familial bliss."

Adam pushed him on the shoulder. "You're definitely miserable at the cousin business, but does this mean the Crow is now my cousin once removed or something like that? Because, you know, hot girl relatives …"

"Adam, you know that line of appropriateness that your Tourettic brain can't usually see?" I asked, narrowing my eyes.

He grinned. "I jumped it?"

I scoffed. "You poured lighter fluid all over it and lit it on fire."

THE WOODS

We waited until after midnight to gather in the solarium. The trap-setters were led by Adam's girlfriend, Alex, and the Shifter Owl mix, Colin Zhang. Ava and Tam were with them, as were Adam, Mr. Shaw, and a couple of other strong guys who could dig holes. Alex and Tom had gone over the plan for booby-trapping the woods in detail, and everyone knew what they were doing and where.

Charlie and I figured we'd try Clocking eight people out into the woods at a time. There were traps to be set and Monger guards to lure into them, and it was going to take a lot of bodies to do both. I had once drawn a spiral on a big granite slab in those woods, and she and I had gone earlier to make sure it was still intact.

"When we land, you might feel a little dizzy or nauseous," I explained to the first group of eight. "Clear out to the sides as quickly as possible, because we'll be Clocking right back to the same spot with the next group."

Heads nodded, and I gathered people around the spiral I had already drawn on the wall with chalk. We made a chain of linked arms that began with me and ended with Charlie. Then she put her hand on the spiral while I traced.

The humming sound rose rapidly, and as soon as I fixed the image of the granite slab in the woods, we were through.

Connor immediately stripped down and Shifted to his Wolf. His job was to prowl through the woods to locate whatever guards we hadn't spotted from the roof. We needed to know where they were so we could set the traps accordingly.

The twin girls, Beck and Bauer, were already circling overhead as Blackbirds. Logan had chosen his big Bat form for nighttime reconnaissance, and the three of them had taken off directly from the attics at school. Colin, the trap-builder, hadn't traveled as an Owl because it would have forced him to work in the buff.

Archer and Tom were both armed with rifles I'd retrieved from the gardeners at Elian Manor, and they were going to act as guards for the trap-builders. Tom looked a little strung out from the moment we landed in the woods, and I caught Archer's eyes and glanced at Tom meaningfully. Archer nodded and turned so that he had Tom in his sight.

Charlie and I returned with the second group, and Charlie immediately scrambled up the tall tree above our spiral. She was armed with a bow and arrow, and her job was to guard our exit. Ringo and I took off into the woods that led away from the school. We were headed toward the gardener's shack where I'd been taken by the Romanian Were with the help of Raven and her brother. I wanted to set wards around it so we could have a safe house for our people in the woods, just in case things went pear-shaped.

The shack was just as I remembered it, if not more empty. Ringo watched outside while I stood in the middle of the room and pushed a wall of warding heat out to surround the shack. In my mind, it was like a sound wave that moved outward from my body, but it was both more and less solid than sound, and a person could only come through it if they meant no harm to anyone inside.

"What if there's no one inside the buildin' when the bad guy enters?" Ringo asked when he came inside after I'd finished.

I was sitting on the floor in the center of the shack, trying very hard not to shiver. Setting wards seemed to leach all the heat from my bones, and I hadn't figured out how to counteract that effect.

"I don't know. It's all pretty th-theoretical to me." I couldn't stop the chattering of my teeth, and Ringo whipped his coat off and wrapped it around my shoulders.

"Th-thanks," I whispered.

He sat behind me and I leaned back into him for warmth. He held me there for a few minutes until the tremors finally stopped and I could sit up.

"Are ye better now?" he asked.

I nodded. "Aislin must have set the original wards around the walls of St. Brigid's in the dead heat of summer."

"'Ave they always been there?" Ringo draped his arms over his legs and leaned back against a crate.

"Yeah, I think they have. I think maybe that's why Seth Walters never came to the school for me, even though he knew I was here." I met his eyes. "It's also why I think I trust Raven."

"Ye mean because the wards let 'er in?"

I nodded. "I guess someone could change their mind about harm once they're inside the school grounds, but they can't come in if they intend to do harm." I shivered again. "I can see the necessity for wards, but I don't like them."

We loped back through the woods with as much stealth as free-running allowed. Once or twice I thought I saw the Shifter Birds overhead, but for the most part, the woods were silent enough to let me think while I ran. Of all the people in the woods with us, I was most worried about Tom. He had seemed okay since we'd been back at school – better than I'd seen him in a long time – but the minute Archer put a rifle in Tom's hands, he'd gotten a wild, twitchy look in his eyes, as though he fully expected the wolves to come out of the walls at any moment.

Ringo and I had been gone less than an hour, and work was nearly finished on the outlying traps we came upon first. Alex had proudly shown us the snares, pit traps, and blinds for bomb-throwing they'd built at intervals a hundred yards back from the perimeter of the woods. Archer and Mr. Shaw were with Alex, and they reported there had been no guard activity anywhere near them while they worked. It was good news for the plan, and we agreed to meet back at the granite slab twenty minutes later.

Connor met us in his Wolf form about halfway between the two crews. He nipped my hand and pulled backwards, and Ringo whispered behind me, "Run!"

Connor's Wolf led us through the woods, avoiding some of the traps that had already been set, and around to the site of a big pit that Adam and Colin had dug in an area that led directly to the road. Adam was crouched down at the edge of the pit, whispering urgently. I reached him, out of breath, and nearly stumbled backwards when I saw what he was looking at.

Tom stood over Colin with his rifle aimed at Colin's forehead. Tom was breathing hard, and it looked like he was trembling.

"Tom!" I whisper-shouted. He didn't look up, so I tried again in my normal voice, pitched low enough that I hoped it wouldn't carry. Ringo immediately put himself on the other side of the hole, facing outward, watching for guards coming from the school.

The trembling in Tom's arms grew more pronounced, as if he was barely controlling his instinct to shoot. Colin lay on his back in the hole, his eyes like saucers, and there was blood on his lip.

I was behind Tom, so I caught Ringo's eyes across the pit, looked down at Tom, then back at Ringo. He nodded.

I dropped into the pit and Tom swung around, rifle-first, exactly one half-second before Ringo dropped in and shoved Tom up against the dirt wall. He yanked the rifle from Tom's hands and tossed it up to Adam, and before Tom could swing at him, I pulled Tom into my arms.

"Tom!" I said in a low voice. "It's Saira." His heart was pounding, and Colin scrambled up and out of the pit while I murmured into Tom's ear. "Shhh, it's me, Tom. You're okay."

I could hear Adam whisper fiercely to Colin, but I paid no attention to the words. I just held Tom in a tight hug from behind. He didn't lean against me but held himself rigid, and his breathing was shallow and fast.

Ringo stood in front of Tom, looking him in the eyes. He didn't break eye contact as he spoke in a voice that was nearly a whisper. "We'll get ye back inside St. Brigid's when ye're ready. Ye just need to let us know when ye can move without startlin'."

Tom's breathing calmed a little more, and I heard someone else running toward us. I shot a glance at Ringo, and he flicked his eyes up, then shook his head quickly. I risked unlocking one of my arms from around him, and I slowly moved that hand up to his hair. I began stroking it like a mother does to a terrified child, and he shuddered, and finally leaned back into me. My hold on him became less restraint and more embrace. Ringo nodded and spoke to him. "Are ye ready to go up?"

Tom nodded, but didn't speak, so I let go of his arms. Adam crouched down at the edge of the pit and helped to haul Tom out. Archer was on the edge behind me and reached for my hand. He pulled me up and into his arms. "Are you okay?" he whispered into my hair.

"Yeah," I said. He let me go, and I went straight over to Tom. I could finally see his face and the wildness that still lurked in his eyes. "Come on. We're taking you back to school," I said.

He looked ashamed, and then whispered to me. "No one else. Just you." I bit back tears and reached for his hand as we stepped onto the granite spiral. "Wait," said Adam. "I'm coming too."

Tom spoke before I could. "You guys should finish what we started. I'll be okay."

I shot a quick look at Archer. I didn't want to take Tom back and leave him alone, but I couldn't think of who should come with us. Archer moved, but Colin stepped in front of him. "I'm coming," he said. I looked at him, then at Tom.

"Is that a good idea?" I asked.

Tom took a shuddery breath and nodded. "Yeah, it is."

I looked back at Archer and saw him consider Colin for a long moment before he gave a curt nod. Other people from Alex's trap-building team were starting to arrive, and they could help finish the traps here. "I'll be right back," I whispered to Archer.

This return trip was harder without Charlie, and both Tom and Colin fell to their knees and took great, gasping gulps of air to keep the dry-heaves down.

"That's normal?" Colin said when he finally stood up and braced his arm against the wall.

"Yeah."

Colin reached a hand down for Tom and helped him to his feet. I eyed them both. "Are you guys going to be okay?"

Colin was a couple of years older than Tom, but Tom was taller. They were both slight men, and I sensed Colin could probably take care of himself in a fight if he didn't have a rifle pointed at his skull.

Tom nodded, still taking shuddery gasps of air. "Yeah."

My eyes flicked between both guys for a moment until Tom finally gave a half-smile. "You're going to be a fearsome mother someday, you know that?"

"Shut up," I said, trying to hold back the relieved smile that threatened. "And clear out of the way. I'll be right back." The two guys were already moving across the room when I Clocked out.

Charlie was down out of her tall tree, and most of Alex's group had assembled by the granite slab when I returned to the woods. Archer raised an eyebrow and I nodded, which was the wordless way of saying 'is everything okay?' and 'yes.'

He stayed behind with Adam to make sure that Connor made it back and could return to his human form while Charlie and I Clocked the first eight people back to the solarium. Tom and Colin had left the room, and the returning group seemed tired, but also a little giddy. I advised them to move out of the way and then Charlie and I Clocked back to the granite slab.

The rest of our booby-trap team had assembled, and a giant Bat fluttered to my shoulder right before I started tracing the spiral for another trip back to the solarium. I jumped, a couple of people muffled shrieks, and then I glared at it fiercely as I completed the spiral.

Logan's Bat was still gripping my shoulder when we landed back at school. The Bat flew up to the roof glass and then out of the solarium with what looked like a grin on his little Bat face. I glared at Connor, and he held up his hands in surrender. "I'm only surprised he didn't Shift and go back with us naked."

After a round of quiet thank-yous and quick plans to meet up the next day, most of the group trudged off to bed. Adam and Ava had gone in search of Tom, leaving Ringo, Charlie, Connor, me, and Archer alone in the solarium.

"Do we know what happened?" I asked.

Charlie nodded, and spoke quietly. "Adam got to work digging Colin's pit traps straight away while Tom stood guard. Colin came to check on them often, always pausing to speak quietly with Tom. Adam noticed Colin's attention on his cousin and said something teasing. The next time Colin came to check on them, he came up behind Tom and startled him. Before Tom had even seen who it was, he had knocked Colin backward into the pit and was standing over him with the rifle pointed at his head."

Ringo sat back. "World's not ordered for 'im anymore."

Charlie furrowed her eyebrows. "What do you mean, it's not ordered?"

Connor exhaled. "It means Tom probably has PTSD." He saw her look of confusion and quickly added, "Everything's been coming at him, trying to kill him since Wilder took him from the Tower of London. He's a little safer now, but he's still ducking and waiting for the time they don't miss."

"He was doing better here, inside the building," I said.

"Putting the gun in his hands started it, but honestly, I think the stress in the woods would have been enough to trigger his response," Archer added.

I exhaled. "Okay, Tom stays here tomorrow night. And then, when we're all done here, he gets some help."

"My mum used to teach psychology. She's the one who got me through the tough parts after France," said Connor quietly.

I rubbed my eyes and sighed. "Somehow I think we're all going to need her help when this is over."

FATE

I was up at dawn despite only getting about three hours of sleep, and I grabbed a cup of coffee from the kitchen before creeping down the hall to Aislin's office.

The door was open and the light was warm and welcoming inside. The last few encounters I'd had with Fate, beginning with my visit to her on the other time stream, had been tense at best and downright terse at worst. I knocked on the doorframe and found her already seated in an armchair. The other chair was pulled out and waiting for me.

"Come in, Saira," she said with a kind smile.

I held up my coffee mug. "Would you like me to get you a cup of coffee from the kitchen?"

"Oh no, I have the kettle on, thank you. Please have a seat."

"You were expecting me?" I asked.

"My dear, despite the tensions we have experienced lately, I do genuinely enjoy your company."

I sighed. "Half the time I feel like I've been thrown in a giant ocean, but with no boat and no life raft. I swim and I swim and I swim, and the farther I think I get, the more I start to sink."

"And the other half of the time?" she asked as she poured hot water into the pot of tea leaves next to her chair.

I scoffed. "I'm pulling my friends down with me."

She smiled. "It is a remarkable thing to have friends, isn't it?"

"Pretty spectacular, actually."

She sat back in her chair, and the light of the floor lamp made her look more like Miss Simpson and less like young Aislin. "Tell me about your friends. I only know those who are students here, and then only as their headmistress."

I smiled. "Are you doing that on purpose? When you sat back, the light changed and made you look more like the kindly older woman. When you sit forward, I see more of the young Immortal from the paintings."

"Whom do you trust more?"

That was an interesting question. Did I distrust Fate? I took a sip of my coffee and thought carefully before I answered. "I guess I trust Miss Simpson more than Aislin."

"May I inquire as to why?"

I exhaled and chose my words. "When you were Miss Simpson, your kindness and generosity felt genuine. Knowing you as Aislin makes the information you gave me access to feel like a carrot dangled in front of a gullible horse. If you guys – the Immortals, I mean – have a request of me, just say it. I'm tired of making every mistake in the book as I try to figure out how to navigate through your world."

Aislin regarded me steadily, and then she sat back into her Miss Simpson light. "Tell me about your friends, Saira."

"Why?" I was being manipulated, and I didn't want to drag anyone else into it.

"Because I believe they are important to the tasks ahead of you and I'd like to understand, as they say, your assets." She smiled at that, and I smiled with her. It sounded like terminology she had picked up from Connor or Ringo and their gaming-speak.

"Okay." I pictured the faces of the people I cared about as I spoke. "Did you know Archer and I got married?" At her expression, I grinned. "Of course you knew. It's very strange, because I don't feel old enough, or even adult enough, but I married my best friend, and I can't imagine ever loving him less than I do now."

Aislin sat forward again with a smile. "I've had forty-seven marriage proposals, and not one of the lovely, wonderful men was ever my best friend. I believe you are quite lucky, my dear."

"Thanks," I said, "me too." I took another sip of coffee. "The interesting thing I've learned about best friends is that you can have more than one. I have two. One I love with passion, the other one I love with complete affection. Archer is my heart, my soul, my reason, and the sum of my experiences, and Ringo is laughter and adventure and strange wisdom that answers the questions that wake me up at two a.m."

Aislin laughed – and it was Aislin, looking even younger and more beautiful than I'd ever seen her look in person. "I understand those questions, for that is the time when Ava wakes me with her visions."

I smiled. "Ava … Ava is like a fairy princess with no filter." I studied Aislin's young face. "And Adam is the biggest, softest *guy* I've ever met."

She sat back again, but this time I only saw Aislin. "Tell me about their cousin, Tom."

I sighed. "Tom hid his pain for so long it became part of his identity. He cares very deeply, but he's terrified to let other people love him because he's sure he'll hurt them."

She tilted her head. "Tell me who else you consider a friend." "Well, Connor Edwards, of course, and his little brother, Logan. Charlie, and Olivia—" I tucked my legs under me and contemplated the people in my world. "I guess Millicent has become my friend too. And Mr. Shaw, obviously. He's part teacher, part father, and part friend."

She smiled, and it touched her eyes and made me feel as though she really heard me. "These are your people, Saira. You found them as you were discovering yourself, and through them, you've gained a much richer experience of this world we both inhabit. You asked why the Immortals haven't made a request of you? Can you honestly say you would have even considered a request had you not experienced every joy and hardship, or met every friend and enemy that the past year has put in your way?"

I looked her straight in the eyes. "One year ago I was freerunning the streets of Venice Beach with only my mother and a few stray cats for company."

"Would you go back to that?"

"Not in a million years."

She regarded me steadily, and I didn't look away. "Our edict against interference with our Descendants has a purpose. Just as telling a child not to touch the hot stove carries far less weight than the burn does, choosing one's own path as the result of experience creates a much more committed traveler than the one who was directed to that path."

"What if the path isn't the one you wish the person would take?" I asked.

"One cannot trust a path, because the path is different for each person who takes it. One can only trust the person to choose the path that best represents their values and experiences."

"Who set me on this path?" I asked.

"You did, my dear. The circumstances that brought you to us only mattered because of what you did with them."

I hadn't realized we were going to have an existential conversation about my life, although what did I really expect, given that I was talking to Fate? "I told you about my friends; can you tell me about yours?"

She knew exactly what I was asking, and I thought for sure she was going to refuse. But after a very long hesitation, she finally spoke. "When the world was younger, I knew them better, so I fear my experiences of them are out of date. Jera was like a sister to me. She had the wisdom of experience behind her, and mine was of things yet to come. Our discussions were lively, and our debates often became like theatre for the others. Goran always sided with Jera, but we never thought anything of it. Because everything about him was so *big* – his laughter, his fierceness, his voice – it overshadowed the signs of a couple falling in love."

She sipped her tea and stared into the cup as if it were a mirror of a different time. "Aeron missed nothing though. He saw every look, every touch, every whisper that passed between Jera and

Goran. Aeron had been in love with Jera since the beginning, you see. He was content to love her from afar, but he withdrew from all of us when she became pregnant with Goran's child."

Aislin's gaze was direct. "And that was what Duncan had been waiting for. In the absence of peace, Death is the only thing that can put an end to War, so long as Aeron remained active among us, Duncan was constrained. But once Death retreated to his island home, Duncan had free reign. He spread rumors that Aeron's jealousy was violent, and that he intended to harm the child and to kill Goran. Even Nature knew that Death could end that part of him which lived in the plants and trees and creatures of the Earth, therefore Goran heeded Duncan's warning that Death should be cast out of our Council and his powers removed."

"By whom?" I asked. "Who was strong enough to take away the power of Death?"

Fate smiled indulgently. "No one, dear. War was spinning a tale to suit his own ends, as War always does. But Goran was afraid, so he threw his lot in with Duncan and demanded that Jera and I do the same. I, of course, would not stand against Death, though I'd Seen the discord the union between Jera and Goran would cause and warned them against it. Jera cared only for the son she carried in her womb and would speak no word against his father."

I was riveted to her story, and Aislin's smile faded as the memories took her. "The babe was three days old when his empty cradle was found covered in blood. Not a trace of the child was ever seen again. Duncan stormed through the world proclaiming Death the villain who had slain the child in rage that the woman he loved had chosen another man. This served Duncan well, because Goran and his Descendants took up arms with War against all who stood with Death."

I stared at her. "He caused a civil war?"

Aislin's expression remained carefully neutral, even as her voice was filled with sadness. "Brother slew brother, friends became enemies, and the houses divided. Jera retreated in mourning and left her Family to their own devices to survive or die in the carnage. Aeron's Family, always the smallest, was nearly annihilated, and any who survived were hunted by every generation that followed. I protected those of my Family that I could, and we remained neutral so that we would be left alone to live. But the discord was sewn by Duncan into the very fabric of our Families, and when Death's Descendants had been hunted to near extinction, Duncan exploited a new fear – the union of Jera and Goran had created a child whose death began the war. Fear is a powerful reason to hate, and hate gives more power to the mongers of fear. Thus, the Mongers became the enforcers, because it was in their interest to keep the fear alive."

"So they got powerful, the Shifters got angry, your Family stayed out of it, the Clockers declined to near oblivion from Jera's neglect, and the Suckers who survived hid from the world," I said.

"Precisely."

We sat in silence for a long moment before Aislin spoke again, and her tone was that of a person confiding a secret. "We are only as strong as our Families believe us to be."

I held my breath. "We who?"

She sighed. "Immortals are like the old gods. Our power lies in people's belief in us, and our strength comes from the strength of our Families. Mongers became strong, so Duncan got more powerful. Clockers have died out, so Jera has become weakened as well."

Aislin had just given me an Immortal secret – maybe the biggest one they had – and with it, I finally understood Duncan's motive for stealing the ring. I swirled the dregs of coffee in my mug and considered her words. "What if Jera's child didn't die?"

I didn't look up until it became clear Aislin wasn't going to answer. So I asked again. "What if the boy didn't die?"

"Then the world would have another Immortal, and Duncan would burn the world to ashes rather than share his power with anyone."

READY

I stopped by my old room and knocked.

"Come in," Raven called.

I poked my head in the door. She sat on her bed using her smartphone while Cole worked on a laptop at the desk.

"Hey," I said, "how's it going?"

Raven just couldn't look at me without suspicion, but it didn't actually bother me. "Everyone goes silent whenever I walk by, so, you know, that's pretty fun." She scowled.

"How'd Slick like your info?" I asked brightly.

"Who is Slick?"

"Your uncle's voice is so smooth and smarmy, it's what I called him before I knew his name."

The corners of her mouth twitched, but she hid the smile that threatened. "It wasn't enough. He wants more."

I came in and shut the door behind me. "I have more."

Cole closed the lid to his laptop and Raven set down her phone. If Raven was suspicious, Cole was downright hostile.

"Whatever information you give Raven is obviously going to be false, and that's going to get my sister hurt."

I shook my head. "Not false. You can ask Tam or anyone else to corroborate. I know what the stakes are, Cole. I'm not going to put Melanie's safety at risk."

"Why? Why help me?" Raven sounded more angry than confused.

367

"Do you really want to ask that, or do you just want to pass the information on and stay out of it?"

She glared at me, so I shrugged and reached for the door. "Okay, see you later."

"What do you want me to tell him?" she said quickly as I pushed the handle.

I didn't turn around. "Archer and I are taking the kids out of here tonight – the young ones. We're stashing them at Elian Manor. It's safe, but still close enough that their parents can get to them."

"What the hell!" Cole growled. "She can't send that message to the bastard. He'll take kids for leverage in a heartbeat, and you two are as good as dead if he gets his hands on you."

I turned around, but I only had eyes for Raven. "Send the message, Raven."

She held my gaze for the space of five heartbeats, and then she nodded once. "I'll send it."

Olivia and Charlie had scoured the attics for every piece of dark clothing they could find, and the group assembled in front of us was dressed in the oddest assortment of vintage clothes I'd ever seen. There was a lot of Victorian-style men's clothing spread around, which gave the solarium the distinct feeling of a Steampunk party. The girls had tried to give me a black topcoat and hat, but Archer's closets held plenty of long-sleeved fitted black t-shirts, and my mom had packed a bag of clothes for me before she came to St. Brigid's, so I was comfortable in black skinny jeans with ankle holsters for my knives, my combat boots, and one of Archer's black shirts.

Ava and Tom were the only ones not dressed in dark clothes. They would coordinate resources inside the building, and Tam would go with the rest of us into the woods so Ava would have eyes on the outside. Tam's green hair was covered by a navy blue balaclava, and without all that distracting color, I found him to be quite handsome. Apparently Ava did too, because they were surreptitiously holding hands.

On Tom's advice, we had gone quietly to people, either alone or in small groups, and told them their part in the plan. Only a handful of people knew the whole picture – partly for security, but also because we really didn't want everyone to know how ridiculous we were for imagining we could pull this thing off. It was a two-part plan. The attacks on the Mongers in the woods to free the school was part one – dangerous, but not outrageous. It was part two that made us feel like B-movie writers with no budget and an impossible task.

It was nearly midnight, and the mood in the room was equal parts solemn and giddy. The first wave of trappers, with Adam, Archer, Connor, and Ringo among them, was ready. Tom came over to us and gave Adam a hug, then he slapped Ringo on the back, and surprisingly, shook Colin Zhang's hand. His tone was stern when he spoke to me. "Five minutes, in and out."

"Yes, sir," I said, grinning at the black knight chess piece in his hand.

I made sure everyone was linked to both Charlie and myself, kissed Archer quickly on the cheek, and started tracing.

We had counted on the moonless night to help conceal our traps, and it was so dark that Adam nearly fell into one when he stepped off the granite slab. Connor quickly Shifted, then led the group away into the woods, where the few noises they made melted into the silence.

Charlie and I were back with the second and third groups as quickly, and by the time everyone was in position, Archer had returned and was ready to leave with me for phase two.

Adam and Connor had been told where the warded shack was, so if things went bad, they could lead people there. Ringo flashed me three fingers – Archer and I had exactly three minutes until everything kicked off.

I blew a kiss to Charlie in her tree, hugged Ringo quickly, then grabbed Archer's hand.

"Let's do this," I whispered.

We Clocked directly into the walled garden at Elian Manor. Beck, Bauer, and Logan, who had flown in as Birds, waited for us there, already clothed with things that Liz had left for them. For this part of the plan to work, our assumption that the garden would be surrounded when we opened the gate had to be right.

It was.

"Hands up where we can see them," growled a man's voice in a tone that sent Monger-induced vomitousness straight to my gut. And just like that, it began.

THE RING

There were four guys in tactical gear pointing weapons at us as we exited the garden, and I don't think any of us was immune to the fear the sight of them induced. Archer stepped out first, his hands high in the air, followed by the girls and Logan, with me at the rear. Knowing that Jeeves and the gardeners were hidden with rifles in the trees above us didn't really quell the terror pumping through my veins.

I protested that they let the kids go free, but the Mongers ignored me, zip-tied our wrists and ankles together, and loaded us into the back of a box truck. I struggled to push down the memory of the last time I was in this position, but my heart rate sped up and panicked breaths began to build in my chest.

"Hey," Archer murmured in my ear. "We knew they'd do this. It's okay, you're fine."

The whites of my eyes must have been showing, because Logan smirked at me. "Put a lid on the crazy, Saira. If I cut you out now, they'll find the knives."

I nodded and swallowed, hard. The truck started moving, and I took a deep breath to shove the panic away. We made a couple of turns, which I tracked from memory, and when we made it onto the expressway, I nodded to Beck and Bauer. "Okay girls, when the doors open, get out of here and fly back to school. As soon as you get there, find Tom and tell him where we are."

They nodded silently.

"I'm really proud of you both for how brave you were back there."

One of them, Beck, I think, whispered, "I just kept imagining them without trousers, and then I had a job not to giggle."

"Me too!" her twin announced, and this set off a wave of quiet laughter that made the panic loosen its grip on my throat.

The truck turned off the expressway, and I closed my eyes to imagine the route we were taking into London. Anticipating where Seth would have us taken was the biggest question mark of the night. There were a lot of variables and things that could go wrong, but others' ability to find us was the key to getting out of this alive.

"All right, it's time," Archer said.

The girls nodded again, and they both curled forward like they were going to do a somersault. When they circled back up, their bodies had Shifted into perfect Blackbirds. The zip ties had fallen off their wrists and ankles, and even though Logan must have been dying to do the same, his expression looked a little like pride as he watched the Blackbird twins hop toward the back doors and settle down to wait.

We slowed to a stop, and the front doors opened and closed. We thought it was likely that the Mongers still believed Archer was a Vampire, which meant they would probably have their guns aimed at him as they opened the door. This was why Logan was lying at the back of the truck. The second the doors opened, the Blackbirds exploded out and Logan began thrashing around wildly as if he was having a seizure. I screamed at the guards, both of whom had their weapons drawn.

"Help him!" I threw a choked sob in my voice for good measure, and Logan's mouth quirked in a grin. I would have kicked him if my legs had been free.

One of the guards shone a torch at Logan, which, admittedly, made him look like something that had escaped Bedlam. They were so morbidly fascinated by Logan's fake seizure and so afraid Archer was going to lunge at them that they failed to notice the absence of the two girls. I decided it was time for hysterics.

"Get him out of here so he can breathe!" I screamed at them. I drew on some of the panic I'd felt during the ride, and my eyes actually filled with tears.

It wasn't Oscar-worthy, but it was something.

One of the guards yanked a knife out of a holster on his belt, and I thought for a second I'd gone too far. But he used it to slice the zip tie at my ankles, and then snarled at me to get out. Headlights hit the back of the truck as a vehicle pulled up behind us, and the two other Mongers who had been at Elian Manor got out of the sedan with weapons aimed at me and Archer.

"Hey, there were two other kids," one of them growled.

The guard who was reaching for Logan stopped and stared around the back of the truck.

"What the …?" He turned to me. "Where are they?"

I said nothing.

The guards frantically shone their torches around the inside. Logan stopped his seizure act and sat up to watch them search, his eyes shining with mischief. I glared at him to remind him to keep his mouth shut.

The guards were starting to panic, and the quiet conversations between them became a debate between telling Walters they'd lost two children or pretending they'd never had them in the first place. They hadn't reached a consensus by the time one of them snarled at the others to shut up.

"The boss knows we're here. He's going to wonder why we're not inside yet."

The men were terrified to cut Archer's ankle ties, but he calmly informed them that he had no intention of harming them while their weapons were pointed at me.

"If either of my friends comes to the slightest harm, however, I will most certainly slake my growing thirst," he said in his most pompously menacing voice. It seemed to work, because the guards kept their distance from all three of us, and although we were surrounded by weapons and had no use of our hands, I felt relatively secure.

I saw immediately where we were, and despite the nasty case of Monger-gut I'd been sporting since they took us from Elian Manor, I was glad. We were outside the building that housed Seth Walters' office, and although it hadn't been the only place they were likely to take us, it was the one I knew the best. Ringo and I had broken in here about a million years ago, and I knew the basic layout of its three floors fairly well. It was also situated on the same side of the Thames River as Kings College, where I knew we could hide with Bishop Cleary if we had to run.

After we'd stolen the ring.

Because that's what this was all about – we had to steal Doran's ring from Seth Walters' hand. On the list of things that could go wrong with our ridiculous plan was the fact that he could use it to compel at least one, or maybe two of us. I was the only one who was immune to its power for sure. Archer had been, when he was infected, but now that he was mortal, we weren't sure how he'd react. And Logan was pure Shifter, and therefore completely vulnerable to the ring's power.

If I had stopped to think about our odds of success, I would have run away screaming.

The guards led us up the central staircase and halted us at the landing. One of them knocked on a door that I remembered was Seth's office, and it was flung open.

Seth Walters moved like an impatient man, but his voice was all calm coolness. "Hello, Clocker." The words sent a shiver down my spine because they were spoken in exactly the same slick tone he'd used the first time he'd said them to me on the road outside Elian Manor over a year before.

He stepped back from the open doorway to usher us inside. Logan was next to me doing his best impression of a meek and frightened child, and Walters stopped him. He put a hand under his chin to lift his face. "And who is this?"

"He's the son of one of the people you kidnapped." I needed to make Walters think we were all immune to the ring's power so he wouldn't try to use it on us.

Walters' eyes narrowed and he looked at his guards. "Surely there was more than one. Where are the others?"

Before they could answer, Archer spoke. "They were Shifter Birds. They Shifted and flew away from Elian Manor when they realized we were caught."

Walters studied Archer for a long moment, and I could see the guards struggling to decide whether to let the lie stand. One had been about to speak when Walters smiled, and he quickly schooled his expression back to neutral.

"All the better if the Council knows I have you. They'll work themselves into a frenzy of fear, and I won't even have to say a word," he said in a voice that reminded me of gleeful James Bond villains setting their plans in motion. All he needed was to tap his fingers together in front of his face to become a giant cliché.

I glanced down at his hands and was very glad to see there was no ring, but I sincerely hoped he hadn't moved its hiding place.

Two of the Monger guards remained in the room with us, which left at least two others, and possibly many more, in the building. I'd been cataloguing every risk factor, and I knew Archer was doing the same. Logan seemed to be the most relaxed of all of us, and I just hoped Seth didn't realize that he was the one to watch.

Seth sat on the edge of his desk and studied us. His eyes landed on Archer first. "I thank you for your donation. It will be quite useful once I've secured full control."

"Useful in what way?" Archer asked. His words were pleasant – his tone was not.

Seth's smile was an ugly thing. It reminded me of a wooden doll with a painted grin that didn't change the glare in its eyes. "I believe in keeping my options open," he said. "My ascent to power is likely to draw the ire of people who haven't yet been subjected to my very compelling speeches. Even with the limitations of your condition, I do look forward to being impervious to assassination."

"Vampires can be killed." I was able to keep his gaze when I spoke, even though the Monger-gut he inspired made me want to puke.

His eyes flicked to Archer and his smile sent a shiver of fear up my spine. "Yes, they can, as my dear, departed brother Wilder can attest."

Wait, what? Wilder? As in *Bishop Wilder*, who had died long before Seth was born? As far as I knew, Seth Walters had never traveled back in time, so how much could he possibly know about Wilder beyond his authorship of the Descendant genealogy?

"Though I suppose it didn't matter in the end, since he failed at the Vatican," Seth said, with a false *tsk, tsk* sound in his tone.

"He … failed?" I asked in genuine confusion. I felt like Alice down the rabbit hole as Seth's words got curiouser and curiouser.

"He failed to steal the ring, which was the entire reason for his presence in Rome," Walters said, his voice laced with derision. "And then he failed use his immortality to find favor with War."

Confusion was making my skin itch, and I stared at him with a million questions hurling themselves against the inside of my skull. "How … how do you know anything about Wilder at the Vatican?"

"The moment of one's *turning* is a noteworthy occasion, don't you think?" There was an odd glint in Walters' eyes that was like light catching the edge of a spring-loaded trap. I couldn't see the jaws of it yet, but I knew it was there, so I decided to step in it to see what was underneath.

"If you knew about Wilder, then you know that *your son* was the one who infected him." Goading him was dangerous, but it might get him to talk.

The grim stillness of Seth's expression melted into a tight smile. "Well, wasn't that fortuitous for me? My father said I was the best of his sons, and my own son helped to secure my favor."

"Your father?" I asked.

The strange tone in his voice hinted at a smirk, but this time he didn't hold back. Seth's grin grew wider. "The Immortal War, of course."

The room swayed suddenly, and I locked my knees to keep from going down.

Duncan was Seth Walters' father?

I forced myself to avoid looking at Archer. I needed to keep Seth talking, and he seemed delighted to oblige as long as he could see the shock in my eyes. He explained. "Duncan's eldest son, Wilder, failed to complete the task he'd been groomed to do, his second son made the fatal error of bringing Weres into the business with the Council, and his third son rendered himself useless by repeatedly drawing the attention of ungifted law enforcement. Therefore, he decided it was time to take a hand in shaping *my* power."

And the shocks just kept coming. "Wilder was Duncan's son?" I breathed, trying not to throw up. "And … you're talking about Rothchild at the Council massacre?" He said nothing, just smiled wider. "Who was the third son?" I swallowed hard, not sure I really wanted the answer.

"My 'grandfather,' George Walters." Seth air-quoted the word *grandfather* like a douchebag, and I might have scoffed if I hadn't felt so sick. I should have let Tom kill George when he'd had the chance.

"But how could you be Duncan's son? If George was his son, you're Duncan's great-grandson." I said, trying to wrap my head around his words.

"No, my brother is the one descended from George Walters. My father – Duncan – decided my mother should be, how shall I say, one of the spoils of War." He actually sounded proud.

"Ew," I grimaced, not bothering to hide my revulsion.

"Like father, like son," Archer murmured, too low for anyone's ears but mine.

My mind was racing, and I felt my world tilt on its axis. All this time I'd believed I was fixing time stream splits to save history – as though my skills and those of my friends were the stars of the show. But now the curtain had been lifted to reveal the Immortal puppeteer in the rafters pulling strings, making all of us dance to the music he wrote, in the theater he built. I felt powerless and insignificant, but I fought to hide it from Seth Walters, who would suck strength from my despair like a leech.

"This whole thing has been about getting power for War?" No matter how fierce I made my voice, it didn't cover my incredulity that such elaborate machinations could be about one very simple thing.

"Absolute power. With no other Descendants to rise up against Mongers, Duncan stands alone at the pinnacle." He smiled again, and anger began to creep into my powerlessness. "And I stand by his side as his soon-to-be immortal heir." He turned the full nastiness of his grin toward Archer, and I felt my resolve snap back into place. No matter how big and overwhelmingly awful War's plan was, the removal of one small ring could undermine all of it. If I kept that in focus, maybe I wouldn't run away screaming.

"What do you want with us?" I finally asked.

"I've taken what I need from him," Seth tossed his head at Archer, "and this one," his eyes flicked to Logan, "is leverage. But, you know, accidents can happen during prisoner exchanges."

Logan went wide-eyed, gave a convincing squeak of fear, and Shifted into the form of a Snapping Turtle that immediately tucked head and legs into its shell and hid.

Seth glared at me. "You said he was a mixed-blood's brat. Mixed-bloods don't Shift."

Mixed-bloods could do all kinds of unexpected things, and some of them, like the Blackbird twins, *could* Shift. I forced a casual tone, "Some of them can."

He was angry, and he stalked around the desk to sit in his chair. He reached under the desk and withdrew the ring from the same place where Ringo had once found it. I needed to distract him a little longer before he could slide it on his finger.

"Why me?" I asked, trying to mask the desperation in my tone.

He did pause, but he kept the ring clenched in his fist. "You and your mother were the last Clockers we could find. Duncan knew your mother had gone forward with you, but until my son Saw you in that Venice Beach slum, we didn't know where she was."

My arms were beginning to ache from being zip-tied behind my back, and I tried to loosen my shoulders. "Why did you need a Clocker?"

He got up and slipped the ring on his finger. My heart sank. Any command he gave now could possibly compel both Archer and Logan into doing something against their will. Seth pulled a knife from his pocket and flicked it open as he approached me. I held my breath, and horrifyingly, closed my eyes.

It was instinct, and I forced them open again, but not before Seth saw me do it. He chuckled under his breath. "Ah, the little Clocker is afraid of me. She has finally acquired some sense."

Archer was so tense he was vibrating with it, and Seth scowled at him. "Move, and I'll cut her." Archer inhaled sharply through his nose, but kept his mouth firmly shut. I felt Seth at my back, and then the knife flicked through the zip tie that bound my hands.

"I needed a Clocker," he said at my ear, "for the same reason I needed a Seer, a Shifter," his eyes flicked down to the Snapping Turtle holed up in his shell on the floor, and he scoffed, "and a Sucker. For the same reason people keep pets – to do their bidding."

He came around to face me, just inches away. "But I needed *you* to neutralize the prophecy." He smiled again, and I almost whimpered.

When he finally stepped back, I could breathe again. "Sit." He waved me toward a chair as he went back around to his seat. "You," he said to Archer, and I went back to holding my breath, hoping that whatever he said wasn't a command, "are not useful to me dead, but I will not hesitate to drain you, am I clear?"

"Crystal," said Archer, and I exhaled softly, and sat when Seth did.

Out of the corner of my eye, I saw Logan's Snapping Turtle poke its head out and begin a slow crawl forward. The two Monger guards were at military ease – the wide-legged stance with hands holding assault-type rifles. One was at the door, and the other was behind us near the big half-moon picture window that overlooked the empty street below. Archer remained standing, his hands fastened behind his back, while Seth turned his attention back to me.

"Your mixed blood, sadly, takes you out of the running to be my personal Clocker. Unless, of course, I have something you want and can use that to compel you to my bidding." His eyes flicked back to Archer with a slow smile.

The callous way he twisted people around for his purposes was disgusting, and I wondered what Death's daggers would show me if they ever cut Seth Walters. I reached down to scratch my leg, and Seth flinched. His eyes narrowed, and he reached into a desk drawer for a small handgun. The red stone in Doran's ring winked in the lamplight as he took the safety off and set it carefully on his desk. So, unholstering my daggers was out of the question.

"Or I could kill you now and remove any possibility of the fulfillment of the prophecy."

It was my turn to flinch, and Seth smiled again. I really, really hated that smile. "Why does the prophecy even matter?

*The child of opposites will be the one
To heal the Dream that War's undone.*"

Seth recited the lines quietly, and he sat back in his chair and slung one leg casually across the other. The hand with the ring draped across his bent knee, which now blocked his view of the approaching Turtle.

I couldn't possibly urge the Snapping Turtle to move faster, but I mentally willed him to get the lead out. Seth's eyes had locked onto mine with the force of laser beams. "That cannot happen," he said coldly.

"What can't?" I might have squeaked, thinking he'd read my mind. "What can't happen?"

His eyes narrowed again. "Is it possible that no one has told you what the prophecy means?"

I shrugged. "It's probably not even about me."

"Oh, it's you. I have combed through every record of every child born to the Immortal Descendants. You and the circumstances of this year fit every piece of the damned thing."

"So? What does it even mean? What's so bad about healing the dream that war's undone?" My heartbeat quickened. He definitely knew something I didn't, and I thought Duncan's interference in the affairs of humans had gone way beyond fathering evil megalomaniacs.

His eyes glinted with menace, and the nausea in my stomach intensified. "Not a dream, like a fantasy, but *the* Dream. The sixth Immortal. The one who should never have been born."

Surprise screeched through me at his words — not that Jera's child was the sixth Immortal — but that he had a name and Seth knew it. The screeching got louder, and I realized it was outside the building — the squeal of tires and brakes, and then the slam of car doors.

And then everything happened in slow motion, and at dizzying speed — all at once.

The guard at the window looked down.

Seth reached for his gun.

The Snapping Turtle, who had finally reached his destination below Seth's ringed hand, lunged at the red stone dangling above him …

And bit the finger wearing it off.

Seth screamed in pain and rage.

He flung his gun away and gripped the table with his other hand to stand. I dove at the guard behind me, and then stared in horror as Seth drove his foot into the Snapping Turtle on the floor in front of him. The kick sent Logan's Turtle hurtling through the half-moon window.

"Nooo!" I shouted as Archer threw himself at Seth. They went down in a tangle of limbs. I had fallen on top of the guard by the window, so the one by the door and I were the only ones who saw what happened.

The Turtle crashed through the glass, shell-first, holding a bloody finger in its mouth. The next moment it Shifted and became a giant Philippine Eagle, which spit out the bloody finger, and carried the ring away clenched in its beak.

I had exactly one second to revel in our success before feet pounded on the stairs outside the office, and gunshots and shouting heralded intruders. The guard by the door broke his apparent paralysis and turned, while the one under me struggled to shove me off him.

I dropped an elbow into his temple in a self-defense move that would have made Mr. Shaw proud, and was reaching for his rifle when the door burst open and more gunshots were fired.

Jeeves stood in the open doorway, panting with adrenaline and holding a hunting rifle aimed at the door guard. Ringo was right behind him with one of the assault rifles the guards had used. And Seth held his pistol to Archer's head. Archer bled freely from a gunshot wound to the shoulder, and Seth was careful not to touch him.

I whimpered, and Seth growled as Jeeves swung the rifle around to aim at him. Seth's eyes searched the broken glass for the ring. "I'm leaving here now, and you won't stop me if you want the Sucker to survive the night."

Jeeves narrowed his gaze. "I'll drop you right now and you might get a shot off, but it won't matter because you'll be dead."

Ringo came into the room and walked right up to the stunned door guard. "Shoot him!" Seth bellowed, but Ringo threw up a leg in a roundhouse kick, and the guard went down with a heavy thud. Seth's eyes widened in shock as he watched his Monger fall.

"You have a choice," said Jeeves, in his most steely-eyed badass voice. "You can leave him and walk out of here on your feet, or I'll shoot you now and take my chances with your reflexes."

Seth's glare was laced with hatred as he laid the gun on the desk and put his hands up. Blood ran down his wrist from the missing finger, and his eyes flicked to mine. I nearly stumbled back from the force of his fury. In that moment I knew that if he ever saw me again, he would kill me in an instant. Archer saw it too and took a step forward. Seth's eyes darted between Archer and Jeeves, and with trembling rage held barely in check, he backed out of the room.

Ringo made a move to go after Seth, and I thought Archer would have too, but Jeeves kicked the door shut behind him.

"Go now," said Jeeves to me.

"Ye 'eard what 'e said 'e'd do to Saira," growled Ringo.

"And he'll do worse to Logan if we don't finish what we started," I said as I leapt to Archer's side and sliced through the zip tie. Ringo pulled off his jacket and wrapped it around Archer's shoulder to stanch the bleeding.

"How bad is it?" I searched Archer's eyes.

Archer grimaced, and his eyes went back to the door. "Just a flesh wound."

I muttered, "I'm sick of your flesh wounds."

"Walters will move 'eaven and Earth to get that ring back," said Ringo.

"Well then, let's go." I gripped Archer's hand tightly, and he finally nodded.

"Where is the ring?" Jeeves asked, as I drew a spiral on the ground.

"Logan took it back to school." I looked up. "Do you want to come with us?"

Jeeves shook his head. "I'll head back to Elian Manor."

I nodded. "We'll see you soon, then."

Ringo crouched down next to me and held on. The next moment we were gone.

WAR

The laboratory was empty when we arrived, and despite a wave of Clocking sickness, I made a move to run toward the door.

"Wait! Saira, help me," Archer gasped. He looked at Ringo. "Find some disinfectant and a bandage. Saira, help me get this off."

Ringo searched the cabinets while I unbound his wound. "You were right. It's a flesh wound," I said, staring at the bloody gash on his arm where a bullet had passed.

"Told you," Archer ground his teeth a little as I dabbed at the blood.

Ringo came back with supplies, and we washed and bound the graze. It was deep enough to scar, but wouldn't affect muscle or bone, and we talked while we worked.

"The girls made it back, I take it?" I said to Ringo.

"Safe, sound, and very proud of themselves. Jeeves was waitin' at the end of the road for me, though I left before all the Mongers were trapped."

When we finished bandaging Archer's arm, we took off for the solarium to find out where we stood against the armed Mongers that had besieged St. Brigid's. We arrived to find Tom pacing like a wild animal while Ava sat very still in her seat, her eyes unfocused and her face pale.

"What's wrong?" I called out as we sprinted into the room.

Tom froze and stared at us. "The ring?" he asked.

"Logan has it. Is he not back yet?"

"I'm here," the young Shifter called as he sauntered into the room. "I stopped to grab clothes so your delicate sensibilities wouldn't be offended by my awesomeness."

He produced the ring with a flourish and held it out to me.

I saw Tom twitch, as if to reach out a hand for it, but he inhaled sharply instead and nodded at me. "You take it."

Logan closed his hand over the ring and made a move to drop it in his pocket. "Or I can keep it while you make up your mind," he grinned.

"Give it," I growled at him. He grinned and dropped it in my hand.

"All yours. How awesome was that mid-air Shift and spit, huh?"

I grabbed him for a hug, which he resisted in proper boy fashion. "Truly spectacular." I dropped the ring in my pocket and turned back to Tom. "What's happening outside?"

Suddenly, Ava shrieked, "No!" She stared wildly around her, as if she just realized where she was. Her eyes found mine and she gasped. "War is here."

Ava jumped up from her seat and raced for the door. I hesitated exactly half a second before I chased after her. I grabbed her arm and pulled her around to face me, but she tried to break free, a panicked look in her eyes.

"I have to tell to Miss Simpson!"

"Can't she see your visions?" I demanded.

"It wasn't a vision. I was seeing through Tam's eyes." Her own eyes were huge, and her breath came too quickly. She tried to pull free again, and I yanked her arm so she'd look at me.

"Ava, where is Tam." Archer and Tom had arrived on either side of us. Ava's wild gaze included all three of us.

"They're in the old gardener's shack in the woods."

"Who's there?" I demanded.

"Survivors," she said as tears filled her eyes. She fled the room.

"Saira! We need to go there, now!" Ringo said. There was a command in his voice I'd never heard, and I realized he was terrified. Charlie was out there in the woods somewhere.

"I'm coming too," said a voice from the door. Raven stood with a rapier in one hand and her phone in the other. "Cole texted me. He's trapped in the shack with Tam." She looked as wild-eyed as Ava did, and for the same reason. "He said the guy outside has a sword."

"A sword?" I screeched. "God! It's Duncan. Your Immortal – War."

Archer grabbed my arm. "I'm getting my swords. Wait for me." He raced from the room, and Raven scowled.

"Why not a gun?" she said scathingly.

"Why do you have that?" I nodded at her rapier. It wasn't the dummy kind – it was sharp and looked deadly.

"Because I'm good at it."

"Exactly," I said.

"Ye are good. And since blades are what Duncan fights with, we fight with blades," said Ringo. Raven considered him, then nodded, and Ringo turned to me. "Saira, get us there. Let us see what's 'appening on the ground."

Tom said grimly, "I need to be there too." He flexed his hand, and it looked like an unconscious gesture. If the possibility of battle set off his PTSD, I couldn't imagine what seeing Duncan again would do. Tom, Ringo, Raven, Archer, and me. Five people to Clock without Charlie's help.

Logan stepped forward and opened his mouth. "No way are you going," I scowled at him.

He scoffed, "Whatever." And he did the same forward somersault maneuver the girls had done, and spun himself into a giant Barn Owl before flying out into the night.

"Ye can't tell 'im what to do. It's the fastest way to make 'im do a thing." Ringo might have smirked if he hadn't been so anxious.

I strode to the spiral on the wall and spoke to Raven. "You have to hold onto me and don't let go. It'll be super cold, and the nothingness of it will freak you out, but it's over in a few seconds, and you're probably going to puke when we land."

"Ugh, why do you do it then?" Raven made a face.

"Because I'm good at it."

Archer sprinted into the solarium, a long leather case slung over his shoulder.

"Took ye long enough," said Ringo, but I'd finished tracing the fourth spiral, and Archer grabbed my belt loop just in time.

My first glimpse of the area where we landed was from my knees, where I was losing the remains of the Moroccan stew I'd had for dinner. Cinnamon and cumin do not taste better the second time, and everyone who had Clocked with me was enjoying the same repeat dinner.

"Jesus, Clocker!" Raven gasped. "How can you stand it?"

I ignored her and crawled off the granite to stumble over to Mr. Shaw. He was crouched down, and Charlie hovered at his side. "Mr. Shaw!" I called to him. He turned at the sound of my voice, and I saw that his shirt was covered in blood. I made a strangled noise and lunged toward him before I realized the blood was someone else's.

"It's about bloody time you came back. Charlie, gather the wounded who can walk and bring them back to the portal. I'll have to carry this one and two others."

Why was everyone wounded? What had happened here?

I stared down at Colin Zhang and would probably have lost my dinner a second time if there'd been anything left to hurl. His lower leg was a mess of smashed bone and tissue and had been bound tightly below the knee to keep him from bleeding out. Fortunately he was unconscious, or I was pretty sure he'd be screaming.

Archer and Ringo immediately followed Charlie and Mr. Shaw as they gathered the wounded mixed-bloods. Tom knelt next to Colin and inhaled sharply. "I'll take his shoulders, Saira, you keep his legs off the ground. Let's get him to the rock."

We moved him as carefully as we could, but he still grunted in unconscious pain. Raven was finally on her feet, and she stared at us in horror. "What did you do out here?" she half-whispered.

"Laid traps for the Mongers who kept us prisoner," I said grimly.

"And they fought back," she said.

"Apparently."

We laid Colin down near the spiral, and Tom supported his head long enough to pull off his jacket and place it under him as a pillow. Archer and Ringo supported a young woman between them and brought her to the spiral. Her name was Shannon, a mixed-Shifter who had the speed of a predator but without the Shifting skills. She had been one of the runners sent out as a lure to draw the farthest guards into the trap zone. She'd been shot in the side, but had kept running until she finally collapsed from blood-loss.

There was shouting from one of the big pits, and Raven ran over. A guy in his sixties stood guard over the pit with a captured assault rifle in his hands. I couldn't tell how many Monger men had been trapped there, but I saw at least four. Something else was said, and then Raven unsheathed her rapier and pointed it threateningly at the Monger in front. She scowled as she spoke, and when the Monger said something in return, she feigned a lunge. He stumbled backward into his buddies, and she smiled grimly. The man guarding them patted her on the shoulder and slipped away into the woods while Raven stood over the Mongers, arms crossed with a menacing glare. When a different man came back and took up the guard position, also with a confiscated weapon, Raven said something cutting to the men in the pit, and then returned to join us.

"What was that all about?" I asked her.

Mr. Shaw came into view carrying Daisy.

"Guys being jerks," Raven grumbled. She got up to help Mr. Shaw lay Daisy on the granite. The young woman was unconscious, and her face was bloody. "What happened to her?" Raven asked him.

"She was guarding two of the Mongers with their gun. They jumped her and beat her unconscious," he said grimly.

"Animals," Raven glared.

"Mongers," Shaw growled back. He surveyed the assembled group of injured people and nodded. "Okay, let's go."

Archer held my face for a brief moment, and then stepped back. "We'll head out to the shack now. Come find us."

"Be safe," I said as Charlie and I linked everyone through touch.

Mr. Shaw's parting words to Archer closed a fist around my lungs. "Alive or dead, bring them back."

I Clocked the wounded directly into the classroom next door to Mr. Shaw's laboratory. Charlie ran for my mom and Millicent while I helped Mr. Shaw get Colin to the table in the other room. He was already prepping for surgery when my mom arrived. I kissed her quickly, then found Charlie. "I need you to come back with me. I can't transport that many people alone."

She glared. "I would get out there on foot if you didn't Clock me."

We were back in the woods an instant later, with as much discomfort as if we'd walked through a door. "Will you go around to all the traps and make sure our people have what they need to keep guarding those guys?" I asked Charlie.

She clenched her jaw, and I knew she wanted to come with me out to the shack. But she finally nodded. "If you take too long, I'm coming to find you."

"I know. I'd do the same. Thank you, Charlie. The last thing we need is a bunch of escaped Mongers coming at us from behind."

She picked up her bow and quiver from the base of her tree and slung them over her shoulder before heading out into the woods. That girl was a good match for Ringo, and I hoped they would get a very long life together.

I stopped long enough to pull both daggers from their ankle sheaths before I ran. The relative quiet of the woods only lasted the first two hundred yards, and then the clash of metal and the shouts of men reached my ears.

I put on a burst of speed, but then slowed as I got closer to the shack. I was going to be the unexpected guest at this party, so I tried to use that to my advantage. The smell of smoke suddenly hit me, and it fueled a spike of adrenaline. I didn't see or hear any flames, but that was somehow worse, and I moved silently through the woods to the clearing.

The burned out shack was still smoking, and small flames continued to burn the bits of wood that weren't already charcoal. The adrenaline rush was quickly turning to panic as whispers of *no, no, no* raced through my brain.

I forced calming breaths into my lungs and then crept around until I could see the source of the sounds of metal-on-metal. Three people were ringed around one, and all had swords. Someone else was huddled in against the trunk of a big tree nearby, and I couldn't spot any others. I snapped at the chorus of 'no' in my brain and told it to shut up as I moved in closer.

I nearly tripped over Adam and had to clap a hand over my mouth not to shriek. He was pale under all the soot that covered his features, and his breathing was shallow, as if the air hurt his lungs. There was a sword next to him, its blade still clean, and I nearly shrieked again when his eyes opened to look at me.

I dropped to my knees next to him. "Adam! Where are you hurt?"

"Can't … breathe. Fire …" His voice came in whispered gasps. "Tried to … fight. Can't … hold."

"Shhh. Where are the others?"

"Woods," he gasped. "Hiding."

God, I hoped so. I kissed Adam's sooty forehead, left him with one of my knives, and grabbed the sword. "I'll be back," I promised him. I skirted the edge of the woods so I could approach the surrounded man, whom I assumed was Duncan, from behind.

My run took me past the tree where I'd seen someone crouching, and I realized it was Tom crouched over a Wolf.

No! I slipped up as quietly as I could without being seen by the others, and whispered to Tom from behind a tree. He looked up as he tied a binding around the Wolf's leg, and I saw that he was covered, head to toe, in black soot. Connor's Wolf whimpered once and looked me in the eyes. His fur was singed, and there were patches that had burned off, but the bloody bandage around the upper part of a leg was the most concerning. Tom threw a glance back at the sword battle in the clearing behind him.

"They can't win this," he said tiredly. He sat back and rubbed his eyes, which were red from smoke and unshed tears. "They can't kill him, and he'll keep fighting until he has what he wants."

"What does he want?"

"The ring."

I put my hand to my pocket in an unconscious gesture, but Tom saw the motion and glared at me. "Don't you dare give it to him, Saira. It's not his!" he hissed fiercely, and Connor's Wolf growled in response.

The clash of metal rang behind him, and then a female voice cried out. I clenched the sword in my fist and rushed forward. Tom's hand shot out to stop me, but I leapt it and ignored his whispered, "no!" as I sprinted.

"Duncan!" I yelled as I hurtled headlong into the battlefield. Archer had engaged him in swordplay while Ringo helped move Raven back out of reach. She was bleeding from several places, but the wound that had knocked her back was one to the thigh.

Raven batted Ringo's hands away and sent him back in to help Archer, then caught my eye and said grimly, "Finish this."

I called out again, "Duncan!" and this time he heard his name. He sent a flurry of slashes at both Archer and Ringo, and even with the two of them battling him, he was clearly winning. He looked up at me with a scowl but didn't break the onslaught of his attack.

"I have the ring you want," I yelled. This made him pause just enough for Archer to lunge. He stabbed Duncan in his sword arm, and it was deep enough to seriously wound.

Duncan roared in pain, but switched his sword into the other hand and dove for Ringo, who just barely danced out of the way in time to avoid being cut in two. All three of them were bloody, and at least two of them were tiring.

"I'll give it to Aislin unless you stop," I called.

Abruptly he let the sword tip fall to the ground, and he breathed heavily as he glared at me.

"GIVE ME MY RING!" he bellowed. I swallowed against the fear his rage inspired.

Archer and Ringo were backing away, out of range of Duncan's sword. Ringo passed close enough to me that I could murmur to him. "Adam is in the woods back there," I jerked my head, "and Tom and Connor are over there. Get them and head to the rock." He nodded, and then the two of them melted into the woods. I began swirling my foot in the dirt below me as I stalled for time.

"It's not your ring, is it? The ring belongs to the Immortal Dream."

"The Dream is dead," he growled at me, and he picked his sword up and held it menacingly.

"Tell that to your Council when I bring it to them."

"Give it to me!" Duncan pointed his sword and me and walked forward. I forced myself not to run. "I will kill you where you stand and take what's mine," he growled.

I heard something in the woods behind me, and I caught a glimpse of Tam, crawling toward me from the bushes, covered in soot from the fire. I breathed a sigh of relief and continued to swirl my foot in the dirt as Duncan advanced.

"It's against your rules," I said as I slipped the ring from my pocket and put it on my finger. "You may be War, but you lose your voice at your Council if you interfere with us." Whatever evil had winked at me from the red stone the first time I saw it in Seth Walters' office had been replaced by something cool and soothing, and I felt calm confidence sweep through me.

"There are no witnesses." He smiled slowly, as if he would enjoy what he planned to do to me.

"Aislin is watching this whole scene play out, Duncan. She can see you, and she can see me, and if you kill me here, the Immortals will know it."

Duncan whipped his head around as if expecting Aislin to walk out of the woods. When nothing happened, he scowled at me. "She's not here. She can see nothing."

I had one last spiral to trace with my foot, and the humming was growing louder. Tam stood up behind me and grabbed my belt. "She sees through my eyes," he said to Duncan, right before we Clocked out.

I took us straight to the granite rock spiral and almost Clocked right into Charlie. She was with six of the mixed-bloods, and they were up on the rock, completely surrounded by about ten Mongers with rifles.

"You're the Clocker Walters wants," one of the men growled at me. Archer and Ringo weren't back yet with the others, and I didn't know if Duncan was going to follow, so this needed to end now.

"Every one of us has been battered by this thing that one power-hungry man started. He told you to hate us, and you believed him," I said. The calm, confidence of the ring still flowed through me, and I hoped I could do this without causing more damage.

"You attacked us." The Monger's voice was angry, and the others murmured their agreement as they began to close in.

"We defended ourselves," I said. "But we're all Immortal Descendants, no matter what Family we come from, no matter what mix we're made of. My blood runs just as red as yours does, and I love and hope and dream just like you do. We are not born better or worse than anyone else, we're born *human*, and we build ourselves up from the same ground floor."

I saw Archer and Ringo emerge from the trees supporting Adam, Cole, and Raven between them. Tom followed right behind with Connor's Wolf slung over his shoulders. A few of the Mongers saw them too, and tensed, but others had lowered the guns they held, and they seemed to be listening to my words.

"This place," I gestured toward St. Brigid's, "is where we have a chance to learn the skills we're capable of. It's also a place to understand what other people can do, who they are, and how we can work together. I'm called a Clocker, but it's a skill I can *do*, not who I am. *I* get to choose who I am, just like you get to choose for yourselves – no one else has that right. It's called freedom, and it's a thing worth defending against those who would take our rights from us."

More Mongers relaxed their tense poses, and two of them put their weapons on the ground. "Any child that's afraid of the dark knows to turn on the light so they can see the thing they fear. Do that now. Look around you at the people you've been taught to hate, because hate is just the cloak that hides fear. The light's on in these woods, and there's nothing to be afraid of here."

There seemed to be a collective sigh, as though the last of the tension running through the Mongers let go. I felt it, and Charlie stood up on her tiptoes to kiss my cheek. "I'm going back now. I think it's time to walk in the front gates."

She stepped down off the granite slab and made her way through the Mongers closest to her. They stepped back to let her pass, and when the other mixed-bloods, in various states of battered and bloody, began to follow her, some of the Mongers fell into step with them too.

I let myself exhale slowly. I was afraid to let too much air out in case it was all just a ruse, but two of the remaining Mongers gathered up the guns and waited patiently for me.

"We're going to take these back to our vehicles and pull out. We don't belong here."

"You *do* belong here — just as much as we do. It's the guns that don't." I said. The man nodded and they started to leave. I called after them. "If any of your people are hurt, bring them inside the school. We have a doctor."

He looked up again, and this time there was a hint of relief. "Thank you, ma'am," he said.

They trudged away, and I flung myself off the rock and into Archer's arms. He held me tightly, and I whispered, "I'm too young to be ma'am."

He chuckled, and then Tam and I got on either side of Adam, Cole, and Raven, and our small family went back to St. Brigid's through the front door.

The Aftermath

Aislin was gone when we got back to the school. Ava told us she'd been white-lipped with anger after she saw Tam's view of my exchange with Duncan, and she'd gone to call an Immortals' Council.

The laboratory and adjoining classroom had been transformed into a makeshift surgery and recovery room, and my mom, Millicent, and Olivia took firm and efficient charge of their patients. Three of the Monger guards had taken me up on the offer of medical care, and a couple others had helped move furniture to get the rooms set up.

Mrs. Arman and Alex were both at Adam's side, and Ava and come to inspect Tam to make sure he truly was uninjured. Cole had been burned getting out of the fire, but he sat by Raven and held her hand while Millicent cleaned the various cuts and slices she'd been dealt by Duncan.

Liz Edwards had rushed over from Elian Manor and was tending to Connor's Wolf. The burns were worse than the cut, but they would all heal faster if he was in Wolf form. Logan had Shifted into a Kitten again and was curled up under his brother's chin, purring softly.

Mr. Shaw was still operating on Colin Zhang's leg in the laboratory side of things, so one of the Mongers, who had been an army medic, stabilized the worst wounds and treated the cuts and burns. Tom clutched the black knight in his hand and sat across the room lost in thought as he watched me clean and bandage Archer's injuries. There was a gash on Archer's forearm that was pretty nasty, but everything else would likely heal well. Ringo had avoided major injuries but had gotten a slice on one cheek that Charlie was cleaning thoroughly so it wouldn't infect.

I leaned over to whisper in her ear. "Bringing everyone back to school through the gates was brilliant, and I'm so proud of you for making it happen."

She grinned. "You gave such a wonderful speech, it needed a grand gesture."

"We make a good team, Charlie. I've never been able to transport so many people on my own, and definitely not without being sick afterwards. Thank you so much for your help."

She looked at Ringo, then whispered back to me, "There's no place I'd rather be."

When Archer was patched up, Tom came over to us and murmured under his breath, "If you can get your mum to take five minutes, I'll get my aunt and meet you in the solarium. We need to talk." His expression was grim, and I knew he'd been thinking about Duncan.

"We'll be right there."

My mom was sitting with Daisy, who was conscious again, and whose wary eyes followed the uniformed Monger medic around the room as he worked on people. When I asked her to join us, my mom moved a couple of feet away from Daisy to speak quietly. "I can't leave her alone. She was beaten by men in that uniform, and she's in shock."

"We'll sit with her," said Raven from the nearby bed. My mom started to shake her head no, but then considered.

"It could be good for her to have a Monger ally right now."

Raven held my mom's gaze. "We won't leave her, Ms. Elian. What happened to her wasn't right. None of this was."

My mom nodded. "Thank you, Raven."

Mom followed me to where Archer waited by the door, then she looked back and surveyed the room. "It's like a war zone," she said sadly, and she was right.

Camille Arman waited with Tom in the solarium. She was studying the chess table, which looked as though an entirely different game had been played on it. I knew Tom had been moving pieces on both sides as Ava fed him information, and it was like a map of everything that had happened in those woods. My mom hugged her. "I'm sorry about Adam's injuries. How is he doing?"

"He'll be better when he gets on some oxygen, but as long as there's no infection in the next couple of days, he should be fine." Camille included Tom and Archer in her gaze. "He told us what you did to get them out of the burning shed. You saved my son's life."

I yanked on Archer's hand. "What did you guys do?" Retroactive fear spiked in me, and I tamped it down as too little, too late.

"I'll tell you later," he whispered.

Tom took a deep breath. "We need to talk about the Immortals."

Camille's expression froze. "I don't think there's anything for us to discuss."

"They're not gods, Camille," Archer said gently.

"Talk to us, Tom." My mom ignored Camille's tension and put on her most reasonable voice.

"Duncan knows that Saira has the ring, and he would have killed her in a heartbeat to get it."

Both women stared at me – Camille with shock, my mom with horror.

"We must make it known that the Descendants' Council has the ring and will keep it safe from any further abuse of its power." Camille had the most pompous upper-class voice when she chose to use it. Unfortunately for her, the voice didn't work on me. Or Tom, it seemed.

"No," he and I said at the same time.

"It doesn't belong to *you*," Camille said.

"No, it belongs to the Immortal Dream." Every set of eyes swiveled to me, and I met every person's gaze. "I'm going to the Immortals' Council meeting."

"There is no Immortal Dream," declared Camille.

"Dream is Jera and Goran's child. Seth Walters knows it, Aislin knows it, and Duncan confirmed it," I looked Camille straight in the eyes.

"Well," she said, reaching for her next argument, "you're a mixed-blood, Saira. They can have you condemned."

"I guess I'll just take my chances," I said with steely-eyed confidence.

"You may need witnesses," Archer said quietly. "Take me with you."

"And me," said Tom. He held up his hand. "I have the battle scars to prove Duncan's interference."

I turned to my mom. "Would you consider coming with me? You'd help with the Clocking sickness, and you're a witness to the Council massacre."

Camille snapped, "What does that ancient history have to do with any of this?"

I kept my eyes on my mom when I answered Camille. "Spencer Rothchild was Duncan's son, and the massacre was orchestrated by him. Bishop Wilder, George Walters, and Seth Walters are all Duncan's sons too. He's been trying to take over for nearly two hundred years."

That stunned Camille into speechlessness, and my mom blanched. "Is this true?"

I nodded. "Seth Walters was positively chatty about his Family history, just before Logan stole the ring from him."

The briefest of smiles touched my mom's mouth. "Yes, I'll go with you." She turned to the Seer Head, "Camille, please reach out to the MacKenzie, or barring that, his younger son – the reasonable one. We'll need to call a Council meeting for tomorrow night, and I have the feeling there will be a general election. Perhaps it's best to have the meeting here, where everyone can attend."

There was acceptance and possibly a little defeat in Camille's eyes when she nodded, and my mom reached her hand out to her. "Can you also tell Bob and Millicent where we've gone?"

"And Ringo," I added. "Please?"

Camille set her mouth and inhaled resolutely. "I will be making a general announcement to everyone at St. Brigid's that you have gone to fight for the rights of all Descendants, regardless of Family, and to expect elections at the next Council meeting, to which everyone is invited."

I beamed at her. "Thank you."

"And then I want to go home. I am sick and tired of living in a dormitory room." The haughty voice was back, but it was tempered with a smile as she left the solarium.

Archer turned to me. "Do you know where we're going?"

I thought of the Council painting that Doran had been working on in Artemisia's studio – the beautiful marble room with the island view out the window. "Yes, I do."

My mom looked down at her blood-stained shirt. "I feel as though I should change into my best dress to go before the Immortals."

"No way. They get us bloody, filthy, wounded, and exhausted. It's Duncan's machinations that set this thing in motion, and it's time to put a leash on War."

THE IMMORTALS' COUNCIL

The Immortals' Council room was even more beautiful than Doran's painting of it had been. It was very similar to our own Descendants' Council room, except everything was made of gleaming white marble. Even more spectacular than the view of the deep blue-green sea out of the windows were the Immortals seated on their simple white thrones. There were five thrones with four Immortals seated, and one Immortal who stood before them.

Duncan turned at our entrance into the room. We had come in through a spiral portal very much like the one carved in our own Council room, and though we were variously battered and blackened with soot, each one of us stood tall and faced the Council on our feet.

"Who dares enter the Immortals' Council?" Duncan roared furiously. He still wore the battle garb that made him look vaguely like a centurion. I half expected to see a plumed helmet on top of his short-cropped hair.

He reached for the hilt of his sword, and I put my hands up. "I am Saira Elian, of Clocker and Shifter blood." Duncan unsheathed his sword and took a step toward me.

"Stand down, War." Aeron's voice was tight with tension despite his outward calm. He expected trouble, and was ready for it. Death was the same, striking dark-skinned man I'd seen on the other time stream who wore, oddly enough, charcoal jeans and a black silk t-shirt, sort of like something Giorgio Armani would wear on casual Friday in Milan.

I nodded to him in an attempt to show respect and cover up my fear, and then introduced the others. "This is my mother, Claire Elian, Clocker Head of the British Descendants' Council, Archer Devereux, of Seer blood, and Tom Landers, a mix of Seer and Monger blood. Both men are also formerly of your Family, sir." I directed the last bit to Aeron, and although his eyes widened slightly in surprise, he scowled.

"No one is formerly of my Family," he said grimly.

"Tom and I have been cured of the infection that causes Vampirism, sir." Archer's voice carried the cultured deference that members of the nobility could turn on like a faucet. It was respectful, and yet confident and strong, and it never indicated submission.

"You have mixed with my blood, therefore I claim you for my own," Aeron said in a similar tone, but without the deference.

Archer inclined his head in agreement or acquiescence — whichever it was, it seemed to work for Aeron and he settled back into his seat.

"What is the point of this intrusion? These mortals have no place in our Council room, and they certainly have no right to speak." Duncan had re-sheathed his sword and now seated himself back on his throne. It was a power move, meant to remind us he was an Immortal and we were cockroaches under his feet. As power moves went, it was more subtle than I would have given him credit for, and also fairly effective.

"With respect, I come with a request." I raised my eyes to Aislin first and found her wearing her young, ethereal face, with long flowing hair and a diaphanous white gown. She looked every inch a Greek goddess, and her face was deliberately expressionless. I'd actually expected that.

My eyes moved next to Jera, a stunning brunette with bronze skin and green eyes that looked at me with interest. "I would like the Immortal Dream to be instated to the Immortals' Council, and

I ask that all mixed-blood Descendants be allowed to choose to belong to either of their parents' Families, or to his."

My mother gasped behind me, and there was unsettled rustling in the room, both behind and in front of me. Duncan's eyes narrowed, and he spat. "There is no Dream."

My gaze shot to him, and I held up my hand with Doran's ring on it. "There is, and this ring belongs to him."

Duncan leapt from his throne and advanced on me. It took every ounce of my courage not to move, even as my mother stepped back reflexively, and Archer's instinct put him in front of me.

"Stand. Down. War!" Aeron's voice filled the room, as though it bounced from every wall. It was a truly awesome thing to experience, and even Duncan flinched. My eyes had been riveted to War, but now Goran commanded the attention of the room when he stood and bellowed.

"WHERE IS MY SON!"

"Dead!" shouted Duncan, as he pointed to Aeron. "By his hand."

I shook my head. "Not dead."

"Enough!" Aeron slammed his hands down on the arms of his chair and rose. "You, child, know not of what you speak." It was chilling to feel Death's attention, but he shifted it to Duncan and I could breathe again. "And you ..." He stood right in front of Duncan's throne and glowered at him. "You left that child for dead, and then incited a war to cover your tracks."

Aeron had studiously avoided looking at Jera the whole time I'd been in the room, and now her eyes sought his. "*Left* him for dead?" she asked him.

He finally turned and met her gaze. He seemed to steel himself to say something, but then he turned and departed the room without another glance at any of us.

Jera sounded wounded, and she turned to Aislin. "What did he mean, *left* him for dead?"

Aislin said nothing, though her expression was full of sympathy. And Duncan was gearing up for another rant, so I opened my mouth, and the words just came out.

"The son of two Immortals is obviously Immortal himself. He couldn't be killed."

Jera's eyes swiveled to me and stayed there. Goran looked sick, and Aislin blanched, while Duncan's face reddened and he looked ready to draw his sword on me again. So I decided to poke the bear. "Duncan hated Aeron – still does – because he's the one with the real power, and Duncan wants it all. You had just created a sixth Immortal, and War's not so big on sharing power, so he decided that killing the baby and blaming it on Death knocked out two birds with one stone. You …" I turned to Goran, "believed him, and between the two of you, started a war among your Descendants. You made Death's Descendants outlaws and nearly annihilated them, and all that drama led to a law against mixing Families that has been used to oppress some of your own Descendants – your actual Family."

Aislin studied me for a long moment before she spoke. "You know Jera's child?" Interesting that she called him Jera's, as if Goran had forfeited his rights when he caused a civil war.

"Yes, I do."

Just then, Aeron returned, and was followed into the room by Doran. It was the first time I'd ever seen Doran appear anything less than completely confident, and I actually wanted to comfort him. Instead, I took his ring off and went up to him.

"Hey," I said softly. He seemed surprised to see me, and then he smiled. I held out his ring. "This is yours, I think?" Doran took it in his palm and then closed his fingers around it. That's what finally made Duncan explode.

"Lies! That ring is mine and everything this *mortal* has said is designed to manipulate and trick you!"

"Uh, no, actually, the ring isn't yours." Tom spoke quietly, and his voice shook, but he looked Duncan in the eye when he held up the black knight chess piece. "*This* is the Monger artifact."

The gasps this time were audible, and Duncan leapt from his seat and strode to Tom. I was pretty sure my own knees would have buckled already, the way Duncan glowered, but Tom stood straight and didn't flinch, even when Duncan snatched it from his hand.

"It has strategic power," Tom began, but Duncan cut him off.

"I know what it does," he snarled, then turned to Doran. "But that ring—"

"—is mine." Doran turned to face Duncan, and his confidence had returned, because he smiled, and though it didn't reach his eyes, it was pure charm. "Thank you for keeping it safe for me all these years."

No one but me had noticed that Jera was on her feet, and her eyes hadn't left Doran since he walked into the room. She took a step toward him, and stumbled. "Doran?" He moved swiftly to catch her, and she stared at him in wonder. "It is really you," she whispered as she touched his face.

And just like that, I felt intrusive and awkward. I took a step backward and then glanced over at Aeron. He watched Doran and Jera together with an expression that looked like pride mixed with unimaginable sadness, and I inhaled quietly. Doran had once told me he'd left Artemisia for two months to do something for his father. Aeron had raised Jera's child as his own, and now he had given him back to his mother.

Whatever impulse moved my feet in his direction, I'm sure it wasn't self-preservation. I reached for the daggers that I'd returned to their ankle sheaths after we'd come back from the woods, and placed them on the floor in front of the Immortal Death. "Your daggers, sir." I said, backing away.

Aeron tore his eyes away from Jera and Doran to look down at the blades, and it took him a moment to register what they were. Then he looked into my eyes. "You may give them to him," Aeron indicated Archer, "or find another who is worthy. It would be useful to have one of my Family with my skill."

"He is my husband," I said.

Aeron studied me. "Then I have gained a daughter with uncommon courage." He looked at Archer. "You chose wisely."

Archer nodded. "Yes, sir. I know I did."

"So did I," I said, pulling myself up straighter.

A hint of a smile touched Aeron's lips, and it transformed him from formidable to completely compelling. He spoke to me. "I have heard your request, daughter. I shall see it so." Then he turned to my mom, "Take word of this back to your Council. You, of three Families," he turned to Tom, "I shall suggest that Duncan return his artifact into your keeping. You, too, have shown courage and wisdom, and I find I am intrigued to know more."

I took a shaky breath, unsure of the wisdom of my words, but going to say them anyway. "Come and visit us then … maybe not in your official capacity, though – Aislin knows where to find us."

His eyebrows rose in surprise, and then he smiled. "Yes, perhaps I shall do that one day." Aeron indicated the daggers on the floor. "Take them and go now. Leave my family to me."

I nodded with deference, handed the daggers to Archer, and returned to my people at the spiral. I caught Doran's eyes for one brief, final second, and he winked at me as we Clocked out.

I knew we'd be seeing him again soon.

GRAYSON MANOR – 1554

The manor house was draped in mistletoe, fir, and yew for Christmas, and lovely decorations of dried oranges and holly wreaths filled the rooms. Archer and I were given a guest room usually reserved for visiting royalty, which, according to Valerie Grayson, we were.

I joined Valerie and my mom in Charlie's bedroom, where a maid was lifting a stunning gold dress over Charlie's linen shift. Valerie dismissed the maid and fastened the dress up herself.

"Oh Charlie, you look so beautiful," my mom exclaimed. She had tears in her eyes when she looked up at me, and I was so glad she had come with us to this wedding, especially since she had missed mine.

Charlie caught my eyes. "I seriously considered searching the Elian Manor closets for something to wear from the 1950s, but it takes a certain degree of fortitude to wear these gowns, and I felt that perhaps I was finally strong enough."

I took her hands in mine, and the diamond band Ringo had made for her sparkled like stars on her finger. "Charlie, you were strong enough the day I met you. The only difference now is that you actually believe it."

Valerie had finished fastening the exquisitely embroidered gown. She studied the young woman she had helped shape, and her gaze filled with tenderness. "My dear, the time you gave me has been the most precious gift I've ever received. Thank you for allowing me to dote on you, and to love you as my own daughter."

She kissed both of Charlie's cheeks, and there were definitely tears in her eyes when she looked away.

"Why is it that weddings make people cry?" Charlie whispered to me as my mom and Valerie sorted through Valerie's jewelry cases for sparkly things to drape on the bride.

I shrugged. "I have theories, but it's more fun to make something up."

She grinned. "Oh do!"

"I think people don't *fall* in love, but instead, love starts as a tiny butterfly, usually in the belly, because that's where we feel it first. And that butterfly multiplies and multiplies, until our whole being is filled with the butterflies of being in love. Then, at a wedding when two people declare and promise that love out loud, the room fills with their butterflies, and people cry with the beauty of it."

"Oh, I like that story! Today, if I feel nervous, I'll imagine the whole room full of butterflies."

I smiled at my beautiful friend who was in love with the brother of my heart. "It will be."

Ringo and Charlie's wedding was intimate and lavish. He and Archer both wore gentlemen's suits from 1889, and mom and I were in Tudor gowns, borrowed from Valerie and quickly altered by her dressmaker. Millicent and mom had thrown them a wonderful engagement party at Elian Manor before we left, but Millicent had declined to Clock with us. We didn't press the issue.

Ringo's eyes shone as he promised to love, honor, and cherish Charlie all the days of their lives, and when Charlie's eyes filled with tears, she looked at me and we both looked up at all the imaginary butterflies that filled the hall.

When I hugged Ringo after the ceremony, I whispered to him, "I'm glad you finally asked her that first question."

He looked at me with the eyes of a man. "I'm glad I loved you first – it gave me a foundation to build on. I just never imagined how high it could go until I saw her again."

"She's a very lucky girl," I said with my whole heart, and then I replayed his words in my head with surprise. "You've lost your accent."

An impish grin lit up his face. "It let me blend in on the streets, but now I have a fine wife, and she deserves a proper gentleman."

The feast afterwards in the candlelit dining hall was fit for a king, but because it was just us, we moved a small table near the fireplace and sat together like a family, telling stories and laughing until late in the night.

Valerie gave the couple her wedding present first. "I've bought a property near Marylebone Park in London. I intend to build a townhouse there, and I will set up a trust that names you, Charlotte, as my heir. As I fear things may become tangled during the next three hundred years, I would like to name Lord Archer Devereux as the executor for the title of the property until such time as Charlotte and her husband can claim it. I'm sure the solicitors in the nineteenth century will be able to find you, Archer."

Charlie jumped up and hugged Valerie, which was no mean feat in all the heavy fabric of her dress, Ringo kissed the back of Valerie's hand, and Archer bowed. "It would be my pleasure, madam."

They had a home, and the excitement that shone on Charlie's face was palpable. My mom stood up and brought a small wrapped package to Charlie, who was clearly in on whatever was inside that box, because she turned and gave it to Valerie.

"My wedding gift to Charlotte is not one that she has the ability to use. You do, however, and I trust that my daughter can teach you the finer points."

Valerie looked confused until she opened the box. Inside, on a bed of dark blue velvet, lay the Clocker necklace. Valerie gasped and looked up at her foster daughter with shining eyes. "I'll be able to visit you?" she asked.

"I can teach you how to focus your travel so that you clock to their house on a certain date. It means you're probably going to have to build a walled garden at the house so we can put a spiral in it." I said.

"Oh!" Valerie's voice was choked with tears and she clapped her hands together in delight. "I might one day see my grandchildren!" She flung her arms around Charlie and Ringo first, and then my mom and me. "It will of course be handed back to the Elian line after I'm gone." And then, just for good measure, she kissed Archer on the cheek. There was happy crying all the way around the table, and it took several handkerchiefs and some manly throat-clearing to get ourselves under control.

"And now, from Saira and myself …" Archer pulled two envelopes out of the inside pocket of his dinner jacket and handed them to Ringo, who held Archer's gaze a long time before he finally opened the first one. His hand shook very slightly as he passed the letter to Charlie, whose gasp at the first line caused Valerie to slide her chair next to Charlie to read over her shoulder. Ringo stood up and came to our side of the table.

He held a hand out to help me up from my chair. "My lady …" His voice choked. "Thank you," he finally managed to whisper. I held his face and kissed him on both cheeks.

"You're welcome."

Ringo embraced Archer in the kind of hug I'd only seen them do one other time – the first time they met again after Archer's infection. It was the grip of brothers, and their eyes were shiny when they parted.

Valerie's voice rose in confusion. "Please excuse my ignorance of modern banking. There is an account set up for Mr. and Mrs. Ringo Devereux at Rothschild & Sons? But that is your name, is it not, Archer?"

"It is my brother's name too," he said with a grin at Ringo. "Open the other one."

"I'm not sure I can," Ringo said, wiping away the tears.

I laughed. "Charlie, Ringo has butterflies in his eyes. Could you do it, please?"

She giggled and slit open the second envelope. This time her gasp was even louder. "Oh, Ringo! It's an admission from King's College London for Ringo Devereux, to study the discipline of his choice, and for Charlotte Devereux to the Ladies Department of King's College for the same."

Ringo stared at Archer open-mouthed. "But King's is for the upper classes."

Archer smirked. "You carry a Lord's name and bank statement. I think you qualify."

There was another round of embraces and some more tears before we all returned to our seats.

"By the way, we've arranged with the modern Rothschild bank to call us any time a letter appears in a certain safety deposit box. You'll have to give us a day or two notice — at least long enough for them to do their daily box-check — but the system should work okay for arranging visits." I had been so happy when Archer told me what he had in mind, based on the way Tom had left us a message. I had actually gone back to 1945 to test it with the Rothschild banker I knew, and it had worked perfectly.

It was the only thing that was going to make saying goodbye tolerable. Our days with Ringo and Charlie had been too brief, and although they did consider staying in our time permanently, they realized they actually did want to experience getting older day by day, instead of all at once with a visit back.

So they were our constant companions during the two months after the Monger battle. They sat in on Council meetings that were open to all Descendants, and experienced the shaping of Descendant politics first-hand. They divided their time between Elian Manor and rooms in the newly opened wings at St. Brigid's, where mixed-blood Descendants were now eligible to send their children to school. Charlie studied botany with Mr. Shaw, and managed to teach him some of the old plant lore she had learned during her time at Grayson Manor. And when he wasn't with us, Ringo spent every minute with Connor, either in the laboratory or playing video games and tinkering with electronic gadgets.

We took Ringo and Charlie with us the first time we visited the house in Galway that Millicent gave us. That had been a working trip spent cleaning and repairing the beautiful old place on the Cliffs of Moher. Ringo was the one who pointed out that a scene from *The Princess Bride* had been filmed at those cliffs, and our running joke of the weekend became answering "as you wish" to any request.

Ringo's friendship with Tom had also deepened. Ringo understood Tom in ways even Adam didn't, and it was Ringo who was able to convince Tom to accept the position as Monger Head on the Descendants' Council. There were full-blooded Mongers from the Rothchild/Walters regime who objected, but when Raven and the soldiers who had fought in the Monger battle stood up for Tom, the dissention quieted to a low murmur.

Probably the most karmic ending of all belonged to Seth Walters, who died from blood poisoning. He had believed until the end that Archer was a Vampire, and had injected Archer's Seer blood into his Monger veins. He was dead for three days before anyone found him.

The engagement party that Millicent and my mom threw for Ringo and Charlie had also been a going away party, and I'd never felt so much love and friendship in one room. My mom confided in me that night that Mr. Shaw had asked her to marry him. He was the new Shifter Head, and I had returned the Shifter bone into his safekeeping. They felt they needed to bring the matter before the Council, but they weren't asking for permission or forgiveness, just acceptance.

After we left Grayson Manor, I took Archer back to modern St. Brigid's before Clocking Ringo and Charlie to 1889. Archer couldn't return to Victorian London because he was already there — and already a Vampire. Except things had changed now, and Archer from 1889 found us at the Baker Street townhouse that Valerie had built for Charlie and Ringo. My mom had gone to Elian Manor to see her sister, so it was just the four of us.

"How much do you want to know, Archer?" I asked him, when we were seated in the drawing room across from Ringo and Charlie.

He smiled at me, and it was my Archer exactly. They all were — every version of him, from every age — he was *my* Archer. "All of it has changed already, hasn't it? This life that I will live is already different than the one I did live because you have changed it."

"It's not a time stream split though, because the only person really affected is you." I said. "I think it's more of a time stream overlay. Whatever happens to you as you move forward in time won't change the fact of what did happen. It all just lays over the top, so that as you experience things now, you'll remember them in my time as well."

"There are differences though," he said quietly as he looked down at the crowned heart ring on my left hand.

I smiled and held the hand out to him. "There are, but we can work around them."

EPILOGUE

"Do you want to drive?" Archer called to me from the bedroom of our Galway cottage. I was staring at the painting of us above the mantel, lost in thought, and I jumped when he came up behind me to kiss my neck.

"I still can't believe your mother bought this before you were born," I said as I spun around to wrap my arms around his neck.

"I can't believe you painted it," he said admiringly.

"I sketched it. Artemisia finished it."

"Which means we have several hundred thousand pounds-worth of art hanging on our wall." Archer kissed me on the nose. "And if I haven't said it enough lately, thank you for speaking to my father."

We had gone to the Arman's townhouse, which Archer had sold to Mrs. Arman's great-grandmother, and told Camille what Lord Devereux had said to me about leaving something for Archer in the house. He thought he knew where to look for it, and she was very happy to let him search.

Camille had mellowed since the Council had become more open and inclusive, and it had been enjoyable to sit in the kitchen with her while Archer went on his treasure hunt. The painting and a letter had been in the first place he looked – a false back in a built-in cabinet – and we'd waited until we came to Galway to unwrap them both.

413

The painting had made me cry. It was more beautiful than I could imagine, and it was exactly how I felt every day that I got to wake up next to my husband and see the world by his side. The letter had made Archer cry, because it was from his father, who told him how proud he'd been of his younger son, and how he hoped Archer would make a good life for himself with someone who showed him the love his father had never been able to.

"You drive," I said, in answer to his earlier question. "I want to sight-see."

"Can I come?" A voice I knew came from the open door, and I laughed to see Doran leaning against the frame. Archer shook his hand warmly and I hugged him.

"It's good to see you, Doran."

He smirked. "You've never said that before."

"Not out loud," I retorted.

He stepped into the cottage and his eyes went straight to the painting. "A perfect spot for it."

"Did you know that Archer's mother bought it?" I asked.

He scoffed. "Who do you think sold it to her? She'd Seen you together though, before Archer was born, so it was an easy sell."

My eyes shot to Archer, and he looked startled and then happy as he gazed up at the painting of us touching each other's faces. He took a breath and tore his eyes back to Doran. "Can we get you something? Are you hungry?"

He smiled graciously. "No, thank you. I'd love to see your studio though," he said to me.

"How'd you know I had one?"

He shot me a look loaded with "duh," and I laughed and led him to my favorite room in the house. It had been a solarium that Archer insulated and turned into my art studio. It had spectacular views of the Aran Islands.

Doran admired my work, sent Artemisia's greetings, and then turned to business. "My parents have finally become friends, thanks to you."

"All of them?" I asked.

He winced. "Maybe not Goran so much – there was no room left for love between himself and my mother when he joined Duncan's civil war – but Aeron and Jera have made their peace with each other. Aeron is seriously considering a visit to St. Brigid's by the way."

"Give us a warning and we'll be there," said Archer from the doorway.

"Good. I think you'll like my father. Underneath the stern, forbidding exterior beats the heart of a kind man who raised a baby by himself to have a part of my mother to love."

"It's a little twisted, Doran, you have to admit."

He scoffed. "It's beyond twisted. The House of Borgia has nothing on my family. But he was a good father, despite his motive for raising me."

Doran studied a painting I'd begun of the Immortals in their Council room. There were six thrones, and six people sketched into their places. Doran was seated between his two fathers, and his expression of peace had been the easiest to draw. I watched him carefully as he studied it, but he said nothing, only stroked the edge of the canvas and then turned to me.

"I came to give you this …" He pulled something from his pocket and held it out. The ruby ring glinted in his hand. "… and to ask if you would become the Mixed-Blood Head."

I hesitated, a little afraid to touch the ring, and yet it called to me.

"The Families have moved away from *Heads*. We call them Representatives now, because we realized we don't need leaders so much as listeners," I said. It had been Millicent who suggested the shift in responsibility, and I was so proud that everyone had embraced the new roles.

My gaze went back to Doran's eyes. "What do you expect from your Representative?"

"The ring's official name is the Ring of Dreams, and its power, as you experienced that day outside St. Brigid's, is the power to inspire. It is meant to stand for what I represent – hopes and dreams of harmony. It is the mixed-bloods who can build the bridges between Families until we are no longer islands alone, but great, interconnected landmasses where all can thrive. This ring requires a principled wearer though, as you learned, and I trust that you are that person, Saira."

I glanced at Archer and found his eyes shining with pride as he nodded. I did pick up the ring then, and it felt warm and wonderful in my hand. "I am honored to be your Representative. Thank you."

Doran kissed me happily on both cheeks. "I leave you to the rest of your day then. I understand there's a spectacular monastery just up the road, on the grounds of Kylemore Castle. You might find it interesting."

He shook Archer's hand on his way out, and I scoffed. "I guess we're going to Kylemore Monastery then."

We took the new Aston Martin up the coast. It was after dinner when we arrived, and it was still winter so no one else was about. We let ourselves inside and stepped into a gloriously decorated main hall.

"It's so beautiful," I whispered reverently. A fire was crackling in the hearth, and stone carvings on the walls were cast in lovely light. I moved closer to examine one that caught my eye when I heard the priest come in behind us. "Ah, visitors," he said graciously in a deep voice.

"I hope you don't mind—" I didn't finish my apology as I turned, because my words had stopped working and a huge grin lit my face. "Bas!"

He and Archer were already embracing like long-lost friends, and we settled ourselves by the fire to catch up on each other's news. During the course of the conversation, Archer convinced Bas to join us at the next Council meeting and to perhaps consider becoming Death's Representative. Bas was intrigued at the idea of meeting the Immortal, and we made plans to get together again later that week. It was nearly midnight when we finally left.

As we drove home along the rugged Galway coast, I looked over at Archer's profile and experienced the most profound déjà vu I'd ever felt.

"We've done this before," I said, as I watched his face in the light of the Aston Martin's dashboard.

Archer took my hand in his and kissed it. "Never like this."

"It was all worth it, even the awful parts." I stroked his cheek gently. I never got tired of touching Archer – it reminded me that he was real, and we belonged to each other. He smiled, and light glinted on his teeth. "You know I used to call you Wolf," I smirked.

The smile got bigger. "Now what do you call me?"

There weren't words big enough to describe how deeply I felt, or how profoundly I'd changed from knowing him, so I used the smallest ones I knew that said everything.

"I call you *my love.*"

THE END

The Bramante Staircase – The Vatican

THE TRUE HISTORY

My favorite thing about writing a time travel series has been weaving real historical facts throughout my invented stories, and there are *a lot* of random truths in the fictional world of *Cheating Death*.

Oscar Wilde was a playwright, novelist, essayist, and poet who lived from 1854 until 1900. He was renowned for his cutting wit, and remembered for his plays, imprisonment for 'gross indecency' with men, and for his death at the age of 45 after emerging from prison ill, destitute, and alone. His quotes are some of my favorites, and I've threaded several of them through his dialogue in *Cheating Death*.

There is no specific evidence, however, that Wilde ever spoke at St. Etheldreda's Church, or that he knew the real Father Lockhart – who was responsible for the restoration of the church in the late nineteenth century – despite the similarities of their backgrounds, education, and beliefs. Father Lockhart encouraged a

418

thriving community of artists, poets, and playwrights, and several important authors of the day were invited to speak at St. Etheldreda's, which is the oldest Catholic church in London.

Mary Shelley did travel through Italy in 1842, and the facts surrounding her life with Percy Bysshe Shelley, the writing of *Frankenstein*, and the deaths of her children are also accurate. A first edition of *Frankenstein*, inscribed 'To Lord Byron, from the Author' was discovered in 2015 and sold for an undisclosed sum to a British collector. The asking price was 350,000 pounds sterling.

The Artemisia of my story is based on the famous Italian Baroque painter, Artemisia Gentileschi – born in 1593 and trained as an artist by her father, also a renowned painter. In 1612 she was raped by her art tutor, and in an unprecedented move, sued her rapist for damages. Despite being tortured in court to determine the truth of her testimony, Artemisia won her lawsuit. Tassi, her attacker, was protected by the pope though, and served just eleven months in prison. Tassi's work has been forgotten now, and Artemisia, whose paintings are remarkable for depicting a violent, feminist point of view, is considered one of the greatest Baroque artists of the age of Caravaggio.

The Tower of the Winds is a spectacularly painted tower in the Vatican that can only be accessed through the Secret Archives, which is closed to visitors. The tower was, in fact, the home of Queen Christina of Sweden for a few months when she moved to Rome in 1654 to convert to Catholicism. Christina was one of the most educated women of the seventeenth century. She spoke eight languages, including Hebrew and Arabic, and had a deep fascination with the study of religions, including Islam, and Protestant and Catholic Christianity. Christina declared herself "unsuited to marriage," and then abdicated her throne to her cousin. She remained politically active and tolerant of religions throughout her life, and in 1686 issued a declaration that all Roman Jews were under her protection.

When Saladin recaptured Jerusalem from the Crusaders in 1187, he summoned the Jews and permitted them to resettle in the city. Saladin was considered an extraordinary leader, a magnanimous statesman, and he died penniless after giving away his fortune. His sword was legendary and disappeared to history, and the technology for Damascus steel remains a mystery to modern science.

Hatton Gardens is the historic jewelry district of London, and the River Fleet that runs under it was covered with brickwork in the nineteenth century to mask the stench of the raw sewage in the water. There is apparently a drain in Clerkenwell on which one can stand and hear the river flowing beneath the street. The Camden Catacombs still exist below the Camden Market, and they were once owned by the British Railway to house the pit ponies that pulled nineteenth-century railcars. NM Rothschild & Sons, founded in 1811, was headquartered in a Victorian building on St. Swithin's Lane during the late nineteenth century. It is the seventh-oldest bank in England.

Thousands of skeletons were exhumed from the catacombs under Rome in the sixteenth century, and sent to towns and cities in Germany, Poland, and the north to be adorned in jewels and finery. They were displayed as saints in the local Catholic churches in order to re-inspire the masses to Catholicism. They are called the Catacomb Saints, and have been documented beautifully in a book by photographer and art historian, Paul Koudounaris.

The Fisherman's Ring was the official seal of the Catholic popes, and disappeared from papal business in 1842, hence my choice for the year in which to set the Italian section of *Cheating Death*. The discovery that Mary Shelley had actually been on tour in Italy that year was her entrée into Saira's world. The other historic event of 1842 included in this book, though altered for location, was the Versailles rail accident. A train traveling from Versailles to Paris derailed, overturned, and caught fire, resulting in 55-200 deaths (the actual number was never determined due to the extraordinary heat of the flames). It was the worst rail disaster in history at that time and ended the practice of locking passengers into their carriages.

As you can see, the true facts in *Cheating Death* are all over the historical map. From Saladin's siege of Jerusalem in the twelfth century to the twenty-first-century discovery of Lord Byron's copy of *Frankenstein*, this book was far less concentrated in one time period than the previous books in the series, and I definitely took liberties with some of the details. The kernels of truth are great starting places to look up some fascinating facts though, and I've set up a page of links to the real history from all five Immortal Descendants books on my website at www.aprilwhitebooks.com.

Although the journey which began with *Marking Time* and now ends with *Cheating Death* is over, I will, from time to time, check in with these characters to see how they're doing. Ringo and Charlie are living in a townhouse that Valerie built for them in central London on what is now Baker Street, if that gives any indication of the mischief they might get up to. Bas has had a *whole lifetime* of experiences on his quest to understand the world's religions. And did you know that Edgar Allen Poe once disappeared for nearly a week and was finally found wandering the streets, semi-delirious, wearing clothes that weren't his own? He died soon after, taking the secret of his disappearance to the grave, and I've always wondered whether there was a spiral nearby …

The best place to discover information about further adventures of the Immortal Descendants is through my once-a-month newsletter, the sign-up for which can also be found on my website at aprilwhitebooks.com/newsletter. I hope to see you there!

Thank You

The story I tell to explain my friendship with my best friend and editor, Angela, is about the first time she came to my house. She walked right up to my bookshelves, studied the titles, and smiled. "Oh, I know you," she said, and a friendship was born.

I am able to do what I do because I am supported by an amazing community of people. Angela, Korry, and Valerie keep me mostly sane; Mom, Tania, Jessie, Maria, Dawn, Jill, and Kelly love me even when I'm not; Dan, Heather, Anneke, Kim, Linda, Kate, Jenn, and Mary-Cathryn make me better; Alexandra, Stella, Shannon, Maeve, Griffin, Wyatt, Aeris, Beck, and Bauer make me *want* to be. And Ed, Connor, and Logan are my mirrors, my reason to breathe, and the loves of my life.

My very favorite quote from an incomparable storyteller is one I wish for all of you:

"May your coming year be filled with magic and dreams and good madness. I hope you read some fine books and kiss someone who thinks you're wonderful, and don't forget to make some art -- write or draw or build or sing or live as only you can. And I hope, somewhere in the next year, you surprise yourself." – *Neil Gaiman*

Thank you for taking this journey with me, dear readers. Thank you for your support, your generosity, and the gift of your time. I feel I can honestly say now, at the conclusion of book five of a series I've poured my heart into, "Oh, I know you," and that a friendship based on a mutual love of stories has been born.